THE ARMS OF
HERCULES

TOR BOOKS BY FRED SABERHAGEN

The Berserker® Series
The Berserker Wars • *Berserker Base* (with Poul Anderson, Ed Bryant, Stephen Donaldson, Larry Niven, Connie Willis, and Roger Zelazny) • *Berserker: Blue Death* • *The Berserker Throne* • *Berserker's Planet* • *Berserker Kill* • *Berserker Fury*

The Dracula Series
The Dracula Tapes • *The Holmes-Dracula Files* • *An Old Friend of the Family* • *Thorn* • *Dominion* • *A Matter of Taste* • *A Question of Time* • *Séance for a Vampire* • *A Sharpness on the Neck*

The Swords Series
The First Book of Swords
The Second Book of Swords
The Third Book of Swords
The First Book of Lost Swords: Woundhealer's Story
The Second Book of Lost Swords: Sightblinder's Story
The Third Book of Lost Swords: Stonecutter's Story
The Fourth Book of Lost Swords: Farslayer's Story
The Fifth Book of Lost Swords: Coinspinner's Story
The Sixth Book of Lost Swords: Mindsword's Story
The Seventh Book of Lost Swords: Wayfinder's Story
The Last Book of Swords: Shieldbreaker's Story
An Armory of Swords (editor)

The Books of the Gods Series
The Face of Apollo • *Ariadne's Web* • *The Arms of Hercules*

Other Books
A Century of Progress • *Coils* (with Roger Zelazny) • *Dancing Bears* • *Earth Descended* • *The Mask of the Sun* • *Merlin's Bones* • *The Veils of Azlaroc* • *The Water of Thought*

THE ARMS OF

HERCULES

THE · THIRD · BOOK · OF · THE · GODS

FRED
SABERHAGEN

TOR®

· A TOM DOHERTY ASSOCIATES BOOK ·
NEW YORK

This is a work of fiction. All the characters and events portrayed in this novel are either fictitious or are used fictitiously.

THE ARMS OF HERCULES

This book is printed on acid-free paper.

A Tor Book
Published by Tom Doherty Associates, LLC
175 Fifth Avenue
New York, NY 10010

www.tor.com

Tor® is a registered trademark of Tom Doherty Associates, LLC.

Library of Congress Cataloging-in-Publication Data

Saberhagen, Fred, date
    The arms of Hercules/Fred Saberhagen.—1st ed.
        p. cm—(Book of the gods ; 3rd)
    "A Tom Doherty Associates book."
    ISBN 0-312-86774-3 (hardcover)
    ISBN 0-312-87776-5 (paper)
    1. Hercules (Roman mythology)—Fiction.   I. Title.

PS3569.A215 A76 2000
813'.54—dc21   00-031715

First Edition: November 2000

Printed in the United States of America

0 9 8 7 6 5 4 3 2 1

ONE

A Blind Man Witnesses

I do not sing this story, for I have neither the patience nor the voice to hold an audience. Rather I will write it down, so I will have the time to choose my words and amend them as I go along. Those who wish to read may do so. Those who do not will be under no compulsion to appear polite.

I have, among other things, this in common with all other members of the human race: that the seed of my life was planted, the roots began to grow, before I could be there to witness any part of the process. Therefore I can tell the first chapter of my story only in the form in which others who were there have told it to me.

Years ago, in the kingdom of Cadmia, there came a certain summer night on which the prophet Tiresias, in vivid dreams, beheld the descent of the mightiest of living gods. A few hours later, when Tiresias awakened to the first birdsongs of the bright spring morning, he climbed from his bed and called unhurriedly for his servants and his guards, sending his young companion to seek them out. The blind seer was an old man then, and he had been an old man for a long time, but the joints of his limbs still moved freely enough, all the vital parts of his body functioned, and he still craved young girls. As a member of the king's household, in a high position, he had the power to indulge his craving. His companion on that morning was a girl, and very young.

The prophet enjoyed the sound of young girls' voices, and the touch of their smooth skins, but whether or not they were beautiful in the world's eyes was a matter of total indifference to him.

When he could be bothered to explain his preferences to anyone, he put it this way: "In the first place, the dear little creatures are more grateful for the attention; and in the second place, very few of them deserve to be called ugly. You are handicapped in your vision by having eyes, and I can see the girls much better than you can."

The prophet himself, on the other hand, was ugly by almost any standard. He had been eyeless since birth. His face had eyebrows, but under them there were no lids to break the smooth expanse of skin, and the skull had no accommodating sockets.

Preparing for their master for that unexpected morning foray out into the world took the servants a little time. For this purpose they arrayed him in his own and his servants' idea of barbaric splendor, garments of bright colors and fine cloth, golden rings around his arms and in his earlobes. Tiresias bore all these procedures patiently, for he wanted to be sure not to arrive too soon at his destination. It was two hours after sunrise when he left his apartment in one wing of the king's palace, and set out on the road.

When he left the palace on that morning of birdsongs and sunlight, he went singing, in a cracked voice, some ancient song that no one else who was still alive in the kingdom of Cadmia had ever heard before. He mounted for his ride with his arm around the bored-looking young girl who had shared his bed. As far as anyone knew, there was no tie of blood between them, though the girl was certainly ugly enough to be his descendant. She might possibly have been a daughter or great-granddaughter, carried to almost any number of iterations that you care to name.

When the ill-matched couple had climbed aboard the mastodrom, it started walking, and the bodies of both passengers lurched with the motion of the howdah that rode just forward of the great beast's single hump. The huge, phlegmatic mastodrom had been brought at great expense from somewhere south of the Great Sea. A wizened little driver, a male of indeterminate age, sat straddling the animal's neck, guiding its motion with slight pressures of his callused feet, just behind its huge fanlike ears.

"Where are we going?" the girl asked, doubtless hoping that the day would bring some break in her routine.

"There is a house that has been visited by a god," the old man said to her. "And the man of the house does not know about it yet. I want to be the first to tell him."

"And the woman of the house?" the girl asked, when the mastodrom had carried them on a few more rocking paces.

The blind man laughed. "Ah, she knows already that she has had a visitor. She knows *that* in much more detail than I do. But who the visitor was—that will be a big surprise, I think!" And his laughter boomed out, as loudly as if he were still young and healthy.

Accompanying Tiresias, besides his youthful concubine, was an escort permanently assigned to him by King Eurystheus, a squad of half a dozen armed men on their own smaller and more agile mounts. The seer did not really want them, or believe he needed their protection, but the old king insisted that they always go with him; and this morning Tiresias had made sure they were alerted for his foray.

The morning's journey was only a few miles. Less than an hour after it began, the chief of the armed escort reined in his own much smaller mount, an ordinary cameloid, and turned closer to the mastodrom to tell its passengers that they had reached their destination. The estate on which I was conceived and born was a large and important one. The manor house was only a few miles outside the seven-gated city wall of Cadmia, whose massive stones were just visible in the distance from our own front gate.

The blind old man seemed somehow to know exactly where he was as well as anyone. Even before the soldier began to speak, the prophet turned from the public road to face the great ornamental gates of the estate, lifted his chin, and called out loudly: "Open, Alcmene, lady of the manor! I bring you marvelous news!" Eyewitnesses of the event confirm that the seer did not call for Amphitryon: thus even at that time he knew that the lord of the manor was not at home.

Amphitryon, who for many years was called my father, was a nephew of the late king Electryon of Megara, and he had been banished to Cadmia as a result of one of the intrigues afflicting that royal family, like so many others. (According to family tradition, Zeus was his great-great-grandfather; and a similar tradition in my mother's family gave her the same god as male ancestor eight generations even further back; in truth almost every family aspiring to high social status claimed divine blood.)

There was a pause while the gatekeeper inside sent some junior servant running for instructions, up the long hill to where the big house stood amid its ornamental plantings.

Meanwhile, out on the road in the sunlight of the summer morning, Tiresias waited patiently, singing. There were moments, even epochs, in which Tiresias seemed but little aware of what was going on in the world around him. The special seats with which his howdah was equipped were shaded by a canopy, which insured that the waiting would be comfortable. His armed escorts, taking their cue from him, were patient also. But what they thought of the quality of his song could be seen from the expressions on their faces.

Tiresias was by far the most famous prophet in Cadmia, or for many and many a mile around. Some said he was a child of Zeus, one of the Thunderer's uncountable bastards who were scattered all around the world, and that this explained both his deformity and his occult powers. Whatever the truth of that theory, I do not remember that Tiresias ever denied it.

The seer did not seem to object to being kept waiting in this way. Every minute or so the mastodrom swayed restlessly, treating its passengers to a soporific rocking. Meanwhile the tuskless creature groped about with its trunk, which was shorter than an elephant's but bifurcated for half its length, and therefore almost as handy. When the time came, the mastodrom would use its flexible trunk to help its passengers dismount.

On that summer morning, Alcmene, she who was to be my mother, awoke stretching on rare and expensive silken sheets, her body luxuriously sated by a night of tempestuous lovemaking, the like of which she could not recall. Somewhat to her surprise and disappointment, she found her bed partner gone when she turned in the direction of the empty pillow beside her own.

Her dreams, when at last her husband's importunities had allowed her to fall asleep, had been vaguely disturbing.

At the time of which I write, my mother was still considered a remarkable beauty, though the first years of her youth were past.

Pulling on a robe, a thin wrap designed to display her superb figure, she went out into the hall. The first servant she encountered was actually on his way to tell her of the unexpected caller at the gate, but she brushed aside this news and demanded: "Where is the master this morning"?

The question earned her a blank look. "Where should he be, mistress? Still a great many miles from home, I fear."

My mother's protests died on her lips even as she heard the news of the distinguished visitor; already a fearful suspicion had been aroused in her heart. There might be something seriously wrong. But what could it be? She knew, unquestioningly, that her husband had come home quite unexpectedly about midnight and had been with her through the remainder of the night, joined to her very closely most of the time. But now his familiar presence had vanished, completely and unaccountably.

Alcmene looked into room after room, but there was no sign of Amphitryon anywhere, nor of his weapons, nor of the clothing and the armor that he must have been wearing when he came home from the wars, must have discarded before coming in to her. She could clearly remember hearing his weapons and his breastplate clang together when they were thrown down on the floor.

Another servant, hurriedly dispatched to reconnoiter, came swiftly back to report that the cameloid Amphitryon always rode was not in the stable.

Now the lady Alcmene had to put her uneasiness momentarily aside to greet her illustrious caller, as Tiresias, the king's adviser, was being conducted to the house and offered refreshment.

When she entered the room where he was waiting, the eyeless man turned his pale face toward her. If he was aware of what effect his appearance could have, at close range, to one who was not accustomed to it, he made no allowance for it.

He said: "I wish to speak to your husband, my dear, as soon as he comes home. That should be soon."

Despite the servants' evidence, Alcmene was on the point of correcting her visitor, telling him that her husband had been home for many hours. But she remained silent, remembering how the servants had already started to react to that claim, absolutely refusing (though silently and subserviently, of course) to believe her.

She never even considered the possibility that the events of the night just past might have been a dream. Whatever else might have happened to her, it was not that. Dreams did not leave the dreamer's body pleasurably sore, and bedsheets stained.

*   *   *

While servants spread through the household in a futile, half-hearted search for a master they knew could not possibly be there, old Tiresias began to explain to my mother the reason for his visit.

"Young lady, last night I saw the great god, all-powerful Zeus himself, descending on this house. I saw the Thunderer enter your bedchamber, and what transpired there, between the two of you."

"Merciful gods!" the lady murmured, low-voiced. Her first thought was that the man who stood before her now was mad.

His voice, though, was horrifyingly reasonable. "But even from me"—he thumped his chest—"from me, Tiresias, the *why* of the matter is still concealed."

The lady drew a deep breath. Her second thoughts were even more frightening than her first.

"If," she began, "*if,* as I say, my lord Tiresias, anything of the kind had happened . . ."

But the lady was spared any effort at deception. The seer had turned his blind head and was listening to sounds from another direction.

A moment later, the unexpected return of Alcmene's husband was announced, by a servant who at least pretended to be joyful as he proclaimed the news.

The fact was, of course, that until the night when my true father first visited my mother, Alcmene had enjoyed a justly deserved reputation for chastity. The great god Zeus knew this, of course, and so for the duration of his visit, which lasted only a few hours, he had assumed the likeness of her husband. If you know anything of the history of Zeus, in legend and in fact, you will not be surprised.

The legends will tell you also that to make sure Alcmene was thoroughly deceived, Zeus gave her a gift of a golden cup, which Amphitryon could have captured from his chief opponent in the war, and also told her of many thing that had happened on the battlefield. Later, when Amphitryon tried to tell her of his adventures, she amazed him by filling in some details he had forgotten. But on the truth of these particular stories I make no judgment.

Usually Alcmene was genuinely glad to welcome her husband home. But this time it was with a heavy, sinking feeling that she first saw

Amphitryon, as he came riding in with two or three companions, all of them dismounting from their cameloids with weary groans. She felt nothing at all of the lightening of spirit with which she usually witnessed his arrival.

The general was really of no more than ordinary size, but so strongly built, with powerful hands and arms, that he seemed larger. He was about forty then, somewhat older than his wife. Much of his long hair had already turned gray, which secretly annoyed him, though it gave him more credibility as a leader. His eyes were gray, too, and they could turn very cold and hard.

"Hello, wife. We've ridden all night." Amphitryon had arrived wearing helmet and breastplate, just as his surrogate had on the preceding night, and his round shield hung from the horn of his wardrom's saddle. The returning general was in good health but looked somewhat dirty, tired, and worn, after a journey of several days.

He came to his wife and kissed her hungrily, locking her in an embrace. If the general had not been entirely without women for the past several months (and he certainly had not), he had endured that time without the one woman he preferred above all others.

Iphicles, my half-brother-to-be, then a mere beardless fourteen years of age (not very large but strongly built; a younger edition of his father), awakened by the stirring in the house around him, came running to welcome his father home, demanding at once to hear tales of glorious battles.

Answering Iphicles, Amphitryon said: "Well enough, I suppose. I suppose we win more than we lose, if we count up all the scores. Well, this is not the first year that this war has taken up our time, and I don't suppose it'll be the last. But enough about battles. I've come home for a rest."

When the tired general finally took notice of Tiresias and his squad of escorting soldiers, he was surprised.

"To what do we owe this honor, soothsayer? Has the king sent you?" Amphitryon tried to keep out of his voice the disgust he felt in looking at the eyeless face.

"I am here by reason of a greater power than King Eurystheus." Tiresias smiled faintly, as if he could still hear the general's loathing in his guarded speech. "Amphitryon, I bring you news of your extraordinary misfortune."

The general's shoulders slumped, and for a long moment he stared in silence at the prophet. Then he looked around him, making sure that the members of his immediate family were all well. But Amphitryon, who did not know yet that he was to be my foster father, was too well acquainted with the seer, or at least with his reputation, not to take him seriously. "If you bring bad news, let me hear it in private."

Giving the prophet his arm, he guided him to an inner room and shut the door.

When the two men were alone, and Tiresias settled in a comfortable chair, he raised his blind face toward the warmth of the cloud-filtered sunlight coming in a window. Then, at the sudden passing of the cloud from in front of the sun, he tilted his head away from the light, as if its new brightness hurt him in some way.

The general half-sat on the edge of a table, folding his arms and swinging one leg. "Well, sir?"

"Last night your house was visited by a god," the prophet told Amphitryon bluntly.

"Indeed." It took the general a little while to come to grips with this announcement. Like the great majority of people anywhere, even those of high rank, he had never in his life seen any god. Had anyone else told him the same thing, he would have laughed. But this was Tiresias.

"Which god?" Amphitryon demanded at last. "And for what purpose?"

"It was the Thunderer himself. As for his immediate purpose, it was the same that generally brings Zeus to the bed of a lovely mortal." The blind man raised a cautionary hand. "You ought not to blame your wife, for the god appeared in a perfect semblance of yourself. Any mortal would have been deceived."

For almost a full minute after the general heard those words, he seemed unable to speak. At last he managed to choke out a brief response: "But why?"

The question got no answer—not then. At that time the seer knew no more than the cuckolded general exactly what purpose Zeus might have had in committing this outrage, beyond relieving his chronic lust. No doubt that was purpose enough for the Thunderer, to whom legend attributed all the fine moral stature of a rutting beast.

Tiresias had to repeat his unwelcome message several times before the general began to believe what he was being told.

Amphitryon's first reaction, when at last he began to believe what he was being told, was violent anger. Jealous rage swelled in him, and he stalked about, muttering.

Then he stopped and looked at the closed door of the room. "Where is my wife now?"

"It will do no good to question her," the seer advised him.

But Amphitryon, angry, would not listen to advice. Summoning Alcmene, he brought her into the room and closed the door again, shutting the three of them off from the rest of the world, and made her listen to the prophet's story.

In a low and deadly voice he ordered: "Tell my wife what you have just told me."

"Tell her yourself." Tiresias, himself more puzzled and uncertain than he wanted to admit, was in no mood to be ordered about.

"What have you to say to that?" the general demanded of his wife.

"Oh, my lord. I don't know what to say." She who had just become my mother felt confused and injured—and at the same time, secretly, gloriously honored at the thought that the greatest god in the universe had chosen her as his lover, if only for a night.

Her first thought, on hearing the prophet's revelation, had been that Zeus had simply lusted after her; only now, as she listened to the two men talking, did it occur to Alcmene that she might be going to bear the god's offspring.

Mixed in with shame and surprise, my mother felt a wonder and a gratitude that she dared not show. She fixed pleading eyes on Amphitryon. "My lord . . . I repeat, I don't know what to say. Last night I was sure that I was with you—as I am sure of your identity at this moment."

Her husband grunted something, a stunned and almost unintelligible sound. "For now," he said at last, "better go on about the business of the household."

*   *   *

Obediently Alcmene bowed her head and moved away. When she was gone, her husband turned back to Tiresias.

"Prophet, I am sorry if I spoke rudely to you a moment ago. I apologize, and humbly I ask your advice."

The blind head nodded slowly. "Your apology is accepted, great general. My first advice is that you do nothing in haste or anger."

Amphitryon might not have heard him. He almost seemed to be mumbling to himself. Another wave of shame and anger had come over him and seemed about to overwhelm him. "The law says—tradition has always said—that a woman so grossly unfaithful can be, even should be, burned alive."

Before he could even begin to pursue that idea, there came what might have been a response that effectively prevented any serious consideration. A burst of savage thunder sounded from not far overhead. Looking out the window, the general gazed incredulously at the thick clouds which had been gathering, with amazing swiftness, since his arrival home.

Moments later, rain poured down. There would be no outdoor fires today, anywhere in this vicinity.

Over the next few hours and days, suspicions of some baser plot began to creep in on Amphitryon, taking possession of his imagination. For a time, even despite the warning cloudburst and its thunder, he almost managed to convince himself that Zeus was not really involved. Rather it seemed to him possible that the king or someone else had been playing him false, and Tiresias was in on the plot somehow.

My young half-brother, Iphicles, moped about for a day or two after his father came home, upset by the knowledge of what had happened, and worried about what might happen next. Any suggestion that his mother might be burned would have terrified him, but fortunately for his peace of mind, he never had to hear it.

Tiresias and his armed escorts took their leave of the estate on the afternoon of the day of their arrival. The ancient seer was accustomed to unpopularity, but he was still unshakably certain that he had seen the god descend.

Of course the seer made sure that his concubine was with him when he left. Meanwhile she had spent the time chatting with the kitchen girls, delaying them in their work; and Tiresias in the intervals of his own conversations had enjoyed listening to their voices, even at a distance.

And that is basically the story of that day as it has been told to me. There are questions which I have never been able to answer to my own satisfaction. For example: Was it Tiresias who told the general what my name was to be? If so, was it his own idea, or did it come from Zeus? And did the seer advise that the name should be well publicized, on the theory that calling the child "beloved of Hera" might forestall the wrath of the Thunderer's jealous spouse?

In any case, I can now assure you, with the benefit of firsthand experience, that the gods, the real gods, are not bound in their behavior by what the legends say they ought to do, how they ought to feel.

The next days—then weeks and months—were difficult for everyone on the estate. Amphitryon, like any other general, was not averse to handing out punishments when he deemed them necessary—he enforced his will firmly enough, but he took no particular joy in making people suffer.

But he was jealously possessive of Alcmene, and he took his own honor very seriously. In this case there seemed no one else to blame for his wife's infidelity, no one to punish except her. But any move along that line had been effectively forestalled.

Once Amphitryon had firmly put out of his mind his first wild impulse to burn his wife alive, he meditated taking a great vow never to touch her again, for fear of bringing down on his own head the jealousy of Zeus. And it is a fact that my mother had no more children.

In later years, when my personal history began to be severely confused with legend, until matters had reached a point where even I could scarcely be sure where one ended and the other began, some stories had it that the mother of Hercules, still "fearing Hera's jealousy," caused me to be exposed, shortly after birth, just outside the walls of Cadmia.

There the goddess Hera herself was said to have come upon me by accident and to have been tricked into nursing me, not realizing that the sturdy infant at her breast was the illegitimate spawn of her lecherous husband.

In fact, the truth about the relationship between the goddess and myself is even a little stranger than the stories. Time and the gods permitting, I will have more to say about it later.

People love wonders almost as much as food and drink, and sometimes more, and so they insist on creating legends. But mere mortals lack the storytelling skill of Fate, and legends tend to be less marvelous than truth.

Some nine months after god and prophet had made their respective visits to our house (visits which were never repeated, by the way) my mother gave birth to me; and an hour after giving birth she was tottering on her feet, sacrificing at the altar of Zeus, giving extravagant thanks that I had not come into the world with a bull's horned head, or any such overt indication of my paternity—such a consequence of the god's mating with a woman was not unknown.

Years later, Alcmene became fond of telling me that for the first few months of my life, everyone around me had the impression that I was entirely normal. Mother always shook her head in wonder when she told me that.

TWO

Lessons Gone Awry

In later years my mother always told me that I had been a gentle child. Somewhat moody now and then but, fortunately for myself and others, almost never aggressive or quarrelsome. I have the impression that my mother controlled me easily, during most of those early years, with soft words and much love. But as the wife of an important general, she had many obligations, and a large part of my upbringing was left to others. As for the general who played the role of my foster father, I saw even less of him than I did of my mother. Only very recently have I begun to develop some real sympathy for this man, Amphitryon, whose own scruples would allow him neither to adopt me wholeheartedly as his son, nor cast me out as a nameless, shameful bastard.

I suppose my childhood was happy enough, as mortal childhoods go. Yet a few unpleasant memories endure, beginning very early. (I am not talking now about the snakes, for on the day they came to kill me I was much too young to retain any memory of the event—more later on the snakes.)

The earliest scene of any kind that I can recall with any accuracy took place when I was three or four. One of my succession of nurses, irked I suppose at having been sternly forbidden to administer even the mildest paddling, locked me in a closet as punishment for some childish offense. Standing alone in the dark was not frightening so much as boring, so I put my hands on the door and gave it one determined but still easy push, which broke it neatly from its hinges and shoved it flying across the room. Standing out most clearly now in memory are the wide eyes of the woman who had locked me in, and the way that I, ready to accept the whole business as some pleasant game, laughed at her astonishment.

Being shut up in a dark place had meant no more to me than brief inconvenience, and I might have continued to assume the whole episode was only one of play, except for the frightened look on the face of the nurse when she heard the loud splintering of wood and saw how I emerged—and worse, the expression on my mother's face when she came in response to the noise, beheld the wreckage, and learned what had happened. The adult reactions, which were more of fear than of disapproval, puzzled me and brought on in me a deep, unsettling anxiety as well.

Very much the same thing happened also some years later, on the one time when Amphitryon beat me, in an effort to inflict punishment. He may have been half drunk at the time.

Up to that point in my life, you understand, I had been given no official account of my true origins. I suppose it was not until late in my childhood that I began seriously to doubt that Amphitryon could be my real father. When the suspicion arose, I found it not particularly disturbing. The man had rarely demonstrated any enthusiasm regarding me—his parental energies seemed to be concentrated almost entirely on Iphicles, for whom he arranged a promising marriage when the lad was only sixteen, and I was only two or three. Not that my half brother and I engaged in open rivalry. As long as I remained a child, there was too much difference in our ages, and afterward I was rarely home. And Iphicles was assured of inheriting the whole estate.

Nor was Amphitryon especially cruel by nature—actually I can only recall him beating me that one time, and for that he had some justification. In the process of testing the strength of a certain object that he valued highly, a fine steel dagger that was a present from the king, I had broken its blade.

As a child I was credited with being stoic, because I had no clear idea of what real pain was like; and fortunately my special powers had always protected me from real injury as well.

Their onset must have been gradual, and at first they were restricted to purely defensive service—I never bit a nipple from the breast of my mother or any of my wet nurses, never crushed an adult's finger in my instinctive baby grip. My seeming stoicism on the day when Amphitryon beat me was not the result of any grim attempt at fortitude, but rather a near indifference to what was happening. Having reached the age of ten or so, I had practically full voluntary control over all my powers. I might of course have pulled the strap out of his hands and torn it into shreds, but I was well aware that any such feat would only have worsened an emotional climate that had already become extremely unpleasant.

As the flogging went on, and on, without having any noticeable effect, the man who had never quite been my father—though I still called him that—grew frightened by my reaction, or rather by my lack of any that he could understand. Suffering and fright on my part would have reassured him, and sturdy defiance would have been understandable. But I remained sullenly unmoved, and he grew fearful. Only then, by contagion, did the experience become frightening for me in turn. Thus, by means of a complicated process, the thrashing did at last have its intended effect, causing me to mend my ways.

As proof of the impact the experience had, the images are with me still. Amphitryon's arm rising and falling, rising and falling, swinging a leather strap, while I stared impassively and wondered at the ritual in progress. I realized that any normal child would have been left bruised and screaming, but I was in no way qualified to play my expected part. Each loud impact on my exposed flesh was met precisely by an involuntary countersurge of invisible power from within my body, a nullifying force that afforded me virtually complete protection. After the beating had continued for what seemed many minutes, I began to be aware of a faintly unpleasant stinging sensation, not enough to keep me awake had I been sleepy, and later in a mirror I noted a slight reddening of the skin.

At last the man who had never been my father cast the strap away from him and left the room in silence. I suppose he must have spoken to me—uttered threats, admonitions, curses, *something*—while the punishment was in progress, but whatever it might have been, I retain not a word. And he never spoke to me of the matter again.

When I had outgrown my succession of nurses, my mortal parents provided me with a series of tutors in their stead. Mathematics, geography, an elementary grounding in certain languages (for language I had an aptitude), literature. Of these instructors the last one, Linus, taught me music. More accurately, he made an effort to do so.

I liked the pure sounds of Apollo's instrument, the lyre, or of a good singing voice—mine was not. I could be entranced by intricate melodies, calling up captivating dreams that went beyond what could be put into words. But the musical details I was actually expected to learn, all the tedious-seeming business of tones and notes and scales, remained as indigestible as bits of gravel.

Linus was middle-aged, and not a large man physically, though he could seem so when he made the effort, which he did fairly often. As far as I knew he lived alone, and whether he had wife or family he never said. He had gray curling hair, very little beard, a fondness for jewelry, and an aristocratic manner, more so than many of us who were supposedly the genuine aristocrats. He knew much about music, and cared much. But I soon learned that he cared about power more. There was in him also a sadistic strain, which he for the most part kept concealed.

I was already fifteen years old when Linus arrived to teach me. For the past few years it had struck me as odd that Amphitryon never said anything about starting me on a course of military training. The other boys with whom I was best acquainted, those of my own age and class, were all now keenly concerned with sharp blades and other military matters. I had never been encouraged to play with weapons, except that practice with the bow was tolerated, and I had acquired moderate skill in archery. Not that I was particularly eager to be a soldier, but the fact of my special treatment left me uneasy, because it emphasized the importance of my difference from everyone else. I suppose I dimly understood that my parents were afraid of what might happen if someone put a sword or spear in my hand and urged me to use it, even in a controlled practice. And now here I was, for some reason expected to do well in music.

I suppose it is hardly necessary to mention that my peers respected me for my strength, although I carefully controlled it when in their presence, using only just enough to outwrestle any one of them when called upon to do so, or lift a slightly greater weight than any other boy could manage. I think my efforts at concealment succeeded, to the extent that none of my companions, with the notable exception of my nephew Enkidu, had the faintest suspicion of the true state of affairs. I myself had reason to believe that my powers went far beyond anything they had yet been called upon to do. But I did not *know* that for a fact. I had no wish to know the true extent of the gulf dividing me from everyone else.

*   *   *

The immediate cause of my problem with the tutor Linus had to do with a certain servant girl attached to our household. Megan had come from somewhere among the savage tribes to the far north; she was a couple of years younger than I, and I had started an affair with her.

In a way I suppose that was almost inevitable. Young masters in manors, from time immemorial, have begun affairs with young servants, slave or free. Down through the years I have often told myself that, more often than not, the menials are rather pleased, at least at first, to be so singled out.

But in contrast with the way such affairs usually progress, I had fallen in love with Megan.

Linus came upon us when we were making love in one of the makeshift hideaways we favored. Perhaps his intrusion was sheer accident. I will not repeat now exactly what he said or what he did (some incidents are not worth telling), but it involved a kind of blackmail—as far as I knew, my mother and foster father were not aware of my serious involvement with a servant.

The girl was much in my thoughts. But she was absent when the crisis came.

There arrived a certain summer afternoon, in the courtyard shaded by trellises and grapevines where I usually had my lessons, when Linus, unwisely going beyond mind games for the moment, struck his unmusical student. It was a casual, contemptuous, almost absentminded slap, of a kind he had administered to me two or three times before. The impact of a music teacher's hand was no more painful to me than a falling feather. But this time the teacher had chosen precisely the wrong moment, had overstepped an invisible line, and the unmusical student immediately, impulsively hit him back.

He ought not to have attempted blackmail and then struck me with such casual contempt. The two together added up to a fatal mistake. He thought he had established a new hold over me that gave him the privilege of inflicting such abuse, but in fact the very opposite was true: he stood in special danger. His words and act together were like a spark in the air of a granary filled with dusty grain. My anger flared explosively.

*   *   *

I knew beyond a doubt that my teacher was dead before his body hit the courtyard tiles, as soon as I felt in my right arm and shoulder the small shock of the backhanded, unpremeditated blow and realized, too late, with how much angry force it had been delivered.

For the space of several breaths, which to me seemed a long, long time, the routine of the surrounding household flowed on just as before. I could hear the steady murmur of incidental sounds. No one else was aware of what had just happened, and I remember realizing that in some sense my world, the world in which I had grown up, was coming to an end. That world had only a minute more to live, and maybe less. I could hear the servants being merry about something, in the direction of the kitchens, and in another courtyard someone pouring water from an urn.

I remained utterly alone in the small, shaded courtyard, with the body of the man I had just killed. In fact I had never felt so utterly alone in all my life. My right fist with the lyre still gripped in it—I have never much cared to listen to the sound of that instrument since—had caught him awkwardly on the jaw, making a breaking noise that seemed quite loud, and my tutor had gone down on the pavement as if felled by an arrow through the heart. Now he lay with eyes open and his head twisted far over. He might have been gazing at the sky, or maybe at the intervening grapevines on their trellis, and there was such a look of complacency on his dead face that I doubted whether he had had time to feel a thing, much less to understand just what had happened to him and why.

Fortunately for me, Linus was not a member of the aristocracy, nor was he attached to the king's household. But neither was he an utter nobody, whose shattered jawbone and broken neck might never be noticed, whose death could be practically ignored and forgotten. His only relatives were . . . who were they, exactly? I could not remember at the moment, but I seemed to remember his saying that they lived somewhere far away.

My trial took place two days later, in an audience chamber of the palace, before Eurystheus the Second, the teenage king of Cadmia.

Following the advice of my lawyer, who happened also to be a friend of the royal family and of Amphitryon as well, I pleaded self-defense, and on that ground I was acquitted. The whole business took less than half an hour.

Eurystheus was a cautious youth, still ill at ease being king, feeling his way into a job for which he had never been properly prepared. He was not one of the lads with whom I had grown up. He was somewhat taller than me, and it was easy to see that by the time he was twenty years old he would be fat. His father had fallen unluckily in some minor battle, and he himself was grandson of Eurystheus the First, who had been on the throne when I was born. In those early months of his reign, Eurystheus the Second, a lifelong slave of caution, went nowhere without a guard of picked soldiers in attendance. I think he had nothing to say during the entire trial without first getting advice from the legal adviser who stood just behind him.

Tiresias was in the room during the trial, along with a score or so of other onlookers, but he had nothing to say.

In the course of the arguments, my lawyer, one of the cleverer of his profession in the city, had occasion to say several helpful things, one of which was: "The truth is, Majesty, this young man is growing rapidly and he does not know his own strength." My lawyer tended to perspire heavily, and yet in fact he was quite calm and confident under almost all conditions.

The truth was, of course, that I knew my own strength better than anyone else who was still alive. But I was not going to argue the point.

The king was only a few months older than I was, and he could sympathize with that. Thinking back, I realize that he also might have had a tutor or two whose violent deaths would not have totally displeased him.

There was learned medical testimony that Linus's neck had been broken, as were certain bones in his skull and in both his upper and lower jaws. The fatal lyre, itself basically undamaged, was exhibited in evidence, and we all stared at it solemnly.

Only one more brief whisper from his adviser, and the king was ready to pronounce his verdict. That I was speedily acquitted was, I am sure, partly due to the fact that the king wanted to retain his general Amphitryon as his loyal follower. It also helped that Linus had only distant relatives alive anywhere, and no one of importance was seriously offended by his death—indeed, his abrasive manners probably caused a number of citizens to feel a certain satisfaction.

Acquitted though I was, it was universally agreed that I ought to go away for a while. As my sixteenth birthday was still almost a month in the future, I was considered still a bit young for the army. The king recommended that I be sent out to tend the herds for an indefinite period—this frequently happened to the youth of prominent families when they grew hard to control. As we were leaving the palace, my lawyer told me confidentially that in practice my stay with the herds would almost certainly be prolonged for at least a year, more likely two or three. But there was no reason why I should not pay brief visits home during my period of exile, provided I was discreet about it.

As we returned home after the trial, my mother was in tears, though she could hardly have hoped for a more favorable outcome. Amphitryon was somewhat grim, as usual, and had little to say. But he appeared reasonably well satisfied.

My lawyer, like most other male adults, was a military veteran, and he shook his head. "Besides, any young man, especially a general's son, who reacts to the first touch of discipline by breaking the neck of someone in authority—that young man would not fare well in the army."

So my official innocence was declared, and in the same breath my punishment, for it amounted to that, was settled. With the king's verdict gratefully received, and a date for my departure set, the household was caught up in a general sense of relief. I scarcely saw Megan, and I had the impression that she was deliberately trying to keep out of my sight; but I would not have known what to say to her had we had a chance to be alone. The fact that everyone, even my mother, seemed ready to ignore me during my last few days at home did not bother me at all: The less attention anyone paid to me in my current state of mind, the better.

But before I turned my back on home and went to learn to be a herdsman, I decided to make a greater effort than I ever had before to probe the uncertainty of my own origins. I waited until I could feel reasonably confident of having Alcmene to myself for a quarter of an hour, and then approached her, when she was alone and reading, or perhaps weaving or spinning.

It did not seem to me a good omen that this meeting was going to take place in the same courtyard where I had killed Linus, but I refused to put off the business any longer.

"Mother?"

She raised her lovely eyes with slow reluctance. "What is it, Hercules?"

"I want you to tell me the truth about the snakes."

There was a long silence, during which my mother refused to look at me at all, and picked at her woman's work with nervous fingernails, and, I suppose, dropped or made a stitch or two. Then at last she raised her eyes to mine again and asked: "What snakes?"

When I only waited wordlessly, standing with hands clasped behind my back, she fell silent again, and it seemed a long time before she sighed. "You've heard the stories."

Of course I had been hearing them, in several garbled and fragmentary versions, from the servants, from my playfellows, year in and year out, from the time that I was old enough to understand any stories at all. Still I said nothing.

At last she gave in, and set aside the fabric she had been holding in her lap. Folding her well-kept hands, she said: "Of course you have. Well, I suppose your father and I should have told you the truth about it all much earlier."

The many stories I had been hearing all my life were of course concerned with more than snakes. *My father?* I thought. *I have never seen the face of my true father, nor heard his voice.* But I said nothing. I wanted to take things in order, and now it seemed that I might hear the truth about the snakes at last.

Another sigh from Mother, another pause. Then at last she began. "It happened in this house"—she turned her head—"in what is now my sewing room, which was then your nursery. There were two snakes that came in—into the house—somehow. One day when you were no more than ten months old."

"How did they come in, Mother?"

"We were never able to determine that. The doors had all been closed, or so the servants swore. There were the drains, of course, but everyone agreed the snakes were too big for the drainpipes. When they were dead the servants measured them, and one was fully eight feet long, the other almost ten." And she repeated: "You were ten months old."

"Some enemy sent them, to attack me? Or could it possibly have been an accident?"

"I don't know." She shook her head and sighed. "No, that's not really true. I was sure from the beginning that it was not a—not a natural event. We've never been able to determine any reason. That anyone would have had."

"Did you try?"

"For a time we did. I consulted soothsayers, but they could tell me nothing."

"Tiresias?"

"No." She shook her head. "I suggested going to the king's prophet, but your father didn't want to consult him."

"You mean it was Amphitryon who didn't want that."

"That is what I said."

"He is my father?"

My mother was silent.

After waiting awhile I asked: "Of what species were the snakes?"

"I think they were not natural snakes, but monsters. Although they might have been vipers of some kind, I suppose. I have never learned much about snakes, but I have no doubt that they were poisonous. I saw their fanged heads later." Alcmene's face was still almost calm, but she made a strange, small noise in her throat. "One of the magicians cut their heads off, so he could use them in his rituals. But he was able to find out nothing."

"Tell me exactly what happened," I pressed her.

My mother sighed loudly, as at a painful but familiar sight. "There's no doubt about it, the serpents were coming after *you*. There was a servant's child, an infant, in the room as well, but they ignored her. Their path into the room took them directly past the cradle where she lay, and they came past it, straight to you. We could see the slimy trails they'd left—not natural snakes, but monsters. And you were still too young to walk. But somehow you had caught one snake in each of your two hands. You grabbed each one just behind the head, just as if you knew that was the proper way."

My witness had tilted her head back now, and her eyes were closed. "Snakes never die quickly, and they were still thrashing about when we—when I heard the noise and came running into the room. Their thrashing had pulled you from your cradle, but you still held on. Your little fists did not seem big enough to grasp those scaly bodies properly. But when we tried to pry them away from you, we saw how deep your tiny fingers had dug in through skin and scales, how you had crushed bones."

I did not know what to say. Of course I could remember nothing.

"You were not crying, Hercules," my mother said. "You were laughing, as babies laugh. You thought it was a game."

There was silence in the courtyard for a time. Finally Alcmene said: "That was when your father and I knew how truly—how truly special you were, Hercules. Though we had begun to suspect, even earlier."

"My father?"

My mother's eyes came open, and their look was sharp. "Hercules, you know who I mean. The lord Amphitryon has been a father to you."

So, it was true. I nodded slowly. "More or less. Most of the time. Some of the time, anyway." I knew boys who had suffered much worse treatment in their homes, and from true fathers; I had seen their bruises and heard their stories.

"He has not been cruel," I had to admit. "But I think he will be glad when I am no longer living in this house. But, Mother, now that you've started to tell me about the snakes, tell me more. Please. Every little detail that you can remember."

While Alcmene talked, confirming what had seemed the wildest rumor as cold fact, I stood before her listening carefully, but most of the time I did not look at her. Instead I looked down at my own hands. They were well kept, sunburned, but not at all callused—it seems that

I never develop calluses, or blisters, either, even from hard manual labor. For a youth of fifteen my hands were not particularly large or muscular, though they were no longer childish.

At the moment they were resting on the back of a heavy wrought-iron chair, the top of the chairback formed by a bar of curving black metal half an inch thick. I thought the bar must have been bent into its present shape when it was red hot, by the blows of a heavy hammer in the hand of a skilled smith. That rod of iron was cold now, and many a strong man could have held it over his knee and strained and groaned and not been able to wrench it out of its congealed shape by so much as the thickness of a fingernail. I knew I could easily—easily!—have tied it in a bow, but I did nothing of the kind. Not for many years had I performed any truly extraordinary feats in my parents' sight, or in the presence of anyone who was likely to report to them.

The story of the snakes was deeply interesting, but now that words and thoughts were flowing I had even bigger questions that I wanted answered.

When my mother fell silent again, I asked her: "How often have you seen my father? When was the last time?"

Her eyes went closed again, and her head was shaking slowly, side to side.

She said: "Hercules, enough. It will be better if you don't try to dig into such matters."

"What will be better? How can it be better?" Receiving no answer, I drew a deep breath, and persisted. "When was the last time you saw my father?"

For a moment I feared that my mother was going to faint. But at least she did not pretend not to know whom I was talking about.

She said: "I have had one meeting with Zeus in my entire lifetime, and you seem to know about that. I suppose there is no possibility that you could not. I swear to you, Hercules, that since that night I have never seen him, or heard from him again. Not ever."

"I believe you," I told her. "Yes, I believe you, Mother." My throat was dry. I had never seen him or heard from him at all.

She nodded. "Amphitryon has always been suspicious, but I have sworn to him again and again, as I swear to you now: That night was the first, and last, and only time."

"I see." After a while I added: "I thought that there could possibly have been some message. Some word for me, even passed on indirectly. Maybe after I was born——?"

"Nothing." Mother shook her head emphatically. "Never again the slightest communication from *him*, the god we are speaking of. You must understand that, Hercules. I have no reason to think that he, your true father, even knows that you exist, or would care if he knew."

My hands were tightening on the iron chairback, and I could feel it begin to give a little, like soft wood, or something no harder than the body of a snake. I knew that what I was doing would leave fingerprints. "Someday I mean to find him, Mother."

Alcmene had been upset by my questions, but now, for the first time, she was frightened. "*Hush!*"

"I mean to find him, Mother. Find him, and talk to him, and learn from him what he knows and cares about."

"*Hush*, I say!" And she started from her chair.

On the day after that interview with my mother, I left home to be a herdsman.

At that time, most of the locally owned cattle were grazed in a district called Nemea, miles from the city. Herds of cattle, mixed in with lesser numbers of droms and cameloids. The animals and the herders who followed them spent eight or nine months of the year wandering among treeless hills, with ribs of rock protruding here and there through a thin skin of soil and grass. If the winter promised to be mild, the stock might be kept out in these fields all year round.

Once again, on the morning of my departure, my mother expressed her great relief that the king had declared me not guilty, and that my punishment had not been more severe.

"You must be thankful, Hercules. A man who strikes a fatal blow by accident sometimes has his right hand cut off."

I was in no mood to be told how I should feel. "I don't suppose that happens very often to any son of any family as important as ours. And I doubt it could happen at all to any son of Zeus."

I remember how she stared at me then, aghast at my dangerous pride. "Perhaps we have spoiled you in bringing you up—spare the rod and spoil the child."

Alcmene had to stop there, probably remembering the day when Amphitryon had tried to beat me. And I suppose she was also thinking of Linus, who had not believed in sparing the rod—not as long as his hand held it.

At last my mother was able to continue. "Hercules, you have a princely pride. But you must remember that you are not a—prince." She hesitated just slightly before the last word, and I thought, with an eerie sensation down my spine, that she had been on the point of warning me that I was not a god.

"I know what I am not, Mother. But what *am* I?"

She could not tell me that. But I was determined that some day my father would.

○ *THREE* ○

A Real Lion

$\mathcal{J}$t so happened that my twelve-year-old nephew Enkidu, the son of my half brother, Iphicles, was also scheduled to take a turn at herding. I had managed to avoid that sort of duty until now, but Enkidu already had a year's experience in minding cattle. Of course when the summer ended I would be required to remain in exile with the herds, while he would return to Cadmia to go to school and to begin his military training.

My nephew was tall for his age, only a few inches shorter than I, and of wiry build. His hair was curly black, and most of his skin, like mine, had been burned dark by the sun. He might have been considered handsome, were it not for the fact that his ears stuck out outrageously. The difference in our ages was small enough, and we saw each other frequently enough, that my attitude toward him was what it might have been to the younger brother I had never had.

There I was, at the age of sixteen—my birthday overtook me on the road—undertaking what was really my first unsupervised trip away from home. Propelled by the well-nigh irresistible force of a royal suggestion, armed with my mother's blessing, and with a bow and arrows presented to me at the last moment by Amphitryon, I put on sandals and a herdsman's long shirt and started out into the countryside, with Enkidu at my side.

The army had taken almost all the cameloids and droms that were of any use, and so the two of us had to walk to the grazing grounds. We made fairly good time, but still the journey took us almost two weeks, on roads that alternated between dust and mud, depending on the weather.

As familiar territory fell behind, and the road ahead opened more or less straight and clear into the unknown, the gloom that had hung over me since the death of Linus began to lift. Enkidu helped to raise my spirits, too; he was a cheerful, energetic rascal most of the time, telling jokes and propounding riddles, looking forward to a repeat of what must have been a pleasant adventure for him during the previous summer. Sometimes during that two-week hike my companion and I were fortunate enough to find a hospitable farm, and sometimes we slept under the stars. One night when it was raining, we were lucky enough to find a hollow tree big enough to let us put our heads inside.

We heard nothing about any lion until the fifth or sixth day out, when we encountered an itinerant peddler who was trekking in the opposite direction, tugging the reins of a llamoid that bore in its panniers his meager stock in trade, tightly covered to protect it from the rain. According to the story this wanderer told us, the herds that we were going out to watch were being steadily depleted by, and one herder had already been killed by, an enormously powerful and savage beast, a great cat whose hide through some unnatural magic was proof against the point or edge of any weapon.

Neither my nephew nor I had ever laid eyes on any feline bigger than the household tabby. And I suppose neither of us was overly imaginative, at least not enough to be frightened by the story the peddler told. Rather we were intrigued—a lion seemed to promise some excitement in what might otherwise have been a boring job.

Enkidu had seen enough of me in recent years, observed enough in the way of occasional secret demonstrations, to have some awareness of my awesome physical strength, a factor that no one else in the city or on the estate, not even Amphitryon, had yet fully appreciated. As I may have mentioned already, there was nothing about me at first glance to give the secret away. At the age of sixteen I was coming to terms with the fact that I was never going to be above the average height. My hands were on the small side for a man's, my wrists still relatively thin, arms and shoulders quite ordinary in appearance, revealing nothing of the invisible might that coiled within. What I had not yet begun to understand was the full extent of my own powers.

Among the few items I carried with me into temporary exile were a quiver of arrows and a heavy bow, both, as I have mentioned, parting gifts from my foster father, bestowed before either Amphitryon or I had any idea that I would soon encounter a lion on which to try them out. The bow was so heavy in the pull that only the strongest men could draw it and shoot with any accuracy. It was elegantly made and decorated, and I am sure that Amphitryon would have kept it with him except that he, who by ordinary standards was far from weak, found it impossible to aim steadily.

Despite Enkidu's having made the long journey to the herding range once before, he still managed to lose his way as we drew near our goal. But after an extra day or two of wandering, my companion and I eventually located the herds belonging to several owners, about a thousand animals in all, gathered in one place. Naturally the grass in the immediate area was rapidly depleted, and the herd had to be kept almost continually, if slowly, moving.

On our arrival, the herdsmen turned out to be a small pack of frightened boys, fewer than a dozen in all. When they saw that newcomers had arrived, they slowly gathered around us.

Their leader, a tall youth called Tarn, gave us a cool welcome and seemed to be determined that we should be properly frightened, at least of the lion if not of him. He introduced us to the others, a scrubby crew varying in age from ten years to about fourteen, of assorted shapes and coloring. Some, like Enkidu and I, were clad in herders' shirts, others wore nothing but belts to hold their slings or knives. They were armed with an assortment of poor-looking weapons, including blades, slings, and simple sticks.

We soon learned that our new colleagues, particularly after dark, spent as much time huddled fearfully together as the animals did. And they were interested in me. Word of what had happened to Linus had already reached them; news of such violent and dramatic events always got around fast. I was only surprised that the truth had not yet been greatly exaggerated.

But talk of the lion naturally dominated everything else. All the boys swore that they had seen the beast again and again, though no two of them gave exactly the same description. All agreed that it was a fearsome monster indeed, and of a gigantic size.

Fear is one of the more contagious ailments, and Enkidu and I began to feel a touch uneasy.

The cattle tattooed with Amphitryon's brand, about two hundred animals in all, were mixed in with those of other owners, several varieties of sheep and mutant cows and steers all jumbled together. Until a few days ago there had been a herd bull, a fierce animal who had challenged the lion and had been promptly eaten.

"We wanted to get the animals all in one place," one of the more talkative lads, who had been on duty for the last few months, told me. As I immediately suspected, the truth was that with the lion prowling almost every night, and sometimes during the day, the boys all wanted to stay together, for which I could hardly blame them.

The more experienced herders among them explained to me that the traditional plan for trying to fend off a large and active predator called for three watch fires to be built each night, and the herd kept inside the triangle as much as possible; of course it was often hard to scrape up enough fuel for one good watch fire, let alone three. The animals were so frightened that they stayed without much wandering. Of course it would not have taken much to launch them all in a stampede.

"Since the lion usually comes at night, I doubt your bow would be of much use," observed the leader of the herd boys, "even if it wasn't much too thick for you. Unless you can see in the dark?" Tarn was determined to hang on to his leadership, such as it was, especially as he was a couple of inches taller than me, though probably a little younger. I think it cost him a valiant effort not to be impressed by the fact that I had not only killed a man—no one else in our crew had done as much—but had somehow escaped serious punishment for the deed.

I thought of demonstrating how easily I could draw the bow, then offering to let him try. But at that tender age leadership had no more attraction for me than it does now; it is a burden I unwillingly assume when necessary and drop again as soon as I am able, because in my view it brings unpleasantness at best.

"Afraid not," was all I said.

"We hoped they would send men this time." This from the second-oldest of my new colleagues.

"All the young men older than me are busy with the war. And none of the old men want to do this kind of work. Besides, when we left home, no one there had even heard about your lion."

"But," I added after a moment, "I might be man enough to deal with it." I suppose it was only the calm tone in which I spoke that forestalled an outbreak of derisive laughter.

Tarn thought about it, then demanded: "If you're sixteen, why aren't you in the army?"

"I just turned sixteen on the way here." I wasn't going to try to explain that my parents had kept me out of the army because of their deep though unspoken fear that I would mangle someone—not an enemy, but some comrade in arms who, according to the rules, ought not to be mangled. Probably it had even occurred to them that whatever violence I might commit in this remote place would be more easily ignored or covered up.

At that age I had as little acquaintance with physical pain as I had with serious fear. No doubt my claim sounded to my new associates like idle boasting, but I meant it only as hopeful speculation. Having lived all my life with my extraordinary powers, I felt confident that they would see me through an encounter with a lion as effectively as they had through confrontations with snakes and music teachers. I wasn't *absolutely* confident, no, not quite—but what doubts I had were no more than enough to excite a certain sense of danger, and only to the level where it was still pleasurable.

One of my listeners, at least, was not convinced by my offhand optimism. "Deal with it how?" Tarn asked, going back to the subject of the lion. He was still looking dubiously at my oversized bow.

"We'll see. I'll do the best I can." And I turned away, avoiding argument. That had become my habit, more than ever, in the weeks since Linus lay in the courtyard with his eyes turned for the last time to the sky.

Unlike most of the other herders, who kept finding various honorable reasons not to undertake the job, I readily took my turn, and even volunteered for an extra one, walking between small watch fires in the dark.

On the next night after our arrival, the lion came again, terrorizing the herd, and killed again. I heard the great beast roar, but wanted to wait for better light before trying to do anything about it.

When the first light of dawn arrived, there the predator still was, great mane and tawny hide and switching tail, crouched in the middle of what was now an otherwise deserted plain. The successful hunter was still feeding leisurely on its kill, a steer with its throat torn out.

Most of the other boys were looking at me, ready to be amused as soon as I presented them with whatever good reason I might have found for not approaching the enemy just now. But I paid my audience little attention and instead began to walk steadily toward the lion. Enkidu stayed with me, only a step behind.

With the impatience of youth, and well aware that my aim was less than expert, I loosed my first shaft at what I considered long range, something more than a hundred yards. My bow was bent far enough to propel the arrow with tremendous force. But unfortunately I missed the mark by several yards, so badly that with majestic scorn the lion ignored my efforts. Not till my third shot did I manage to hit the beast, squarely on its wide flank, with a broad-blade hunting arrow. The boys behind me drew in breath with a collective gasp as the keen-pointed shaft only bounced off.

The lion turned its head, gave us a look, and unhurriedly went back to feeding.

Now we had solid evidence confirming the rumors that this was no purely natural beast. Odylic magic was involved.

In a quiet voice, Enkidu, standing beside me, said: "Then it's true, what the stories say, about sharp points and edges, how they can't dig into its hide."

I grunted something. We might indeed be facing powerful magic, but I had no intention of giving up. The other herders stayed where they were, well in the rear, watching, desperately gripping their inadequate weapons.

"If I bend the bow any farther," I muttered, "it'll break. Or the string will." And that was exactly what happened on the next shot. The tough cord snapped and lashed me, imprinting a line of what would have been fiery pain on any mortal human arm save mine.

The boys squinted at me from a distance, as if getting a more detailed look might help them understand just how I had managed to break the string on a bow that none of them could have begun to pull. Tarn, who had been anxious about maintaining his leadership, was now as silent as the rest. Eventually, on his making a reasonably courteous request, I had let him try the bow, and he had strained his thin arms to draw it without having much effect.

Now I violently blasphemed the various bodily parts of several gods and cast away the useless stick, trailing a length of broken bowstring. Clenching my fists, I looked around me in frustration.

Had I had any experience with a shepherd's sling, I suppose I would have borrowed one and tried it; as matters stood, I had no reason to think that I could hit the beast with a slung stone in more than one out of a dozen, or maybe a hundred, tries. I would be at least as likely to brain one of my companions, no matter where they stood. With a little imagination, I could picture that kind of performance rendering the great beast helpless with laughter—I supposed it was not entirely impossible that a magic lion could laugh.

Still, such missiles did not depend on sharp points or edges to do their damage, and on thinking the matter over I doubtless would have tried to borrow a sling, except that the lion had turned to look at us once more, with an attitude of speculation, and when I looked around again the other herders had all retreated to an even greater distance. Except, of course, for Enkidu, who, though far from cowardly then or later, was careful to stay close to my side.

When the lion had made its latest kill, the herd had scattered, as it usually did when one of its number was brought down. The others had dispersed quickly to a distance of a couple of hundred yards. But once the predator settled down to eat, some instinct evidently told them that they were safe again for the time being, and they stopped running and resumed their life's work of turning what grass they could find into meat and milk and dung.

After the shot that broke the bowstring struck near the lion, kicking up dust from the rocky soil, the beast coughed a little roar and regally prepared to withdraw. But there was no thought of abandoning its dinner. Once more sinking its fangs into the fresh carcass, it gave a single heave and slung the inert mass over one shoulder. Then it walked away, carrying the dead weight greater than its own with the ease of a man wearing a small traveling pack.

Shrugging off the useless quiver of arrows, in my frustration I hurled them scattering to the ground. "I'm going after the beast," I told my nephew. "You can stay here with the others, if you like, and watch the cattle."

"No need to watch the stock while the lion's gone," Enkidu protested. "I'm coming with you. I know how to track," he added hopefully, after a moment.

Obviously my nephew's confidence in my abilities was at least as great as my own, and I found that somehow reassuring.

"All right," I agreed. At the moment the lion was still in sight, and I did not need a tracker. But before going after it I wanted to arm myself with some more effective weapon.

The twelve-year-old looked back toward our timid colleagues, then suggested: "One of these others might loan you a sword."

"I've seen their swords; you borrow one if you want. And bring a waterskin. No, if an arrowhead won't pierce the damned thing's hide, I'll bet a blade won't, either."

"You could try thrusting right down its throat."

I looked at my helpful colleague. "I'm going to try a club." I might have thrown rocks at the lion, of course, but again I distrusted my aim.

"Are you sure?"

"No, I said I was going to try."

Pacing away in a direction opposite to that taken by the beast, I climbed a nearby hillside where there were scattered trees. Such fallen trunks as were available proved on close inspection to be soft and rotten, so I soon found myself engaged in the difficult business of cutting and tearing a big club out of a live tree. Picking up an edged rock as the best tool available for severing and breaking wood, I hacked and splintered the green, live trunk of a wild olive into an approximation of the shape I wanted. The task took me the better part of an hour, while Enkidu stood watching in near silence.

My weapon, when I had finished shaping it, tearing away with my fingers the last unwanted bark and splinters, was about five feet long and almost straight. The thick end was as big around as my leg, the small end much thinner, enabling me to grip it comfortably. The wood was springy and heavy, and when I swung it hard it sighed nicely in the air, with faint whistling overtones.

*   *   *

By the time I had finished these preparations, the lion of course was out of sight again. Silently my nephew led the way to the spot where we had seen it last. Casting around there, he soon picked up its trail.

We had to follow the beast across half a mile or so of barren ground, and around another hill or two. In this effort my nephew's tracking ability proved of considerable help.

We came around yet another hillock in the great plain, and there the lion was, not a hundred yards away. It had dropped its burden and was once more chewing contentedly. We were close enough to hear the bigger bones crunch sharply, as if a man were cracking nuts. A few scavenger birds had begun to circle overhead.

This time when the lion raised its head, displaying a bloody muzzle, I had the feeling that it recognized me as the one who had been shooting arrows; and by now it was tired of being pestered. The beast once more coughed a short roar in our direction. I suppose our antagonist viewed two young humans more in the category of dessert than as a serious challenge, but was gentleman enough to give us a warning anyway.

As we began our final approach, Enkidu's sandaled footfalls, which at first sounded only a pace or two behind me, fell more and more slowly, and farther and farther to my rear. That was fine with me; I needed no tracker at this point, and if my club swung wildly, I did not want my kinsman to be at risk. He was a brave lad, with a lot of confidence in me, but a real lion is a real lion, and I had to admit that this one seemed to grow ever larger as I approached.

I suppose that if my former mathematics tutor had been at my side, and I discussing the business with him, I might have described my state of mind at that moment as 90 percent certain of victory. If there was only a 10 percent chance that the lion would be able to rend me limb from limb and eat the pieces—well, that chance did not seem real at all. Sixteen-year-olds are almost universally convinced of their own personal immortality.

Now only a hundred feet separated me from my quarry, and I plodded steadily on. The lion looked away from me again and around the barren landscape, as if in search of witnesses who might later be called to testify to my insane behavior. Then it looked back. It raised its head and coughed once more, seemingly puzzled by this two-footed creature of less than half its size, who kept inexorably advancing.

Something in the way the animal turned its head to one side suddenly reminded me of Linus. And like Linus, it felt perfectly confident of its own authority, even when confronted with things it did not understand. Or was my own confidence all a horrible miscalculation, and was I going to be eaten? But it was now much too late to entertain such doubts.

Now there were only forty feet between us, now no more than thirty. As I continued my methodical advance, with club upraised, the lion crouched and sprang.

I swung my five-foot log with two hands, and all the power that I needed was there to draw upon, unfailing and seemingly unlimited, as I had never really doubted it would be.

But on that day, in my instinctive reaction to the onrushing threat, I must have called upon more than I really needed, far more than I had ever tried to use before—though the surplus was not so extravagantly disproportionate as it might have been. Under the impact of heavy green wild-olive wood striking its extended forelimb, head, and shoulder, the massive tawny body changed direction instantly in midleap, ricocheting almost at right angles. It was as if I had swatted a large insect out of the air. The lion hit the ground ten yards away, rolled another five, and lay there with its four legs sprawled. Its body was convulsed by violent spasms, which even as I watched declined into a sporadic twitching.

My greenwood weapon had survived intact the crushing impact, though the force of the reaction, descending through my body, had driven the heel of my right sandal, on which my weight was braced, several inches into the hard, dry ground. Neither my heel nor any other part of my anatomy was bruised, or even tender. Power had simply flowed from its mysterious, invisible source through all my joints and tendons, bones and skin, seeming to turn my modest muscles momentarily into steel, the flow protecting my own frame even as it worked destruction on another.

Warily, somewhat awed at my own success, I approached the

lion, club upraised. But it was easy to see at once that no second blow was needed. The tawny hide was still amazingly intact, but my one stroke must have created chaotic internal ruin. The body on the ground looked shrunken and half-boneless. One eye had been popped out of its socket, leaving a raw hole, and dark blood was trickling past the white fangs of the open mouth to form a little pool on the bare ground.

There was a sound of running feet, and Enkidu came up, panting, to stand in awe beside me, muttering in a high childish voice the names of gods and demons.

"I saw it. But no one will believe it," he observed after a moment. I looked around and saw that the other boys were only now coming back into sight, atop a little hill two hundred yards away.

"They will if we show them the hide," I said.

We drew our knives and got to work upon the grotesque, almost boneless corpse. Or rather tried to get to work. Our blades could make no more impression on that skin than had my useless arrows.

Belatedly the bright idea occurred to me that it might be possible to skin the beast using its own claws or fangs as tools. We soon discovered that the claws of a great predatory cat were ugly things, filmed with rancid grease from rotting bits of raw meat. Whatever the special nature of those sharp, stained points, they worked. Skinning the cat was still a clumsy job, but no longer impossible. Gradually the other herders came to gather around, trusting the evidence of their eyes that the lion was dead.

Soon I decided that the job of skinning would be more easily completed back at camp. With a single heave, I lifted the beast's dead weight easily onto my shoulders and went stalking away with it.

The other herd boys soon rejoined us. After a quarter hour or so of near speechlessness, they began to be generous with praise, and with advice on how to cure the hide.

A couple of them claimed to know something about the process. "We'll just stretch it in the sun for the time being." And some began to gather poles of wood to make a frame.

*   *   *

"See?" Enkidu was poking at the dead, misshapen head. "You could make the jaws into a kind of helmet. So you'd be looking out through the open mouth."

"Sounds uncomfortable." And so it proved to be, when at last I was able to try it on. But by that time, I had other matters to worry about, of far greater moment.

Later, as months and years went by, a legend somehow spread far and wide that had me wearing the lion skin as my chief garment from that day on. In truth I tried to do so for a while, but the smell of a hide so crudely tanned was hideous, and there were other inconveniences. The poor beast's pelt survived in legend vastly longer than it did in fact. Before long I parted with it in disgust, and I have no idea whether anyone ever picked my discard up.

⚬ *FOUR* ⚬

A Visitor

*N*aturally the flurry of questions continued. I grunted responses, and Enkidu kept thinking up new answers. To begin with I had told the simple truth, that I hit the lion and it died. The only trouble was that no one was going to believe that. All right then, so be it. Actually I felt uncomfortable about letting the simple truth be known. I could not forever keep my terrible strength a secret, but I wanted to postpone as long as possible the day when everyone knew about it.

None of the other boys had actually seen me kill the beast, though some were puzzled by having heard, from beyond the hillock, a single sharp jolt of sound, reverberating from other nearby hills to give the impression of something like a thunderclap. It came to me that they meant the impact of my club.

"Was the lion struck by lightning?" one naked urchin demanded of me.

"No." Ready to give up attempts at cleverness, I repeated in a few terse words the plain truth of how I had killed the beast.

Still it did not really sink in. "We heard a noise," remarked another. "Like a big thump."

But Tarn only shook his head. "No, seriously, Hercules. What happened?" He seemed convinced that I must be joking; but now there was a certain deference in his tone.

"All right, then," I agreed. "Enkidu and I walked around that hill and found the animal dying. Maybe a big rock fell on it out of the sky."

"What?" Boys looked up, startled, craning their necks and hunching their shoulders as if they feared a shower of stones was on its way. "What rock?"

"All right." I shrugged my shoulders. "That couldn't have been it. Then someone or something must have poisoned it."

"What?"

By this time most of my other colleagues were gathered closely around the carcass, beginning a detailed inspection. Soon a couple of them were waving hands smeared with lion's blood and reporting that many of the big cat's bones were broken. How could that happen, one wanted to know, if the beast had died of poison?

If my fellow herders had scarcely known what to make of me before I killed the lion, they were now totally confused. But gradually the conviction became established among them that I must be somehow responsible for the monster's death, and soon no one any longer disputed that idea. As long as they ceased to pester me for explanations, I did not mind. In later years, of course, when my fame had grown, the legends never left room for any doubt about how I had slain the beast. And in this case the legends were remarkably near the truth.

It was soon plain that the boys who had boasted of their skill in curing and tanning animal skins had stretched the truth considerably, as boys are wont to do. In fact, none of us knew much of anything about the process. Gloriously magic that tawny hide might be, but it stank so that even a pack of unwashed ruffians like us could not endure it. We stretched it on a vertical frame made from thin logs, using the lion's teeth and claws as tacks or points to hold the skin in place. Then—I had some eager volunteers to help—we scraped the inner surface clean, as thoroughly as possible, and rubbed it down with sand. After that we left it exposed to the sun and rain. A day passed, and then another, but still the hide retained a prohibitively powerful stench.

The lion's carcass was scarcely cold, and we were still working on the skin, when the business of tending the herd, exciting a few hours ago, already began to seem to me excruciatingly dull. At first, saying nothing to anyone, I contemplated sallying out into the great wide world to seek my fortune in some form of high adventure. The animals I had been sent to look out for were no longer in any particular danger, so I thought I could hardly be accused of violating any important trust if I simply left.

About all that held me back was my uncertainty over which way to go, what to do next when I did leave. Unlike many young men, I had no wish to go to war; there had been a certain satisfaction in crushing the lion, but my memory of killing Linus had nothing pleasant about it, and I would have given much to be free of the dreams in which I relived that scene.

On the other hand, if I went home, I could expect to lead a dull and controlled life. Not only would I be subject to parental authority again, but, as in my last few days under Amphitryon's roof, everyone would be walking around me on tiptoe in fear of some fresh act of violence. Within a year or two I could expect to be pressured into an arranged marriage with some woman or girl from one of the families with whom Amphitryon wanted to cement an alliance. And I was afraid I knew just which girl the general would have in mind.

Moodily I tried to explain all this to my nephew. We were both chewing on straws, sitting in the shade of one of the few live trees that dotted the grazers' landscape.

"What will they make you do?" Enkidu asked, wrinkling his forehead in an evident effort to imagine parents compelling anyone as strong as me to do anything.

Downwind from us, the lion's skin was stretched out. It seemed to be willfully ignoring the bright sunshine that was supposed to cure and dry it, and was continuing to poison the air. Maybe the magic that kept it from being pierced was going to keep it from being tanned as well.

I said: "Get married, I expect, for one thing. To someone . . ."

"Who you don't want to marry."

"Right."

My confidant thought that over a bit. "She's not good-looking, hey?"

"If it's the one I think it is, she's a couple of years younger than you are, and already ugly as Cerberus. No reason to think she'll be any handsomer when she grows up. And then I'd have her whole family for my relatives, and that . . ." I made a helpless gesture, despairing of being able to explain. My private thoughts had turned to Megan, as you might suppose, and in a persistent daydream I imagined myself standing beside her in a formal wedding ceremony. But of course nothing of that kind would be tolerated.

Enkidu wasn't listening to me anyway, but shading his eyes with his hand, gazing into the distance. "We have a visitor," he said.

* * *

That happened to be the evening when a traveler, no doubt worried about lions and glad to find any honest-looking company, approached our fire and asked to be allowed to spend the night. We had no objection, being always ready for some news of the world. He was a burly, bearded man, and now and then he would suddenly look back over one shoulder or the other, as if he had just heard behind him a certain footfall that he had no wish to hear. He was wearing a short sword, in itself nothing out of the ordinary.

Naturally the first thing our visitor took notice of on his arrival was the lion's pelt—it was not an easy object to ignore, stinking as it did, and framed as it was, held up like a banner. He claimed to have heard, in a city many miles away, about the famous lion whose hide was proof against edged weapons, and he said he had come our way deliberately, detouring many miles into the remote backcountry, hoping to encounter someone who had actually seen the beast.

But now he squinted dubiously at the stretched-out hide. "This is the one that was killing so much livestock?" He sounded unconvinced.

"The very same," said Tarn, sounding as proud as if he were the slayer.

Our visitor frowned at it critically. "I expected it would be bigger."

"Maybe it's shrunk," Enkidu put in. Then he was inspired with what he thought was a better idea: "Actually there were two lions, and the really big one got away." But I was the only one listening to him, and that only with half an ear.

"Any lion can be a killer," the stranger admitted, still considering the stretched hide. "Of course not the worst monster I've heard about. Not by a long bowshot. Lucky for your little lion there it didn't try hunting in the eastern swamps. Likely it would've been eaten if it went there. Swallowed whole, even if no tooth could pierce its hide."

"Eaten?" Tarn's jaw dropped. "What could eat a lion? What do you mean, swallowed whole?"

And the stranger began to tell us.

Around the fire in the herders' camp that night, we sat with open mouths, listening to the traveler's exotic stories. When the wandering stranger found how ignorant we were on the subject, he began to entertain us with stories regarding the Lernaean Hydra, which he claimed was terrorizing folk who lived near the marshes of Lerna near Argos, which lay hundreds of miles overland from where we were. None of us had ever been there, of course, or anywhere near.

Aye, there were great things being done out in the great world! Privately I came near deciding that I would be gone with the first light of morning. I could see that Enkidu's mouth was hanging open as he listened, and I decided to invite him to come along.

Our informant swore to the truth of another item that also stuck in my memory: that a wealthy man named Augeus had recently offered a reward, of what seemed a truly fantastic sum of money, to anyone who could rid the land of the Hydra. So far, only two men had tried to claim the prize, and both of them had promptly disappeared into the swamps, not to be heard of again.

At this point all my colleagues simultaneously turned their heads, as if unconsciously, to look at me. Our visitor seemed to take note of this, but his only reaction was a frown, as if he resented the fact that momentarily he had ceased to be the center of interest.

One more quick look over his shoulder into darkness, and he who had been telling us the wondrous news was ready to expand on it.

"Compared to the Hydra in the Lernaean marshes, your upland lion is nothing," he concluded. His tone and attitude, as he glanced once more at the stretched skin, seemed to say that it couldn't even have been much of a lion if a couple of herd boys had taken off its hide.

Enkidu spoke up sharply, suggesting that our visitor try his own knife on the hide. But the traveler seemed to be paying him no attention.

"What is a Hydra, anyway?" asked one of the younger herd boys, too humble to worry about seeming ignorant.

The visitor was eager to reply to that one, in some detail. "The Hydra is enormous. It has twenty heads, and each head has a set of jaws filled with teeth as big as my hand. It eats lions as readily as it eats deer, or cattle—or people. What I'm telling you lads about is a monster born of monsters—they say that Typhon was its father and Echidna its mother." On the last word, he tossed one more quick look back over his shoulder into darkness.

"Typhon was a Giant," put in the tallest herd boy. Tarn was gradually beginning to feel secure in his leadership again, seeing that I had no interest in the job; but he had made no attempt to give me orders.

"Still is, as far as I know," put in someone else.

"What's Echidna?" asked the smallest urchin.

"Another monster, of course," I replied. But I think none of us really knew.

It was on that night that I encountered in my sleep, for the first time, one of the strangest figures I had ever met, awake or dreaming. And the oddest thing about it, as it seemed to me while I lay lost in slumber, was that the apparition bore no resemblance at all to any of the creatures of wonder we had been discussing around the fire.

In my dream I stood surrounded by high stone walls, so close on every side that I could not help feeling closed in, very nearly trapped. He who stood confronting me was very tall, looming over me as if I were a child. The figure stood on two legs, and in general it was very manlike, strongly built and wearing a kilt and sandals. The chief exception to its human appearance was the head. That was a bull's head, complete with two long, sharp, curving horns; the head of a creature that, if discovered in the herd, might have given even our lion pause. And when the man, if he was indeed a man, opened his bull's mouth to speak, the voice that came out of it was very odd. Still, every word was clear.

"Come to me, Hercules. Come to me and learn. Bring your great strength to me and I will find employment for it."

And I awoke, sweating, and afraid of I knew not what.

In the morning, the traveler moved on, leaving us with a few words about the marvelous country he was bound for, where he said he expected to find giant birds capable of impaling people with their beaks. He might have been hoping that one or more of us would volunteer to come with him, but no one did. And even as he cast a last nervous look back over his right shoulder, I had a sudden flash of insight. I understood, as surely as if I had suddenly been granted the gift of prophecy, that as soon as the wanderer reached the glorious land he spoke of, he would begin to tell its inhabitants about the fabulous lion whose stretched skin he had just seen, more wonderful than any creature they had ever beheld or imagined. And he would tell them also about the godlike strength of a youth called Hercules, who had felled the monster with a single blow.

My restlessness had not abated overnight. The traveler's stories, though I understood that they might be mostly lies, had only made it sharper. I began to tell my nephew what I was thinking. A little later on that same morning, Enkidu and I took leave of our fellow herders, whose lives had suddenly become much safer and more peaceful, and went heading out in the opposite direction from that our visitor had taken.

When I issued my invitation, Enkidu was willing and even eager to abandon his assigned job with the herd and come adventuring with me. And why not? So far, his time away from home had all been fun.

"If people come asking after you—" Tarn began, when he understood that we were really leaving.

"Tell them Hercules and Enkidu have gone out to see the world."

We had not been an hour on the road again before my nephew asked me: "Herc, what are Giants like? If one of them could father a monster like the Hydra."

"Huge, I guess. Well, of course, that's why they're Giants. But I've never seen one, any more than you have."

"But where do they come from?"

"How in the Underworld should I know?" He might as well have asked me what kind of people lived on the far side of the moon.

It bothered me that I knew so little about Giants. Sometimes I found it disturbing that the number of subjects on which I was ignorant seemed so vast.

Our minds held only the vaguest kind of map, based entirely on hearsay, of the strange lands before us, but we were satisfied with that. We told each other that we could always ask directions, and we were willing to work for our keep as we went traveling.

Enkidu asked: "Shall we go first to see that man who's offering the reward for killing the Hydra?"

I had been thinking about that. "I'm not sure we can find him. I'm not even sure that there's really any reward." I cast a glance back over my shoulder, a habit I seemed to have picked up from our recent visitor. "The messenger, or merchant, or spy, or whatever he was, just wanted to talk of marvels, and maybe half of what he said was true. *Maybe*. When you think about it, he told us nothing of any practical use."

My nephew looked disappointed. "He told us about the reward! We can try to find the man who's offering it. He said the man's name is Augeus; I remember that plain enough."

I thought some more. "The pair of us don't look much like monster slayers," I said at last. "If we tell people we're going to kill this Hydra, they'll only make fun of us."

"You *could* kill it, couldn't you? If you hit it the way you hit the lion."

I let my feet carry me on a few more strides before replying. "I don't think there's anything living in the world that I couldn't kill."

"That's what I thought, Herc. But you don't sound happy about it."

I grunted something.

Enkidu persisted. "So if anyone laughs at us, you could show them how strong you are."

"Yes. But . . ." But that was the very thing I had spent most of my life trying to conceal. Any such demonstration of superhuman strength, it seemed to me, would inevitably lead down roads I did not want to travel. "No, Enk. I say we find this Hydra monster, kill it if we can, and *then* go to the man who's put up a reward—if we can find him. Bring him the thing's head, or one of its heads, to show as evidence. Then he'll have to pay us off."

Not much of a plan, true. But it was enough to keep us going.

o   F I V E   o

A Dirty Joke in the Stable

$\mathcal{A}$s we traveled, I talked with Enkidu about what my mother, though she knew better, hopefully thought of as the secret of my parentage. Of course it was no secret at all. My nephew, like everyone else in Cadmia, seemed well aware that I was the son of Zeus, even though Amphitryon had never mentioned the subject to me, nor had Tiresias in any of our brief encounters. My mother had only admitted the fact to me reluctantly. But my paternity, if far from secret, was still not something my family wanted advertised to the world, or even discussed openly within the family. This at least was the attitude I had absorbed while I was growing up.

I had brought along my club, of course, when Enkidu and I abandoned our duties as herders to go Hydra hunting. After thinking the matter over, I had also brought along my foster father's last gift to me, though the great bow still lacked a string and I had only a few arrows. You never knew. Actually Enkidu carried the bow and arrows for me most of the time.

Our other resources were very limited, consisting of the few coins we had happened to have in our pockets when we left home. And naturally the distances on our mental map were all quite hazy, but we agreed that a journey of some hundreds of miles would be required to reach the swamp where the Hydra was said to live. That of course did not seem much of a problem to us at the time. Shortly after leaving the grazing range, we departed Cadmian territory, but fortunately the lands that we traversed were peaceful.

To earn our keep, on the days when that was necessary, we stopped at farms and in villages along the way, asking for odd jobs. Sometimes people had no work to offer but fed two wanderers out of charity; and sometimes there were days when we went hungry. Once we killed snakes for our bread, in a village that was overrun by them, but they were only ordinary snakes, and we dealt with them by means of ordinary sticks and rocks. More typical was the farm on which we worked to build a wall of rocks.

The construction work went quickly. I suppose that my speed of movement and my endurance, as distinguished from pure strength, were no better than average for an active youth of sixteen. Certainly they were nothing superhuman. But sheer strength makes most physical tasks much easier, and less tiring.

As we traveled, the country around us had been gradually changing, so that my nephew and I now walked a road that wound among wooded hills, and now and then crossed a fiercely plunging stream. And everywhere we stopped, we asked where we might find the man who had posted a reward for the Hydra; so far, everyone we spoke to had heard of the monster, but only a few had heard any rumor of a reward. Still, the number of helpful responses increased.

We came at length to a considerable estate, where the house and its chief outbuildings only became visible after we had walked a long alley of cypress and other trees.

This estate, according to the people we had most recently spoken to, belonged to the man who was putting up the Hydra reward. Augeus was his name.

"Sure, lads, he lives up there." The man who answered our latest question looked as if he wondered why in the world we might be looking for the man we had named. But then he closed his mouth and said no more.

"Is there work available?" I pressed him.

"I'd say so. Ought to be real shorthanded, right about now." And the man seemed to be absorbed in some private amusement as he watched us walk away.

The next people we talked to were workers on the estate, field hands who only stared at us when we asked questions. For a time I thought they might be slaves, but I saw no metal collars. They had a general appearance of unhappiness, and none of them looked well fed, and had we been older and wiser we might have taken warning from those facts.

One of them, speaking in a dull and lifeless voice, told us where we could find the foreman.

The foreman was a heavyset man of indeterminate age, who carried a cudgel at his belt. Seated on a tree stump, he had a stylus and a tablet in his hands and appeared to have been working his way through some problem in arithmetic. He looked us over quickly as we approached, and did not appear to be impressed.

Some instinct was trying to warn me to turn around and walk away. But, having come this far, I stubbornly pushed ahead. "Sir, they tell us you need workers. We're just passing through, and—"

"You'd like some work? Sure, lads, we'll give you a good day's pay for a good day's effort."

The food we were given was poor, and the beds likewise, but in our brief time on the road we had already encountered worse. After a hard day's work of digging and planting, I fell quickly into a deep sleep. And in that sleep there came a dream of birds, like those of which the traveler had told us: iron talons and feathers sharp as arrows. It seemed that Enkidu was clashing an enormous pair of bronze castanets to frighten the birds out of the thickets, and when they flew out I was doing my best to shoot them with arrows. But I was not having much success . . . the flying things were the size of cranes, and closely resembled the ibises which I had seen only in illustrated books. Except that the beaks of my dream birds were straight, not hooked, and the voice of someone I could not see warned me that they could pierce a bronze breastplate.

The bull-headed figure who had appeared in my dreams before was back again. This time on awakening I was able to remember some of what he had said.

"I would bring you dreams more practical than this one, Hercules. This one is not of my devising, but I have entered it, because it is important that we talk."

"And who are you, dream bringer?"

The answer was unclear, but perhaps that was only because I did not want it to be plain.

The speaker's imaged appearance was perfectly distinct, and in my dream I knew that I ought to be able to name him, but that the name I had for him, that was hovering just beneath my conscious knowledge, was wrong. I awoke feeling as close to fear as I had in a long time.

On our second day of work for Augeus, the foreman assigned Enkidu and me to a new task. The foreman had a certain surface joviality about him, but we both liked him less the more we saw of him.

"Come with me," he commanded, and led us out of the farmyard and down a hill.

When we halted, we were still within easy sight of the main house. "Master's just taken over this land." The foreman seemed to take satisfaction in the claim, as if it benefited him personally. Perhaps it did.

It was plain that the previous owner had allowed things to deteriorate.

"Stables have got to be put in order," our boss observed laconically.

The stables were built in a kind of ravine, below a reservoir. Here the enterprising new landowner, Augeus, had already employed clever artisans. His engineers had obviously come to work with many men and animals at their command, and they had dammed a stream, creating a huge pond to give his livestock water, and also to hold a stock of fish. I could see that there was even a kind of waterwheel under construction, eventually to be incorporated into the dam that held back the water of the pond. Augeus was a rich man now, and he meant to be wealthier in the future.

Even at a distance, I could see that a monumental task awaited us.

The stables, a row of low, ramshackle buildings, were in considerable disrepair, but an even more immediate difficulty was that they were horrendously dirty. For some reason the simplest chores had been long neglected. I saw before me a long structure, whose stone walls had once been painted white. There were between fifty and a hundred stalls in a row, with a roof partly of thatch and partly of tile, that had fallen seriously into disrepair. None of the stalls were occupied at the moment, but there was plenty of evidence that they had been, in the recent past.

Enkidu and I were handed shovels and brooms and told to get to work. New piles of manure were to be created, in a place from whence it could be eventually hauled away for distribution on the fields.

We put in another hard day's labor, and then another after that, shoveling and carrying muck. Experience on our own estate at home assured me that no cameloids or droms could be safely housed here until the cleanup was accomplished. Not only dung, but the nests of rats and mice had to be removed. There was nothing particularly enjoyable about the task, but as farm work went, it was not the hardest or most uncomfortable. We gritted our teeth and told ourselves that it would last a few more days at most, and we would be on the road again with food in our bellies and some coins in our pockets.

As we cleaned out stalls, other hollow-eyed workers from time to time brought in animals to reoccupy them. None of these stable hands had much to say.

About halfway through the third day of our labors, I suddenly paused in my work—breaking off some irritable talk with Enkidu—and for a moment came near forgetting where I was. I had just caught a glimpse of a girl riding by, a slim young figure elegantly dressed, mounted on a fine cameloid, with silver ornaments upon the saddle and bridle—an elegant vision that seemed to belong to an utterly different world from the one in which I labored and fought off flies.

At first I was sure this glorious apparition had not noticed me at all. But then in passing she turned her head, just once, and looked at me, while I continued to gaze at her. I am sure that my pose and my expression were unconsciously more those of a general's son, or perhaps even a god's offspring, than they were those of your ordinary stable boy. It must have been my manner that caught her attention and caused her to prolong her silent gaze for the space of two or three breaths. For surely there was nothing else about me that might have done so, as I stood, pitchfork in hand, dressed as I was in a tattered herdsman's shirt, and standing up to my ankles in manure.

That evening, when Enkidu and I reported to the foreman that we had finished our day's work, he stalked over in the gathering dusk to inspect the place. The moment he saw fresh droppings in one of the

newly reoccupied stalls, an anger grew in him visibly. I understood
later that he seemed to be able to turn his anger on and off at will.
"Look at that! I said you make it *clean*. This here place is still
shit-dirty!" And he aimed a halfhearted kick at Enkidu, who dodged
nimbly away.

"We want to leave in the morning," I said on a sudden impulse.
Until that moment I had been planning to stay on another day or two
and earn a few more coins. But Enkidu had already begun to push for
a quick departure.

Eyeing me from under his lowering brow, the foreman only
grunted.

"So," I asked in a clear voice. "What about our pay?"

"Pay? *Pay?* You be paid nothing until the stables are all *clean*,
like I tell you in the first place. Meanwhile, what about all the food
you been eating? There's a cost for that. And what about the place
where you been sleeping?"

"What about it?" I was dumbfounded.

"You owe us for that, too."

"*Owe* you for it? We've been sleeping here, among the animals."

"This is not a charity! You got that, dimwits? Now I want to hear
no more about pay until you've earned your keep."

Before I could close my gaping mouth and begin to think again,
the man was gone.

When the two of us were alone again, my nephew said: "Damn it all,
Herc, a stable is never going to be spotless. Not with live beasts
penned up in it. And they'll be moving more back in tomorrow. The
way he talks, we could spend our lives here shoveling and still owe
him money."

I grunted and nodded. The true state of affairs had begun to dawn
on me some hours ago, but I had said nothing until I could decide
how best to deal with it. And for once Enkidu had been a little slow to
catch on.

"Does he think we're stupid or something?" Enkidu steamed.

"I guess he does. Or at least he's sure we're scared."

On top of everything else, my valuable though not very useful bow was suddenly missing, and naturally none of the other workers whom I asked knew what had happened to it—or so they said. Most of them seemed afraid to talk to me at all. Neither did anyone seem interested in anything but their own immediate survival.

Not for the first time, I wished that I was six and a half feet tall and muscled like a god, with thick, dark stubble on my cheeks and a frowning brow. Then, I thought, no one would have touched my bow.

When we next encountered the foreman, he also suggested, in the manner of a calculated afterthought, that we should not think of running off before we got the stable cleaned out properly—there were a couple of large fierce dogs that the master employed to find those who departed without paying what they owed. With grim satisfaction at what he assumed to be our helplessness, he took his leave.

"I want my bow back," I said in a low, thoughtful voice, when he was steps away.

Almost eagerly he whirled around again. His ears were keener than I had thought, and he evidently thought that we were not worth trying to deceive. "S'pose you don't get it. What'll you do about it?"

My fists were clenching automatically, but I remained silent, backing away from a physical confrontation.

When the man was gone, my nephew looked bitterly disappointed. "Why'd you let him do that?" he demanded.

"Because. If I fight one man, I'll have to fight another, and another. And if I fight I'll break someone's bones . . . and someone else would draw a weapon . . . there'd be all kinds of trouble. It's no fun killing people."

Enkidu was silent for a time, trying to assess my mood. At last he asked me: "Hercules? What will we do?"

"Let's forget about our pay and hit the road. We'll head out about midnight, when they're mostly all asleep. We can live without the pay."

"What about the dogs?"

"I'll take care of them, if they come after us. But I don't want to start killing people and have to fight a war." Yet, having said that to my friend, still I dallied; neither did I want to leave without relieving my anger.

*   *   *

Shortly after dark on that evening, the girl we had seen riding reappeared. Obviously some relative of the owner's, I thought. Maybe his mistress, though she seemed too young.

This time she came deliberately to seek us out. She rode her cameloid straight up to where Enkidu and I were standing, and sat in the saddle looking down at us as if we were a problem that duty required her to solve somehow. Straight brown hair, parted in the middle, framed an entrancing face. Seen at close range, her green eyes and slender body were more fascinating than ever.

"My name is Hercules," I volunteered, to start a conversation. "And this is Enkidu, who happens to be my nephew."

The girl appeared to have no interest in our names, nor did she tell us hers. Well, I had to admit it was really none of our business.

"I just happen to be visiting here," she said at last. Her tone was almost that of one offering an apology. She sighed and seemed to come to a decision. "I heard them talking, up at the house, about you two. They were making jokes."

"Is it your father's house?" I asked.

"It belongs to Augeus, who is my uncle. I don't like him much. He's a cruel man. So are his foreman, and his slave drivers."

"I had begun to form that impression myself," I said. And Enkidu put in, indignantly: "We're not slaves."

She turned her gaze in his direction. "My advice to you is, if you don't want to *become* slaves, you'd better make some plan to get away from here."

"He owes us money!" Enkidu piped up furiously. "Three days' pay! No, now it's four!"

The girl fumbled out a small purse from somewhere and dug into it. Then she whispered a fervent oath. "This is all I have with me." She held out her hand with two substantial coins on her soft palm. "Take this and go!"

I could feel the warmth of her body in the two coins when they came into my hand. "We're planning to head out around midnight," I said.

"That would be wise."

"But there's one more thing," I said. I was intent on prolonging the conversation, though I hardly had any rational reason for doing so. "Would you happen to know, my lady, what has happened to my bow? I had it with me when I came here, a special gift from my step-father. And now it's gone."

She took thought. "What does it look like?"

When I had described the sturdy stave as best I could, she let me know, shaking her head solemnly, that it was now in the master's collection. "I fear you'll never see it again."

I felt an urge to contradict the dear girl on that point. But she was not the one with whom my disagreement lay. Instead I only said: "Your uncle must be a strong man if he can draw that bow."

"He is indeed. And a dangerous one. Take my advice: forget your bow and leave as soon as possible." She turned her cameloid and rode away while we called our thanks to her back.

As soon as we judged the hour had come, the two of us quietly left our wretched sleeping quarters. When we came to where we had a choice of paths, Enkidu hesitated. "What about the bow, Herc?"

"Forget the bow, let's get away from here." I did not turn toward the house, but instead set out in the other direction. After turning this way and that several times, the path climbed to the top of the wall confining the great pond.

No one now, in the middle of the night, was fishing in the pond or working on the waterwheel. The place was deserted by all human activity, but noisy with its frogs. There was a steady murmur of falling water from the dam on the other side, over which the big pond continually drained itself.

"What're we doing?" Enkidu demanded eagerly. By now he was well aware, from my look and the sound of my voice, that I had something in mind more exciting than mere flight. But he had not yet discovered what it was.

"This," I said, and only finally made up my mind even as I spoke the word. Having now confirmed for myself the structure of the dam that made the pond, I laid hands on one of the great stones in the topmost tier. The anger that I had suppressed was suddenly running fierce and high in my blood; at such a moment had Linus died. The rock I grasped was almost big enough to have filled the stall in the stable where we had been assigned to sleep. While the smaller stones above had doubtless been dragged into place by teams of powerful droms, struggling and suffering under the whip, this one looked as if it might have been here since the creation of the world.

"You can't move *that!*" For once my nephew was seriously taken aback.

I only grinned at him. As soon as I had found a satisfactory grip, I braced my feet on lower rocks and tugged. By all the gods, but it seemed to be stuck! I gritted my teeth and pulled harder. The softer rock on which my feet were braced began to crack, and I shifted my stance a little and tried again.

Enkidu was making a little whining, whimpering sound, half protest and half amazement but then suddenly he fell silent.

There was a heavy grating noise.

Moments later, I could hear the water bubbling and laughing to itself, finding a new way out of the pond, this one right in front of me. Only a light gurgle first, but then as I moved a couple of additional rocks it deepened into a heavy rushing sound.

Later, legend had it that I had diverted two entire rivers through the stables to flush them out. But in this case legend, as usual, overshot the mark. There was no need for any such complicated feat of engineering. One pond, of medium size, with a lively stream behind it, was quite sufficient. All I really had to do was to break through the wall, or dike, of the reservoir, which stood in effect holding back a river. There was only one key point that needed to be attacked.

The flood, when it burst out, took me by surprise and came near to bearing me away, but I grabbed a nearby tree branch with one hand and hung on.

The water poured violently down the narrow ravine, sweeping brush and small stones and fallen trees before it. But the full fury of the flood was not unleashed until about half an hour later, when a big section of the constructed wall, undermined by rushing water, suddenly gave way. By that time a watchman had discovered the leaking dam, and Augeus himself and several of his officials had been roused from bed to deal with a disastrous flood. They were gathered in the area of the stables, making plans for a new dam, when they were swept off their feet. The master and several others were borne downstream screaming and swearing, almost drowning in a torrent heavily flavored with liquid manure. Some stone walls were undermined and went down, too, and when, hours later, the flood finally subsided, the stables were smaller than before.

But most of the stalls were practically clean.

Naturally, none of the people who were so absorbed in dealing with the disaster had any reason to connect it with a couple of itinerant laborers. Stone blocks that ought to have taken a team of droms to move had been flipped about like small mud bricks, and the explanations put forward varied from earthquakes to the sudden displeasure of some god.

For a brief time Enkidu and I watched the fun from a high place near the broken dam. Then we moved on. My blood was still up, and this time I chose the path leading to the big house without particularly caring whether anyone tried to get in my way or not; as it happened, no one did. Two big dogs came running out from somewhere, but the beasts that might under other circumstances have been fierce defenders seemed too upset by the general turmoil to care if strangers approached, and only bounded past us howling.

The two of us marched on, and moments later entered the house through a back door carelessly left open. A cook fire burned low in the hearth, giving light enough to see that there was no one else in the kitchen.

"Look at this, Herc." Enkidu's nose had led him to some almost-fresh baked bread.

There was other good food available as well, all of it much better than the stuff Augeus fed his workers on. We helped ourselves.

Curious Enkidu, half-eaten sandwich in hand, pushed open the door to an adjoining room, which proved to be almost entirely filled with sporting weapons. Evidently Augeus, or someone in his household, fancied himself as quite a hunter. There was my bow, leaning against a wall, and I thought that I was entitled to a new bowstring as part of my payment for days of hard work. I bent the bow of Amphitryon easily enough, between my two hands, while Enkidu slipped on the heavy cord.

Then I saw him stiffen, and I looked up. The girl, whose name I still had not leârned, stood in the doorway. This time she was wearing a thin, fine wrap she must have grabbed up on leaving her bed, a scanty costume that made her look even younger than before.

"Why are you here in the house?" she demanded in an urgent whisper. "He might whip you to death if he finds you here, but luckily there's been some kind of flood. You should be on the road. Take this lucky chance the gods have given you."

"We are going," I said. "Right away. We're practically out the door."

"Actually," Enkidu added, "we left two minutes ago."

I hesitated briefly and then, swept by an irresistible impulse, burst out with an offer: "Do you want to come with us?"

Something lighted in the girl's eyes, and for a moment it seemed that she was actually on the point of accepting my impudent overture. But then she shook her head.

"It wouldn't work. They'd come after you and kill you for sure if I did that. Go, quickly; I'll be all right. I'll soon be going back to my own home anyway."

Yielding to a sudden impulse, I cross the space between us in two swift strides. Before she could try to avoid me, I had taken her in my arms and kissed her. She stiffened and turned her head at the last moment, so my lips fell on her cheek.

A minute after that, Enkidu and I were once more on the road, well fed for once and unmolested.

Swamp Games

*T*he threatened dogs never materialized, nor did any other kind of pursuit; I assumed that the noble Augeus had his hands too full with more urgent problems to give any thought to two missing laborers, or to connect them with the ruin of his dam, or even the disappearance of his fine new bow.

Another couple of weeks on the road carried us well into autumn. The heat of summer faded swiftly, and the colors of the trees were changing, it seemed even as we watched.

Sometimes Enkidu and I tried to count up how many miles we had walked since leaving home. But there was no sense of urgency about the calculation, and the only time it caused me uneasiness was when the memory of Megan crossed my mind. I thought of her clear eyes, her soft voice, her warm and generous body, and I regretted the fact that I had come out into the world adventuring without having one more chance to lie with her, or to speak to her at least.

The more closely Enkidu and I approached the great swamp where the Hydra was supposed to have its lair, the more extravagant were the stories we heard regarding its appetite and ferocity. We were told that the monster was quite capable of devouring whole herds of sheep and cattle at a sitting, along with anyone who was rash enough to try to defend his livestock. What impressed me most was the intensity of the terror the creature had inflicted upon many who had not even seen it—some of the locals were ready to swear that even the smell of the monster could be fatal.

It was said to be the size of an elephant or greater—I nodded wisely when someone told me that, though at the time I had no idea of what an elephant might be. The smallest number of heads that anyone was willing to credit the Hydra with was nine. All agreed that the central head was perfectly immortal, though it struck me that that would be a hard claim to prove, short of cutting the head off and then seeing if it died.

Our strange visitor at the herders' camp had told us, and a number of local informants had confirmed, that the great beast we were seeking was indeed the offspring of Typhon, an awesome Giant, and Echidna, who was said to have the torso of a woman, along with a serpent's tail.

Not that we believed very much of this. We were young, but not that young. Probably, I told Enkidu, about a third of it may be true. The difficulty lay in knowing which two-thirds were false. We were still eager to press on.

The nights were growing cold, and since my companion and I had been so generously rewarded for our few days' work as stable hands, we sometimes paid our way into an inn or private household, and slept indoors.

During an evening at one such inn, it happened that tales regarding the Hydra and its parentage were being told in the common room when we came in. I was just in time to hear one of the locals say: "What I want to know is this—at what point on her anatomy does the woman skin stop and the serpent scales begin? Or vice versa. Must be right around her crotch somewhere, and this could be an important question, if you see what I mean. From ol' Typhon's point of view."

As always, when there seemed even a slight chance of gaining information, I asked questions. "Have you seen the monster, then? Where? How long ago?"

"Seen it? Oh, aye. I have. If *you'd* seen yon Hydra, you'd not be looking to see it again."

And that was about the best we could do in gaining any serious information.

We took it as a good indication that we were getting near our goal when we passed through first one village, and then another, that had been totally abandoned for no apparent cause. All of the forsaken houses stood intact, with most of their furnishings inside, undamaged. This, when I thought about it, was a grimmer warning than any tales of monstrous depredations.

After spending a comparatively comfortable night in one of these deserted dwellings, we came out on a brisk morning to meet a well-dressed, substantial citizen of the district, trundling a barrow along a road. He was accompanied by a woman who could hardly be other than his wife, and two small children. It seemed obvious that they were abandoning their home, bringing with them such remnant of their flocks as they had been able to save, one or two animals.

When the crofter saw us, he set the handles of his barrow down and wiped his face. "You're not from these parts, are you?" he demanded as we came up. His speech sounded strange in our ears, for though he spoke the common language, by now we were what we considered a long way from our homeland.

"No sir," I admitted. "We are not."

The man went on: "I must warn you, lads, you've chosen a perilous road. If you ever want to see your homes and families again, go elsewhere."

I shook my head. "If this road leads to the Hydra," I said, "it's the one we want."

The man's eyebrows went up. "And just what do you plan to do when you've located the monster?"

I paused to give the question due consideration. "I think I'll milk it," I decided at last. "I've heard that Hydra cheese fetches a great price with the city traders."

"*I've* come to kill it," put in Enkidu. He flexed his scrawny arm and frowned critically at the muscle that became barely visible in that position.

On hearing our replies, the woman only gave us a weary look and trudged on ahead, tugging her two children with her. But the man kept staring at us. He said nothing at all for several seconds, and his eyes were wide. It seemed we had come across one of those folk who take all statements seriously, no matter how incredible. Finally he got out: "Oh? And how do you propose to accomplish that?"

"We'll think of something," I assured him.

"You are mad, children. Did your parents never tell you that you are both totally mad?"

"They tell us that all the time," said my companion. "But we never listen."

Enkidu would have been happy to stand for a long time debating earnestly with the wide-eyed man, but I was growing impatient, and we moved on. For the next couple of days the two of us kept poking around the edges of the swamp, accomplishing little, except that the deep mud irretrievably swallowed Enkidu's sandals, which were not buskined on like mine. Fortunately his soles were virtually as hard as leather.

Eventually, by persistence and sheer luck, we stumbled across a trail that a blind man could scarcely have ignored. To my untutored eye, it looked like some body much bigger than a lion's had been dragged through the swamp by main force. Enkidu at once proclaimed that it could belong to no other creature under the sun or moon. "This is a Hydra's track!" he announced, and slapped one bare foot in the ooze for emphasis, spattering us both with mud.

"How in the Underworld do you know?" I demanded. "You've never seen one before."

"Never mind what I've never seen; I can see this plain enough. What else could it be?"

My colleague had a point there, I had to admit, as we turned to follow our discovery. Whatever beast had left this giant spoor, it was easy to tell which way it had been traveling by the direction in which the trampled growth was bent. We advanced slowly, looking over the crushed underbrush and the deep ruts, and I was holding my club ready.

This time no expert tracking was needed to locate our prey. In an hour or so we had come to the end of the trail, which led into the mouth of a low cave, a scooped-out cavity just at water level, big enough to accommodate a couple of Augean stable stalls. This, we were certain, could be nothing but the Hydra's lair.

As we stood on the other side of the narrow, sluggish creek that separated us from the cave, gazing into the dimness and wondering what to do next, there came a heavy scraping sound from deep within the watery recess. Then I caught a glimpse of something moving, a huge thing, far back in shadow. Whatever it was gave an impression of dull scaliness like a fish's skin. But the part I could see was definitely above water level, and the creature seemed to be moving in ways I thought no fish could ever move.

"It's in there, all right," I decided.

We both shouted into the cave, hoping to provoke its tenant in to coming out, and Enkidu threw a flat stone hard, skipping it on the water across the little channel and right into the dark cavity. But there was no response.

"It seems we must lay siege," I said.

"Then let's get to work."

The high ground nearby held a generous supply of dry wood, and with the aid of flint and steel we soon had a small fire going. And at last my great bow became useful, as I fired one burning arrow after another into the creature's lair.

"Look there, Hercules," Enkidu said.

Pausing in my labors, I turned in the direction where he was pointing. A couple of hundred yards away, a small audience was gathering to watch the struggle. Eight or ten people, all facing in our direction, stood on a kind of low bluff overlooking the marshes. Some of these onlookers, to judge by the variety and brightness of their clothing, were no mere peasants and herdsmen. A minute later I caught sight of a second group of watchers, observing us from a different angle. These last were in a fairly large boat. They were equipped with oars but at the moment neither rowing nor paddling, being evidently intent on maintaining their distance.

"Where in the Underworld did all those people come from?" my companion marveled.

"Well, we've been bragging to all the folk for miles around what we intend to do, and some of them must have believed us, enough to get their hopes up, anyway. We may not look like much, but they're probably desperate to get rid of the Hydra, and we're their only chance. And its trail sure isn't hard to find. Let's get on with the job."

My next burning arrow might have hit a sensitive spot, for it seemed to cause the occupant of the cave considerable irritation. The Hydra came out in a rush, splashing muddy water about as if it meant business, and we got our first good look at the thing we had been hunting. It filled the mouth of the cave completely in its passage. At once I could feel the hair rising on the back of my neck. *Here,* I thought, *is some magic power truly as strange as my own.*

And as the beast's monstrous body emerged into full view, any lingering idea that it might turn out to be purely natural had to be abandoned.

It made a noise like steam, hissing and bubbling out from under the lid of some boiling, giant cauldron. Its skin was scaly, mottled in shades of gray and fishbelly white. A body as big as a full-grown mastodrom's, or an elephant's for that matter, came wading and swimming on four massive legs, with clawed feet of appropriate size.

Moving straight in our direction, the Hyrda reared up its heads and towered over me. The number of necks, if not twenty, was certainly not less than half a dozen—I didn't try to count. Each neck ended in a head that would not have looked out of place on a good-sized alligator. More red eyes than I cared to total up were looking at me balefully.

Stepping forward to the very edge of the swamp, I met my foe halfway, swinging my club with a good will, and now with something of a practiced aim. My first hit smashed a head into a spray of blood, with flying bits and pieces.

I had killed one head, but three more instantly came snapping and lunging for me. Fangs ripped at me from two sides at once, but a moment later I felt justified in my confidence that they would be no more than a distraction. Their sharp points could find no purchase on my body, but caught a grip on my tunic, a substantial garment I had recently acquired to see me through the chill nights, and immediately tore it away.

Equal strangeness I was willing to concede this enemy, though I still felt confident that it would not be as strong as me. My belief in my own general superiority was somewhat shaken when, while sparring with the remaining necks, I saw the first head that I destroyed begin to grow back. At first I could not believe my eyes, but it was so. In a matter of seconds the neck stump had healed itself into a scaly, swelling lump, and in no more than a minute new eyes were glowing a sharp red, and a mouth full of new teeth was snapping.

One blow had settled the lion, but I quickly learned that now I was competing on an entirely different level. Not until the fight had lasted for several minutes did I begin to keep count of heads as I destroyed them, and when I got to eight there still seemed as many glaring eyes and slashing jaws in front of me as ever.

I raised my club and advanced a little farther, splashing knee-deep in the slimy water. Somewhere deep inside, I was beginning to grow frightened, and it was a strange and unpleasant sensation, not least because it was so unfamiliar.

Again and again the Hydra struck at me with its claws, which were larger than the lion's and just as sharp. But the power of Zeus still flowed in my nerves and veins, and the beast could not break or bruise my skin, or even knock me down. My swinging arms brushed out of the way more lunging heads and the thick necks that tried to entangle me like tentacles.

So far I had remained unhurt, but still there were moments when I feared that I might have met my match. Despite what I was doing to it, the Hydra was not at all disposed to flee. I stood my ground and kept on flailing with my club, but this creature was capable of harmlessly absorbing, on its necks and body, blows even harder than the one that had killed the lion.

The trees rang back with echoes, as if someone were pounding a giant drum. This monster seemed to shrug off the impacts, and kept on coming. Not only that, but the heads continued to grow back as fast as I mashed them. Even faster. On some of the long necks two heads were now growing where only one had been originally.

Changing tactics, I directed my attack at the body, but the springy necks, each as thick as my own body, kept coming in between, carrying their inexhaustible supply of heads to the unavailing slaughter. The great legs pawed at me, pushing me off balance.

Calling upon reserves of power, I added yet more force to my blows. (Later, Enkidu, indulging his chronic curiosity, discovered one of the beast's long fangs embedded in a tree by the energy of the stroke that had smashed its head.)

But still the damned monster was growing new parts, restoring itself by some odylic magic, as fast as I did damage.

I was becoming winded, all my clothing gone in shreds, and my swings with the club grew wild. At last I retreated, backing out of the swamp, naked except for my lashed-on sandals. Part of me wanted to turn and run, and keep on running; but I fought down the urge.

When he observed my withdrawal, my small ally was disappointed. "We're not giving up, are we?" Enkidu panted. When he was not dashing back and forth along the shoreline, shouting encouragement, he had been gathering more wood and building up our fire.

"Flames of the Underworld, no!" I got out between gasps. "But I need to take a breather. And I have to think. There's got to be some better way to go about this."

Heaps of dry, fallen timber lay nearby, on small islands of high land adjoining the marsh. Taking a break in the combat, we withdrew a few yards to one of the larger islands. There I stood guard on shore, leaning on my club and trying to catch my breath, while the Hydra, writhing and hissing, seemed to be debating among its assortment of heads whether to follow me onto firm ground or let me get away. I could have sworn that there were now more heads than when the fight started; and as far as I could tell at that point, the monster was little the worse for all the pounding it had taken, or all the blood that it had lost that was now spattered up and down the shoreline. Now I could well believe that the thing I had challenged in its lair was capable of feeding on lions as well as cattle.

Enkidu soon had an even bigger fire going, up on the high ground where there was a plentiful supply of wood. By this time it was necessary for me to fashion a new club, having worn out my original one. And this took time, prowling among the live trees and the dead, then hacking and shaving at the wood.

Now it was Enkidu who, in a sense, came to my rescue. It was he who had the key inspiration: "Let's try fire, Uncle!"

"You mean more burning arrows?"

"No. I mean, when you mash a head, if I had a good-sized torch, maybe I could get close enough to sear the neck stump. Then maybe the head wouldn't grow back."

So far no better idea had occurred to me. "All right, it's certainly worth a try. Be sure you stay clear of my swings when you come dancing in with your torch." And I practiced a few swirls of my new club.

"You don't have to tell me that." Fortunately some of the available wood was naturally oily enough to burn with some intensity, and a search produced a few good torches.

I suppose Enkidu's chances of surviving the next phase of combat would have been small indeed were it not for the fact that the beating the monster had already taken had actually slowed it down considerably. That became apparent in the next round. Wading into the marsh again, I pummeled and pounded my antagonist some more. I suppose that each of my blows falling on the monster's body, rather than the springy necks, had done some internal damage, and the Hydra's movements steadily grew weaker. The end of the fight was at last in sight, and we no longer felt any temptation to retreat. Doggedly I smashed more heads, while Enkidu, a burning brand in each hand, darted in and out, scorching and searing the raw neck stumps. As we had hoped, this proved an effective means of keeping the heads from growing back.

Time passed, and as the bright daylight of afternoon began to wane toward sunset, even the monstrous vitality of the Hydra was exhausted. The creature was down, sprawled all but flat in the mud and all but helpless, right on the shoreline, barely able to hold up one or two of its remaining heads, while others dragged in the ooze. The process of regrowth had entirely stopped, and most of its necks now ended in charred stumps. Feebly it tried to drag itself entirely into the water, but that we were not going to allow.

And now the eyes of all the heads, save one, were dulled with death. At last, when my great antagonist was almost motionless, I threw down my club. Then, exerting strength behind the blade of one of our poor knives, I severed the last head from the body. Enkidu with his torch was quick to scorch the stump. Then he threw back his head and let out a long, yodeling scream of triumph.

Moments later I posed with one foot on the scaly body, holding up the severed head. It had been the central one, supposed to be immortal, and indeed its eyes still held life, and its jaws still tried to snap. There came a faint cheer from the distant watchers, and then awed silence.

I found their voiceless scrutiny somehow unsettling. "What's wrong with them? The monster that they feared so horribly is dead;

you'd think they'd be jumping up and down with joy. Why don't they at least come over for a close look? Don't tell me the thing's mate is still around here somewhere."

For a time Enkidu gazed in the direction of the silent watchers. At last he said: "They're not coming over here, but they're not going home, either. It's almost like they're afraid to leave. I don't think it's another Hydra they're worried about, Uncle. I think it's you."

"What do you mean, me?"

"They've been watching; they saw what you just did. They could hear the sound of the blows. Now they're almost as scared of you as they were of it."

"But I mean them no harm."

"You can be scary, Herc," my nephew said. Not knowing how to answer that, I mumbled something.

A few minutes later we buried the head, still hissing weak, lungless gulps of air, on solid ground, under an enormous rock. Later, it was said by many that arrows, when dipped in the creature's poisonous blood or gall, inflicted wounds that were invariably fatal. Possibly so, but they were never my arrows; from that day when the lion survived my shots, I have rarely used any bow.

Just as I finished working the big rock into position, Enkidu called to me again, this time in a different, quieter voice. "Look, Hercules."

It seemed that, after all, one of the onlookers was not too timid to approach. The man was standing in a second boat, and where he and his craft had come from exactly, I could not have said. One moment it seemed that he did not exist, and the next he was right there, no more than thirty yards away, much closer than the other onlookers, a tall, solitary figure poling a small, narrow boat in our direction.

I expected the stranger to land directly in front of us, but instead he stopped his small craft just offshore, where he remained standing in it. Effortlessly he kept his body erect and the boat steady, with one hand holding the pole, its lower end stuck hard in the muddy bottom of the swamp.

Ignoring Enkidu entirely, the tall man fixed his gray eyes on me. The light of the setting sun struck in under his hat's broad brim, creating there a curious appearance of small, folded wings above his forehead. But still something seemed to prevent my getting a clear look at his face.

"Greetings, Hercules, son of Zeus." Our visitor's voice had a resonant, faintly echoing quality; I had never heard anything exactly like it. For a moment I recalled the bull-man's speech that echoed in my dreams, but this voice had a very different sound.

"Greetings, sir," I replied after a moment. The man was wearing a long robe or cloak of some fine, smooth material—I remember thinking that I had never seen a garment exactly like it. It covered his broad-shouldered body almost entirely, but I had the impression he was vigorous. At first I assumed he was young, then old, then young again—and then I simply did not know.

I had seen other men as tall as the figure before me, a few even taller. And yet I was somehow certain, before our visitor had been with us a full minute, that for the first time in my life I was looking at a god. Beside me, my nephew, reaching the same conclusion at practically the same time, had lost his accustomed boldness and was suddenly trying to hide behind me. Enkidu, more upset than I had ever seen him, was whimpering words I could not understand. I put my hand on his shoulder and made him face our visitor—wasted effort, I suppose, for the god was steadfastly ignoring my young colleague anyway.

The resonant voice of the deity rang out across the swamp: "Hercules, I have a new task for you to undertake. Will you accept it?"

For several moments I did not answer. I was naturally impressed by the fact that a god had come to talk to me, but I think it is only honest to say I was not overawed. Perhaps my pride was foolish, rooted as much in ignorance as in justifiable self-confidence, but whatever its cause it was substantial.

I said: "You know my name, sir, but I do not know yours."

Our visitor did not seem offended by my boldness. "Humans call me Hermes. Or sometimes Mercury, or the Messenger. Today I have come in that capacity."

Now the pole with which Hermes had propelled his boat seemed to have turned into a long rod something like a herald's staff, except that it was entwined with two carven serpents, and I remembered that it should be called a caduceus. And the boat was closer to shore than it had been, though I had not really seen it move.

Now I was more impressed, but I persisted. "Whose messenger are you, Lord Hermes?"

Broad shoulders moved a little under the cape. "Again, I suppose you have the right to ask. Your father has sent me to you, Hercules." Suddenly most of the shadow had cleared from our visitor's face. The orange light of sunset showed me the countenance of a man who might have been thirty years old. Handsome, yes, but I had seen mortals who were at least equally so. A face perfectly human—and yet with something in it that was more.

When I said nothing, the god added quietly: "Your payment, for accepting and performing this new task, will be something more magnificent than you can imagine."

At this second mention of my father, a great anger welled up unexpectedly within me, confused with a surprising longing.

All I could think of to say was: "My imagination has never been strong."

"Will you accept the new task?" Hermes persevered, standing a little taller than before.

"You must tell me what it is." I have no doubt that at that moment, in my ignorance, I was convinced I was invincible. I had just killed the Hydra, and I was my father's son. All things considered, I refused to be cowed by the mere presence of a god—not of this one, anyway.

The Messenger was still patient. Letting go of the pole with one hand, so he could point, he said: "Hundreds of miles to the north and east of here, on the slopes of Mount Erymanthus, a monstrous boar is ravaging the land. The beast is as much a curse to the countryside around it as the Hydra has been around this swamp."

"A boar?" I think my jaw dropped open. Whatever I had been expecting to hear, it was not news of yet another monster. "A giant *pig*?"

Gravely our visitor inclined his head. "A boar like no other that has ever lived."

"And I suppose you want me to kill it."

Then Hermes surprised me again. "No!" His voice was suddenly commanding. "You are to capture the beast alive and carry it to a place that I will specify."

"Alive!" I marveled, and felt Enkidu's shoulder move under my hand as he raised his head; evidently my nephew's wonder at this dialogue was getting the better of his fear.

"Alive, Hercules," warned Hermes. "And when you have caught the Boar, you are to bring it—still alive, I emphasize, and if possible uninjured—to the port city, called Iolcus, that lies on the northern shore of the Great Sea. Do you know the place?"

"I have heard of the Great Sea but never seen it. Nor do I know any city called Iolcus. That will be totally strange to me."

"But you will undertake the task?"

"I would do much for my father," I surprised myself by saying. "I would do more than that, if he would only do a thing or two for me, in return."

Mercury seemed to sigh, as if in relief that I had agreed to what he asked. "So much to be taught and learned, so little time," he mused aloud. Then, raising his voice again, he said to me: "You should have no trouble in finding people to tell you where Iolcus is, for it is also where the Argonauts are gathering."

My mind was still engaged in trying to imagine the attributes of this monstrous Boar, and how I was to overcome it without doing it serious injury. So for the time being I ignored the puzzle of who or what in the world might be called Argonauts, why they were gathering, and what they might have to do with me. But in passing I seemed to remember that our talkative visitor at the herders' camp, he who had refused to be impressed by our dead lion, had also said something about Argonauts. That man had spoken of many things that none of his hearers understood.

But Hermes/Mercury was still talking, and now I had to pay close attention to what he was telling me.

"Before you hunt the Boar, Hercules, I strongly advise you to seek out the centaur named Pholus. He can tell you much that will be of use to you in the hunt."

"Centaurs? I know nothing about any centaurs."

"You will learn," said Mercury dryly. "I have told you there is much to learn." And he went on to give me some further details, including a geographical description of a place where centaurs were likely to be found. "Visiting the centaur first will require a detour of several days' travel, perhaps more. But it will be well worth the effort. Pholus can tell you the best way to go about capturing the beast. And he may have other information that you will find to your advantage."

Hermes seemed to have finished with what he had to say, and a silence stretched out between us. My nephew at my side stirred slightly, probably, I thought, trying to get up the nerve to leave the clutch of my protecting arm. Small waves lapped at the shore and at the sides of our visitor's boat, and in the distance the onlookers still gazed in our direction, as if they expected to witness some new marvel. I wondered if any of them were able to identify the tall man in the boat.

At last, in my pride, I demanded to know: "If it is really my father who wants me to do all this, why doesn't he come and give me these instructions face-to-face?" As I dared to speak so boldly to the god, I felt Enkidu's shoulder twitch again.

"You may ask your father about that when you see him," the Messenger responded imperturbably.

And in the next moment Hermes surprised me. I had had the impression that he was ready to leave, but now it seemed he intended to accomplish one more small task first.

He turned his head this way and that, for all the world like a man nervous about being seen (and who, or what, I wondered, might have the power to make a god so nervous?). Then, with a smooth thrust of the caduceus, which was also his boatman's pole, he brought his boat in closer to the shore, right beside the Hydra's huge corpse.

He bent toward the silent mass, and a short, bright blade suddenly appeared in his immortal hand. He braced one foot upon the body, and with a faint shock I noted that his shoes were winged, like his hat. Neatly Hermes sliced off a fragment from one of the charred neck stumps, and then another from a Hydra head that, although stone dead, was still attached to the body. These ghastly souvenirs quickly vanished, along with the knife, somewhere into the god's pocket, or his sleeve.

And in the next moment it was evident that Hermes, with divine assurance, had decided that our interview was at an end. If I was not overwhelmed by him, he did not appear all that much impressed with me. Gracefully he lifted the long pole out of the water, whose surface was blackening steadily with the approach of night. The last rays of the sun had faded now, and the god's face was all in darkness. But he was not yet quite done with me. "Remember, Hercules, what I have told you of the Boar. I will speak to you again after you have brought it to Iolcus. Do you swear that you will bring it there?"

"If that is what my father truly wants of me, I swear that I will do my best to accomplish it."

I was starting to form the words of one more question for the god, but his back was already turned to me, and I had the feeling that it would be useless.

And with that the Messenger turned in his boat and moved the pole in his two hands; and somehow the few thin trunks of trees that rose through the dark water seemed to provide concealment, for neither the god nor his boat were any longer to be seen.

At last I did call after him. "When will I be allowed to see my father?"

No answer.

I raised my voice: "Also, if I am being hired like a laborer to do a job, I have a right to know just what payment I am being offered. I know you said it is 'greater than I can imagine,' and that sounds very generous, but all the same . . ."

I allowed my voice to die away, for I was shouting into the empty swamp.

Saurus

*T*he first breath of real winter soon overtook Enkidu and me as we pressed steadily on, up into the high country. That, we had been told, was the place to look for centaurs; but so far we had not seen so much as a hoofprint of that legendary race, let alone gained any clue as to the whereabouts of the individual named Pholus. Again and again I regretted not having pressed Hermes for more detailed information; and again and again I wondered whether I had been completely foolish in agreeing to the pledge that Hermes had demanded of me.

As for my earlier determination to confront my father and demand some answers from him, my failure was so complete that it pained me to think about it. I had not abandoned the idea, but of course had made no progress at all in carrying it out.

Several weeks had passed since I had beaten the Hydra into a mass of fish food and Mercury had carried away his samples of the creature's flesh. Enkidu and I had gratefully accepted the food and clothing bestowed on us in gratitude by some of the people who had watched the fight. On the day I wish to speak of next, we were trudging along a high mountain path, in accordance with the only clue we had that might help us locate Pholus. My chronic impatience was made somewhat the worse by the realization that we were getting farther and farther from Mount Erymanthus, where we must eventually hunt the Boar.

Our new clothing was somewhat warmer than the garments that had been lost and torn away while we were chasing down and killing the Hydra. But, coming from the warm lowlands as we did, we had failed to appreciate what real winter on a mountainside might mean, and whenever we stopped walking we began to shiver. What we needed were furs and hats and boots.

My nephew's teeth were chattering as he asked: "Herc, do centaurs speak the same language we do?"

"I wouldn't be surprised if Pholus speaks ours, along with maybe a dozen others. I've heard that some of his race are very well educated." In childhood Enkidu and I had both learned a smattering of a couple of tongues besides our own, and in our ignorance I suppose we felt beautifully equipped, linguistically, to make our way anywhere in the wide world.

As Enkidu and I strode along, now and then swinging our arms to keep warm, my mind had moved ahead to future difficulties, and I kept trying to think of what would be the best way to wrestle with the Boar. If the creature we were soon going to hunt was in any way comparable in strength and ferocity to the two terrible beasts I had already conquered, catching it alive promised to be fiendishly harder than clubbing it to death.

My companion's thoughts were running on a parallel track. "Herc, we still don't know just what this great Boar looks like."

"True, but that should be the least of our problems. I don't doubt we'll recognize the cursed thing when we see it. It must be a special beast indeed."

Actually, Hermes had given us practically no description of the Boar. But, having seen farmyard and pasture boars, of a more or less ordinary variety, I thought there would be no problem of recognition. I could picture fearsome tusks, of course, but I didn't really suppose that they would hurt me, when the Hydra's fangs had failed to inflict so much as a scratch. Maybe I thought, I could first stun the great pig with my club, or with my fist, if I could calculate just the proper amount of force.

I felt sure that the cloaked figure who accosted me in the marsh had been a god. But for some reason, as I continued to mull over the experience, I was no longer entirely convinced that our visitor had been Hermes. Nor could I understand why Hermes—if he had been Hermes—had been so insistent that the Boar was not to be killed.

Enkidu and I were striding along with our minds on these and related topics, also speculating on the nature of centaurs, as I recall, and paying little attention to our surroundings, when a huge, heavily armed man surprised us totally by stepping out of concealment behind a tree and onto the road just ahead of us, where he stood blocking the way.

At his first appearance, the man's face was contorted into a scowl of menace, but as we remained passive, that soon smoothed away into a gap-toothed smile. I suppose his age might have been thirty, though it was hard to judge. He was clad in leather trousers and a leather vest with boots to match, his reddish hair hung in two pigtails beside large earrings, and his face and his enormous arms, quite bare in total indifference to the cold, had been heavily tattooed and ritually scarred. His barrel-like torso was festooned with belts and holsters, from which sharp weapons sprouted like thorns from a cactus.

I saw with faint, unreasonable disappointment that there was nothing of the centaur about him, though at first glance he was not much smaller than a horse. A robber, certainly, I thought; and I realized that we were lucky not to have encountered others of his profession in our wanderings to date. Somehow I retained presence of mind enough to take a quick look around, and I was vaguely surprised that he had no band of ruffians with him. Any lone bandit was going to have a hard time of it, I thought, if his potential victims tended to travel in groups. But perhaps this one made a specialty of lone travelers, or feeble-looking pairs—like us. I was of course carrying my latest version of a club, but I knew that it looked too big and clumsy to be an effective weapon, especially in hands no more impressive than mine.

Meanwhile the huge man had put his fists on his hips and was regarding us with satisfaction, as if we might have been two mushrooms he was about to pick and eat.

"Good morning, lads." The voice of our new acquaintance was suitably large and deep, but well controlled. And indeed, he sounded truly pleased to see us.

"Good morning, sir," I said. It seems to me now, as I look back, that half my mind must have been still on centaurs, and the Boar. I kept looking about, still more than half expecting a dozen or so of the robber's henchmen to come springing out of their own ambushes. But we three were still alone, so I turned back to him. "Do you know where we might find some centaurs?" I asked, on the off chance.

The man did not appear to hear the question. "My name is Saurus," he announced, then paused, as if expecting a reaction. When none came, he went on, frowning. "You both look cold. I think you should come along to my cave—it's nice and warm. I have some warm clothes there that would just fit you."

If these were the words of genuine hospitality, the tone certainly had a false ring to it. I exchanged glances with Enkidu, who shrugged minimally. As long as he was standing close to me, he was no more frightened than I was, and his eyes actually brightened at the prospect of adventure. I looked back at the man, who no longer seemed quite so satisfied. I suppose our reactions, neither innocent gullibility nor craven fear, were odd enough to awaken some uneasiness.

"Which way is your cave, sir?" I asked politely.

As if reluctant to be outdone in courtesy, Saurus made a motion with his head, then stepped aside to let us precede him. A small path, practically invisible from the road, led from behind his tree of ambush into the woods. I turned my back on the man and walked along the path, without really stopping to think about what other options might be open to me.

I did, of course, take the precaution of making sure that Enkidu was safely in front of me; he had scampered at once into that position, making sure to keep me between him and the big man. My stick rode in its usual place on my right shoulder. If Saurus, who was now walking behind me, should try to wrench it from my grasp, or more likely, to strike me down from behind with one of his own weapons . . . well, he'd be in for a surprise. But I still was not absolutely sure he meant us any harm. Very likely he did, I thought, but simply had no respect for any weapon so big and clumsy as my club, especially in hands as small as mine.

"Been traveling far, boys?" asked the large voice behind me, retaining its joviality. "Is home a long way off?"

I turned my head back slightly to reply. "All the way from Cadmia, sir. Thanks for your concern."

He did not reply, and I wondered if he had ever heard of Cadmia.

We had not quite gone a hundred yards along the path when the cave suddenly appeared in the form of a dark oblong window in a natural limestone wall, the opening covered by a hanging stitched together from the hides of large and furry animals. Saurus stepped up to push the hairy curtain back, and moments later we were all inside. I left my club outside, thinking there would probably not be room enough to swing it in a small cave anyway.

Enough daylight to see by came in through high crevices in the rock. It was a surprisingly warm chamber, roomy but snug, but despite the promise of comfort it was hard to relax, because of the dozen or so human skulls and other bones which the proprietor had incorporated into the luxurious decorations, and which ran like a frieze, up high around the irregular and slanted walls.

A small fire was burning, making an optimistically merry sound, in a recess in one wall of the cave. A hole in the rock above the fire made a fair chimney, and the stone floor formed a handy natural hearth. On a flat stone near the fire, a lidded pot was keeping warm, sending out a vaguely appetizing aroma. Had it not been for the charnel-house decorations, the place would have been quite cheerful. Much of the stone floor was actually covered with a carpet, incongruously fine.

Even a robber can have a home, I thought. And suddenly, I suppose because of the image of coziness and home, I thought of Megan. But she was far away, and I thanked all the gods that she would never be anywhere near this cave.

Something much larger than a mouse went scampering near my feet, and I looked down, startled, to see a couple of exotic little animals, lizards of some kind, the size of rabbits, running around inside the cave. At first their dark-scaled bodies moved too fast for me to get a really good look, but when they paused I saw that they were wearing collars, like pets. One of them was carrying a bone in its monkeylike forepaws and chewing what looked like the last fragments of meat from it. The bone looked ominously like a human ulna. Crouching on the hearth, the creatures stared at us with their large yellow eyes, and it seemed to me that they looked hungry.

"Your pets?" I asked.

"Meet Deimos and Phobos. They keep most of the vermin out. And they're better company than people."

I said nothing, but only shook my head. If a man prefers the companionship of lizards, what use is there in arguing with him?

Saurus invited us to shed our packs and sit down. But as soon as

I had slid mine from my shoulders, he snatched it up, opened it without hesitation or comment, and dumped out the meager contents on the single, narrow bed that stood against one wall. Enkidu's burden followed quickly.

"Not much," the robber observed in disappointment. "Too bad, lads, that you're both so poor."

"Help yourself," I offered. "If you see anything there you like." Then I drew a deep breath, feeling for some reason that I owed the man fair warning. "But if you empty my pack, then before I leave your cave I'll likely fill it up again, maybe with things more valuable. Like some of those warm clothes you mentioned. And I suppose you have a good supply of food."

Saurus gave his imitation of a laugh. It would need more practice if he wanted it to be convincing. He was still watching me with amusement, but now with caution, too. Most likely my continued calm suggested to him that I was mad, and the mad, no matter how small or poorly armed, are always dangerous opponents.

"As for clothes," the huge man said, "you lads won't need to worry about such things anymore. I understand they're just not needed in the Underworld. In fact, you'd better take off the ones you're wearing—that'll keep 'em from being damaged and save me the trouble later."

I was glad to see that Enkidu had already done what he could to remove himself from harm's way, scrambling back as far as he could get in a blank corner of the cave. Now I would not have to worry about protecting him in the conflict that seemed likely to begin at any moment.

Still, with the image of Linus before me, I felt a need to make the whole business thoroughly explicit, so I asked our host: "Don't robbers usually have helpers? I mean, don't you like the odds to be in your favor, as a rule?"

Saurus looked at me almost pitingly. "Why, bless you, lad, I don't need any helpers. Not in dealing with anyone I might invite into my home. Maybe you've heard of me by my other name. Some call me the Lizard." Again he paused, as if expecting that the name would produce some effect. But Enkidu and I had never heard of him.

Now the robber was growing angry. "And the odds *are* in my

favor, boy. If you doubt it, try me. What do they call you, by the way?"

"Hercules," I said. But that name meant no more to him than his had to me.

"And my name is Enkidu!" came from the corner, in a brave, piping voice.

"All right, Enkidu," said the Lizard equably, turning his head a little toward the corner, while he kept his narrowed eyes on me. "I'll let you live until later, so you can clean up the mess that it seems I am going to have to make. But it'll be outside. Little Hercules is going to come out there with me; I dislike staining my good carpet."

The Lizard had scorned to draw his sword for me but already had one of his big knives out. When I reached to grab his arm he was far too quick for me—not that being quick did him any good at all. Before I could get hold of him, the blade came slicing through my tunic, and I felt it slide cold and sharp along my ribs. There was a biting sensation, but, as I verified with my own eyes later, sharp bronze or steel in a man's hand was no more able to break my skin than the Hydra's fangs and claws had been. And in the next moment I had managed to catch his arm, and the fight, if you could call it that, was effectively over.

When Saurus felt his muscles crushed in the power of my grip, his bones about to break, and he saw in my eyes that he was soon to die, he said, in a changed voice: "A god has come against me, and I can do nothing."

I wondered if someone, sometime, had given him a prophecy to that effect. For he believed what he said, and he said no more, and put up almost no further struggle. Somehow the Lizard's calm acceptance only made me the angrier, so far was his behavior from what I would have said and done in his place.

He did not scream but only grunted twice, once when I broke his arm, making him drop the knife, and again when I snatched from its scabbard another of the blades that sprouted from his leather-strapped torso, and awkwardly pushed the keen point through his heart. It seemed to me fitting that death should come upon him through one of the tools of his evil trade. Deimos and Phobos screamed and ran away, and bright red stained his good carpet after all, and no one was ever going to clean it up.

In that manner died the second human being that I had ever killed. I found my second slaying less upsetting than my first—and had I been wiser, that fact would have troubled me.

But could I have been so cruel to the world as to allow such a robber and murderer to live? The skulls nailed high on the walls grinned down at me—victims having the last laugh on their killer after all, for they had told me beyond a doubt what manner of man he was.

A god has come against me. But no, I had seen Hermes, and I knew that *I* was not a god.

As soon as he saw Saurus crushed, Enkidu came out of the corner of the cave where he had taken shelter, and stepped carefully over the robber where he lay, no longer breathing, on his good carpet. Then the two of us unhurriedly went through the cave, looking for useful supplies and miscellaneous loot. Most of it we found in a back room, its entrance half-concealed by another curtain of animal hides. Here were the stores I had expected and hoped to find, of dried meat and fruit and fish, and warm clothes enough in different sizes, including fur-lined boots, to complete our outfitting.

After a little searching, I dug out another tunic for myself, one lacking a knife slash, and some leggings and a fur hat. While we were rifling the storeroom, my nephew picked up a fine, fur-lined hooded cloak, which I suppose might have once belonged to some elegant lady, and better footwear. But he thought all this was incidental, and kept on looking anxiously for treasure.

There was indeed a considerable store of gold and silver. This was cunningly buried under the floor, but Enkidu searched diligently until he found it. I pocketed only a handful of coins, which would be useful in buying provisions on the way.

"Look at this, Herc. And this! By all the gods, it's gold!"

"Heavy stuff to carry." I was trying on some boots, of which there was a good selection.

"But *gold!*"

I shook my head. "I've got all I need. You take what you want.

But don't expect me to lug an extra load, or defend a big pile for you." Coins and jewels, gold and silver, in themselves have never seemed to me a great prize, or worth much trouble to accumulate; the world contains vast quantities of such things, after all, and enough to meet immediate needs can usually be found when they become really necessary.

For a minute he was quiet, rummaging around. Then: "Look: earrings! I wish I had my ears pierced, Herc. Are yours?" I suppose my hair hung thick and low enough to keep my ears from being a familiar sight to my companion.

"They're not," I said. "I doubt that anyone could find a tool to pierce them with. But Saurus's ears have large holes." I could remember that detail of the body in the other room.

I doubted also that the boy was paying any attention to what I said, for he did not reply. He tried on an assortment of golden armlets, rings, and necklaces, one after another, as well as belts that carried jeweled swords and daggers. But in the end, under my disapproving stare, he contented himself with a bag of coins of comparatively modest size.

Then my nephew looked around the little space and sniffed the air. "Do we want to spend the night in here? It'd be warm."

"I don't want to spend the night with him," I said, nodding toward the curtain and what lay in the room beyond.

"We'd put him outside. We could even bury him."

That was widely supposed to make the walking of a ghost less likely. "Burial might be a good idea, but I'd rather not stay in his cave at all. We're in no danger of freezing to death, especially with these new clothes. We'll find somewhere."

Enkidu shrugged. "All right. The stew in the other room smells tempting, though."

So the Lizard had turned out to be hospitable after all. Before leaving his cave, we tasted the contents of the simmering pot, decided that it was nothing worse than it first appeared to be, stewed rabbit, and dined on it heartily.

As we were leaving, I stopped just outside the entrance to the cave, tore down the furry robe that kept in warmth, and put my hands on the edge of the doorway, trying out this grip and that. Soon I found one that I thought would do the job. Pulling steadily, I dislodged a few key supporting rocks from the limestone cliff so that a portion of the steep hillside shuddered, and my nephew and I had to jump briskly to get out of the way. Nearby trees vibrated as in an earthquake, shaking dark leafless branches, and the whole front of the cave collapsed, belching a cloud of dust and dirt into the chill air. It was just too neatly situated for a robber's roost.

Meanwhile, on the death of their master the two little lizards had fled the cave, screaming in their high small voices. When we got outside we found their tracks marking the thin snow. But I doubted that Deimos and Phobos had run far, and supposed they would come back before long. The collapse of the entrance had still left room for their small bodies to pass, and the inside of the cave would stay warm at least until the fire went out. And there they would now find fresh bones to chew.

○ EIGHT ○

Centaurs

After leaving the robber's cave, Enkidu and I resumed our quest for centaurs, in particular the one named Pholus. We roamed about for several weeks, seeing few people, zigzagging back and forth across the region in which we had some reason to believe we might be able to locate our quarry. More than once I was on the point of giving up our intermediate objective and trying to get back on the direct road to Mount Erymanthus, where the Boar was supposed to be. I was impatient to find the damned monster, whatever it was like, deliver it as instructed, and then get on with my life—Hermes, after all, had not insisted that the centaur's help was absolutely essential.

Several times my nephew and I thought we were completely lost, and the fact that we were now warmly shod and clothed no doubt saved our lives.

Among the other treasures contained in the robber's cave had been a small arsenal of captured weapons, and we had picked up slings, almost as an afterthought, along with our other booty. My nephew, putting in long hours of practice in the following days, became skillful enough to bring down some small game to tide us over when we could not find a hospitable farm to give us food and lodging.

Our wanderings during those weeks took us well away from Erymanthus, whose snow-capped peak we could glimpse in the distance now and then. But we persisted.

At last we found ourselves among settlements where people did not look blank when we mentioned centaurs, or speak of them as fantastic marvels. In this rugged country of wooded hills and deep ravines, there were few human settlers. None of the people we encountered in this region had any doubt that centaurs were real enough. But they insisted, almost to a man, that they knew nothing about such creatures, and wanted to know nothing. It seemed that in these parts, at least, the two races were well aware of each other's day-to-day presence, but still good at keeping out of each other's way.

Eventually we met one woman, an elder and also a healer, who not only had seen centaurs but claimed to be personally acquainted with the very one we wanted. She confirmed that Pholus was much more likely than most of his tribe to seek out human contact.

Our informant not only described the appearance of Pholus in great detail but (once she was convinced that we were not out to hunt and kill him as a form of sport) advised us where we were likely to find him.

Armed with this information, Enkidu and I stubbornly pressed on. On the afternoon of the second day since leaving the house of the helpful woman, we came upon a strange trail that at last sent our hopes rising.

Every one of our informants, including Hermes, had assured us that we might track centaurs by looking for what seemed to be the prints of horses' hooves.

The marks before us had clearly been made by hard hooves that were certainly not a goat's, or a deer's, nor belonged to any animal that my nephew and I had ever seen.

"Are these horse tracks, Enk?"

The expert tracker squinted at them carefully. "Maybe. Or maybe a centaur's. What do you think?"

"Could be a demon's for all that I can tell."

Despite difficulties, at last we had some success. The ground again was covered in light snow, which made the tracks easy to follow, and even one as little skilled in the art as I was could study them in some detail.

Having proceeded on some further distance, through moderately thick woods, we began to hear a chopping sound.

I stopped in my tracks, holding up my hand. "Hear that? Sounds like a woodcutter up ahead."

"Maybe he's seen the one we're looking for."

"Maybe. Or . . . centaurs have arms, don't they? One of 'em could swing an axe."

Moving on as quietly as we could, we soon came to a stop at the edge of a small clearing and stood there, hardly daring to breathe.

My first impression was that a horse was standing at the far side of the little clearing, facing away from us, tail switching now and then, broad flanks steaming faintly in the cold. I thought it was an ordinary man, his torso naked despite the cold, who sat astride the horse. It was an awkward position for chopping, but the man's arms were vigorously wielding an axe against a thick dead branch projecting from a tree. A moment or two had passed before I noticed that the human legs of the apparent rider were nowhere to be seen. Nor were the horse's head and neck.

I snapped a twig underfoot about that time, trying to move to get a better look; but the being on the far side of the clearing did not turn around. Either he had not heard us coming, or he was indifferent to the approach of a mere pair of humans.

At last I called out in a loud voice. "Greetings!"

Now he who was standing with his back to us did take notice at last, and turned gracefully on his four hoofed legs, and answered with a nod, as if he were loath to be interrupted at his work. He had long hair and a long beard, adorning a face as fully human as the rest of his upper body. All of these made him a good match for the description given us by the woman.

Moving forward a few more steps, I called out boldly: "My name is Hercules. This is my nephew, Enkidu. And if you are Pholus, we have walked a long way indeed to find you."

The centaur pushed back long hair from his face. "I am Pholus. But why have you gone to all that trouble? And just how far is a long way?" His voice was deep and pleasant.

"All the way from Cadmia. I have gone to so much trouble because a god commanded me to do so."

Pholus frowned, as if he were thinking over very seriously what I had just said. Our new acquaintance now grabbed up and pulled on some kind of shirt or jacket, which I supposed he had earlier taken off in the heat of chopping. His arms looked brawnier than those of most entirely human men—he could easily have been a match for the late Lizard.

When he had his shirt on again, he picked up a bow and quiver of arrows from the ground and slung them over his shoulders, just as a normal man might do. The fresh carcass of a deer lay at his feet, I saw now; evidently his hunting had been successful. His mode of carrying a deer was different, of course, as he tucked it behind his human torso.

I am sure that you who read this must have seen pictures of centaurs, if not the thing itself: the head and arms and torso of a man, in the case of Pholus strongly built and in the prime of life. But where you might expect to find the hips, the body as it were began over again in its equine stage, as if the man's torso were a horse's neck. Human hair and beard were the same color as the horse's tail—there was no mane on his human neck or upright torso.

Only later, months and years after this first meeting with one of their race, did I begin to realize how hard the life of a centaur truly was.

For one thing, the huge body requires much nourishment, and it all must pass in through the small human mouth, where whatever chewing was necessary had to be done by small human teeth. Centaurs eat meat, when they can get it—to chew and swallow enough vegetables to support the massive body would be well-nigh impossible. There were of course other problems, too, including those that come of having two stomachs—but in my ignorance none of them occurred to me at that first meeting.

When we had introduced ourselves and had at least begun to discuss the Boar, Pholus invited us to his house, actually only a kind of hut. It was a mile or two away, and our host courteously slowed down his normal cantering pace to one that we could match.

The little house with its thatched roof stood by itself in a modest clearing, with no other buildings near. The front door was large enough to fit a stable, and the place smelled faintly like one, though it was as clean as any house might reasonably be expected to be—in fact cleaner than I have seen the palace of the king of Cadmia, especially on the morning after a late revel. There was little in the way of furniture inside—natural enough, I realized, when I considered that the owner and his usual visitors must rarely sit down and commonly slept while standing. A couple of tall, shelflike tables, skillfully made, offered space for reading and writing, and there were some books, stored on even higher shelves. At one side of the large room a fire of modest size, built on a stone hearth that was raised chest-high to a man, gave out comforting heat and light. There was no sign of any other occupant, and the look of the place strongly suggested that Pholus lived a hermit's life.

The interior was not as cheerfully lighted as that of the last dwelling that my nephew and I had been urged to enter; but in this case we were urged by a gesture of genuine hospitality. Almost involuntarily I cast a glance around to reassure myself that here there were no skulls.

Enkidu volunteered to play the role of butcher and cook, and dragged the deer outside. After some rummaging in a large cupboard or closet built into one wall, Pholus brought out one ordinary chair, which was I suppose the only one he had, and offered it to me. Enkidu, looking quite content to be almost ignored, sat tailor-fashion on the floor against a wall. Obviously the lad was fascinated by our host, and he could not keep from staring at him.

There was a notable jar of wine here, our host informed us, and at once began to tell us the story connected with it. The huge container had been in his house—which, he assured me, was older than it looked—for generations.

According to this ancient tale, all totally new to me, the wine was to be kept, unopened, until a son of Zeus should come for a visit.

"Since you make that claim," said Pholus, "I will take you at your word and open it. Another reason is that I have always been curious about the wine."

By now Enkidu's efforts had born fruit, and the smell of roasting venison enriched the air. When Pholus rolled the wine jar into view, tilting and balancing it on one side of its bottom edge, I saw that it was indeed huge, and made of clay. The top was dusty, the lid closed with a seal of wax so dark and crusted that it might well have been as ancient as he claimed. Pholus grappled it with powerful arms and rolled it out of its closet to a position near the center of the room.

Next he wished to lift the barrel up, into a kind of rack that held it in a position where it could be easily tapped. I could see that this was a job that would ordinarily take two men to accomplish, and I offered to give him a hand.

When I did, of course the great cask went up easily between us. He stepped back, wiping his brow and frowning at me. "Where does your strength come from, lad?"

"An inheritance from my father."

"I see."

When I heard how long the wine had been there, I was not optimistic about its quality, having learned that any left aging for more than a few decades would turn to vinegar, or worse.

Returning to my chair, in which it seemed impossible for a human to get comfortable, I asked our host: "Folk don't usually keep their tuns of wine that long, do they?"

Rummaging in another closet, he had come up with a mallet and a wooden spigot, which he was now holding, one in each hand. "I am the wrong one, Hercules, to question on the habits of humanity. Are you then a good judge of fine wine, Hercules, son of Zeus?"

"Nothing of the kind, good Pholus. But of course we had wine in the house where I grew up, and now and then I've listened when people were talking on the subject. I might repeat some of their words, if that would amuse you."

He laughed and gave me all the details he could of the ancient prophecy, which were not many. According to the story passed down among the centaurs, bad things would happen if this cask was tapped before a son of Zeus arrived—and some catastrophe even worse might be expected should it *not* be broached when the proper time was reached.

When he had driven in the spigot with a few sharp blows and turned it properly, he handed me a flagon, filled with a liquid that looked rich and almost solid red, save for a tiny froth of bubbles on the top.

As my nephew began to serve us dinner, the centaur filled another cup for himself. Nor did he completely forget Enkidu, but tapped him a little wine as well, in a broken clay cup, the only other vessel that seemed readily available. Evidently drinking parties were not a common occurrence in this house. The boy looked sourly at this poor share, but brightened as soon as he tasted it.

For my part, I had to admit that my drink was as far from vinegar as any that I had ever tasted. Even to my uneducated palate this wine was superb, and I wanted to have one more cup at least, to wash down my bread and meat.

I began to tell Pholus of our adventure with the robber. Our host heard me out with close attention, and he was openly impressed. He said that the Lizard was locally quite infamous, and that the folk for miles around would rejoice that we had finished him.

"Congratulations, son of Zeus, on your escape."

"I'll drink to that."

We both smacked our lips with satisfaction.

Now the centaur was squinting at me intently. "Just how *did* you manage to foil the Lizard's plans for you? If you have no objection to explaining?"

"None in the least." Realizing that my previous demonstration of strength had been insufficient, I picked up an iron trivet that lay as a decoration on his table, and with my fingers twisted the thick bar that formed it into quite a different shape. Then, reminding myself that my host had not much furniture to spare, and even this trinket might have value in his eyes, I bent it back again.

Pholus said: "Ah," and leaned his human torso back, like a man settling himself more comfortably in a chair, though of course his body remained standing on its four strong, stable legs. And I thought his manner altered subtly. Not that he was suddenly afraid of me, but now I thought that he truly began to believe what I had told him about being a son of the Thunderer.

The strong wine was certainly beginning to go to my head, and I was on the point of asking Pholus rudely whether there was not a stallion or mare in his immediate ancestry. But our friendly conversation was soon interrupted by a noise outside, the thudding on hard ground of many hooves, and it was plain that either more centaurs had arrived, or else a group of men riding on horses.

Getting up from my chair, I peered out at the side of a window and saw the heads and shoulders of about a dozen men, and the dark bulks of the same number of horses. In the dim light I could not be absolutely sure that I was really looking at a gang of centaurs until one cantered closer to the house. At least half of those I saw were armed with bows and arrows, and some were carrying other weapons, too.

The one who had come near the house now called out in a raucous voice: "Pholus, we see by the trail that you have company. Two of those ugly creatures, so-called humans, that have only four limbs, totter and toddle on only two feet, and move not much faster than rocks and bushes. Ugly and clumsy monsters, they must be."

These words were hardly reassuring, and I thought the tone of the newcomers' voices boded ill for the success of my mission, though I was not personally afraid. Their mood was obviously less than jovial and seemed to resent my presence. So far they had not taken any particular notice of Enkidu, and he had shrunken so far into a corner that he seemed on the verge of utter invisibility.

Pholus looked worried and seemed uncertain of what to do; I opened the door of the house and stood out where the newcomers could see me plainly.

One centaur—later I learned his name was Nessus—conspicuously the rowdiest of the group, for some reason seemed to hate me on sight, more than any of the others did.

On getting his first clear look at me, Nessus declared: "So, this is the spawn of Zeus, of whom so much has been prophesied! What do you say, god-bastard, are all the things that the prophets say about you true?"

I remained standing in the doorway, leaning on my club, as if it were only a walking stick. Feeling the wine, and arrogantly conscious of my own strength, I called back: "It would take a wiser man than me to answer that. Especially since I have no idea what your prophets say. They may be only ranting fools. In fact, that seems quite likely."

A round of jeering answered me.

Without the further warning, one of the gathering loosed an arrow at me. It struck me before I saw it coming, and stuck in my winter jacket. I pulled it out and looked it over negligently, then broke it between my fingers.

Another individual, whom I heard the others address as Chiron, cantered out to a spot midway between me and my opponents and attempted to be a peacemaker. Pholus added his pleas in the name of common sense, but the peacemakers were only two, while all the others, ten or so, seemed bent for some reason on doing me great harm.

Chiron bravely, even foolishly, I thought, tried to keep himself between me and the angry ones.

I shouted at him that I didn't need his help and that he should look to his own safety.

Another well-aimed arrow came at me. I ignored its stinging impact and responded by hurling back a small rock that I snatched up from the bare ground at my feet. It missed the archer I was aiming at, and went on to crisply snap off a branch somewhere in the dark woods beyond.

A moment later, Chiron sidestepped at the wrong moment, while endeavoring to head off a threatened charge, and went reeling back with an arrow through his upper chest, shot at me by one of the mob behind him. I must correct the legendary error that the shaft was one of mine. I was no longer carrying a bow and had not done so for some time. I had traded the gift of Amphitryon for food, in the hungry days before we reached the cave of Saurus.

Rocks were fairly plentiful on the ground before me, and I let fly with a barrage that effectively dispersed the mob for the time being. As soon as the crazed centaurs had been temporarily driven off, I went to where the fallen peacemaker lay, and tried to help him.

The wound in itself ought not to have been fatal, but he warned me, between gasps of his dying agony, that the arrow must have been poisoned. And he gave me another warning, too, that at the time I failed to understand: "Hercules, do not get any of my blood on you."

Of course I could have picked him up and carried him, but the horse-sized body would have been an awkward burden, and I might have hurt him in the process. Also I realized that it would do little good to carry him inside the house.

The fumes of wine seemed to have been driven from my brain, and now I regretted my shouted insult. And I still wanted to know, from anyone who was capable of telling me, why the centaurs had grown so angry. Had they somehow realized that Pholus had broached the wine? Was it simply because they wanted that good red stuff for themselves?

Neither Chiron or Pholus gave me an answer. Perhaps they were unable.

But before I could learn anything more from the dying Chiron, there came a thunder of hooves in the middle distance, and the mad ones renewed their attack.

So much for any hopes I might have had for an evening's enlightening conversation. Now I found myself engaged in another all-
out fight.

Looking back over the years, I can now see that, yes, it is quite true
that with more maturity, more sense, and a little diplomacy on my
part, the worst of the trouble might have been avoided. But three
cups—perhaps even a little more—of that strong wine had made me
first irritable, then irascible, then launched me well on my way to
drunkenness. Naturally, I was no stranger to wine, having been brought
up in a well-to-do household, but at home my consumption was invariably quite modest. And the drink in that aged cask was truly
something wondrous.

"What the hell are they so upset about?" I again demanded of
Pholus, when another brief interval in the fighting gave me a chance
to talk. Looking around, I noted that his house was being ruined in the
process. A fire had started in the thatched roof, and I tore down a
burning reed bundle and scattered it into dying sparks.

"Sorry about your house," I added. "But I'll be damned if I'm
going to turn tail and run."

"And I am shamed," he said at last, "that this could happen while
you are my guest." After a pause he added: "It is the wine, of course."

"Are they afraid I'm going to drink it all? The whole damned jar?
There's enough to take a bath in. It's great stuff, but I'm only good
for . . . well, maybe one more cup."

My host, I seem to remember, counseled moderation.

I was having none of it. "Moderation, is it? A bit too late for that.
By the balls of Mars, I've half a mind to go out there after 'em. But
they're safe enough from me. I'll never catch 'em while they all can
run like racehorses. But they'd better not come within my reach."

And I seem to remember gulping yet another draught of the red
wine, which seemed to be running like liquid fire in my veins. No
damned horse was going to tell me what to do. Horses in general
were a strange, exotic species, and horses like these, that seemed
half-human . . . angrily I began to express my contempt.

With the renewal of the attack, Enkidu once more took shelter in
a corner, first thoughtfully refilling his small clay cup to the brim and

taking it along. If he was going to die soon, he would have some measure of enjoyment first. Unhappily I thought that the corner was not going to do him much good—the walls of this house were not as sturdy as those of the robber's cave—but I had nothing better to suggest.

Once more the attack swept in on us, and this time it was better organized. Our assailants had armed themselves with rocks, dead tree branches, and axes like the one that Pholus had earlier been wielding. They charged the house. At the sight of this determined onslaught, Pholus turned away and fearfully tried to hide himself.

Throwing rocks at me was a mistake, for it only provided me with a supply of ammunition. When a couple of logs were knocked out of the walls by the battering from outside, I used one after another as a swinging club, and then pulled another wall apart to gain more missiles. Horrible screams, half-human and half-animal, went up from the wounded creatures when my thrown logs, coming with the speed of spinning arrows, hit them squarely or scraped them and knocked them down. Had I not been somewhat drunk, I would have killed more of the attackers than I did.

Among the centaurs whom I failed to kill that night was Nessus, who here conceived a great enmity for me, so that ever afterward he remained determined to do me some lasting harm.

Enkidu, who somehow came through the fight unscathed, and I spent the remainder of the night with Pholus, in what remained of his house, expecting at every hour that our enemies might return, perhaps with reinforcements, and try again to wipe us out. For an hour or so after the last clash, we could hear them intermittently in the distance, bellowing like drunken men and crashing through undergrowth somewhere. Our host had sustained a couple of minor injuries, and we tried to help him with his bandaging.

All the centaurs I had yet seen were male, and I wondered if the whole race was of one sex. If so, I thought, reason enough for them to be chronically angry.

Pholus, when he could pull himself together, did what he could to explain.

Some of the males of his race, he said, on occasion mated with mares. Some undetermined number actually preferred that sort of coupling. The great convenience, of course, was that the organs of centaur and horse were well matched in physical size. As far as he knew, no issue ever resulted from such unions.

But, he explained, the majority of male centaurs, himself included, found such intercourse fundamentally unsatisfactory, as their own essentially human minds persisted in regarding women as infinitely more attractive than horses.

"That seems to me only reasonable," I said. And Enkidu nodded wisely.

At about that point, it also occurred to me to wonder how any female, even a mare, could give birth to such an odd-shaped body as my host's. But then I supposed that if droms and cameloids could manage, Mother Nature would find a way in this case, too.

Pholus went on with his explanations. Unions between male centaurs and women were sometimes fertile.

It was not a subject I cared to hear any more about. In the gray light of morning, the fumes of wine had all but completely evaporated from my brain. I was tired, and my garments were torn in several places where my enemies' weapons had struck home, but otherwise I had sustained no damage.

No, there was one exception, and excited as I was with wine and violence, I finally had to take notice. On the back of my right hand, a red spot burned, smaller than a small coin, but sharp as fire. Looking closely, I could see there was no wound, but definitely a blister. Something, somehow, had caused me injury. I rinsed the place in water, which did not help much.

My host took no notice; he had graver matters than my blister to be concerned about.

He said: "But to couple with a goddess, now . . ." And with a sigh he left the comparison unfinished. At the time, I took his behavior for a subtle kind of bragging; in my callow innocence I thought it would be difficult indeed to find any goddess willing to pair with a centaur.

Delivering a Boar

*B*efore Enkidu and I left Pholus, we helped the noble centaur start to rebuild his ruined house, at least to the extent of clearing wreckage and salvaging materials that could be used in reconstruction. After that, I labored for another hour, cutting and carrying wood, including parts of the house that had been reduced to wreckage, to make a suitable funeral pyre for Chiron. Our host informed us that few centaurs ever found their final resting place in graves—I suppose the reason is that huge holes would be necessary, and the bodies of that race, their arms so high above the ground, are ill-suited for digging in it.

The moderate chill of early winter soon gave way to bitter, freezing cold as my nephew and I made our way across the high country. We were working our way steadily toward Mount Erymanthus, aided by the fact that the peak itself was now and then visible through a frame of tall pine trees. The mountain above the timberline was covered in pure white and displayed a plume of blowing snow on windy mornings. Even at the lesser altitude where we trudged along, snow lay deep in places and looked as if it intended to remain for many months. The stories we heard from the natives as we toiled through the high country confirmed what Hermes had told us about a wild boar of exceptional size and ferocity, ravaging the land.

If I had ever been inclined to curse the Lizard, I was almost ready to bless him now for having, however unintentionally, furnished us with warm clothing. My special powers had never afforded me any protection against the common discomforts of heat and cold, though in my more optimistic moments I thought that my father's blood might prevent my actually freezing to death, or perishing of sunstroke. My only other chance to demonstrate a soldier's fortitude, and that in a very minor way, was to stoically ignore the pain of the blister on my hand, and in a few days that had faded, leaving only a small scar.

Enkidu, too, still clung to the memory of the Lizard and his store-room, but chiefly as a reason for continued grumbling. My nephew's unsatisfied craving for wealth had transformed that rustic chamber, in his memory, into something like a royal treasure vault. He still regretted that we had left behind any of the gold and gems. I failed to respond to these sullen protests, and in time, to my relief, he gave them up.

Besides, there were current problems that demanded our continuous attention. For a time we were much concerned that Nessus and some other angry centaurs might be on our trail, determined to cause more trouble. I could not rid my memory of the expression of hatred I had seen on the face of Nessus when I got my last look at him.

And still the words that Mercury had spoken to me on parting, at our last encounter, lay clear in my mind. The god had been very specific in his instructions—in passing on to me what he said were the commands of Zeus. According to those, it was very important that the beast we were now hunting should be still alive when we carried it to Iolcus. As we traveled, my nephew and I speculated endlessly on possible reasons for this requirement, but as you might expect, we got nowhere.

Another question that nagged at me from time to time was exactly where we were supposed to bring the Boar, supposing we did manage to capture the beast and carry it as far as Iolcus. Who, if anyone, would take delivery of our strange cargo when we got there? And, beyond that, what precisely was it wanted for? Hermes had left me with the impression that he intended to meet us there in person, but I had trouble imagining any god making an appearance in the middle of a busy city.

We continually worried at these and related questions, but came no closer to finding answers.

Other delays compounded those brought on by weather. We wasted, or so it seemed to me, another month or so in an effort to equip ourselves with suitable nets, some of which had to be woven. Only when these problems had been surmounted did we turn our efforts to actually tracking down the Boar.

All reports agreed that our new quarry was a very big animal. They were in accord also that it left no Hydra-sized trail across the rugged high country, and in this they were proven right. All of Enkidu's tracking skill was necessary. We were by no means always blessed with fresh snow, good for tracking.

We had now been gone from home approximately five months. Deep winter had come upon us, and the hours of daylight were short indeed.

After spending many days in a patient, methodical effort to locate the animal, our efforts were at last rewarded with the discovery of tracks that Enkidu swore could have been made by nothing but some kind of giant pig. The size of the imprints was somewhat reassuring, in that the animal producing them could not have been the size of the Hydra, or even much bigger than the lion. And when we actually caught sight of the Boar at last, I was relieved to find this reading of the trail proved correct.

By dint of much effort, we finally chased the beast out of its hiding place into deep snow—we were high on the mountain by that time—and there trapped it with nets.

Enkidu's nimbleness and courage were a great help, necessary complements to my strength. Oh, I could tell you in more detail of the various stratagems, involving much patience and many ropes and nets, by which the Boar was subdued and imprisoned, but I have no wish to turn this chronicle into a monotonous catalog of monsters. Finally I had to stun the creature with a series of sharp, comparatively light, blows to its shaggy head.

One of the local ranchers, overjoyed to see the beast removed (though it caused him much anxiety that I did not kill it while I had the chance; he said he had sworn an oath to boil it into soup), donated a large, strong cart, and another loaned us a team of droms to pull it, with his son as driver. Still others chipped in still more ropes with which to bind the beast, once it was entangled, and some stout timbers from which we cobbled together a crate, or pen, in which it might be carried. And presently we were on our way to Iolcus.

The air steadily grew warmer in the course of our long, tortuous descent toward sea level, and before we had been on the road for many days the land was free of snow again. Partly this was because we were at the same time moving steadily southward. We did our best to feed our captive and supply him with water, but any merely natural beast confined as the Boar was would probably have expired. As matters actually stood, the odylic force that had made the creature huge and formidable operated also to keep it alive, though caged and bound. Whenever I came in view, its red eyes glowered hate at me.

We asked directions as we progressed, but actually that would hardly have been necessary. All roads seemed to tend toward our goal. Hermes had been right, and we had no trouble locating the port of Iolcus, on the northern shore of what was by far the largest body of water that Enkidu and I had ever seen.

When we first came in sight of the Great Sea, we marveled that we could not see the other side of the vast watery expanse that lay before us, slate gray, under a gray sky—although of course we had known all along, from travelers' stories, that it must be so.

Even before we actually passed through the gates of Iolcus, Enkidu and I found ourselves immersed in a kind of country fair, or carnival, atmosphere.

As we drew near the city, we encountered more and more evidence that a remarkable gathering of noble heroes was in progress. Some six months had now passed since Enkidu and I had left our homes in Cadmia. Behind us the high country was still deep in winter, and snow capped the peaks of Erymanthus and its neighbors. But here, many miles to the south and at much lower altitude, the weather on the northern shore of the Great Sea was already as mild as spring. Here were green palm trees, pelicans, and other wonders for two country boys to marvel at.

The city of Iolcus was not as large as Cadmia, nor were its walls as formidable, being mainly logs and not stone; but it still held by far the largest gathering of people we had seen since leaving home.

As we drew near the chief inland gate, our progress was slowed by the numbers of people who stopped to marvel at the Boar, and at the way we were carrying it alive.

But our arrival, though it drew a considerable crowd, was not the only or even the chief cause of excitement in that town.

"Jason himself is here!" more than one of the locals excitedly informed me.

That name meant something to me, as I thought it must have done, at the time, to almost everyone in the world. Jason's fame as a warrior and adventurer had spread swiftly during the last few years. All sorts of heroic deeds were attributed to him, and probably he was even more famous than Theseus, and had not the same piratical reputation. When it became widely known that Jason was seeking forty or fifty volunteer adventurers to accompany him on a special quest, men had come from everywhere, seemingly from every corner of the earth, certainly from as far away as the news had had time to travel. I suppose there is really no need to say that very few of those who applied without a special invitation were accepted.

Speaking of Theseus, almost everyone we met expected that the youthful adventurer, sometimes called King of the Pirates, would sooner or later put in an appearance. But there was no sign of him yet, and no one knew where he might be. Many assumed that his name was on the list of those to whom Jason had sent personal invitations; if Theseus was not a hero, who could claim that title? True, his remarkable career consisted of little but acts of piracy. But if a consistent concern for others' property was made a qualification, Jason might have a hard time filling his roster.

Someone had posted on a wall, on one side of the town square, an impressive list of other heroes, whose presence was confirmed.

No one who observed our entrance into the town would have mistaken me for one of those summoned—at least, not until they saw what freight was carried on the cart that I was driving (our borrowed driver, unnerved by the constant red-eyed, bristly presence of the Boar, had defected before we were halfway to the port). One look at the creature in my cart was enough to assure any observer that I was probably no ordinary teamster.

The crowd that had begun to gather around us and our cargo was growing larger, minute by minute.

Once within the city walls, I drove on to the city square, in part simply because I wished to avoid blocking the narrow street. On the edge of the square I reined my team of droms to a halt, not exactly sure where to go or what to do next.

I was only slightly surprised when, true to his promise, Hermes materialized, seeming to come from nowhere. One moment I was unaware of his presence, and the next he was standing right beside me. The god was wearing the same winged hat and long cloak in which he had appeared to us in the swamp, and bearing in one hand his caduceus, the staff with the twined serpents.

Before I could decide for myself the proper degree of respect to offer him, Hermes announced that he was ready to take delivery of his fresh, live monster.

Traffic in the crowded square flowed by us without pause; and I soon realized that the other people must see a totally different image than Enkidu and I did when they looked at the god Mercury. Perhaps they also heard different words, if they could hear his speech at all. Not that the Messenger was totally invisible in their eyes; they walked around him instead of bumping into him, while they continued to marvel at our captive pig. But it was as if some spell prevented them from paying him much attention.

What really surprised me about Hermes/Mercury was that this time he had a mortal man as his companion. This fellow was middle-aged and of impressive bearing, though garbed in the clothing of a common workman, a mere loincloth, cheap vest, and sandals. He stood close beside the god, and the two were in earnest conversation.

I was about to ask the Messenger who his associate might be, but before I could do so, the man himself turned to me and extended a hand in greeting.

"I am called Daedalus," he announced in a brisk voice. His hand felt callused, hard as wood, against the permanent softness of my palm and fingers.

It was a name that I had heard before, while still living at home. Indeed, who in the world had never heard it? The name seemed to me to belong to some legendary character and was vaguely associated in my mind with feats of great skill and wisdom; I could not at the moment recall the details of what Daedalus was supposed to have done, but I was sure he had accomplished marvels. Was this indeed the same, the legendary Daedalus? But why should this man not be of legendary fame, if he consorted on friendly terms with Hermes?

No doubt my surprise showed in my face. "The master Artisan?" I asked.

Daedalus smiled faintly, like one who found it gratifying to be recognized. "There are those who call me that," he said. And he promptly shook hands with Enkidu as well, having evidently determined quickly that my companion was no mere servant—or, perhaps, his attitude suggested, not caring whether he was or not. And then he turned his attention to the Boar, which obviously interested him more than either of us mere humans.

The name of Daedalus, if shouted in the marketplace, would not have created nearly as much excitement as that of Jason, but was perhaps just as widely known. Trying to recall everything that I had heard about the Artisan, I finally remembered hearing that he was a widower. I saw before me a lean man of about forty and of no more than average height, with a large nose and brownish, gray-streaked hair tied behind him with utilitarian string. His fingers were ringless as a slave's, though there was no reason to believe his corded neck had ever worn a collar. Both hands were scarred, as if from the use of every kind of common tool.

As soon as Hermes and Daedalus got their first look at the Boar, they put their heads together and began what was obviously an intense discussion concerning the monstrous beast. They poked and prodded its legs and ribs, and tugged at handfuls of its hair. Meanwhile, as its flanks rose and fell in great, shuddering breaths, my living trophy glared back at them with its red eyes and seemed to yearn to get its huge tusks into their flesh.

Presently the Messenger turned back to me. He inclined his head toward me very slightly; and I understood that, from a god, this was an impressive mark of favor indeed.

When Hermes began our serious discussion, he was standing closer to me than on his previous appearances, so I was able to get a better look at his face. I understood that what I saw was not, of course, the actual Face, the indestructible object of transcendent power that conferred all the powers of a god upon the human who happened to put it on. The Face of Hermes, like that of any other god, had to be inside his head, where it must have been ever since the day this avatar slid it over his eyes and nose, and where it was certainly going to remain until the day he died.

But what I was able to see at close range helped me to fully realize what I had known in theory, that he who was now Mercury had begun life as a mere human being. Naturally it must be the same for all gods and goddesses. As usual, I found myself wondering particularly about the case of Zeus.

He said: "Congratulations, Hercules, on your success. This beast should be of considerable value to our cause."

"Thank you, Lord Hermes." I drew a deep breath and was about to inquire regarding my payment, but Mercury was already speaking again and paid no attention to what I was trying to say.

"Having accomplished this," the Messenger informed me, "you must be considered worthy to undertake another assignment for the one we both serve. This new task is of an importance that would be difficult to overestimate."

When he paused for my reply, I said: "Before we talk of new assignments, what about our reward for struggling to bring in this huge pig? The last time we met, you assured me that it would be marvelous, beyond the range of my imagination. Your exact words, as I recall, were: 'Your payment, for accepting and performing this new task, will be something more magnificent than you can imagine.'"

The god stared at me with divine hauteur—or maybe the look that I interpreted as such was no more than godly indifference. "What reward would you consider fitting?" he inquired.

"I think, Lord Messenger, that I have already made this clear. To begin with, I want to see my father, and speak to him, face-to-face."

Mercury seemed not to have been expecting any such demand. He was silent for so long that I began to wonder whether he meant to ignore my request altogether, or was perhaps trying to devise some ingenious punishment for insolence. But then at last he only said: "You do not know what you are asking."

"It seems simple enough to me."

"But it is not. Is there any alternative reward that would please you?"

"Not until my father agrees to see me and to let me have a talk with him."

"I see." The god sighed and shook his head. "Meanwhile, I am prepared to offer you a reward anyway, for what you have done already. The gift of Zeus is one that I think you will not refuse."

"Perhaps. How soon will I be allowed to see this different gift, and know whether I will refuse it or not?"

"You will see a portion of it very soon. Be patient."

Few people in the great world knew the name of Hercules as yet. But it did not hurt my local reputation any when I lifted crate and boar and all from cart to ground unaided.

Once Hermes and Daedalus had officially taken possession of the Boar, the God of Thieves magically whisked the animal away, crate and all, by some means that I could not detect. Still no one else in the square seemed aware that anything out of the ordinary was happening. In the process, the Messenger and Artisan disappeared as well, along with the cart and draft animals.

"I don't understand," I brooded, when my nephew and I were once more alone. "Why couldn't the mighty Hermes have laced up his winged Sandals, and flown up there onto the snowy mountain, and plucked the Boar out of its cave himself? And I wonder what plan it is that requires the presence of Daedalus as well?"

When my nephew wondered aloud who Daedalus might be, I did my best to enlighten his ignorance. By then I had begun to remember a few details of the Artisan's career.

Then I added: "Who knows why gods do what they do?"

The boy shrugged. "I don't. This one never even seems to notice that I'm around. But maybe that's just as well." Enkidu continued to puzzle over it all for a moment, then asked: "And what was all that about giving you another assignment? It sounded like he thought he was doing you a great favor."

"It sounded that way to me, too. Well, I don't doubt we'll find out before long what the great Messenger had in mind."

"And what was all that about giving us a reward? Do you think he will?"

"I suppose. He said it would come 'very soon.' All right. But maybe to a god, 'very soon' means something like a hundred years. Damn him, anyway. Why can't he just give me some straight answers?"

Enkidu looked around nervously. "Hercules, be careful. He might hear you."

"Let him hear. That's all right with me. Gods are only people wearing Faces. Anyway, you were complaining only a minute ago that he never pays you any attention."

"Yes, but . . ."

The more I thought about my situation, the more annoyed I became. "I tell you, Enk, I'm not going to stand around and wait to be given a handout, like some attendant at a stable. If Zeus is really my father, that ought to count for something. I'm fed up with this crawling and climbing through all the swamps and brambles and useless places of the earth. I've had it with endlessly digging and chasing after monsters."

Enkidu sighed. "All right, Uncle, whatever you say. But what are we going to do instead?" Then he brightened. "I know what I'd like to do, if we could choose. If only we could join the Argosy! That's what Jason calls his expedition."

The same idea had already begun to take root in the back of my own mind. One alternative of course would be to go home; but I never seriously considered returning to Cadmia, where I thought I would certainly be ordered into a marriage I did not want to make, or into the army, now that I was sixteen and old enough. Probably both.

What few scraps of news we heard from our homeland indicated that the war—I supposed it was the same one—was still on, afflicting the land like some lingering skin disease. And we learned also that everyone was getting so tired of unending struggle, endless lists of casualties, that some kind of an arranged peace might soon be possible. I was now well into my seventeenth year, and were I to go home, no one would object to putting weapons into my hands when the army faced real enemies.

But I had no wish to subject myself again to the authority of my foster father, or even of my mother. Having come this far, I meant to take whatever further steps were necessary to dig out the truth of my relationship with Zeus. Whatever that truth might be, the gods were evidently taking a special interest in my affairs. Hermes was an impressive presence, to say the least, but still I was not awed, and I wanted him to stop ordering me about, so I could get on with some kind of life of my own.

Mercury had seemed to assume that I would not be able to do this even if I tried. And in this case Mercury was proven right.

Entering a prosperous-looking, busy tavern, with Enkidu tagging along behind me, I put a couple of the Lizard's smaller coins down on a table. Immediately a well-dressed young man nearby, whose size, confident attitude, and youthful vigor made me assume he was probably one of the heroes, announced that he was buying this round of drinks and I should save my money. When I had saluted him with thanks, he presently came walking over, his arm carelessly around one of the giggling tavern girls, so that he dragged her with him, apparently without really noticing the fact.

When he stood beside me, he introduced himself as Meleager.

"Those who know me well call me Mel." His great hand swallowed mine.

For a moment there seemed something familiar about his greenish eyes, and I tried to remember whether I might ever have met him before. But that seemed unlikely, as he had never been to Cadmia, or so he said, while I in my early years had rarely been anywhere else.

He went on to explain that I had been pointed out to him as the lad who had carted a gigantic, somehow magical Boar into town, and he wondered if this were really so.

When I admitted that it was, Meleager proclaimed himself an experienced boar hunter, too, and one of some renown. He had some technical questions about the feat I was supposed to have accomplished, queries about ropes and knots and so on that I tried to answer. His accent seemed to me strange, but with a little effort I could make out everything he said. I did my best to explain what I could about the

Boar, but in the general din (the tavern was becoming crowded) I could not be sure that I was being heard or understood.

We had been talking for several minutes when he suddenly paused, a hand to his forehead as if it ached. "Hercules, Hercules—it seems to me I've heard that name before."

"Really? Was it in connection with a beast called the Hydra? Or maybe with a lion?"

Mel seemed to have no idea what I was talking about. "Are you coming with us on our little trip?" he demanded. "I mean the one that Jason's cooking up. Maybe your name's familiar because I saw it on one of his lists."

"I don't know if I'm coming with you or not. Tell me about the trip." But now another huge young man, Meleager's equal in heroic stature, was bellowing something at him from his other side, and he had turned away again and in the noisy tavern failed to hear me.

Meanwhile, strong drink of an unfamiliar kind had been set before me, in a foaming tankard. I was young, but looking around I could see that I was not the very youngest being served. Tasting the beverage cautiously, I reminded myself that what had happened when I drank wine among the centaurs must not be allowed to happen again here.

Two women were dancing on a kind of platform at the far end of the room, stripping off their clothes one garment at a time, while patrons shouted and whistled encouragement at them. Even I could see that they were not good dancers, nor was the music pleasing, but their bodies were young and taut and healthy, and the sight threatened to distract me from everything else. In only a few of the farmhouses where we had slept on our long walk had any female company been available.

Meleager had turned back to me again, and soon I learned that he was the son of a noble family who lived very close to Iolcus. Again he went out of his way to point out that he was something of a famous boar hunter in his own right.

That, I thought, would explain his continued curiosity, while leaving unexplained the strange sense of familiarity evoked by his green eyes. Meanwhile, he was still asking questions.

"What happened to the creature, by the way? I mean, where is it now? I spoke to several people who were there in the town square when you brought the animal in, but no two of them could agree on who took it away or where. One said you sold it to a butcher."

"I doubt you'll find it in a stew pot anytime soon." I took another long pull at my foaming tankard. My eyes kept turning back to the wiggling women.

"Then where?"

"I sold it, got a good price." Later, a time came when I realized that curious ears other than Meleager's must have heard me say those words.

"Wish I could remember where we've met before," said Mel. Then, as if in professional curiosity, he began to question me again on the technical details of hunting and capturing the Boar. Distracted by the dancers, I responded to his queries as truthfully as I could, but I could see that he was having trouble understanding. Naturally his mind was working on the assumption that no mortal man could be strong enough to handle such a beast in the way I seemed to be describing.

When Meleager, letting the matter of the Boar drop for the time being, kindly asked me how things were going in my life in general, I tried to express my dissatisfaction. "One of my parents is a god. And one of my gods is a parent. What a combination!" Well, it seemed a profound statement at the time. Meleager must have thought so, too, for he frowned and appeared to be giving it serious thought.

Though I ignored the fact at the time, others were observing both of us. Anyone, even an insignificant-looking outlander like me, who was engaged in such a serious conversation with a hero must be someone worth knowing, too.

The performance at the far end of the room was over now, the musicians devoting themselves to drink. One of the girls who had been dancing on the platform came up to me and commented on how nicely my beard was beginning to grow in. Something about it must have caught her eye from clear across the room. Her hair was yellow and thin, her face sharp-featured, and in the warm room she had not bothered to resume even a single stitch of clothing following her dance. As she stood near me the tip of one of her small breasts brushed my arm, as if by accident. And brushed again.

I rubbed my cheeks and chin, feeling the scratchy, bristly patches that had recently developed. "It's been a long time since I've seen a mirror," I admitted.

Enkidu, having been given no tankard of his own, had sipped more than was wise at mine. Now he was tugging at my tunic and telling me that his stomach felt queer, and he would wait for me outside. I nodded and brushed him away.

Meanwhile my very latest acquaintance was still speaking to me in her soft, eager voice. "Ah, but you must look in one, for you are very handsome."

"Look in one what?"

Her laughter tinkled pleasantly. "A mirror, you silly man! I can show you a room upstairs, in this very house, where there are many mirrors, all clear as air—big ones, on the walls and ceiling."

My head was whirling, dancing. I saw, as in a vision, a centaur dancing on a stage, then coupling with a mare. "So, you think I'm handsome, hey?"

"Oh yes," she said, and added: "They say you are also a strong man, and I can see that they are right." She reached out and squeezed the modest-looking muscle of my arm.

"No, you can't. See it, I mean. But I am. Even stronger than I am handsome."

The dancing girl laughed and put her hand on my arm again, more lightly this time, and the stroking touch of her fingers burned like fire.

Argonauts

It was midmorning when I emerged from the tavern, rubbing my eyes and blinking in the sunlight, with the sights and smells and sounds of a strange city all around me. At once I spotted Enkidu, sitting on the step of a market across the street, eating some toasted bread and waiting for me.

Evidently the youngster found something amusing in my appearance as I shuffled across the street, wincing at what seemed to me the inordinately loud noise of cartwheels thundering past.

"Did you sleep well, Uncle?" he demanded impertinently as I approached. "Or was that upstairs room with all the mirrors too bright for you?"

I sat down beside him with a groan. Holding out both hands in front of me, I marked how the fingers trembled slightly. My head was throbbing faintly, too, a phenomenon almost totally unknown in my young life. Something strange indeed must have affected me, more than putting down a mere half-gallon or so of wine. The drink had not had anything like the exotic, intriguing taste of the centaurs' ancient vintage.

"I slept passably well," I grumbled. "Though I could have done with another hour or two."

What had deprived me of sufficient rest, apart from the energetic activities of certain dancing girls, had been the insistent presence of strange dreams, prominently featuring the strange, bull-like figure who had now been intermittently invading my sleep for several months. Again I thought the bull-man had been trying to convey some warning to me, but my dreaming mind had been too fuddled for it to come through clearly.

I started to try to tell Enkidu about my latest experience of these puzzling visions, but he had heard me speak of similar things before and was not much interested. He said he had spent most of the night in a nearby barn, where he slept well and got over his troubled stomach. Fortunately for our fortunes, he still had most of our money safely with him. But he was not now in a mood to do much listening, once he realized that I was not going to relate in great detail my adventures in the room of mirrors.

And now, in a sudden change of mood, my nephew no longer seemed at all amused. For once he was unhappy enough to be serious, and even glum. Looking listlessly at the remnant of toast he had been chewing on, he complained: "I wish I was strong."

"You're quite strong, for your age."

"You know what I mean, Herc. Strong like you. And I wish that girls and women came flocking around me."

"We all have things we'd like to change. I wish my head would cease to ache. A philosopher would say that sooner or later all our wishes will be granted." As soon as I had made that pronouncement, it did not sound quite accurate to me. It was close, though. I was sure I could remember hearing something of the kind from the most philosophical of my former tutors. At least my version was encouraging.

My nephew told me, in a few disapproving words, what should be done with all philosophers.

Now only a few of the Lizard's coins remained to me, and those only by accident, a few that had become stuck in the lining of my tunic, where they were almost impossible to find. It seemed the wrong time to ask my nephew for money. I thought of looking about in the market for food and drink, but decided not to. Enkidu offered me a fragment of his toasted bread, but at that moment my stomach was too queasy. Getting up, I made my way carefully to a nearby fountain, where I slaked my newly raging thirst in the jet from a stone dolphin's mouth, and soused my head. That helped some, but still my head and belly were not right.

Only at that point, I think, did it occur to me to wonder whether my companions in last night's revelry might actually have put some foreign substance in my drink, with the intent of increasing its potency far beyond that of the natural power of wine.

Thinking it over, I realized that there might well have been some plan under way to drug me into a stupor and then rob me. I had talked in the tavern about selling my great pig for a good price, which meant I would be carrying money. It would have been no trick at all for one of the girls to drop something in one of the several—all right, one of the many—drinks I had consumed upstairs, or even in the one I had started on before ascending to the room with mirrors.

Well, if their plan had indeed been to knock me out and rob me, it had certainly miscarried, because here I was, and my few coins still with me. I had remained reasonably alert, and certainly functioning, for hours after going upstairs . . . though when I had awakened in midmorning and had decided to get up, everyone else in the upper room had been still totally passed out.

While I was struggling to sort out my more reasonable memories of the last twelve hours or so, and to see if any of even the clearer ones were worth retaining, Enkidu tugged at my sleeve. A familiar figure was making its way toward us across the square.

Out of courtesy I got to my feet as Daedalus came up.

One shrewd glance from the experienced Artisan allowed him to deduce my condition. "Bit of a hangover, young man?"

"I believe that's what it's called, sir. I don't have a lot of experience along this line."

With a shake of his head he expressed his sympathy. "Being young has great advantages. But of course there are drawbacks, too." He paused, then added expectedly: "I have a son at home, somewhat younger than either of you lads."

Enkidu was still gloomy. "I'm not very big. I was just telling Hercules, I wish I was six feet tall, and strong like him."

"I'll never be six feet tall," I said.

Daedalus nodded thoughtfully. "Having a wish not immediately granted is often grounds for sorrow. Unhappily, having one granted often produces the same result."

That sounded like a more accurate version of the philosopher's precept I had been trying to remember, and my nephew began to repeat his prescription for practitioners of that art. But in the midst of it he was suddenly struck by an idea, and broke off to ask a question.

"Daedalus, sir? Could Hermes make me strong, do you suppose?"

"I doubt it, lad," the Artisan responded absently. "That is, he might, but I doubt he will." Though he spoke to Enkidu, he was looking at me now, and he began to frown. "Hercules, I feel I should warn you about something."

"Sir?"

"I myself have some experience of celebrity—though not nearly as much as you seem destined to endure. It can be a dangerous drug, more dangerous than wine."

My stomach gave a queasy stirring at the thought of wine, and my head felt in no shape to cope with sage advice. "Thank you, sir—Daedalus, if I may—actually there's something else I'd like to ask you about."

"Ask away."

I began to tell him of my strange dreams. As soon as I described the horned figure, Daedalus said unhesitatingly that it was Prince Asterion of Corycus whom I had met.

"Who's that?"

The Artisan seemed mildly surprised at my lack of knowledge. "There are some—ignorant people in many countries—who do not know him, and who call him the Minotaur."

Enkidu, who was listening, let out a faint gasp—and I said: "Ahh." I said it thoughtfully, for certain things that had not quite made sense suddenly began to do so.

Daedalus was still talking. "But you are very fortunate, Hercules, if Prince Asterion takes an interest in your welfare. He is a friend of those gods who are most friendly to humanity. Had he any special message to convey to you? Perhaps a warning?"

I clenched my eyes tight shut and tried to think. "He had a message of some kind, I think. But I was too fuddled, even in my dream, to understand it."

Meanwhile Enkidu's attention had been captured, and he was still quietly marveling, repeatedly whispering that other name. *The Minotaur.* In his mind, and in mine as well, the word called up more legends: of the island kingdom of Corycus and its fabled Labyrinth; of a queen who had lusted unnaturally for a bull, and of the grotesque offspring that had resulted.

Daedalus, taking note of the boy's mutterings, suggested sternly that he had better not use that name at all. Then the Artisan looked around, as if to make sure that we were not being overheard.

"I assure you," he said, "it was no ordinary bull, but great Zeus himself, who visited Queen Pasiphae some twenty years ago and is the father of the prince. May the good queen's spirit rest peacefully in some quiet corner of the Underworld. If any such place actually exists."

"You doubt it does?" I asked.

"I have seen too much of the world to be very certain of any part of it. But one thing I know is that the monster called the Minotaur is a creature of legend, and very little more than that. The prince, on the other hand, is very real."

"The figure I have seen in my dreams, and who has spoken to me there, is certainly more than legend, Artisan. Having seen centaurs, I am more ready to believe in him."

Daedalus nodded reassuringly. "The prince Asterion, the real visitor in your dreams, indeed has the skull and horns of a bull, though the heart and hands and brain of a man. He almost never leaves the Labyrinth, but he has the power to roam the world in his dreams, and also to enter the dreams of others. If the prince has given you a warning, you had better heed it."

Presently Daedalus squinted up at the sun and announced that there was business he had to be about. After saying that he would probably see us soon, the Artisan took himself away.

My nephew and I soon got up and, for want of anything better to do, strolled in the opposite direction.

"Oh, Hercules." It was a faint whisper, luxurious, weary, and admiring, all at the same time. Looking around, I saw the girl who had spoken my name in passing, and who was now retreating in the direction of the tavern where I had spent the night. She had now clothed herself for an appearance on the public street, but my brief glimpse of her face was enough for me to identify one of my bedmates of the mirrored room. One of those who might have been trying to rob me. What was it that Daedalus had said about celebrity?

Having turned our backs on the street of taverns and easy women, my nephew and I kept moving in the opposite direction. Our feet seemed to carry us automatically toward the nearby harbor. After all, water lay always downhill, and that was the easiest direction in which to carry an aching head.

There was no doubt as to which of the ships along the busy docks was the one being prepared for Jason's much-celebrated expedition.

That was plain even before we came close enough to see the name of *Argo* painted on the bow. And presently, working our way through a scattering of idle onlookers, we got our first close look at the ship, resting unguarded against the quay.

Long and narrow, with places for fifty oars, her every line breathed adventure, and a great, challenging, staring eye was painted on each side of the prow, just forward of the name.

The *Argo,* the ship in which the heroes planned to accomplish their great adventure, was an impressive sight. There was a notch in the raised central deck where a mast could be mounted, though neither mast nor sail were visible right now.

I fell into conversation with some local idler—or perhaps he was a worker, for there were brushes and a paint pot at his feet, suggesting that he or someone else might have just completed the job of painting on the giant eyes. My curiosity was greatly stimulated. "And the object of this expedition is—?"

The man looked at me as if he thought I might be having fun at his expense. "To find the Golden Fleece and bring it back."

Overhead a gull was screaming, as if in derision. But I was just bewildered. "Back where? Here to Iolcus? And what is this Golden Fleece?"

My informant shrugged. "That's what everyone tells me, but I don't know what it means."

I thought that my new acquaintance Meleager would surely be able to tell me, and I supposed I would see him somewhere in town today. But I hesitated to betray my ignorance by pestering everyone else with questions.

Enkidu was tugging at my arm. "Look, Unc. What the man is carrying. That must be the compass-pyx for Jason's ship."

I had wondered what sort of navigational instrument the heroes would be provided with, and now I could see. It looked like something special indeed.

The man I had been talking to explained. "That's one of the heroes, the steersman Tiphys. Last night he carefully removed his compass-pyx from the ship, to make sure it wouldn't be stolen. Hah, who would dare swipe anything from that bunch?"

Tiphys, a very solid-looking fellow though not especially large, now came carrying the device onto the pier, obviously ready to reinstall it, a job that I had always heard was easily accomplished with a few simple, routine rites of magic. He acted as if the instrument belonged to him, treating it with the familiar care of a man who handles a treasure that has been passed down in his family for generations.

By now a little crowd had begun to gather onshore, just behind Enkidu and myself, as we stood there on the narrow pier. There was a murmuring from the crowd, and it gave me a strange sensation to hear people I had never met, or even seen, using my name, pointing me out to one another as someone worthy of notice. It seemed that word had finally reached the people of Iolcus regarding what had happened to the Hydra in its swamp, and how the Boar had been carried into town. And I had been observed to be in earnest conversation with a hero. Many now presumed me to be of that company.

I could hear some muttering behind my back: "Is it true that he clubbed a lion to death as well?"

Soon there came a louder murmuring among the crowd as a small group of young men, most of them taller than the average, made their way into it and through it. Now the pier swayed slightly underfoot with the weight of several heavy bodies moving briskly along it.

I turned around to face the shore just as a deep voice approaching from that direction asked: "You are the one called Hercules?"

"I am."

The speaker, perhaps ten years my senior, towered over me. He was arrayed in fine garments, and his whole head seemed a dark, luxuriant mass of hair and beard. "My name is Jason. And do you think yourself qualified to join us in our quest?"

"I don't know the answer to that, sir. I'm not sure just what qualifications you expect."

The mass of dark hair nodded judiciously. "A reasonable answer."

Jason explained that he and some of the others had begun just recently to hear of a certain youngster named Hercules, who was said to have achieved great things. They all assumed that I had come to Iolcus to join the heroes on their quest, and by the time they joined us on

the crowded pier, it was obvious they had already decided among themselves that the next step must be to test my worthiness in some way.

Various murmurings around me soon informed me that the gods
only knew how many other youthful would-be heroes had already
been disposed of in the same way. In most cases, a bout or two of one
of the milder forms of wrestling had sufficed to do the trick. I have no
doubt that a majority of the qualified heroes on hand thought this
would promptly eliminate me.

I felt relieved, having been worried that some bloodier test would
be suggested.

"A little arm wrestling, then?" Jason was proposing jovially. "It's
a warm day, whoever loses shouldn't mind a little swim." Actually, as
we were all quite fully aware, the water just below the pier looked
quite foul, a state of affairs only natural for a busy harbor that received much of a sizable city's waste. Today the wind and tide were
doing a poor job of flushing, and it was not the place that any of us
would have chosen for a refreshing dip.

Before the test could actually get started, more of the Argonauts appeared and introduced themselves to me. Eventually it seemed that
their whole number came crowding onto the quay, forcing the retreat
to shore of an even larger number of spectators. Among the newcomers I recognized Meleager, evidently no worse for his own visit to the
tavern last night—of course his visit had probably not lasted nearly as
long as mine.

Meleager asked me how my head felt this morning, after my adventures last night. "My own skull feels a bit thick," he added.

And then there happened that which I had not expected—and my life
was changed forever. First I heard her voice, talking at a little distance, utterly unexpected, tantalizingly familiar . . .

. . . and then I raised my eyes and saw her, standing on the next
pier over, only a few yards away, beyond a gulf of noxious water. She
was looking, I realized, not at me, but directly at the man who stood
just next to me. A pair of green eyes that I had seen only three times
before, and then in very different circumstances, but could never have

forgotten. The last time I looked into them it had been by candlelight, in a dark kitchen.

Looking at Meleager now, and at the family resemblance between them, I realized why I had thought his face familiar at first sight.

She was dressed differently now than on the last occasion when I saw her, but I did not doubt for a moment that it was in fact the same girl who had helped two young itinerant laborers who had been badly cheated.

Now she was calling to Meleager in a familiar way. He waved back casually and then turned to me to make the introduction.

· "Over there you see my sister, Deianeira, informally known as Danni. Danni, this is Hercules, who says he wants to come chasing the Golden Fleece with us."

Then he paused, awareness slowly dawning in his honest face. He smote his forehead with his palm—then seemed to regret the act.

"But no, what am I saying? Of course you two have met before. *That's* where I heard the name of Hercules!" He raised his voice again. "By Hades, Danni, I ought to have remembered what you told me!"

The other heroes were meanwhile wrangling among themselves, so far good-naturedly, about which of them was to administer the test of wrestling. No one was that eager, for testing an undersized recruit was not the kind of trial that seemed to offer any chance of glory. Danni took advantage of the delay to come around and join us on the same pier. When she came near, I took her hand gently, as a man of quality does in Cadmia when introduced to a fine lady of his own rank.

She nodded a greeting to Enkidu and then turned back to me. Her straight brown hair was blowing a little in the breeze. "I see, Hercules, you and your friend have abandoned your earlier profession of farm laborer."

"The hours were long, the pay not great—though that improved toward the end, and I felt well rewarded by my stay on your uncle's estate. How is he, by the way? In bad health, I trust?"

I was rewarded with a giggle. Soon she was explaining to her brother, in more detail than before, her version of what had happened at the estate of the wicked Augeus.

Of course in Danni's version of events, which she unquestioningly believed to be the truth, the destruction of the dam, and the resulting flood, were put down as merely a coincidental stroke of good fortune that had allowed my nephew and me to get away without being noticed.

"Anyway," she concluded, "the remains of Uncle's stables are now clean. He tries to take some comfort from that fact."

Meleager stared at me for a long moment, before finally deciding that the whole story was worth a hearty laugh. Evidently he and his greedy uncle were not on the friendliest of terms.

Then he clapped me on the shoulder in good fellowship, a blow that would have staggered any ordinary man. "Lucky for you and Enkidu that there was such a flood that night!"

"Yes," I said. "That was very fortunate for us." But I was already looking at his sister again, and all I could think of was the depth of those green eyes.

"I hope you're able to come with us," Meleager said. He was sincere, but his tone made it clear he thought it wasn't likely, given the test that had been proposed.

I had looked at Danni only briefly the first time my eyes fell on her. But then I found myself looking back at her, again and again, over what must have been a period of several minutes.

When she turned her eyes to me again I said: "I think I ought to go back and arm-wrestle with your brother there."

What she said in response somehow failed to register with me. Green eyes—or were they after all some oceanic shade of gray?— quickened my pulse, seeming to convey a kind of wordless promise. I have seen something of the same seeming change of color on the sea in troubled weather.

But she was so young. Of course I was actually not yet very old myself. Perhaps she was not every man's ideal of great beauty, and perhaps she would never be . . . but I considered her a vision of loveliness, despite her youth, her age less than mine, body barely rounding into womanhood. A quotation, gleaned from some romantic tutor, drifted into my mind: ". . . upon whose neck was still the verdancy of youth. Nor was she yet familiar with the ways of Aphrodite, charmer of men."

But however great an impression Danni had made on me, I had little time to talk to her just then.

The Argonauts, after some prolonged though low-key wrangling, had finally decided on what test I was to undergo. In a general murmur of heroic voices I learned that it would be the same one that had been used on several others who had recently applied to join their company.

Jason, taking the lead in administering the test, as he did in almost everything else, stepped forward, smiling, and stuck out his big hand. He was almost a head taller than me, and his hand seemed to swallow mine. I thought there was a genuine friendliness in his attitude; he would not try to hurt me as punishment for my impertinence.

"We must make it a fair, strict trial," Mel warned me, half-apologetic.

"Of course. I understand."

And in the privacy of my own thought, I reminded myself strictly that I must be careful not to crush the hand of the brother of the girl who had been of such help to me. Nor should I do permanent damage to any of her brother's friends—of course, in truth, her green eyes would have saved *him* whether she had been my friend or enemy.

Whether I was to be invited to join the glorious quest or not was suddenly not so important to me as the chance that I might be able to impress a certain girl. But luckily the two goals were not exclusive. When the signal was given, and the match began, it was Jason who, tugged irresistibly forward, swayed and moved in a couple of helpless running steps before going off the pier and into the cool, refreshing water of the harbor. I thought the expression on his face was richly comical, and I heard my nephew's giggle plainly in the shocked silence of the watching crowd. Danni was also stricken dumb for a count of four, but then she added her own scream of delighted laughter.

Other Argonauts, suddenly alerted to the fact that something unexpected was happening and that they had better be prepared to do their best, followed their leader into competition. After four or five had copied his dive over the edge, the shallows beside the quay began to look even uglier than before, churned up as they were by the thrashing of brawny arms and legs.

When the next two contestants were disputing briefly as to who was next, pride, the heady fumes of sudden celebrity, at least as strong as those of wine (yes, Daedalus was right) once more got the better of me.

I shifted my stance and stuck out my left hand as well as my right. "Two at once?"

That was a dare such men could not refuse, and a moment later there was a double splash. In such a competition I found it hard to distinguish the strength of heroes from that of herd boys.

There were more than forty heroes present (I made no attempt at an exact count) and before my test had been completed, all of them had stepped up manfully to take their turns. There was some grumbling among my victims, and I received some formal congratulations when the farce was over, but mostly the crowd onshore and on the other piers looked on in an awed silence.

My credentials as a hero had been established beyond any shadow of a doubt, but in my foolish pride I had brought some who might have been my friends into the stage of envy, first stop on the road to being enemies.

○ *ELEVEN* ○

A More Pleasant Swim

*T*hat afternoon I was welcomed aboard the *Argo* by Jason personally, in effect formally granted heroic status. The leader of the Argosy seemed a trifle reluctant, and at the time I could not understand why. But following the exhibition I had put on that morning, I suppose he could hardly have done anything else.

Each qualified and accepted hero was allowed to bring aboard one companion, who was not required to pass a test, and so Enkidu came with me. No one bothered to ask whether he was present in the capacity of friend, relative, servant, catamite, or some combination of those categories, all of which were already represented among the chosen adventurers and their various associates.

That very day the expedition got under way, taking advantage of a favorable midday turning of the tide. I pulled an oar with the others, a few minutes being long enough to acquire the necessary skill. Some of my new shipmates, who had noted the soft skin of my hands, looked forward to seeing me quickly blister; but they were doomed to disappointment. Most of my body was already tanned from almost lifelong exposure, and the sun reflecting from the sea did no further damage.

Within an hour or two we had run into some choppy seas, and after half an hour of that I was unheroically seasick; my only consolation on that boatload of heroes was that I was not alone in my suffering.

Some of those who were not sick seemed to find amusement in the plight of us who were. Before my wretchedness had persisted for an hour, my anger at these mocking ones, and at myself, grew great enough to drive out seasickness from my guts and brains. Yet fortunately it was not great enough to goad me to violence.

As we rowed, the conversation around me touched on many things: women and the sea, Giants and gods. I listened mostly, now and then contributing a word or two; but to my surprise what I had vaguely expected to be the chief subject of conversation was scarcely mentioned. That was of course the Fleece itself. Neither I nor my nephew had yet been able to discover just what kind of treasure this might be, and gradually it dawned on us that some considerable number of those who were now on their way to seek it did not know, either.

Our first night out we spent at sea, mostly dozing at our oars, while clouds covered the stars, and Jason, who apparently did not completely trust Tiphys and his elaborate compass-pyx, decided to wait for dawn to push ahead.

On our second day at sea we raised some hills around noon, and soon came ashore at a different place on the mainland for a scheduled final outfitting and to once more refill our water jugs and jars and waterskins. This was, of course, another part of the world that I had never seen before.

Before landing, we rowed up into the mouth of a good-sized stream, and one of my shipmates informed me that this was the river Chius, and the land that we had reached was Mysia.

Most of the crew might still have had some lingering taste of Iolcus harbor in their mouths, for none of us were eager to restock our water supply in this muddy stream. The party split into several groups, and most of the groups went inland, searching in several directions for a clear pond or stream.

At the time I assumed it was by sheer accident that Enkidu and I were separated, assigned to different parties; but before long I realized that it was nothing of the kind.

I was the chief subject of the following conversation but did not hear it, for it took place in a water-fetching party of which I was not a member. But it was later reported to me by a source I considered reliable.

Jason was shaking his head as he trudged along, carrying several empty jars, like all the other members of the group. "I am a strong man," he announced matter-of-factly, and others nodded. "But when he gripped my paw, I might as well have been a child." Jason raised his own right hand, large-boned, thick with muscle, callused in certain telltale spots that indicated a habitual use of weapons, and stared at it as if he beheld some troubling flaw. Then in a lower voice he mused: "Do you know, that wasn't the worst thing of all."

"No?" prompted one of his companions.

"No. The worst thing of all was—and it was easy to see—that Hercules wasn't even trying very hard."

"And he's not at all large," someone else put in, after a pause in which they all considered the implications.

"Wait till he gets his full growth," another voice speculated ominously.

For a while after that, no one said anything at all.

The heroes of the Argosy, every one of them having personally tested the strength of this upstart Hercules, knew that not one of them could stand against me for an instant in any direct contest. Later I learned that whenever I was not present, they tended to sulk and scowl and mutter among themselves, trying to devise some way to be rid of me. From accounts I was able to piece together later, the business went something like this:

The group of which my nephew was a member had gone ashore like the others, everyone carrying appropriate containers, in search of clean water.

When Enkidu's party had made their way inland half a mile, one member of it suddenly recalled having heard where a suitable pool might be.

When they had reached its shore, one muscular young giant approached Enkidu casually and asked him: "Are you *sure* your uncle's not some god in disguise?"

"I'm sure." The boy was calmly matter-of-fact about it. "I've known my uncle all my life, and he wears no Face. Zeus *is* his father, though."

The little squad of heroes who had casually managed to separate us muttered and discussed it among themselves. A number of the Argonauts also claimed divine ancestry, in one form or another; sometimes it seemed that half the people in the world, at least those who hoped to advance in society, did that. But among this boatload of adventurers, a great many of their claims might well be true, to judge by the various powers they could demonstrate. They were not overawed by me. But they were worried.

By now, Enkidu's group had come out of the woods to stand beside a long, broad serpentine of water, almost an acre in extent. Its grassy shores were shaded by the trees of a grove the local folk deemed sacred to some ancient god, a deity whose name had been forgotten. For the moment, the party seemed to have the place all to themselves.

Enkidu asked the others, innocently enough: "Why did we have to come all this distance for water? I heard someone else talking about a clear stream a lot closer to where we came ashore."

"Clear, yes. But not with water like this one. This is a very special pool." This was said with such a winking emphasis that my nephew's suspicions were immediately aroused, and he refrained from drinking from the pool until he saw several of his companions stretched out on the bank, slaking their thirst with no apparent concern and starting to fill their water jugs. Then Enkidu in turn bent down and drank. The water was cool and refreshing.

And very special it proved to be.

When we had all been in the boat, and I had tried to pin Jason down as to exactly where the expedition was headed, his response had been a little vague. The most I could learn about our destination was that it lay somewhere in the East, and that we were going in search of a reputed Golden Fleece. For guidance in the details, he told me, they meant to rely on visions and omens.

Later, I began to wonder if Jason had withheld details because he knew I was not going to remain with the Argonauts for very long.

A sizable faction among the Argonauts, having been convinced of how strong I really was, seeing for themselves confirmation of the wildest rumors, feared that I would hog all the glory of their quest for myself if they allowed me to come along.

I was ready then to give Jason himself the benefit of the doubt, to believe that he was too noble a soul to be involved in such chicanery. In later years I became more cynical about the likely motives of all human leaders.

But whether he was personally involved or not, there is no doubt that a certain clique among the Argonauts decided among themselves to throw Enkidu into the pond of nymphs, the Pool of Pegae. They were in fact reasonably careful not to do the youth any real harm.

Before Enkidu could say or do anything else, two of them had him by the wrists and ankles, their four hands locking him in a quadruple grip no ordinary mortal could possibly have broken. Another hero began a chanting, lightly mocking count: "One, and—"

"What're you doing? Let go!" the boy cried out, beginning to be frightened. The water under the overhanging trees, while much cleaner than the harbor, was somewhat darker and more mysterious than most people would choose for a casual swim.

"You *can* swim, can't you? Good! Fear not, lad, there are no monsters in the depths. Only some girls who say they want to meet you."

—girls?!

"—two, and—"

"You'll find it cool and refreshing, much better than that damned harbor water."

"—three!"

So it seemed to Enkidu that he was only in for a dunking; nothing so terrible about that. And what could they possibly mean, about girls who wanted to meet him? He even managed to relax a little as he went in with a splash. Even while still in midair he caught a glimpse below him of a slender, silvery body, quite dramatically female; and when he opened his eyes, under the clear water, he saw drifting before him a girlish face framed in wild wet hair and wearing an expression of devilish anticipation, as of some delightful game about to be played.

And now, close beside this first apparition he beheld another, at least as beautiful; and then another, and . . . with a strange feeling in his gut, he realized that there must be at least a dozen of the water sprites in all, and that they had him thoroughly surrounded.

He was swimming freely now, but was suddenly not so much concerned to get out of the pool as to investigate the wonders that its depths had so unexpectedly revealed. And the more he saw of those wonders, the more willing he was to be detained by them. He had never met a naiad before, though I would not be surprised to learn that he had dreamed of them without knowing what they should be called. Had my nephew known what sort of welcome awaited in the pool, it might have taken several heroes to keep him out of it.

Before long, I was quietly tipped off by the companion of one of the other heroes. The information came in the form of vague and disconnected hints that something might have happened to Enkidu. My informant told me he had last been seen alive on the shores of a certain pool, called the Pool of Pegae, which lay more than half a mile inland. At that point the name of the pool meant nothing to me.

Paying little attention to the suggestive fact that none of the heroes were coming with me, I dashed in that direction. I have never been able to manage anything out of the ordinary in running speed, but still I soon located the pool, which was easily approached by a couple of well-marked trails.

When I reached the shoreline, the boy was nowhere in sight, and for a moment I was totally convinced that he was drowned. Detecting some kind of disturbance below the surface, I threw off my clothes and dove into the pool to see what I could find. I was far from being the best of swimmers, but I was determined to do all I could.

Even in a pool that size, the tumult under the water was violent enough to be easily discovered. To my great relief, I soon saw and heard him sporting in good health.

Soon I had joined Enkidu in his watery sport. We both enjoyed the romp.

I quickly noted, with considerable relief, that nothing like scales and fish fins were in evidence, either on his body or those of his new playmates. The nymphs' bodies below the waist were as fair and womanly as they were above.

While we were both still below the surface, his voice reached me with the sound of a stream of bubbles.

"Uncle, Uncle! There's great magic in this pool! These girls can fix it so we can breathe underwater!"

I thought about it, then bubbled back: "That can't be good for you, in the long run."

But a moment later I was trying the technique myself, under the guidance of a fair instructress. The long run always seems very far away when you are young.

The naiads offered superb sport, I must admit, and it might have been possible for a man to spend years in that pool, coming to the surface only now and then, or not at all if that should please him, so long as the fair natives were on hand to protect him with their special magic; but I had other aims in life. Several hours had passed before I finally succeeded in disentangling my nephew from the silvery bodies of the naiads. We surfaced among a stand of lily pads, I retrieved my clothes from the border of the pool (Enkidu's had all permanently disappeared somewhere underwater) and we went looking for the Argonauts.

But by the time we had returned to the landing place, the sun was setting, and the *Argo* and its load of heroic voyagers were long gone. Only a couple of the less sophisticated natives stood and gaped at us.

For a time I stood on the muddy riverbank, now and then chucking a pebble into the stream, my mind busy with unsettling thoughts and mixed emotions.

When Enkidu told me what the men who threw him into the pool had said, I realized that the heroes' whole object in so treating him had been to delay me.

I had to face the fact that the Argonauts, or at least a strong faction among them, did not want Hercules adventuring with them. They were jealous of the glory that I would win when their serious adventures began; and resentful of the fact that they would appear weak whenever they were compared to me.

"So," I said aloud, when understanding finally forced itself upon me. Now I felt resentful, too, and yet buoyed up with a strange, sullen pride in my own peculiar nature.

"What do we do now, Unc?"

"I don't know."

He brightened slightly. "Well, we could just walk back to the—"

"No! That's one thing we're not doing, just walking back to the Pool of Pegae. We are not going to spend our whole lives there." Tiredly I looked up and down the riverbank. "I wonder if there's a real port around here somewhere?"

"We might not need one, Herc. Because here comes a boat. Maybe we can ask whoever . . ." And Enkidu's voice trailed off.

Yes, indeed there was a boat. Here it came, a small, strange, trim, single-masted craft the exact like of which neither of us had ever seen before. It came sailing silently around the nearest upstream bend of the little, nameless river to put in just where we were standing.

I had no need to look twice to recognize the tall figure that stood up in the boat and stepped ashore.

Hermes, the patron of thieves and honest merchants, as well as travelers and athletes, was still carrying his staff with its carven serpents, but was no longer using it as a boatman's pole—this craft was moving under some other, invisible, means of propulsion. He had discarded his long cloak in favor of a simple tunic, and I could see again that he wore winged Sandals, as well as the familiar winged and broad-brimmed hat.

"Hail, Hercules," Hermes greeted me in his resonant voice as he drew near. "I bring you the reward I promised—and also a message from your father."

"Hail, Lord Mercury," I responded. "When am I to see him?"

"That is difficult to say."

"I thought it might be." Suddenly the memory of the day's sport in the deep pool seemed only tiresome, a distraction best forgotten as soon as possible. "Well then, where is Daedalus?" I asked the god. "There are matters I would like to discuss with him."

"He is busy working on the Boar," Hermes answered shortly. "And both man and beast are far away from here by now."

"Working on it? Do you mean butchering the creature, for some feast or sacrifice?"

It seemed to me odd that Mercury had to consider that question before he answered it. "Neither sacrifice nor feast," he allowed at last. "But there is a kind of butchery involved."

Moments passed, in which little waves slapped at the small hull of the new boat, which had been painted a plain white.

"All right." I sighed, and felt my shoulders slump. "I cannot compel a god to answer questions."

"I am glad, son of Zeus, that you realize that fact."

"What message does my father send?" I asked.

The Messenger seemed to relax a bit. "He wishes you well and urges you to travel on as quickly as possible to the island of Corycus."

Once more Hermes had surprised me, and for a long moment I could only stare at him blankly. I of course knew something of Corycus, where grew the legend of the Minotaur, and where the real Prince Asterion, who was my counselor in dreams, must live; but I could see no connection between this new demand and any of the other efforts I had made so far.

Mercury seemed ready to take my silence for agreement. "Also, I am pleased to offer you the first part of the reward you have been promised." With a gesture he indicated the little boat. Though neither anchored nor grounded, it did not drift off in the current, but remained just where the god had stepped from it, its prow barely touching shore.

"A boat?"

"Yes."

I gazed at the small vessel without understanding, while it bobbed lightly in the water. "Whose is it?"

"Yours, if you will accept it as the promised portion of your reward."

"It is not what I have asked for. You still refuse me that."

Mercury did not reply.

I sighed. "Somehow I was expecting that great gods, like yourself and Zeus, would offer more than just a boat—something in the nature of a fabulous treasure."

"Would you prefer a fabulous treasure?"

"I have told you, Lord Hermes, what I would prefer. Well, I suppose the boat may well be useful."

"I assure you, son of Zeus, it is no ordinary craft." The Messenger's voice was solemn.

Once more I studied the vessel, but still it looked quite ordinary to my untutored eye. I saw the name, *Skyboat,* emblazoned in two languages on the prow. "Just what makes it so special?"

"For one thing, it will help you to complete your journey to Corycus very speedily."

"I see. A gift to the workman of a new tool—so he can more quickly accomplish his work. Well, what sort of monster am I to wrestle with when I get out to that island? Maybe an octopus, or a bat? Where do you want the creature delivered, and should it be alive or dead?"

"When you are on Corycus, it will be better if you can avoid wrestling, and highly advisable that you do no fighting at all. You are going there to meet a being of very unusual appearance, but he is no more a monster than you or I."

"I assume you mean the man some call the Minotaur," I said. "More properly known as Prince Asterion. Daedalus, before he rushed away the last time, did his best to enlighten me about the prince."

"I am glad to hear it," said Mercury. "For in fact Prince Asterion is your half brother."

I had already been vaguely aware of that fact, but to hear it stated plainly made me stop and think.

Now Hermes seemed ready to depart, leaving the boat behind; the wings on his Sandals and his hat were twitching, and now he rose effortlessly into the air, graceful and easy as a hummingbird.

"Who is to pilot the boat for us?" I called after him, in something like alarm.

"No pilot will be needed," Mercury responded calmly.

I looked in bewilderment at Enkidu, who was looking back at me with a similar expression on his face.

"But neither of us knows anything of the sea," I protested to the god. "We're likely to drown ourselves before we're out of sight of shore."

Hermes paused momentarily in midflight. "You do know something of the compass-pyx, and of its use?"

"I've never touched one, nor has Enkidu. We saw a little of the instrument they were putting aboard the *Argo*. All the sailors on board remarked how fine it was."

"The one in your new boat is finer still. It will serve you well no matter how great your ignorance. But to save time I will detail a certain sprite to help you."

"A sprite, Lord Hermes?"

"A creature usually attached to the Twice-Born, Lord Dionysus. You will not see it, but you will have help with the boat when you need help. Also your new servant can do duty as a messenger. If you should happen to make some great discovery, you will be able to communicate it quickly to the gods or humans who are your friends."

And Hermes pointed toward the boat.

I found nothing new to see in that direction, and when I looked back again to where he had been standing, the God of Merchants and Thieves was gone.

Enkidu could hardly have known any more about boats than I did, but he was desperately impatient to give this one a trial cruise. We climbed in and gingerly shoved off into a river that invited the experiment by being almost calm.

The boat drifted in a straight line, or so it seemed, with none of the aimless turning I had been expecting.

Enkidu was enthralled. "Uncle, this is even better than the *Argo!* This is a damned sight better!"

"Not as big, not by a long way."

"But this boat we don't even have to row!"

Mercury had been out of sight for some time before Enkidu and I got around to wondering exactly where the Argonauts might have got to by this time. They had talked of heading east, but that was about all we had been told.

"When we have finished whatever we are supposed to do on Corycus," Enkidu suggested, "we might get in our boat and look for them. If this compass-pyx is as good as it looks, it could probably find the *Argo* for us."

"No, they sure don't want us with them. Certainly they don't want me, so to the Underworld with them. Besides, I suspect that when we have finished whatever is to be done on Corycus, my father will have thought up yet another task."

My nephew nodded, and let drop the matter of the *Argo* and its crew, so jealous of their fame. Enkidu hardly seemed to care where we were going next. I think I might have ordered him to set course for the Underworld, and he would have complied, so long as the journey could be made in our beautiful new boat.

TWELVE

Visiting a Queen

*B*efore heading out across the sea, my nephew and I put in at a small settlement a quarter of a mile downstream from where the *Argo* had landed, almost at the river's mouth. It seemed about the only place approximating a real port on that sparsely inhabited coast. Here we were able to obtain some decent clothing, that we might present a proper appearance at our arrival on Corycus, and also some food for the voyage. Small lockers aboard the *Skyboat* already contained jugs of water and several days' supply of fruit, dried meat, and fish. But Hermes seemed to have ignored all other needs that a crew or passengers might have.

The townsfolk stood staring after the two of us as we carried our purchases aboard, and that night we slept in the boat. Early in the morning, with our audience reassembled and gaping at what they must have supposed to be our folly, we awkwardly (and doubtless incorrectly) hoisted our small sail. Enkidu closed his eyes and pressed his forehead to the compass-pyx. The *Skyboat* began to move, propelled directly by its own magic, and we set out boldly through the mouth of the river and into the open sea.

Our destination, the locals had warned us, lay about two hundred miles to the southeast, half the width of the Great Sea away. They marveled at what they thought was the stupidity of two landlubbers, attempting such a feat in a small and practically open boat.

In the press of other concerns, I came near forgetting what Hermes had said about detailing a sprite to help us through any difficulties we might have with navigation. But so far it seemed we might be managing on our own. When Enkidu had moved away from our compass-pyx, and I cast my untutored eye at it, it seemed to me that Hermes had been right, and it might surpass even the model they were carrying on the *Argo,* of which Tiphys had been so justly proud. Our navigational device was just as big, and the box that housed it was made of real ivory, as far as I could tell, and the carved and painted patterns on the surface of the box were more complex.

The style of construction of our craft provided a tiny cabin, just about large enough to shelter two people, if they crawled in on hands and knees and could endure each other's closeness. The sail proved to be almost entirely for show—fortunately, for neither of us knew the first thing about sailing—though later it proved perfectly capable of functioning in the ordinary way. It also filled itself out with a phantom breeze when there was no real wind in the direction chosen by the steersman. There were no oars, but a couple of paddles had also been shipped aboard, again mostly, as I thought, for show. *Skyboat* was perfectly capable of propelling itself by sheer magic.

At this time, I sorely missed the company of Daedalus. I was keenly aware of my need of a wise counselor, but the only confidant I had, had now attained the ripe age of thirteen. So far, for my nephew, our wandering had been mainly a series of glorious adventures, culminating in a chance to sport with naiads. And to top it all off, he had now been provided with a wonderful new toy in our magic vessel. Small wonder that at the moment Enkidu was perfectly convinced that the world was an endlessly wonderful place.

As the two of us put out to sea, I caught a brief glimpse of a girl with hair almost the same color as Danni's, hard at work bending her slender, nude body over a fishing net on a nearby beach. It was of course not Danni. But I found myself wishing fervently that Meleager's sister might appear onshore and wave good-bye to me; far better yet, that she should be waiting to greet me when I landed somewhere. But alas, she was naturally nowhere in sight, being miles away.

Somehow the sight of one girl, and the thought of another, evoked in my mind the thought of yet another very different one. The face and body of Megan, our unhappy household servant as I remembered her, appeared briefly in my imagination; but as I sat in our little boat, Megan seemed to me to belong to a different world, one that had little or nothing to do with the one I now inhabited, away from home adventuring. And at the moment, her very remoteness invested her with a kind of glamour that made her all the more desirable.

* * *

The weather at the start of our voyage looked a trifle ominous, and had either of us any real experience of the sea, we might well have been frightened at what we were about to attempt. But in this case our ignorance was a shield. While Enkidu, clutching the compass-pyx and gloating over the power it gave him, confidently set our course, I sat thumping my hand gently on our new boat's solid side.

So, this construction of wood, canvas, and magic was the reward I had been promised. Certainly not what I had asked for, but real and solid, and if the Messenger had told the truth, quite marvelous enough to be the gift of some benevolent god. Solid proof, if any were needed, that Hermes was no mere impostor, or creature of my imagination. The whole game had now been raised to a different level.

We had been under way only a few minutes, gradually picking up speed, before all land had dropped from sight behind us. But still our boat, under the control of the magical device given us by Hermes, ran straight and with unhesitating speed. Since my life now depended on it, I wanted to find out as much as I could about how it worked. I reminded myself to ask Daedalus when next I saw him. Possibly the compass-pyx was too magical to fall fully into his realm of expertise, but I would try him anyway.

It was installed in a containment box, or binnacle, very near the exact center of the boat, and the four side walls of the ivory compass were connected, with magical effect, to the corresponding walls of the binnacle in which it rested.

The first time I put my head near the compass-pyx, the air nearby sounded with a thin whining from some invisible source. I jerked back nervously and looked about, one hand raised to swat a giant insect. But there was no such creature to be seen.

"You hear some buzzing, Herc?" Enkidu was grinning at me. "I did, too. But it didn't do me any harm."

Sudden realization dawned on me. "Lord Hermes said that he was leaving us a sprite to help us navigate." And as I spoke, the humming sound peaked sharply, then fell abruptly away.

My nephew looked more interested than worried. "What will it do?"

"Not much of anything, I hope, unless we need its help." Actually

I knew no more of such beings than Enkidu did, but I wanted to be re-assuring. "Try to use the box again; the less help we need, the better."

He followed my advice and had such good success that both of us were able to forget for the time being about our invisible companion.

My main concern was with more basic and important problems, on which I doubted that the sprite could give me any help. Nor could Enkidu, surely. All the great business of my life lay between me and the gods. I kept turning over in my mind what facts I thought I had made sure of, and those I only suspected, regarding my past life and what I might expect in the future.

Whatever faint doubts I might once have had that Zeus was really my father were becoming harder and harder to sustain—from what other source could I derive my special powers? And everyone agreed that the Thunderer's children were legion, scattered around the world along with his more remote descendants, all products of his obsessive lechery down through the ages. But rarely if ever, according to legend, did he sustain any interest in any of his bastard children. So I was less than confident it was really Zeus who had sent the Messenger to give me orders and to provide a magically powered boat. Mercury, speaking with all the lordly authority of deity, had clearly said as much—but was the God of Thieves and Merchants always to be believed?

Soon I began to share my thoughts with Enkidu, who was wondering what made me so silent and thoughtful. My nephew and I speculated as to whether we might someday be treated to an interview with Helius, the Sun, or maybe Apollo himself. Or possibly Hera or Aphrodite.

Of course the gods, as usual, provided an inexhaustible subject of conversation.

"Herc? I've been wondering."

"What?"

"If your father is . . . who he is . . . then why does he need to send you all around the world, beating the shit out of these monsters? He could just . . . just smite them with a thunderbolt."

"How in the Underworld should I know? Why did he insist on our hauling the Boar around, alive, if they were going to butcher it anyway? Maybe it just amuses him to watch. He never tells me anything."

"But now you're making a great effort to do what he wants you to do."

"Well. He is my father. Though he's never spoken a word to me since I was born."

"I know, you keep telling me that."

And that put an end to conversation for a time.

"Corycus is where the Minotaur lives," Enkidu observed, after a period of thoughtful silence.

"Are we back on that again? You should have been paying attention when Daedalus was talking to me, and Hermes, too. You'd better not use the word *Minotaur* at all when we get to Corycus. He's Prince Asterion, half brother to Queen Phaedra, and like me, he's a son of Zeus. And Hermes wants me to talk to him."

"But he's really got a bull's head?"

"So it seems."

"But he talks like a human being? And all you have to do is talk with him?"

"That's the way I understand the business so far."

"I was just wondering if maybe they expected you . . ." Enkidu didn't finish.

"If they want me to pack the Minotaur in a crate and cart him off somewhere? No, listen, Enk, we'd better get this straight, once and for all." And I did my best to pass on to my nephew the information that Hermes had conveyed to me.

When I had accomplished that, or thought I had, we were silent for a while. Then at length Enkidu said: "Corycus will be really different, though, won't it, Herc? If Lord Hermes said we don't have to kill anything there. How long are we going to stay?"

"Not having to hit anything with a club will be a pleasant change, as far as I'm concerned. Not having anything trying to bite me will be even nicer. I don't know how long we'll stay."

Again long minutes passed, and then my companion offered: "I wonder where Jason and his pals are now."

I turned my head and looked out over the empty sea. "A good many miles west of here, I'd say. And getting farther away from us all the time. It'll be all right with me if they just keep going, on and on, until they fall off the edge."

"But wouldn't it be neat if they could see us in this boat? I bet we could run circles around the *Argo*."

Even two passengers as ignorant as we were of seafaring could hardly fail to recognize how marvelous our *Skyboat* truly was. As we gained more experience of its capabilities, Enkidu was ecstatic, almost literally entranced, and went through spasms in which he seemed to be bubbling over with joy. "They gave it to us. They just *gave* it to us!" And he drove us swirling in circles on the surface of the great calm sea, while gulls went screaming past above us, never having seen the like before.

"Just gave it to us? No. It represents a partial payment; weren't you listening?" My gaze went sweeping around the empty place where sky rimmed water.

Finally I added: "And when we reach Corycus, Hermes will show up again and tell us there'll be more to it than talking. We'll be expected to do something else—something pretty difficult and dangerous. Now get us back on course."

"Difficult and dangerous? What'll that be?" But he obeyed my order, as if reluctantly.

"I don't know what, or why. All I do know is that the great god Zeus has never—never—paid any attention to me. Until only a few months ago. Then, good old Dad seems to have suddenly decided that the world is suffering from a plague of monsters. And that I, just one of his innumerable bastards—I suppose one of about a million that he's never even seen—I am just the one to clean it up. And to speed up the job a little he sent one of his helpers to give me a boat."

"You can be scary, Herc."

Despite the vaguely threatening aspect of the sky and sea when we set out, the weather actually remained fine for many hours. Evidently, if Poseidon did not belong to the cabal of gods who were supporting us, he had not become an active enemy.

After we had been for a time out of sight of land, and of all other craft, I took a second turn at crouching over the compass-pyx (I almost had to drag Enkidu away, to get a chance) and with the aid of its powers called up a vision of our destination. This time I heard the sound of no invisible companion.

Soon I discovered that it was sufficient for me to whisper the island's name while resting my forehead against the ivory box. On each trial the device showed me, behind my closed eyelids, a new view of the island, very slightly nearer than the time before but from the same angle.

With a superb instrument like this, even a landlubber who had never used a similar device before had no trouble in navigation. When our course seemed well established, in a general southeasterly direction, I urged our new craft to full speed.

I supposed we might even be able to go faster in the case of dire emergency.

Even now we were going so fast that a white bow wave sprang into existence, and the small waves could be heard slapping the bottom in a regular rhythm as they raced beneath. On the rare occasions when we came in sight of other craft, I insisted that we limit our speed to something less than the apparently miraculous. Still, the cool wind in our faces was strong enough to tear our breath away.

But now we had a vast open stretch of water all to ourselves. Dolphins appeared to challenge us, and raced along, but soon they, too, were left behind.

As I have said, our destination was no less than two hundred miles from our starting point, but we made the voyage, straight across open water, in no more than half a day. When eventually a line of squalls blew up across our course, I took the compass-pyx with me into the tiny cabin. Our boat slowed its speed considerably, and with no human hand upon the helm maneuvered itself among waves to minimize their impact and the roughness of our ride. But still I thought that we were making steady progress.

Soon we raised the mountainous, partially wooded spine of Corycus above the waves. The island was more than a hundred and fifty miles long, but very narrow. Only about an hour later we were cruising, at a much reduced speed, into the busy harbor of Kandak, the capital. It was clearly, as I had expected, much larger than any city I had ever seen before. Plainly visible in the middle distance was the sprawling palace, where less than a year ago, as everyone knew, young Queen Phaedra had ascended to the throne—I remembered how much excitement had been generated in Cadmia at the time, by news of the strange and violent events leading up to her succession.

By the time we reached the mouth of the harbor, much of Kandak had come into view. Also in sight, adjoining the palace, were the outer walls of the famous Labyrinth, sprawling over what was claimed to be four square miles of land.

Laborers and craftsmen of several kinds were at work, and folk with more leisure in their lives were strolling along the waterfront, but few took much notice of a small boat carrying a young man and a boy and looking utterly normal. Our sail put up a convincing show of being driven by nothing but the breeze.

But one man at least had evidently been expecting us, for he came walking along the pier before we had finished tying up, and bade us welcome in the queen's name.

We were hardly ashore before we learned that the gossip of current affairs on the island included considerable speculation as to whether Queen Phaedra might be going to marry. So far there seemed no certain answer to that question. People still spoke in hushed tones of the recent marriage of her sister, Ariadne, to the newest avatar of the god Dionysus.

The guide who had been sent to meet us happened to glance back along the dock, as we were walking away, at the place where we had tied up the gift of Hermes.

"What happened to your boat?" was his bewildered question. "It was right there, but now . . ."

I could still see it, and Enkidu told me later that he could, too, though only as a kind of transparent wraith of a small boat. At the time, we reassured our guide as best we could, and followed him on.

We were conducted first to the palace, where we had scarcely arrived before being told that Queen Phaedra had been informed of our arrival and was awaiting us impatiently.

As Enkidu and I walked along, we kept half-expecting to catch a glimpse of the divine Dionysus somewhere; but then we were told that neither he nor his bride, the princess Ariadne, were on the island.

The queen of Corycus received us privately. She was an attractive woman in her early twenties, with dark hair and a compact figure. The general assumption among her people was that she would not long remain unmarried, but naturally any match she made would have to be carefully considered.

Given the prominence of some of our relatives in Cadmia, neither Enkidu nor I were utter strangers to royalty, or to the procedures expected of visitors at court. So we were not as completely awed as many youths of our age might have been; and the young queen seemed to go out of her way to be friendly and gracious.

The queen concluded: "My brother feels an urgent need to see you, and I must send you on to him. But there is one other here who must speak with you first."

Now a familiar voice sounded, and a figure appeared whom we immediately recognized. And Enkidu and I saw, to our considerable surprise, that the Artisan had somehow got to Corycus ahead of us and was watching us with some amusement.

At first I blinked at Daedalus and was unable to believe my eyes. In the next moment, anger and suspicion surged up in me, and I was convinced that the apparition before me had to be some kind of a deception.

Jumping to my feet, I grasped the figure by one arm, taking care not to crush flesh and bone, but forestalling any attempt the man might make to pull away.

"Majesty," I cried, turning to the queen, "this cannot be truly Daedalus. We left him behind on the mainland, and we came here faster than any other boat could travel."

The queen and her attendants were at first greatly alarmed at my energetic action, and guards with spears leveled came bustling in. But in a few moments the cooler heads in the royal party had understood where the difficulty lay. They left it up to the Artisan himself to explain it to me.

"Swift as your little boat must be, Hercules, you should accept the fact that the transport which brought me here was even faster."

"How can that be?"

He looked around before speaking, and lowered his voice. "You should keep the matter a secret for now, but I actually came here in the chariot of Dionysus."

For a moment I thought the Artisan was joking; but then I saw that he was perfectly serious. It was evidently not the first time that Daedalus had ridden in the chariot, for he seemed to take the whole business with amazing calm.

And a little later, I was actually able to catch a glimpse of the supernatural leopards and the chariot, waiting inside the palace, at the end of a dim hall, even though the god whose property they were was somewhere else.

"Where is Dionysus?" I heard myself whispering to Daedalus, who walked beside me.

The Artisan looked at me severely. "I do not question the comings and goings of such a one. He may be very far away by now; the chariot will not be his only means of getting around."

I walked on in silence, past uniformed guards and lovely statues, all the panoply of wealth and power. Enkidu, trailing me by a step, had not uttered a word for a long time. We had come a long way from the herders' camp in Cadmia.

THIRTEEN

Talking to the Minotaur

*W*hile I was waiting to hear word that Prince Asterion was ready to see me, I took the opportunity of seeking out the Artisan. Though I knew Daedalus only slightly, I had begun to trust him, and there were several matters on which I wanted his advice.

Meanwhile Enkidu, who was usually not given to worrying about anything more profound than the size of his muscles or the amount of gold he might someday manage to accumulate, had disappeared into the palace kitchen. I felt confident of being able to find him there, telling stories, eating, or chasing wenches, when I wanted him.

I had no problem locating Daedalus. He sat alone on a rooftop terrace of the palace, staring blankly at the surface of a table before him, on which he had arrayed an assortment of small objects, none of which I could recognize. I took them to be the parts of some cunning machine. They were of divers shapes and sizes, some carved of a substance that looked like bone, while others appeared to be polished wood, and yet others were clear glass.

Not wishing to break the Artisan's concentration, I remained standing quietly at a little distance until he noticed me, and then I apologized for interrupting him. But he seemed glad to see me, and bade me sit down. The elevated site provided us with a fine view of the Great Sea, beyond the palace and the harbor of Kandak.

The objects arranged on the table, Daedalus told me, were parts of an antique device with which he hoped to be able eventually to make some astronomical observations. But the problem of properly assembling the device had so far baffled him.

"Maybe some are missing," I suggested

"I fear that's all too likely." But then he seemed to put the matter aside with a gesture of his work-hardened hand. "How do matters go with you, Hercules?"

"The *Skyboat* is a great help in getting from place to place. It does marvelous things. I hope you can examine it eventually."

"I hope so, too. If I had time . . . but there are only so many years, days, and hours in the life of any man. What else?"

"I have no real complaint about any of the tasks the gods have asked of me so far." I paused, and let time pass. In the distance, two servants were quarreling about something. The scar on the back of my right hand itched, and I scratched it absently. At last I added: "The truth is, matters do not go as well as I would like."

The man across the table nodded slowly. "I understand that you are determined to have a meeting with your father."

"I am."

As I began to make my usual complaints about my father, Daedalus listened intently, and a frown grew steadily upon his face.

"Is that how the situation seems to you?" he asked at last. "I did not realize you were so angry."

"How else should it seem?"

The Artisan sat for a time, still frowning. But now he gazed out at the distant waves, obviously deep in thought, while in front of him the collection of small parts lay totally forgotten for the moment. At last he sighed deeply and turned around to me again.

"Hercules, there are some things I dare not tell you, and other things that I simply must not. But I can tell you this: I have seen your father, and spoken to him, and—"

"You have seen Zeus?" I was impressed, and at the same time not totally convinced. For Hermes the Messenger to appear openly before mortals was one thing; for Zeus himself to do so would be quite something else. But neither could I wholly doubt. He who sat before me now was only a man—but a man who had ridden at least once in the chariot of Dionysus.

Daedalus responded calmly. "Yes. I have seen the Thunderer and spoken to him, not many days ago—"

"Where?"

"On the mainland—let me finish, Hercules—and it is my belief that not a day has passed since you were born when you have been absent from his thoughts."

"He must have a thousand bastard offspring, scattered around the world."

Daedalus nodded his grizzled head. "That may well be. But you are one of those he thinks about and particularly cares about. Do not forget that Zeus, like all gods, is first of all a human being."

Now it was my turn to sit silent, trying to digest a bit of information. I was staring at the sea but did not see it. At last, turning back to my adviser, I told him: "By all the gods, I wish I could believe that."

"You can."

"The man who currently wears the Face of Zeus is the man who sired me?"

"That is my belief."

"So, what have you heard my father say about me?"

But the Artisan was shaking his head.

"Tell me!"

"Let your anger fall upon me if it will, Hercules, but now I must say no more. Probably I have said too much already."

After that, we spoke for a time of other things. Within an hour a messenger came to tell me that Prince Asterion was ready to see me. Soon the Artisan, forgetting his clockwork puzzle for the moment, was guiding me into the Labyrinth. Enkidu had emerged from the kitchen, evidently sated for the moment, and came tagging at my heels; no one objected to his presence.

Our guide led us out of the palace by one of the small side doors, then along a small gravel path that curved across a corner of the parklike grounds. Now I could see that we were headed straight toward one edge of the mysterious Labyrinth, which here immediately adjoined the palace grounds. The Maze's outer wall of stone, tall and slightly curving, loomed up ominously ahead of us.

And then we were inside, following a curving, stone-walled passage, barely wide enough for two to walk abreast, that branched, and branched, and branched again. Some sections were roofed, and here and there a stair went up, and another down. There were small courtyards, with ponds, and plants, and statuary.

It was, I learned, easy to find one's way to certain destinations within the Maze by following a series of painted spikes, which had long ago been driven into the pavement.

Not that my guide seemed to need them. I soon realized what I should have known all along, had I given the matter even a moment's thought: Here Daedalus was on familiar territory, having labored in the Labyrinth for many months on a project for Phaedra's predecessor on the throne. Many fascinating stories were connected with that effort, and some real events seemed to have been already transformed into legend. I told myself that when the time seemed right I would ask the man himself to tell me the truth of all those marvelous events.

But that would have to wait, for now we were moving rapidly into the depths of the great Maze. Unlike many other famous sights in the great world, the Corycan Labyrinth, with its thousand miles or more of knotted narrow passages, most of them open to the sky, was truly as impressive as I had imagined it might be.

I had been told by several people that the prince dwelt alone in the middle of the Labyrinth, continuing by choice a style of life that had once been enforced upon him. He lived simply, with almost nothing of the panoply of rank, and was attended only occasionally by servants. He had spent almost his entire life within these walls, relying chiefly on dreams to keep him informed about the great world outside. He welcomed us even more eagerly than his sister had.

I had been told on good authority that Asterion, only a few years older than myself, was like me a child of Zeus. I had to repress a shudder when I saw for the first time with waking eyes just how the divine power had expressed itself in this, my half brother. Somehow this version of a composite creature, with the outward appearance of the head so totally inhuman, was more disturbing than the horse-bodied centaurs had been.

The prince was every bit as large as his image in my dreams had shown him, seven feet tall if an inch. Even a little more, I thought, if you were to count the horns, which went curving up one on each side of the inhuman skull, in graceful symmetry. His feet and legs as they showed below his kilt were very human, no hairier and no bigger than those of some normal men. In the course of his brief life, he had become known to most of the world only as a monster, a kind of bogeyman who feasted on human flesh. The reality of course was very different, and in fact the prince ate no meat at all. He also differed from ordinary men in having been born a eunuch.

The prince bade me be seated beside him on a simple bench, under a trellis of mutant grapevines, whose fruit looked more like miniature peaches. Enkidu, after being introduced, hung about uncertainly. Daedalus warned him sharply not to wander off.

"The Labyrinth is not the worst place in the world to go wandering, but it is one of the very easiest in which to lose yourself."

Enkidu flushed, and bowed in acknowledgement of the order.

When I had recovered somewhat from my first embarrassing but uncontrollable reaction to the sight of a man with a horned beast's head, I questioned the prince eagerly on the subject of the father we were said to share; but Asterion could not, or chose not to, tell me anything on that subject that I did not already know.

I sighed and moved on to other matters. "Do you know, Lord Asterion, why Hermes sends me to you?"

"Yes. Because we have important things to talk about, and communication is much more reliable when both parties are awake. You know I have the power to visit the dreams of others, and also to draw others into mine. But those contacts made in sleep are too uncertain for the proper conduct of some kinds of business."

The prince paused for a few moments and seemed to be gathering his thoughts. Then he said: "Hercules, you have done well so far. But all that you have done till now is as nothing to the tasks that still remain."

He paused again, then added: "I hope that you will trust me, Hercules, when in the future I intrude to speak to you in sleep. I will never do so without good cause."

The idea that anyone could so invade the privacy of my own thoughts did not sit well with me. I said: "So far I have no reason not to trust you, Prince Asterion. But then I have no proof that I should trust you, either."

He shifted his great weight on the bench beside me, so that the woodwork creaked. "You speak boldly, son of Zeus."

"Because there is little that I fear."

"No one here on Corycus bears you any ill will. Certainly I do not. But I advise you to fear Zeus, if no one and nothing else."

"And what is the Thunderer himself afraid of?"

"Giants."

Had the prince answered with the one word *nothing,* I would not have been surprised. But the word he actually used astonished me enough to quiet my simmering resentment for a time.

"What do you know of Giants, Hercules?"

It was not the first time since my leaving home that affairs had taken an unexpected turn. First gods, then centaurs, and now this.

"Very little, Prince."

"Have you ever seen one?"

"No."

The prince pressed on. "And have you heard of a war between the race of Giants and the gods we know?"

"Something of such a conflict, yes. But only in nursery tales, when I was very small."

Asterion leaned his head back into the vines that grew behind our bench, as if he were trying to rest his neck from the weight of many dreams, or worries. He said in his strange voice: "I wish that the war was only a matter of nursery tales, and of dreams. But no, it is very real, and very terrible, though for most of the humans on the earth it is still invisible. That will not always be the case."

The Artisan, who was sitting in on our discussion, nodded his head in confirmation.

"The prince and I have decided," he said, "that it is time, and past time, that you know more of what your father Zeus is planning, what problems he and the other gods who stand with him must face. We can only hope that they will approve of our decision."

"Understand, first," said Prince Asterion, "that all the gods, whether they admit the fact or not, are deadly frightened of a terrible and secret weapon that the Giants use against them. Like Apollo's Arrows, it can strike at a distance of a mile or more. But it is completely invisible, even to divine eyesight. It has never been known to injure a mere mortal human, like you or me"—for a moment I thought the bull-face smiled, at including us both in such a category—"but on a god or goddess the effect is devastating."

"What sort of weapon?" I demanded, my throat suddenly dry.

"One that is hard to identify precisely, or describe." The prince raised both hands in an odd pointing gesture. "The projection from their very fingertips of some invisible beam, or force, which ravages the memory of anyone in its path who happens to be wearing a god-Face."

Each Giant, or at least a great many of them, possessed some form of this weapon, which must be somehow built or grown into their very bodies. Therefore any god who came within a mile of any Giant was at risk of losing part or all his memory, temporarily or permanently, even to the point of forgetting his own identity.

Then the prince and Daedalus led me into a different corner of the vast Maze, where a massive door was set into a thick stone wall. As I approached the door, the smell of the sea grew very strong, and I marveled at this, for I knew that the shore was more than a mile away. My guides indicated that I should look through a small hole in the door, and when I did I saw beyond it a room that had been converted into a stone prison cell.

The furnishings of the cell were simple. Its single inmate, a middle-aged man, was clad in a simple garment that might have been fashioned from a fishing net, and he sat on a simple bench studying his own hands, a blank expression on his face, like a man trying to remember what hands were for.

"Hercules, do you recognize that god?" asked the prince, who was standing at my side.

I had had no idea that I was looking at a god. "I do not, should I?"

"He is Palaemon, called by some Portunus, the God of Harbors. Now he is a horrible example of what the Giants' mind weapon can do. He has been so badly affected that he has forgotten what it is to be a god. I'm not sure that it still makes sense to call him a god, though the Face of Portunus is still buried in his head."

I was aghast at the sight. Now Enkidu came to the door to get a look.

"He cannot see us or hear us," the prince assured us. "Dionysian magic has sealed him off."

"Why is he imprisoned?" I asked in a low voice when we were headed down the twisting branching corridor again, back to the room where we had begun our conversation.

"For his own protection. Palaemon has been so enervated mentally that he neither knows nor cares where he is, or what might be happening to him."

"Terrible," I said.

"We are trying to find a cure, of course. But so far none of our treatments have much effect."

I was more shaken by the sight of a fallen god than I could have been by any fabulous monster or towering Giant. "But—if the Giants prevail, and all the powers of the gods should fail—how will the Universe endure?"

"It is not the fate of the Universe that worries me," said Daedalus grimly. "The Universe can take care of itself. The real problem is what is going to happen to ordinary, mortal humanity, should the Giants win."

"I don't understand. If the Giants' weapon doesn't hurt ordinary people, then what is the special danger to them?"

The Artisan spoke convincingly about the monstrous ways in which the Giants treated ordinary humanity whenever their paths crossed those of ordinary people. Fortunately such encounters had so far been fairly rare, because of the Giants' fondness for desolation. But the numbers of both races were increasing, and more contact was inevitable in the future.

"And then there is the problem of monsters. Some cases of severe deformity"—he looked around, I supposed to make sure that the prince was out of earshot—"are the result of interbreeding between gods and mortals. But others come from experimentation by the Giants. Your Hydra and your Boar are good examples."

"And the centaurs?"

Daedalus frowned. "I am not yet certain about them. They have an ancient history."

My pair of tutors also told me about their examination of tissues from the Hydra and the Boar; they both regretted never getting any sample from the Nemean lion.

"There are grounds for believing that the lion, too, was a monster created by the Giants. You say that no weapon could pierce its hide."

"Quite true." Enkidu and I both nodded.

"What do you know, Hercules, of the Golden Apples of the Hesperides?"

"I have never heard of them," I said, after exchanging glances with my equally puzzled nephew.

Hermes and Daedalus and their assistants were also struggling with the problems of learning exactly what the Golden Apples of the Hesperides meant to the race of the Giants, and of obtaining a sample of this mysterious fruit.

"For all we know, the Apples may have something to do with the Giants' secret weapon."

Our talk drifted on to other matters. The Artisan observed casually that he had analyzed some of Prince Asterion's blood and would like to be able to analyze some of mine as well. But, considering my impervious skin, he was not sure how to go about trying to draw a sample.

I was not sure whether I ought to be worried, annoyed, or only amused. "So, you'd like to see me bleed?"

"Yes indeed," he answered absently. "Of course, were you a female," he mused, "there would be your monthly cycle as a source."

"Yes, and were I an olive, you could squeeze me for my oil." The idea that my skin might actually be broken, my blood flow like that of other humans, grew more disturbing the more I thought about it. No doubt my feelings were so sensitive because nothing of the kind had ever happened to me. Not for me the scraped knees and cut fingers that normal children suffered without much thought, being inured to such damage from earliest childhood.

The thought was frightening, and I began to bluster.

"Yes, and were I a duck, I would probably lay eggs. But as I am, I think you will not get any of my blood."

The Artisan said there was nothing urgent about the matter; he was willing to wait until he could think of some good method of collection.

Asterion went on: "Sooner or later, Hercules, we are going to discover just what effect the special weapon of the Giants has on you. You are no god, but you are hardly an ordinary mortal, either. Nor am I, of course, but I am not going to leave the Labyrinth."

Asterion raised a very human palm in my direction, forestalling protest. "No, we are not asking you to volunteer for any experiments. We would all like you to avoid the test as long as possible, but in the end it will not be possible to escape."

We all of us rested overnight, and in the morning we held another lengthy conversation.

Meanwhile, I had still seen only a little, here and there, of the great Maze. I found it deeply fascinating. Daedalus pointed out the spot where he had labored for the young queen's predecessor, and other places where marvelous events had happened, many of them over the last two years.

I discovered that on Corycus, spring came early—more accurately, that there was hardly any winter. Now sunshine striking through the tangled vines made patches of bright translucent green, leaving caves of shadow within the roofed-over sections of the endless, intertwining passageways that comprised the great bulk of the Labyrinth. Somewhere just out of sight, perhaps in the next open courtyard, or maybe in the one after that, water was trickling musically from one of the Maze's many fountains into an adjoining pool. While we remained within those walls, the sound of running water, far or near, was almost never absent. The curving walls and tunnels, most of their surfaces hard stone, sometimes played games with sound.

Asterion surprised me with the claim that he had recently been able to enter the dreams of certain Giants.

"It was not an experience that I would willingly seek to repeat. I felt as if my mind, my nature, was in danger of being absorbed into the earth."

And Asterion, as was so often the case, had dreams of his own to tell. Rarely had his physical body ever left the confines of the great Maze, but in sleep his mind roamed to the ends of the known world, and sometimes beyond.

As our conversation went on, digging deeper into the topics of the previous day, Asterion and Daedalus explained a little more of the ongoing problem between the gods and the Giants, until I began to understand why even Zeus was fearful.

Speaking of the Giants, Asterion said: "Even if we could find some way to nullify their special weapon, they would still be, in many ways, as strong as the gods we know, or even stronger in some cases. They would be formidable antagonists. But as matters actually stand now, Zeus and his colleagues, the beings we have been taught to think of as the rulers of the Universe, are doomed to eventual defeat."

After hearing that, I walked on for some time, slowly and in complete silence. That Zeus, the greatest of gods, with thunderbolts at his command, could be afraid, of anything or anyone, was a new idea to me and required some digesting.

At last I said: "Then we know that our father Zeus lives, whether or not still in the avatar that sired you and me."

"He lives indeed, I can testify to that. Though in recent decades he has been exceedingly hard to find."

"It sounds better if we simply say that Zeus and Apollo and the rest are simply behaving prudently."

"I don't care how it sounds."

Prince Asterion also told me that he had been warned in a dream that it would be important for me to know something of the Underworld.

"Is this some foretelling of my death?"

"There is an implication of danger, certainly. And death waits for us all. No, there was some warning apart from that. But too vague to be of any real use."

"What have either of us to do with the kingdom of Hades?"

"As little as possible, I hope," said the odd voice from the bull's mouth. "Speaking of formidable gods, the Messenger also expressed a hope that you would be able to talk to Apollo while you were visiting our island. But Apollo is not on Corycus now."

"Oh," I said. At the sound of that name, so casually uttered, something inside me seemed to cringe a bit and make an effort at withdrawal, turning inward even farther. True, we had just been speaking of almighty Zeus himself, and it was also true that I had confronted and even argued with great Hermes face-to-face. And I had now been privileged to catch a glimpse of the chariot of glorious Dionysus.

But . . . Apollo.

Far-Worker, Sun God, the Lord of Death and Terror and Distance. And of many other things besides. Shiva the Destroyer was known as a god of tremendous power and was feared by many—but on Corycus, people said that Lord Apollo had shot down Shiva's most recent avatar with the authority of a man swatting a fly.

Beside me, Enkidu was now sitting still. The sound of Apollo's name seemed to have knocked him into the attitude of a chastened child, very nearly afraid to move.

At last I asked the man who was sometimes called the Minotaur. "You *know* Lord Apollo? The Far-Worker himself?"

"He calls me friend," said Prince Asterion simply. "It was his Arrow that struck down Shiva—was it only about a year ago? Sometimes I tend to lose track of waking time—not far from where we are standing now. The Face of Shiva was of course not destroyed, but it fell into a pit—I will soon show you where—with an Arrow still protruding from its Third Eye."

For a moment or two I was silent, not knowing what to say. No doubt to be a child of Zeus was a glorious distinction, even if there were more than a few of us scattered around the earth. But to claim *Apollo* as a *friend* . . .

When I remarked on this to Daedalus, he, too, claimed some familiarity with the Far-Worker, though the Artisan was generally more interested in solving problems without magic than in consorting with the gods.

Now Prince Asterion strongly recommended that I should leave Corycus as soon as possible and set out on a voyage to try to discover the truth about the Apples of Hesperides. Daedalus strongly concurred.

"*Hesperides* sounds to me like a chain of islands," was Enkidu's comment this time. Our tutors quickly explained to both of us that the three Hesperides were women, or perhaps nymphs, named Hespere, Aegle, and Erytheis. But in any case, the Apples might really have nothing to do with them at all.

"This task is different, Hercules, from any you have undertaken yet. This time we can give you but little in the way of specific instructions."

Enkidu was, as usual, ready for new adventure. But reaching the land where the Apples were thought to grow would involve serious traveling.

Even with *Skyboat* to speed us on our way, a journey of that length would take us many days.

But before leaving the island of Corycus, I wanted to make sure that it afforded no possible passage down into the Underworld; Asterion had suggested this as one possible meaning of the blurred dream-message. Daedalus also was strongly curious about what lay just underground; and Prince Asterion agreed that it was only reasonable that I should be the one to make the attempt.

He and the Artisan both accompanied me to the very rim of the pit, with Enkidu as usual tagging along.

We were standing in a kind of courtyard, created by a partial destruction of the Maze and larger than most of those located within it by design. In the center of this space of devastation was a crater, perhaps fifteen yards wide, and at the bottom of the crater a dim abyss of uncertain depth. The bottom, some ten or fifteen yards below us, was piled with rocks of such size that the crevices between them might very well offer passage to a much greater depth.

Glad to accept advice from Daedalus, I allowed Asterion's attendants, supervised by the Artisan, to wrap my body in layers of thick wool, then drench me in water, against the heat, before I started down.

Now I had reached the lowest depth yet attained by mortal men since the formation of the crater. From that point it was my decision to go on alone. I worked my way lower for a little distance, using natural handholds and steps in the rough rock wall of the great cavity. Descending cautiously a little farther under the Labyrinth, I felt the heat increase steadily with every step I took.

Enough daylight still came down through the opening to let me see my way. I called up to my friends that I now saw a kind of tunnel, seeming to lead farther down.

I entered this aperture but could advance for only a few yards before it narrowed so drastically that it became impassable. Where the passage narrowed, I began to widen it by breaking chunks out of the walls with blows of my fists.

Progress by this means was painfully slow because of the difficulty of concentrating the force in precisely the way I wanted. And not many minutes passed before I was brought to a halt, then driven into a retreat, by the tremendous heat of nearly molten rock not far ahead. If there had once been a passage leading farther down, it was certainly closed now. Whether the shadowy realm called Tartarus was anywhere nearby was more than I could guess.

I might have tried to force my way through, at what appeared to be considerable risk; but there was no real reason to believe that I would encounter anything but greater heat, and more rock, behind the layers that were now visible in front of me.

Whether my special powers might be equal to the challenge of protecting my body from damage by molten rock, I did not know, but I had to assume that the pain of such a contact would be terrible. Beside this, the dangers posed by lion, Boar, and Hydra were shrunken into insignificance. Here, it seemed, I was at last beginning to encounter the powers that really ruled the world.

Slowly I climbed back to the rim of the pit, where the onlookers expressed their relief at seeing me emerge alive. Enkidu especially was grateful, and the Artisan had a dozen questions about the nature of the rock below.

As to what might have happened to the Face of Shiva, I could only speculate that it could have been picked up by one of the minions of infernal Hades and carried off to some stronghold deep in Tartarus. I wondered if the Lord of the Underworld might have made a secret alliance with the Giants, and by concealing the Face intended to keep any human from regaining its powers and putting them to work on the gods' side in the great conflict. But I supposed a more likely possibility was that Hades meant to create a new Shiva by giving the Face to some mortal he thought he could trust to be his ally in the uncertain times that seemed to lie ahead for gods and men alike.

Enkidu and I now prepared to depart on our next mission. Again I wished fervently that Daedalus might come with us, but again he declined—reluctantly, I thought. He had essential tasks to perform elsewhere.

FOURTEEN

A Place Called Ilium

*U*ntil the last minute I hoped that Daedalus might change his mind and agree to accompany us on our quest for the Apples. By his own admission he was eager to get his hands on one of those strange fruits. Also I thought he would have given much to be present at my first encounter with a Giant, which seemed likely on my current mission. The true nature of those creatures, the gods' Titanic enemies, seemed to be what now interested the Artisan above all else. But Daedalus only repeated regretfully that he had very important work to do elsewhere. I did not doubt that; but I strongly suspected also that he was deeply afraid of such things as Giants, as every man has a right to be.

Enkidu and I found the *Skyboat* just where we had left it, at the quay in Kandak harbor. Larger vessels were now tied up on both sides, but our boat continued to occupy its small space, invisible to any eyes but my nephew's and mine, until we came to claim it.

The Artisan had taken the time to walk with us to the boat, and as we stepped aboard he gave me some final words of advice.

"Your strength is awesome, Hercules. But you are not immortal."

"I know that," I responded impatiently. But deep in my heart I thought I was immune to death, as all strong and healthy young men are wont to do.

Voyaging boldly out from the island of Corycus, with the full confidence of youth, in our small boat that seemed, happily, almost immune to the adverse effects of wind and wave, Enkidu and I set about trying to fulfill the expectations of the gods.

I was determined, at the very least, to keep the bargain that I now seemed to have made with Zeus, and with that faction of the gods who were allied with him.

Would you believe that we were so young and foolish as to entertain every expectation of success?

*   *   *

Had the Artisan been with us in our little boat, he could have told us much more, in the long hours of our next days of travel, about the gods and about the Giants, too. Though his usual concern was mundane matters, still he knew more about the Olympians than almost any other human being on earth, by reason of the fact that he so often had dealings with them.

On Corycus, Enkidu and I had learned some disturbing things: not only how frightened the gods were of these same Giants, but how little Zeus and the others knew, how much they seemed to have mysteriously forgotten, about their ancient enemies.

I also had at least begun to have some understanding of the special role that I was required to play. How I had been designed and bred to order, as it were; created as a handy tool to carry out the will of Zeus.

We soon discovered that the tutelary sprite assigned us by Hermes still accompanied the *Skyboat.*

Our voyage this time was much longer than our previous trip from the mainland to Corycus. We sailed even at night, trusting to the work of the gods to keep us on course under the stars. Blessed as we were with a superbly reliable compass-pyx, we felt no need to creep along the coast, keeping land in sight at all times, to avoid getting lost. Even so, the great irregularity of the northern shore of the Great Sea several times brought land into our sight on our right hand; and so it happened that our route took us close to the seaside plain and city of Troy, which some prefer to call by the name of Ilium.

At one point, several days into our journey and hundreds of miles from Corycus, where the shoreline curved out near our almost straight westerly course, my eye was caught by the sight of something there on shore, a spot of pink, of a shape appropriate for a human form. I tapped Enkidu on the shoulder and told him to steer in closer yet. The pink spot was moving, or rather wiggling about in the same place.

"Steer in closer," I ordered again, shading my eyes with one hand and squinting into the sun-glare. Enkidu, with one hand resting on our compass-pyx, thought the appropriate thoughts, and our small boat steered itself according to his will.

When we were near enough, the spot of tawny pink began to look for all the world like a long-haired human being chained naked to a rock, halfway up a small cliff and only a little above the sea. It might be expected that any victim left in such a spot would drown if the tide came in high enough. From the top of the little seaside cliff, the barren land sloped gradually inland for half a mile or so, to a kind of crest. Along the elevation, many tents had been erected. At a distance, I could not yet tell if there were people on that ridge, but there were what looked like piles of stone, purposefully arranged. It was evident that a huge construction project was under way.

And when we had slowed our *Skyboat's* speed and come a little closer still, we could see plainly that the chained human was in fact a young and comely female. Soon we could be sure that she was completely unclothed, and also that she was still very much alive, for she began to move her arms and legs, as much as the burden of her chains allowed, and began to cry for help, sounding a thin wail of despair that raised the hairs on the back of my neck.

"What in the Underworld is the meaning of this?" I demanded of the world in general. I had heard of human lives being offered to the gods, but never seen the business before.

"Must be some kind of sacrifice," Enkidu suggested. "Or this girl's done something that deserved one monster of a punishment. Or maybe both."

Meanwhile, our sprite seemed agitated, buzzing invisibly about my ears. This conveyed a sense of urgency, but was no help in choosing a course of action.

"Whatever it's all about, I'm putting a stop to it." I suppose a majority of men in my place would have been afraid to interfere, not wanting to risk insulting any deity by thwarting an intended sacrifice. But I felt I was beginning to grow accustomed to the gods, and Enkidu was generally brave enough for anything, provided no Olympian was actually present.

"So what are we going to do, Herc?"

"I'm not sure yet. But put us in to shore, and we'll do something."

We beached our small boat amid some lively surf, and I more or less tucked it under my arm and carried it up above the current level of the waves. My club I carried on a little farther, before putting it down at the base of the cliff so that I might have full use of both hands. Then I began to climb the small cliff toward the girl. Enkidu as usual was close on my heels.

The cliff was less than thirty feet high, and its face was rough enough that no great climbing skill was required. In fact as we drew near out goal, I observed just above me a fairly well-worn path, which must have been used by those who had placed the maiden in such a perilous state, to bring her down from the cliff top to the ledge where she was bound. One branch of the path swung down the cliff, and I changed course slightly to reach it, making swifter progress possible.

Walking erect again, coming around the last bend of the small trail, I found myself close enough to the victim to read the expression in her eyes, which were now locked on me in desperate entreaty.

"Who's done this to you, girl?" I demanded. "But never mind, I'll have you free in a moment." And Enkidu did his best to reassure her, too.

"Hurry, oh hurry! In a few minutes it will be too late!" And I could see where her wrists and ankles were raw and bleeding from struggling against the chains.

She seemed very near my own age. Her body was shapely, or would have been had not the metal fetters stretched and pinched her into an awkward position. But I was not too much distracted to observe that, contrary to my earlier estimate, the site where she was chained stood substantially above high tide, as was plain from the appearance of the beach. Obviously it was not the ocean itself, not Poseidon as represented by a rising tide, that was expected to receive the sacrifice.

The girl was whimpering. Now that help was at hand, she seemed ready to dissolve in helpless tears.

"Don't worry, I'll have you out of there in no time. What's your name?"

"Hesione. Oh, hurry, hurry! But my chains are welded on, and you have no tools."

I was almost within reach of the intended victim when her gaze suddenly moved past me, and she screamed out: "It's coming, I see it! Quick, help!"

*   *   *

Murmuring something meant to be reassuring, I turned to behold the sea monster, a great blackish shape breaking the gray-green sea, heading in from deep water toward the shore. It looked at least twice as big as the Hydra, but I was glad to see that this time I would have only one head to contend with.

Turning my back briefly on the horror again, I started to break the girl loose from her shackles. That job was more difficult for me than you might suppose, reluctant as I was to do even the slightest harm to her tender wrists and ankles. Also I had to shield her soft skin from flying fragments when the links gave way. But still, in less than a minute it was done.

Meanwhile, Enkidu had gone sprinting back down the path to the foot of the cliff, where he snatched up my club. In a few moments more he had lugged it up the hill again and handed it to me.

Thinking I might as well discourage further human sacrifices as much as possible, I tore out of the rock the bronze rings and spikes to which Hesione had been chained. Then I broke the links of the chains near to the wristlets and anklets that had been welded on by some skilled smith, who had somehow managed not to burn the soft skin. Very considerate of him, I thought.

"Run, get up the cliff, the beast is coming!" I commanded the girl. And at the same time I turned to face the sea, ready for whatever it might bring against me. Still there was only the one great beast, now standing in the shallows, its head on its long neck looking levelly at me where I stood halfway up the cliff.

The young woman's limbs were so stiff with being chained that she could barely stand and walk. Enkidu did not run ahead but gallantly pulled off his own tunic and draped it around Hesione's pale shivering shoulders. Then he began to help her up the path toward the cliff top.

"Everywhere we go," I growled, "it seems the world is full of monsters." Hermes had given me no instructions regarding this one, so I felt free to deal with it as I thought best. Picking up a chunk of broken rock the size of my own head, I slung it with some violence toward the serpent. Unhappily my aim was no better than usual, and the missile missed by several yards, only kicking up a small splash a quarter of a mile out to sea.

Then it would have to be the club again. As a rule, I did much better with the club. Sliding down the steep slope to the strip of beach, I took a couple of warm-up swings and waited.

I had not long to wait. When the beast came out of the water, I could see that its entire body was darker than the Hydra, and vastly larger, but similarly reptilian in its overall appearance. Again I reassured myself that indeed this creature possessed only a single head, though its jaws looked large enough to seize and crunch up our boat in a bite or two. I thought I could feel the sand beneath my feet jar slightly each time one of its feet came down.

And the huge head came swinging toward me, mouth agape, letting out a wave of foul breath almost enough to send me staggering. It seemed that at first the monster expected to be able to swallow me at a gulp, for I was evidently standing below the rock that served as its regular feeding tray, or trough. But as its head swayed near, instead of tender food it got a good knock from my club, which broke its lower jaw—all it managed to swallow on that particular attempt was a few of its own teeth.

In the end this vast sea creature proved not as hard to finish off as the Hydra had been. Its single head, large as it was, evidently lacked enough brain to try to find a strategy, or even to know when it was time to retreat. Three or four more solid whacks on that ponderous skull were enough to crack thick bone into fragments, and in no more than a minute the whole vast body was down in the surf, where it twitched a few times and then lay still.

The sprite came buzzing around my head, invisible as some benevolent mosquito. Perhaps it was offering congratulations. But I only shook my head in irritation. After a moment the humming presence moved away again.

"Well, Daedalus," I murmured, in imaginary conversation with my mentor. "I suppose you might be eager to examine samples of this beast's flesh, as you did the Boar's. You missed out on the lion, but Hermes brought you some pieces of the Hydra, didn't he? I don't know if you might want this one—but if so, you're out of luck. It will all be eaten by little fish before I ever see you again."

But a moment later a new thought occurred to me, and my actions contradicted my words. Picking up a new rock to use as a tool, and thinking that raw flesh would certainly spoil, I broke out a sample of the sea monster's bone, intending to take it when I could to the Artisan, on the chance that he might want it for his continuing investigations.

Later, the story would spread that I had actually leaped, fully armed, down the sea monster's throat and had spent the next three days fighting in its belly. Some folk are eager to believe anything, provided only that it be marvelous enough.

Briskly I climbed to the top of the little cliff, and asked the girl, who had already named herself Hesione, some questions. She proved to be the daughter of Laomedon, king of Troy.

"And where is the king, that he allows his daughter to undergo such treatment?"

The only answer to that question was a burst of tears.

Now, standing at the top of the cliff, I could get a better look at the enormous construction project on the crest half a mile inland. Up there, someone had made a start at erecting huge, thick walls of stone. Below the walls I could now discern a mass of color that I supposed might be a throng of people. At either end, the foundation tiers of the wall curved back over the crest and out of sight. I decided that there was probably going to be room for a great city in the space they were enclosing. Here and there I began to imagine I could discern some scaffolding of logs. How tall the walls in general were intended to be could be seen by the impressive height of a certain tower that stood already virtually completed. A little farther inland I could just make out the roofs of what seemed to be many tents and other makeshift dwellings.

It seemed to me very doubtful that the people who were building their city on the hill would not know that such a terrible sacrifice was being made right on their doorstep.

Whoever might have been watching from the high ridge would not have been able to see what happened to the monster down below the level of the cliff. But someone up there might have been able to see the reappearance of the girl atop the cliff, accompanied first by Enkidu and shortly afterward by me, and that would certainly have riveted their attention.

Soon a squad of uniformed spear-carriers, followed by another of seeming dignitaries, the latter moving more slowly, appeared on their way down the long slope from the unfinished walls. When they got closer I could hear some of them shouting loudly, but whether they were inflamed with joy or outrage I could not tell at first.

"There is my father," said Hesione, muffling a final sob and pointing to someone in the latter group, now only a couple of hundred yards away. "King Laomedon."

As soon as I faced the advancing people boldly they grew cautious in their approach—and they stopped in their tracks when they came close enough to look over the little cliff and see that I had already killed the monster. Their angry cries faded to a cautious, marveling murmur as they saw the vast body rising and falling in the crashing surf. A few people ran down to the shore, and soon a clamor of voices went up, demanding to know what had turned the creature's head into a bloody ruin.

The group led by Poseidon's priest reached us before the group surrounding the king.

The servant of Neptune was garbed chiefly in seaweed, and he seemed a hybrid of priest and warrior, carrying weapons as well as what were obviously ritual objects, dishes and stalks of wheat, I thought him on the verge of apoplexy when he saw that the girl had been freed, and his rage was directed at me when he determined that I was somehow responsible.

Not stopping to talk, or even, I fear, to think things out, he commanded one of his warriors to attack me.

"Hector! Deal with this man!"

Burly Hector's blade came down hard on my left shoulder, before I could try to argue my way out of the situation. Even as I reached to grab the swordsman's arms, I felt the now almost-familiar sharp sting, the signal that my body, had it been no more than human, would have suffered a serious wound.

I had not done much killing, by a warrior's standards, and I had no wish to do more. Grabbing my assailant around the middle, I lifted him into the air, turning his body parallel to the ground. Then I held him that way, tucked under my left arm, as I might have carried a squalling child of two or three. My left hand gripped his right wrist, and his left arm was pinned between my forearm and his body. It was a comfortable position for me, leaving me with one arm free, though I had to lean far sideways to balance the additional weight, somewhat greater than my own. By the time we reached that situation, Hector's sword had fallen from his grip, and he could do no harm to anyone, unless they happened to stray in range of his violently kicking legs. My captive writhed and strained, to little purpose, and a strangled sound, compounded of rage and fear, came from him in short gasping bursts.

"He'll do no harm to me," I assured his countrymen, "but he might be dangerous to bystanders. Is there somewhere I can put him safely down? Or must I hurl him into the sea?" With my free hand I pointed out toward the blue horizon. "I fear he'll sink like a rock, with all his armor on."

The priest of Poseidon could only gape in stunned silence at me as I stood leaning sideways, and at his helpless champion. Eventually two of Hector's comrades stepped forward, hulking men who swore that they would hold him securely; and so I was relieved of my burden.

Talking with the more peaceful citizens of Troy as they gathered around while I stood leaning on my club, I learned the reason for Hesione's being in the terrible situation from which I had rescued her. Somehow the idea had spread among the people that Poseidon was angry with the city because Zeus had compelled him to help build its walls. Therefore the Sea God had sent the monster. Somehow the king had been convinced that the monster would be appeased if it received his daughter as a sacrifice; his only reason for such a belief seemed to be that some soothsayer had told him so. I thought that any king who was so spineless would probably not be long on his throne.

I suppose I should note here what I heard later: that the Trojan princess, once she had been set free, behaved in such a shrewish way that I could begin to understand how everyone had been willing to get rid of her.

Once it seemed certain that the natives had given up trying to attack us, Enkidu began to mingle freely with them. People eyed him with wary respect; no doubt they were more than half convinced that he shared my godlike strength. I noticed that he said and did nothing to correct their error.

When I told the Trojans that my nephew and I had sailed out from Corycus, someone asked our purpose in making such a lengthy voyage in a vessel far too small for trade. Naturally I raised the subject of the Apples of the Hesperides.

Somewhat to my surprise, this brought on a veritable buzz of marveling and speculation, with the graybeard counselors exchanging knowing looks.

Immediately my hopes leaped up. "What is it? What can you tell me about them?"

At length, several of our new hosts brightened and told me that a sample, at least, of one of those very Apples was much nearer than I suspected.

Enkidu and I exchanged a hopeful glance. "Just what do these Apples look like, then?" I asked.

A man who had the whitest and longest beard that I had ever seen seemed to take his role of wise counselor very seriously. He made vague gestures with his hands. "They are not unlike ordinary apples, young man—you are familiar with that fruit?"

"I am."

"Not unlike the common fruit, I say, save that each one grows to about the size of a man's head."

"I suppose the tree must be gigantic?"

That seemed to be the general consensus, though a few minutes' additional questioning convinced me that none of these people had actually seen the tree, knew what it looked like, or were even certain where it grew.

"But someone started to tell me, earlier, where I might find a sample of the fruit, at least."

After holding another conference among themselves, the Trojan counselors assured me I could find a specimen of this strange fruit inside a certain cave, which also seemed to be the regular dwelling place of someone named Antaeus. When they spoke his name their voices dropped, and their faces fell, as if in dread.

Persistently I tried to dig for solid information. "This Antaeus keeps an orchard and grows the Apples? He eats them? Feeds them to his animals? Or what?"

The people gathered around me proposed a variety of answers. No one knew.

"I see," I said, nodding as if I actually understood. "And you yourselves have seen this marvelous fruit inside this cave?"

No, as it turned out, actually none of these people had ever been near the cave. And they thought it only right to warn me that no one who went into that den had ever emerged from it alive.

"Is someone watching the entrance day and night, to make sure that never happens?"

My informants did not seem to hear the question. But eventually one of them told me that a few daring souls, keeping watch from a distance, had seen Antaeus carry the Apples into his stronghold, and had recognized them for what they were.

"May I speak to one of these daring souls myself?"

"Alas, sir, they are none of them here now. They have gone voyaging again. One went with the Argonauts."

If they thought I was going to be much impressed by that, they were mistaken. When they told me the man's name, I failed to recognize it.

One point upon which my informants were eagerly agreed was that the den, or cave, of the formidable Antaeus was only about a hundred miles away, westward and northward along the irregular coastline.

After squinting uselessly toward the watery horizon in that direction, I turned back to my informants. "You interest me greatly, my friends. Now tell me, just who, or what, is this Antaeus? You speak of him as if he were something more than merely human."

The answers I was given to that question were not terribly enlightening, but they confirmed me in the opinion that anyone who lived within a hundred miles of the fellow might be anxious to get rid of him.

After an afternoon and night among the tents and lean-tos of the builders of the new walls, enjoying wary Trojan hospitality, Enkidu and I were ready for a few hours of sound sleep, during which time we took turns keeping one eye open—it was an arrangement we practiced more often than not during our travels. By an hour after sunrise we were getting back into our boat again.

FIFTEEN

Antaeus

he rosy-fingered dawn had come and gone before my nephew and I put out to sea again, shoving our boat off from the beach that lay half a mile below the rising walls of Troy. By the time of our departure in full daylight, no trace of the sea monster's body was any longer to be seen; I supposed the great ugly mass had been washed away by waves and tide during the night. And in the talk I heard in Troy that morning, from those who had witnessed the event and others who had not, the beast had already grown to twice its authentic size.

Enkidu and I piloted the *Skyboat* more or less steadily along the coast in the direction that our hosts had indicated, searching for the cave of the strange being, known to them by the name of Antaeus, that they had described to us. We took turns at the helm. Progress was slow at first, because the compass-pyx kept giving us contradictory indications. This, I had been told by Daedalus and others, was a sign that the pilot could form no clear mental image of his goal. We had both tried our hands at piloting, and I could believe that was our problem, but there was nothing we could do about it.

When we had crept along the coast for twenty miles or so, we put in to shore at intervals and began to look seriously for likely caves, and also for people to question on the subject, on the theory that our informants' estimate of distance might have been wildly wrong and some of their other information unreliable.

In one respect, the legends concerning the being we were looking for proved to be ludicrously inaccurate. My brief stay in that savage and little-populated land convinced me that Antaeus was really king of nothing, not even of the tribe, or guild, of bandits—assuming any such organization could exist. A bandit he was, I suppose, preying on humans whenever he could catch them, though we found no hoard of gold and jewels as in the Lizard's cave. But his predatory nature was the least remarkable thing about Antaeus.

Another falsehood concerning him, told and believed by many

who had never come near his cave, was that he was the son of Poseidon and Mother Earth. Other claims, both quite untrue, were that he forced strangers to wrestle with him and that he saved the skulls of his victims to roof a temple of Poseidon. In the course of our brief visit, I had a chance to examine the interior of his cave thoroughly. There were indeed some skulls about, human and animal both, but only as part of a collection of general organic garbage that made the whole place stink. It was nothing like any temple that I ever saw—more like the lair of some wild animal, much danker and gloomier than the Lizard's cheerful parlor.

I had been solemnly assured, by the folk who were building the walls and towers of Ilium, that I could find a specimen of Golden Apple, the very kind that I was looking for, inside the cave of Antaeus. But about the time we were getting close to our goal, it occurred to me to wonder if the Trojans might have said that simply to get rid of me. No doubt I would be welcome back at Troy again, or anywhere else, whenever there was a sea monster to be slain; but I was beginning to realize that at other times I tended to make most people uncomfortable.

"Enk, do you think they might possibly have done that?" I asked, discussing the matter with my nephew after our third or fourth cave had turned out empty. "Given us a wild story about this bandit and his magic Apples just to get rid of us? You tell me I can be scary sometimes."

"Well, you can be, Herc. And yes, I guess they might have been anxious to see us on our way."

But that was one problem we need not have worried about. Antaeus and his strange fruit turned out to be as real as any of the other monsters I had faced.

It was a forbidding stretch of coastline along which we slowly labored, patiently asking directions of each of the few people we chanced to encounter, poor fisherfolk and gatherers of birds' eggs. Eventually, from certain individuals who were not too terrified to speak of Antaeus at all, I heard confirmation that he indeed lived in a cave, where he slept on the bare ground as a means of maintaining his strength in readiness for any eventuality. And these informants even gave us a fairly precise idea of the cave's location, along with urgent warnings that we had better stay away from it.

When we identified the beach we had been told to look for, we pulled our boat a little way up on shore and simply left it there, trusting to its own mysterious powers to protect it from thieves or destruction by the waves. Then we started making our way along the rocky shore as best we could on foot. It was a strange, wild region dotted with seemingly innumerable caves, through many of which the waves went drenching and thundering at high tide.

Enkidu pointed out to me some signs of our quarry's presence before we saw him.

My nephew had been bending over, studying the ground, but suddenly raised his head to tell me, in a very low voice: "I realize now, Unc, what the people back there at Troy forgot to tell us."

"What's that?"

Enkidu made a show of giving it thoughtful consideration before he answered. "I suppose it was for our own good. They didn't want to discourage us, not when we were doing so well."

"Are you going to tell me *what,* by all the gods? Or am I going to have to strangle you?"

"Hush. This character Antaeus is a Giant." And my nephew stepped back and pointed with a flourish at the ground.

I was shocked into silence for a moment. Then I was on the point of angrily commanding my companion to stop clowning and get on with business. But then my eye fell on the sign that he had seen. Wet sand along the shoreline bore the clear imprint of a giant foot, human in shape if not in size, the five toes clearly marked.

"Indeed he must be," was all that I could get out, at last, in a whisper. The track was fully twice as long as one of mine, and my feet are not particularly small.

Carefully we moved on, in the same direction the marker of the footprint had been going. I half-expected to come upon some Titanic dung droppings among the rocks, but we found no such spoor. I had known humans who were much less fastidious in such matters.

We had gone only another hundred yards or so when Enkidu suddenly stopped and laid his hand upon my arm. His whisper was almost too low for me to hear. "Unc, there he is."

I looked where he was looking, and saw the shaggy brown back of a gigantic head, just visible above some rocks some thirty yards away. And I in turn whispered the names of several gods, in awe.

Cautiously and quietly we stepped sideways until we could get a full-length look at our discovery. Of course the first thing that struck us both about the man, the creature—at first glance I was not sure how to classify our discovery—was his abnormal and truly gigantic size. Imagine a human figure, or rather the crude outline of one, about twelve feet tall and sturdily built.

The second thing that struck me was that there seemed to be something vaguely wrong, out of proportion, with his overall shape.

Continuing to study our quarry from a distance of some thirty or forty yards, I wondered at first whether this might be some mutant man, imbued with earth magic, instead of one of the real, and yet legendary Titans/Giants, supposed to be the sons of Poseidon and Gaia. Considering the matter as coolly as I could, I decided that if Antaeus was a real Giant, and the legends had any truth in them at all, he was certainly one of the smaller ones.

Still, twelve feet in height is a very great deal more than six, and I stood less than that. *That cannot be a human being,* was my inevitable conclusion, after only a brief observation. I came to that evaluation even though the one before me was clothed after a fashion, wearing a rude, patchwork garment that seemed to have been stitched together from the skins of different beasts.

And the more I looked at him, the more certain I became that his body was not only larger than that of any man, but made of some different stuff. I had no doubt at all that this was one of the fearsome beings that Daedalus and Hermes had tried to describe to me.

The next most notable thing about Antaeus was his skin, which was mostly dark but with the appearance of a grainy, earthy texture. It was somehow surprising to see that it gave and stretched with his movements, as any practical skin must do. The few wrinkles that it bore were at places where in humans wrinkles are slow to form.

Rather than advance at once to confront this strange figure

openly, I decided to watch him for a while. There was always the possibility that others of his kind were nearby. Working our way slowly inland so we could observe from a better angle, then peering out from between two rocks on the next hill, we watched him kill a full-sized sheep, wringing its neck as if it had been a chicken. Then he roasted the carcass whole over a fire, and then he ate it, bones and guts and all, avoiding only the woolly skin, which he peeled off and used to wipe his hands. I saw no other sheep around, and we assumed that Antaeus kept no flock of his own and that the one he killed was stolen.

Now and then, during the minutes we spent observing this rude feast, Enkidu and I exchanged whispers, but for the most part we watched in silence. Presently, watching our chances, we were able to move a little closer without being seen. This Giant looked less and less human the closer I got to him and the longer I watched. The difference, as I have mentioned, was not entirely due to the discrepancy in size. His forehead sloped back more sharply than that of any god or human I had ever seen.

His hair, on head and body, emerged from the skin in awkward tufts rather than in the more even distribution generally to be seen upon a human.

The face, which bore no trace of beard or mustache, was almost completely expressionless, and remained that way through all that followed. The massive jaws worked steadily, pausing now and then so the Giant could spit out some morsel he found less than tasty. His eyes were dark, and I thought that there was something wrong with them.

The creature, or thing—I found myself less and less able to think of it as a living person—was so eerie that it made my flesh creep.

Enkidu and I continued to stalk the Giant, gradually working our way closer. I wanted to see, among other things, how keen my enemy's senses were and how alert his mind. In the course of this stealthy maneuvering, I found it convenient to leave my club behind, tucked into a crevice between rocks, handle uppermost so I could grab it quickly if need be.

Eventually, inevitably, we pushed our luck too far. This Giant, the first I ever encountered (had he had his way, he would have been also the last) finally caught sight of Enkidu at a distance of some forty feet, sprang up, and ran after him, obviously with no good intention. It was as if a man who had no love for mice or beetles had spotted one of those vermin in some place where they were particularly unwelcome.

Naturally the boy took to his heels and sprinted away, and I jumped from concealment and dashed forward. The Giant, his back to me, gave chase to Enkidu, and was within a few feet of seizing him, before I could get close enough to intervene.

"Antaeus!" I bellowed at him. "This way!"

At the sound of the name, the huge figure stopped in its tracks. In the next moment it had turned, quickly enough; the huge mouth opened, showing a ragged interior whiteness that might have been a row of teeth. A rumbling bass voice came from it, uttering what sounded like words in some language I did not know. How can I describe that voice? I cannot. But I have heard it often, since that day, in nightmares.

Now our enemy came lumbering toward me, long legs devouring the intervening space.

His first ill-advised and rather clumsy attempt to squash me by stamping on me failed when I grabbed his raised foot in midair and twisted his leg until he fell with a great crash on his back. Thinking over the matter later, I realized that at that moment Antaeus must have assumed, not unreasonably, that I was a god.

Still lying on the ground, he tried to use what I had to assume was the magic weapon described by Prince Asterion—pointing all ten extended fingers of both hands at me and glaring. The gods had planned well, and the Giant's deadly instrument had no effect on me. Stepping close to the enormous body, I kicked it hard in the ribs, lifting it from the ground and spinning it over, so that a sound like a drumbeat issued from the Giant's mouth.

If I cannot describe the voice of my first Giant, how can I even attempt to convey the effect produced by a first close look into his face? Here the appearance of graininess was more pronounced. In that brief moment it seemed to me that his countenance might have been carved from clay, or perhaps sandstone, with two hard, dark pebbles set into it for eyes.

While still sprawled on the ground, he persisted in his gesture of unleashing magic. Somewhat unnerving, as you may imagine. But in practical terms, all his finger pointing and glaring had no discernible effect upon my memory or any other faculty.

Though I felt no ill effects, I still retreated, something I had not done while fighting any of the other monsters. Now I wanted to gain a better understanding of my enemy before I tried to utterly destroy him.

As I moved back, the Giant clambered to his feet, an awkward-looking, stiff-bodied series of movements. He swayed on his huge feet and clutched his middle awkwardly, as if my kick had broken a rib or two and now they hurt.

Meanwhile, Enkidu was hurling fist-sized stones from a point of vantage he had gained among high rocks. The boy's aim was not bad, and I saw one missile bounce high from the Giant's shaggy skull, but I do not think Antaeus even noticed it.

Now my antagonist and I were stalking each other once again.

The huge body proved able not only to move, but to change directions, with surprising speed. My club was too far away for me to reach it handily, and so I simply waited. In the next moment my opponent's hands had closed on me and grabbed me up into the air.

My earlier success in twisting him off his feet ought to have prepared him somewhat for my strength. But still, there followed a few moments in which he seemed almost paralyzed by surprise. After exerting what he must have thought would be a crushing grip, Antaeus tried to dash me down upon the rocks. But he quickly discovered that my smaller grasp, which I had fastened on one of his great arms, was quite unbreakable. Next he attempted to crush me in a hug, but the heel of my right hand under his chin forced his arms straight and his head back.

The Giant dropped me to the ground, stepped back, and uttered a few more words of peculiar speech, which I could understand no better than his earlier remarks. Then he threw himself prone on the ground, in what I first thought was a gesture of submission. But in the space of a few heartbeats he had sprung to his feet again and hurled himself upon me. To my amazement, his strength seemed even greater than before.

Never had I felt anything like his grip. His strength was truly enormous, compared to that of any human wrestler. I was still not afraid of being overpowered, but the brief struggle had left me gasping with exertion.

Meanwhile, keeping track of Enkidu as best I could from the corner of my eye, I saw that he had now scrambled from one pinnacle of rock to another even taller. He also maintained a steady barrage of rocks and kept on shrilling insults at Antaeus, who paid no attention to either. Some of the rocks came close to hitting me, but I thought I would probably not be hurt if one did land.

In the intervals between acts of attempted violence, the Giant barked words at me, phrases that somehow had the sound of questions, though they came in a language I had never heard before.

Again we broke apart, and again we closed with each other. I made no attempt to kill him quickly, because I was rapidly becoming convinced that I ought to ask him some questions, and insist on some answers, before he died.

The hands of Antaeus that would have crushed me were instead broken themselves when I pounded them on rocks. The bellow he let out when his knuckles were smashed seemed more of astonishment than pain. But I was staggered by his strangeness. His skin did not feel like skin, but more like the hard surface of bone, or even rock, with flexibility only at the very joints, where it was essential.

And for a second time during our wrestling match, the Giant flung himself down of his own accord, not waiting to be thrown. Fearing that when he sprang up again he would be even stronger than before, I seized him by the seat and collar of his shapeless garment, lifted him as high as I could into the air, and held him aloft, meaning to keep him well above the earth until he died.

Antaeus was not too strong for me to manage. But he was too big for me to keep him from the earth—my arms would not stretch far enough to let me maintain a grip on more than two of his limbs at once. Stretching and thrashing in my grip, he managed to get one foot on the ground, and when I lifted that away, one of his hands came down to grasp the earth.

Simply holding him aloft was not going to work. Shaking my head, I hit him with my fist once or twice, seeking to diminish his boisterous energy. His flesh did not seem to yield and bruise, so much as it simply crumbled. I followed with a good kick that had the same effect.

I might say that he screamed and bellowed with pain and rage— but those are not really the right words to describe the sounds he made. He seemed to fall on me as if he meant to smother me, and once more we were grappling. Of course he was so large that I had to fold him, almost like a parchment scroll, in order to hold him in a position where no part of his body dragged on the ground. When I exerted myself strongly, part of his body burst open under the stress, spilling out versions of muddy-looking blood and wormlike guts, for which my mind was unprepared.

I was so astonishing that for a long moment I could not move but only stood and stared.

When at last I had broken the great figure into complete helplessness, I stood over it, panting, while it lay impotent on the ground. What remained was not yet still, you understand, but writhed and heaved. The lower half of the face was gone by then, and the staring eyes above seemed to have turned into mere glassy pebbles.

By this time Enkidu, unable to restrain his curiosity any longer, had come scrambling down from his high rock. One knee was bleeding where he had scraped it in his jumping about, but he was otherwise unhurt.

Surveying the ghastly ruin that had once looked almost like a man, my nephew sounded even more shaken than I felt.

"Herc, what is all this? What does it mean?" Now that the practical danger was over, he sounded almost tearful, really frightened for the first time.

I could only shake my head in wonder.

"For one thing," I told him, "It means that the world is stranger than I ever imagined it might be."

"This is stranger even than the Hydra. Because—because it's almost like a man."

"If only Daedalus were here," I muttered.

"He's not here," said Enkidu. "But we'd better take him some of—some of this."

"Nephew, I think that is one of the better ideas that you have ever had."

The Giant's rude garment had come loose in the course of the fight, and when I turned the body over again, we saw that he lacked pubic hair but that his male organs were, as might be expected, of a size for a centaur. Immediately an image sprang to mind of Antaeus ravaging human women.

For what seemed a long time we stood there marveling, unable to decide just what to do next. At last I said: "It is as if a sculptor wished to copy the proper outward form of humanity—but didn't bother to get it completely right. Close enough was good enough for this designer."

"Yes, that's it." Enkidu nodded. "What this creature looks like. But what it really *is* . . ." He shook his head.

"But why a clumsy imitation?" I went on. "And who was the designer?"

I doubted that even Daedalus could give me answers to such questions. Perhaps my father could.

When I examined the ruin of Antaeus's dead mouth, looking at the teeth with which he had chewed up the sheep, I could see that they, too, were rocklike. His tongue was small and, by human standards, deformed.

"Herc. I think I'm going to be sick." And indeed my nephew looked pale under his tan.

This was worse than dealing with dead centaurs. I could feel the same impulse lurching in my belly, but grimly fought it off. "No, you're not. We don't have time for that, we have too much to do."

Now that I had time to think, questions came swarming, like the flies that had already gathered. Were all the Giants in the world built on this same plan? Or was Antaeus a kind of dwarfish monster, an odd shape and strange material even for his race?

Feeling dizzy with a mixture of horror and relief, and with my own stomach on the verge of rebellion, I backed away and sat down on a rock to think.

I would now be able to make a serious report to those who had sent me to discover the truth about Giants. One part of the report ought to make them happy, I thought—I had been exposed to the weapon that somehow scrambled the brains of gods, and it seemed to have had no effect on me at all.

"Enkidu, whether you are going to be sick or not, take a close look at our friend here, so you can confirm what I say when I report back to Hermes and Daedalus."

"I saw you beat him up and kill him, Uncle. I can see what he looks like now, not much more than a pile of clods of dirt. I don't know if I'd believe it if someone else had told me. Can all Giants be like this?"

"I think it must be so."

Seeking to gather all the information that we possibly could about Anateus, Enkidu and I searched his cave as soon as we were sure that he was dead.

"Suppose his mate is hiding in the cave?" Enkidu suddenly piped up, looking over his shoulder toward that dark mouth in the rocks.

"How could a thing like that have a mate?" I demanded. But then I thought better of my answer; the situation was already alive with what seemed impossibilities, so why not one more? And where did Giants come from, if they did not breed?

"No one said anything to us about a mate. But we'd better find her, or it, if such a creature exists." And I hefted a rock and held it ready to employ as either club or missile.

But there was no living thing inside the cave—except the Apples, which I suppose must be counted as alive. Without much trouble we found, in a kind of chest or locker at one side of his cave, a true sample of what had to be one of the Apples of the Hesperides. It was a dried fruit that when fresh must have been fully the size of a human head. The stump of a stem protruded from the amplexicaul curve at the top, as if it had been a real apple.

Also the cave held almost nothing in the way of ordinary furnishings, as if its occupant preferred the dry, bare rock of its floor to sit or lie upon.

In a dark corner we found more Apples. Antaeus had been keeping ten or a dozen of the fruits in all.

Holding up one of the bulbous, yellow, almost head-sized shapes, Enkidu commented: "I wouldn't call this thing an apple, Herc. If it is, it's like no apple that I have ever seen before."

"I'll call it that," I said. "Until I learn some better word." And it did look more like an ordinary apple than like any other fruit or vegetable with which I was familiar.

We slept that night in the *Skyboat,* rocked and lulled by a sea that was almost calm, pulled out a little distance from the shore. I dozed off feeling that I was at last making some real progress in my great quest, and when I awoke in the morning, I found I had somehow come to an unexpected decision while I was asleep. If dreams had played a role in it, I had forgotten them.

"Little nephew, I think this would be a good time for us to return home for a visit."

Before replying, Enkidu, who had been poised for a refreshing morning dip, dove off into the water with a splash. When he surfaced, shaking wet hair from his eyes, he did not seem much surprised at my suggestion. "What about Lord Hermes, Unc? He'll be wanting a report about this Giant. And there's the bone from the sea monster that we ought to take to Master Daedalus. And these Apples, too; our clients will want to get a look at them."

"Lord Hermes has never had any trouble finding me. I think he'll catch up with us again whenever he is ready, whether we're in Cadmia or anywhere else. Besides, he'll probably send me on some new adventure, and I'd like to get in a visit home before that happens. I'd like to see my mother."

All that was quite true. What I did not fully admit to myself at the time was that in the back of my mind was the idea of another one who lived in our house, whom I also yearned to see—and you are quite right; I was not thinking of Amphityron.

Enkidu and I had made our decision, and he was doing his best to enjoin an image of Cadmia upon the compass-pyx, when Hermes came, this time materializing out of thin air to perch on *Skyboat*'s small stern seat.

We showed him the materials we had gathered, and told him of the fight with Antaeus, and its outcome.

Hermes came ashore with us to view the body, but when I first pointed out the spot to him, I thought for a moment that I was mistaken. The remains of the fallen Antaeus now resembled a mound of earth more than a rotting corpse.

The Messenger was much pleased and expressed to us the thanks of great Zeus himself for collecting the samples we had gathered. He also relieved us of the burden of responsibility and carried them on to Daedalus himself.

Besides the Apples, the collection we were carrying included samples of the hair of Antaeus (more human-looking than any other component of his body), and fragments of his strange skin and flesh. I would have liked to pack the latter in salt, to preserve them during what I expected would be a long voyage, but the best I could manage was a kind of pickling in jars of sea water, which shortly reduced the specimens to the appearance and consistency of thin mud. I could only hope they would still be of some use to Daedalus and the gods.

Hermes praised us for our discovery and for the proof we had provided that Zeus's secret plan was so far successful—I was immune to the Giants' most terrible weapon.

And as he was about to depart, he added one important statement to his congratulations.

"Your true father is greatly pleased in you, Hercules."

Almost despite myself I felt a thrill of pride rising against my chronic anger.

○ SIXTEEN ○

Megan

ℋaving been relieved of responsibility for our collected trophies, my companion and I rearranged our meager store of other belongings securely inside *Skyboat*'s tiny cabin, and hoisted sail. Enkidu crouched before the binnacle, laying his forehead against the ivory side of the compass-pyx, and directed it to lead us home.

The course it chose for us turned out to be quite roundabout. We first spent days traversing a thousand miles or so of open ocean, in a great curved path. This was followed by an intricate, time-consuming passage through a number of streams and lakes—some broad, some narrow—and one canal. The latter was an adventure in itself, of which I may have more to say some other time. Then we were guided out into the open sea again. But the gift of Hermes had so far served us so well that I did not hesitate to put my trust in it. For all I knew, our compass-pyx might be avoiding great storms or other dangers in its choice of routes.

Finally, it directed us up a large river, then a tributary, and then a tributary of that again, at last running the boat gently aground when we were still, by my best estimate, more than a hundred miles from homes and families.

I stepped ashore and stretched, shouldered my club and a sack containing some food and an extra pair of sandals, and looked about me. "Well. It seems we walk from here."

"All right, Herc, but my feet are tired. Let's see if we can find some way to ride."

We abandoned the boat only with reluctance, though we assumed that it would once more be invisible to any eyes but ours and would be waiting when we came back. No immortal messengers appeared, and our attendant sprite seemed to have deserted us. For the time being at least, the gods seemed content to leave me alone, and now, having just gone to the trouble of providing them with trophies from a Giant, I found this irritating.

We had to walk only a few miles before coming to a large village, where it was possible to buy cameloids. We were carrying money, gifts and rewards from those who had wished to show their gratitude, and we purchased two animals, along with a little extra gear, and so were no longer forced to walk.

From there our journey overland, occupying several more days, took us past the margin of Nemea, where lay the grazing lands where I had slain a lion—by all the gods, but that seemed a long time ago! Counting up the months, I realized that nearly a year had passed since then. The herds had evidently been moved to a different grazing ground this summer, and Tarn and his colleagues, if they still followed the herdsman's calling, must have gone with them.

The closer I got to home, the more impatient I was to encounter its familiar scenes and people. Still, by the time my nephew and I once more came in sight of the walls of Cadmia, full summer had come around again. From a distance, so little about the city appeared to have changed that it seemed we might have been gone only a day.

But we soon discovered that very much had changed. For one thing, something of my new reputation had preceded me. Everyone who had known me before looked at me now in a different way, and some were glad to see me again, and some were not.

But at first I paid little attention to such matters, for I was shocked by the unexpected news that my mother was dead.

There had been some attempt to send me word of her death, some six months earlier, but as no one at home had any idea where I was, it was little wonder that the message had never reached me. I supposed Hermes might have told me, but he had not. And I was long past expecting any communication from my father. The period of formal mourning had now expired, and there was little required of me in the way of ritual. Such real grieving as I did was very private.

Amphitryon formally welcomed me home, and I thought he was actually pleased to see me, but as usual we had little to say to each other. I no longer called him "Father," but I remained respectful, and thought he did not notice. Nor did he ever ask me what had happened to the bow, his parting gift to me when I went off to be a herdsman. Possibly he had forgotten it.

*   *   *

Iphicles, my elder half brother, who was now more than thirty years of age, met Enkidu and me on the day of our return and marveled at how his son had grown.

"Another year or two and the lad will be ready for some military service," the proud father proclaimed, thumping him heartily on the shoulder.

Enkidu offered no open argument against that statement, but it was plain to me that he had a different future for himself in mind.

"We've heard some interesting stories about you," my brother observed when he decided my turn had come to be evaluated.

"Some of them may even be true," I answered carelessly, and did not bother to ask what any of the stories were. And I thought that he was bothered by my indifference, which was mostly genuine.

I had been home now for a full day, and one of our neighbors was giving me a reasoned explanation, full of clever deductions, as to why the accounts of my miraculous victories over incredible monsters could not possibly be true. "Now, the lion, for instance . . ."

I listened in polite silence for a little while, then walked away, no doubt leaving the arguer with the conviction that he had shown me up as a fraud.

In fact my account of how I had killed the lion, though basically true, was widely disbelieved. Later, I heard that many of the gods themselves had doubted the report at first—though I doubted whether those who told me that had ever seen a god.

"You look different, too, Hercules," said another old acquaintance on seeing me again.

"I suppose I do." I was a few inches taller than when I had lived at home—certain homely benchmarks, in the form of scars on tree trunks and on doorposts, provided confirmation of that fact—and definitely more mature. And my beard was starting to grow in nicely. Critically studying my arms, I decided that I really did look stronger now than I had when I went off to herd cattle. Perhaps I actually was more powerful; offhand I could think of no way to make an accurate test.

Weighing myself on a familiar balance scale, in one of the familiar barns of the estate, showed that I had gained some ten pounds, though my body still showed very little fat. But certainly no sculptor would have chosen me as a model of the ideal.

While I was on that visit home, I took part in my first crocodile hunt, joining my stepfather and my older brother, by invitation, in an expedition they had been planning for some time. It was a dangerous kind of game that warriors played on occasion, to enliven their intervals of peace.

The three of us were in a rowboat of shallow draft, and I was leaning over, trying to see the bottom, while my two companions were busy catching fish. The fish were going to be useful in our hunt, as bait.

"The best bait for crocodile, Hercules, is something bigger," Iphicles was explaining. "Like a sheep or goat. But fish are cheaper."

"You try to lure the creature into the shallows and then surround it with men armed with sturdy spears," Amphitryon added.

I nodded my understanding, and father and son took turns adding explanations.

"We won't use the boat for the actual hunt."

"When the croc's in shallow water, we'll get five or six men and come at it from all sides at once."

"You've got to watch out for the tail, as well as for the head."

The experts had judged that we had enough fish on the string, and the servant rowing the boat had us almost back to shore, when I heard the last bit of advice, this delivered in tones of some urgency. "Don't lean over there, Hercules. Watch out!"

The sight of what I thought was a large fish, moving underwater, had captured my curiosity. I had no more than an instant's warning, in the form of a swirl beneath the surface, before the enormous gray-green shape came lunging up out of the muddy shallows, jaws spread to clamp my shoulder and neck. My startled, instinctive withdrawal was a forceful move that dragged the big croc with me; the boat overturned, and I was standing hip-deep in water.

While my companions screamed and splashed, waving their barbed spears ineffectually, I got my feet solidly planted, then brought both hands up, forcing my fingers in between the large teeth that were vainly trying to puncture the skin of my face and shoulder. There was no odylic magic about this creature, but mere nature could sometimes be quite monstrous enough.

The people in the water around me were still thrashing uselessly. Meanwhile the servant, who had already reached the shore, was running for help. Ignoring them all, I found the grip I needed and peeled the beast's jaws loose—it was no more trouble than folding back a tough fruit rind. Flipping the crocodile lightly in the air, I caught it by its thick tail, called out a warning for onlookers to stand back, and swung the great mass forcefully, sending the head end hard against a massive rock that happened to be standing conveniently near.

I made my relatives a present of the valuable hide. From then on I heard no more doubts expressed about my other feats as they had been reported. And the subject of crocodile hunting was dropped for the duration of my visit.

In the course of my visit I naturally kept encountering familiar faces. Yet one face in particular, the very one I had come looking for, was not to be seen anywhere.

"Where is Megan?" I finally inquired, making a conscious effort to be casual. I chose to ask the question when I was away from my close relatives.

The people who were with me at the time exchanged glances that I could not read. Someone finally told me that they thought the young woman I asked about had been seen at the palace.

"But what would she be doing there?" I wondered aloud. In response, people hesitated, coughed, and changed the subject.

It seemed it would be easier to go and see for myself than to get anyone to give me a plain answer.

The palace grounds were busy with a casual flow of people coming and going on all kinds of business, and no one challenged me as I wandered about. At the moment when I laid eyes on Megan, she was seated in a kind of arbor in a garden behind the servants' quarters. In her arms she was holding an infant, some two or three months of age, while it nursed at her breast. My mind began automatically counting up the months of my absence from home; and in the space of a few heartbeats, before a word had passed between us, I felt certain that her child was mine.

Megan was clad in a simple, familiar garment, of a type commonly worn by female servants, loosened from one arm and shoulder to enable her comfortably to nurse. Her wide brown eyes were fastened on me, but at first, neither of us said a word as I approached. The infant's hair was scanty, but in color much the same as mine. A diaper concealed its sex. I put out a careful hand and turned back the blanket from the tiny face, which stayed nuzzled against Megan's tender breast.

"Our child." I did not make the words a question.

"Yes." She looked at me, as I thought, reproachfully. "I have lain with no one else."

I shook my head; that had not been what I was concerned about. Somehow it had hardly occurred to me that she might have done so. "Is the baby—?"

Now she knew what I meant to ask, before I had decided just how to put the question. "He's a fine healthy boy, Hercules. If there is anything strange about him, I haven't found it out yet."

"All the good gods be thanked for that," I said sincerely. "What is his name?"

Megan told me that the baby's name was Hyllus. She had to spell it out for me.

I thought about it. "I know of no one else called by that name," I commented at last.

"It means 'a woodsman.' And it was my father's name. If my lord Hercules wishes to change it—"

I had stuck out a finger where Hyllus could grasp it, and now he clamped his tiny hand on with surprising strength. Only later did I realize that this was not very convincing proof of our relationship, that all babies could exert a powerful grip. I said, "No, no, let his name stay as it is. His mother gave it to him, and I like the way it sounds."

I must have been with Megan for almost a full minute before my mind fully registered something that my eyes could hardly have failed to see at once—the fact that she was wearing a slave's metal collar. It was a simple ring of iron, such as the lowest of the low would wear, rather than decorative silver, or even gold.

"But what in all the hells is this?" I suddenly demanded, touching the offending object with one finger.

"Just what it looks like, lord."

"'Lord' is not my name. Let there be no use of titles between you and me."

"As my lord wishes." And she smiled in a way that let me know that she was teasing me.

"Now, tell me who in the Underworld has put this thing around your neck. You were never a slave, and you are not going to become one."

"I had no intention of becoming one."

"Then tell me, whose hands put this on?"

Now she looked at me with something like alarm. "They were a slave's hands, Hercules, those of a simple blacksmith, and he liked the business no more than I did. I hope you don't hold him responsible."

"All right. By whose orders, then?"

"It was done, they told me, by order of His Majesty the king. Although the king himself has never had anything to say to me. So far they have only given me easy tasks to do here, sewing and taking inventory."

"But *why?*"

"No one has bothered to give me an explanation. But it seems that servants, like me, whose agreements with their masters are not perfectly in order, as mine with the lord Amphitryon perhaps was not, may sometimes be forfeit—"

"Hush! Never mind. The laws can be a greater labyrinth than Corycus has ever seen. But whatever the laws say, or the king, either, you are not going to be forfeit to anyone."

"It may have had something to do with the lord general Amphitryon's failure to pay taxes."

"Hush."

I wanted very much to kiss her, but even before doing that I reached with both hands and with gentle fingers cleanly, safely tore the iron collar from her neck. It seemed to me that the spot where, as I saw now, the royal seal had been stamped in, was likely to be the weakest, and so I chose that place to rip it right across. Somehow my hands, that had doubted their skill to do as much for Hesione on her seaside cliff, were certain in their power now. I crumpled the heavy scrap of metal into a ball and threw it on the ground, and in the same motion turned at the sound of footsteps to confront whoever was approaching. In that moment I hoped it might be the very one who claimed to have made slaves of my son and his mother.

Instead, I found myself looking into the blank face of blind Tiresias. The prophet looked more infirm than when I had seen him last, and he was walking with a cane in one hand and his other arm around the shoulders of a young girl, who I supposed served him as a guide around obstacles so small and practical that they fell below the scope of his inward vision.

"Hail, Hercules," he greeted me, coming to a stop at a few paces' distance. "I see that you are healthy."

"Hail, Lord Tiresias. I hope that you are the same."

"I am not healthy, young man, and in fact I will soon be dead. You stand in danger of death from a centaur."

That was something of a surprise, and I felt Megan grow tense beside me. "Do I indeed?"

The blind man smiled his faintly horrible smile and offered no explanation.

When I saw he did not mean to speak, I said: "I thank you for your concern, prophet. But it has been shown over and over that no point or blade can pierce my skin. I doubt that any hoof can kick me hard enough to do me harm. Besides, centaurs have had their shot at me already."

"Not everything that does harm, Hercules, is hard and sharp. Beware the soft and subtle."

"Again I thank you for the warning, Lord Tiresias. . . . Speaking of the soft and subtle, whose idea was it to make a slave of this woman who nurses my son?"

"She has already told you almost as much about that as I could tell you." The blind man paused. "What will you do now, Hercules?"

"Do you need to ask? Are there some things you can't foresee?"

"There is much."

"This is my woman," I said, putting my arm around her shoulders. "And I mean to have her for my wife." And as I said that I turned and met her eyes and kissed her.

Tiresias offered no comment. His girl was staring at me in evident fascination. Turning back to him, I asked: "Do you think the king will want to exact some kind of purchase price? If he does, tell him he may deduct it from my share of the estate of Amphitryon, of which I assume some part will come to me."

Tiresias was smiling in amusement now, silently laughing, which made his blind face truly hideous. "You may tell Eurystheus that yourself," he said. "He has sent me to tell you that he wants to see you."

An hour later, I was standing before the young king in the great hall of his palace, the very room in which my trial had taken place a year earlier. This time Eurystheus received me in the oddest way. In place of the throne I had seen in this room before, there stood an enormous vessel of bronze, approximately rectangular in shape, all of its outer surfaces decorated with gods and humans in high relief. This casket, or box, was the size of a large sarcophagus or bathtub, and was topped by a hinged lid, also of heavy bronze. The opening of the lid was in my direction, and it was propped up several inches with wooden wedges. Peering out at me through the small gap thus created were a pair of human eyes that I soon recognized as those of King Eurystheus. On each side of the box stood an attendant, holding one end of a cord whose other end was tied to one of the wooden wedges. The arrangement allowed these to be yanked away at a moment's notice, removing the last chink from the king's brazen fortress—and dropping the lid resoundingly on his head if he failed to duck in time. When, in the course of our conversation, one of the guards' spears accidentally bumped the lid of the great casket, it vibrated softly but richly, like a huge gong.

Of course the box in which the king seemed to be trying to hide was flanked by ranks of armed warriors, a dozen spear-carrying men who eyed me nervously. Those I had more or less expected.

So absorbed was I in attempting to guess whether the king had gone completely mad, or what the meaning of his strange behavior might be, that now I can hardly remember exactly what words I addressed to the king, or he to me. But our conversation went something like this:

"Your Majesty has sent for me."

"We would like to hear the story of your adventures, Hercules, from your own lips." The young king's voice had an odd metallic echo to it, coming out of his cave of bronze. "But first, is there anything we can do for you?"

I wasted no time in raising the subject of Megan.

The result of our talk was that the king, with an air of graciousness, granted me the girl and her baby as a free gift.

Politely I expressed my gratitude. The audience did not last long after that. When it was over, and I encountered Tiresias while on my way out of the palace, I asked him if I might briefly speak to him alone.

The seer motioned with his head, and I fell into step beside him. This time his arm was draped around the shoulders of a different girl.

He said to me: "Someone, a certain prophet of great reputation, fell into a trance. And while in a trance he prophesied, in the king's hearing, that 'Bronze is protection for the most powerful.' And the young king, in his natural arrogance, assumed that the phrase 'most powerful' must refer to him."

"I see. That might begin to explain the bronze casket. Is it safe to assume that the prophet was yourself?" Tiresias did not contradict me, and I went on: "Would it do me any good to ask who the prophecy *does* refer to? Well, never mind. But tell me this, Tiresias. Why should the king think he needs protection when I'm around? Why should he think he's in any danger from me?"

"Many people fear you, Hercules. And are jealous of you."

Slowly I nodded. "At the moment I can't think of anyone who has cause to be afraid. But you are right, I do sometimes see the dread in people's faces, though they try to hide it with a smile of friendship. Still, it seems to me that the king must feel some special terror, to cause him to go to such lengths to fortify himself." I shook my head and made vague gestures.

"Hercules, your strength does not extend to your perceptions.

The king only hides in his bronze box when you are present. He believes that you are determined to have revenge on him."

"Revenge? For what?"

My face must have shown my stupefaction, but I don't know whether the blind man could read my face. Probably my voice gave the same evidence; and now I think it equally likely that Tiresias was past dreading or even caring for anything that anyone might do to him.

This time he answered me directly enough. "For having cheated you out of the throne."

My feet unconsciously slowed to a stop, while I tried, without success, to sort that out. "But what have I to do with thrones?"

"Some eighteen or twenty years ago there was, or may have been, yet another prophecy, to the effect that the next descendant of Zeus born in the land would rule all Cadmia. Eurystheus believes himself to be, like you, a descendant of the Thunderer. Also the king believes his own development in his mother's womb was somehow magically accelerated, and yours possibly retarded, to move him ahead of you in the line of succession. And that you are fully aware of this course of strange events, and must resent him for it."

Again it took me a little while to digest the information. "That last, about my resenting him, is wrong, now that the business regarding Megan has been settled. Totally wrong! Is there any truth in the rest of it?"

"Very probably."

"Then some god or goddess is my enemy?"

"Rumor says Hera."

That was bad news, if true. "Is there any use in my asking why the consort of Zeus should have taken a dislike to me?"

"No use in asking me."

I shook my head. Here were more questions that I could put to Zeus, someday. Or to Hera, if I should ever meet her face-to-face. I could try Hermes when I saw him next, but I had no real hope that the Messenger would be of help.

To Tiresias I said: "But there was no reason to think I'd be a king anyway, was there? Amphitryon's not royalty, nor is there any such thing on my mother's side. I've never been in line for the throne, or anywhere near it."

The blind man shrugged. He seemed gently amused. "I only said there was a prophecy—certainly that was not one of mine. You know what prophecies in general are like—or perhaps you are still too young to have heard very many of them. The less sense they make, the more people are impressed by them. And the harder it is to tell whether they are fulfilled or not."

"But, I repeat, I don't want to be a king. I wouldn't have his throne or his crown if you gave them to me."

"I know that." A pause. "The truth is that you were destined for greater things."

"Such as what?"

"Time will tell."

Now we were walking on again. I thought that in any case the old man would tell me what he wanted to tell me, no more and no less, so I did not bother to press him.

I said: "So, let His Majesty hide himself in a bronze pot, if it makes it easier for him to talk with me. Very likely I will want to talk to him again." At the time I fully expected there to be some opposition to the marriage I planned.

And on that day I left the palace wondering whether the bronze casket did not simply represent a great joke by the blind prophet, who had chosen this means of making the king look ridiculous, and thus getting even with him for something.

Before leaving home again, I took care to make Megan legally my wife, in a full public ceremony, so both she and my son would have such social standing and protection as my name could give them.

The loss of one slave could hardly make much practical difference in the vast royal household. And the young king must have been pleased to see me taking a wife who could not, according to any rational calculation, be of the slightest help to me in any dynastic struggle.

Meanwhile Amphitryon and Iphicles, though they raised mild formal objections to the wedding, I think were secretly relieved to see me marrying so far below my station. What could have been a thorny problem for my foster father, of negotiating alliances by arranging a marriage for me, was thus taken out of his hands. But I knew that my mother, if she still could watch me from the Underworld, would be sad to see me united with one who had worn the collar of a slave. The gods alone knew what dreams of greatness, as she understood greatness, she had still been cherishing for me.

On the night after the ceremony, when my bride and I were in bed together, the one I loved, who I had thought for a time was sleeping, suddenly turned over and whispered to me.

"You are so gentle, Hercules. As you always were."

The gods knew I had tried to be gentle, with her especially. "You do not fear me, then? My strength?"

"Fear you?" she seemed astonished. "No."

And the baby in his nearby cradle cried, a tiny whimper first, swiftly building to a lusty yell. And Megan caught him up and began to nurse him at her breast, which brought quick silence; and in that peaceful bed I slowly drifted off to sleep, in what seemed the most perfect rest that I had ever known.

Apollo

$\mathcal{I}$ was happy to enjoy a week of dalliance with my new bride and to amuse myself with speculation about what happy achievements my son might someday be able to attain. But of course I was not going to remain peacefully at home in Cadmia for any considerable length of time. Even had no summons come from great Zeus himself, still I doubtless would soon have found some other quest to carry me away from the peace and security of home.

Attached to the house, which had been a wedding gift from King Eurystheus, was a small staff of servants, none of whom were slaves; no doubt some were the king's spies, but that did not worry me, as I had nothing to conceal. It was no less luxurious than the manor in which I had grown up, even if it was smaller than I would have liked. Actually I felt somewhat reassured because it was not too close to the palace. The upper strata of Cadmian society would never be really open to this former servant girl and slave, I supposed. I expected that they would be for my son, someday. But that was a matter he would have to work out for himself when he was grown.

Enkidu had dropped in for a visit, and stood frowning thoughtfully at the baby I was holding. Then he asked me: "What will he be, do you suppose? A warrior?"

"I hope not," I said, without thinking. My nephew gave me a puzzled look.

So far he had not enjoyed his stay at home nearly as much as I had. Enkidu chafed under the close attention of his father, and on the day after our arrival was already suggesting to me that it was time to be off again on some new adventure.

But then in succeeding days I heard no more suggestions from him along that line—being busy with my own new family affairs, I gave the matter little thought at the time.

Our visitor had only just departed when a shadow fell across a window, and I thought for a moment that he had come back. Megan, peering out of the house, was tremendously impressed when she caught a glimpse of the one who had come calling.

Her mouth and eyes were round with astonishment, and she pointed toward the outside with one finger, seemingly almost unable to speak. "Hercules! It is . . . it is . . ."

I had been trying to estimate the strength with which my son could grip my finger. But now I came to the window and caught a glimpse as well. "I know who it is, my love." Gently I put her aside. "Wait here, while I go out and talk to him."

"Hercules—?"

"It's all right." I patted my wife's arm. "No harm will come to me. The Messenger and I are required to have these little conversations every now and then."

But my jaunty attitude began to drain away when I stepped out into our small rear courtyard and beheld the somber expression on the face of Hermes.

"Daedalus and Vulcan," Hermes assured me when we were quite alone, "both send their thanks for the sample of Apple you provided them. And of course for the other objects also."

"That's good." I had hoped that the other objects would be more than mere jars of mud when they reached their destination. "They are quite welcome. . . . Lord Hermes, did you say *Vulcan*? Do you mean the god Hephaestus? The Smith himself?"

Hermes seemed faintly pleased that he had managed to startle and impress me. "That is who I mean. Hephaestus vouches that all the samples you have furnished them have been of inestimable help."

"I rejoice to hear it, even if I don't begin to understand just what Vulcan and Daedalus are doing. Now, Lord Messenger, will you answer another question for me?"

"Perhaps."

"Perhaps you can also guess what it is: When will my father see me?"

"Before he does, Hercules, there is one more task you must perform."

"Ah." I put my hand on the branch of a fruit tree but restrained myself from breaking it off. "Does it surprise you, Lord Hermes, that I am not astonished by your answer?"

As usual, Mercury remained imperturbable. "What Zeus asks of you now is a mission more important than any you have previously undertaken—I am quoting your father's very words. And he solemnly assured me that he is ready to see you as soon as you have completed this next assignment."

I had been perfectly prepared for any kind of an indefinite answer. This sudden acceptance of my demand, even qualified as it was, left me not knowing what to say.

Again Hermes seemed to be smiling faintly.

At last I got out: "I promise to undertake any task that my father may set, if he will promise to meet me immediately afterward."

The Messenger raised an aristocratic eyebrow. "Do you not want to hear first what the task is?"

I could feel my face reddening. "I have said what I have said."

Mercury nodded slowly. He turned his head this way and that, studying our surroundings, eyeing the open windows of the house. Then he said: "Let us find a place where we can be comfortable while we talk. It is not a matter that can be spelled out in a dozen words."

Turning out of the courtyard, we moved through a small passage, screened by arbors and grapevines, leading to the small orchard in the rear of the house. There my distinguished visitor adopted a thoughtful attitude, strolling with his hands clasped behind his back.

Hermes said: "You have of course heard of Mount Olympus, home of the gods from ancient times. It was long the favorite dwelling place of Zeus."

"Yes, of course I've heard of it. But do I understand you to say that Zeus lives there no longer?"

"Sadly that is true—but where Zeus dwells now is not our immediate concern. I mention Mount Olympus because somewhere in the vicinity of that place there lives—I should say exists—a man called Prometheus."

I shook my head: No, I had never heard of him.

Mercury went on. "This Prometheus has for a long time suffered a strange and terrible punishment, of which confinement is only the lesser part. Your father sets you the task of locating this sufferer, ending his torment, and setting him free. In the process—and this is the most important part—you must learn from Prometheus whatever he knows about the nature and whereabouts of a Giant named Atlas."

"I see," I said slowly. "And then, having done that much, I am supposed to find Atlas. And then—?"

Hermes held up a restraining hand. "Your father may want you to look for Atlas also. But that will come later. I meant what I said, Hercules. Zeus will see you, face-to-face, as soon as you have found Prometheus and gained his knowledge. Your father will want to hear from you directly what you have learned."

Briefly I considered this, while the god and I kept walking. Then I stopped in my tracks. "I have said I'll do it and I will, whatever it takes. But tell me more about this Prometheus. How is he confined, and what are the other parts of his strange punishment?"

The Messenger picked some fruit from a tree and tasted it with appreciation. For a moment or two he looked no more than human.

Then he said: "Long ago—no need to worry about exactly how long ago, or why—Prometheus was an enemy of Zeus. Of some earlier avatar of the god, I mean, long before your father's time."

"I see. And the nature of the man's punishment?"

"I believe he is chained to a rock." Mercury suddenly seemed oddly uncertain and, I thought, uncomfortable. "There is also, I think, a large and ugly bird involved. Or maybe several of them. Kill the birds if they get in your way. Now I have told you all I really know. You are going to have to deal with the details as best you can."

But then the great god suddenly recalled one detail that he wanted to convey. "Oh, and one more thing. When you set the man free, Zeus wants you to leave some small fragment of the chain attached to him. That way, a certain oath once sworn by an earlier avatar of Zeus need not be broken."

We had resumed our pacing under the fruited trees. I said: "And oaths, of course, are tremendously important."

"Of course."

"All right. I can do all that." The story of the oath and the strange punishment intrigued me, but I was not going to pursue it now. "Tell me where I can find Prometheus."

"That I cannot do."

Once more my feet stopped moving in the grass. For the space of several deep breaths the Messenger and I studied each other in silence. Then I said: "Lord Hermes, I have promised to perform this task. Now, tell me, are you playing some kind of game with me? Or giving me a test? Do you have some reason to want to make the job more difficult?"

"Not at all, Hercules. I will answer any other questions you may have, if I can."

I drew a deep breath and let it out.

"Very well, I do have several. To begin with, why send me, or anyone? Either you or my mighty father could reach this Prometheus much more swiftly than I can, even if I use the *Skyboat*. Especially if you really do know where to find this chained man, which I suppose you must. Either of you gods, I am sure, would make short work of any difficulties the man may be having with rocks and chains and birds."

Hermes was silent, staring gloomily at nothing.

"The chief reason we are sending you instead of a god," he said at last, "is that there are probably Giants in his vicinity."

"I see. And Giants really do pose that much of a danger to you, or to Zeus, that you are not going to risk your necks by going near them."

Gray eyes turned on me with such a look that at last I began to be a little frightened. Mercury said: "We would not pretend that it is so, if it were not. I thought that on Corycus they had explained these matters to you." At last the god was starting to grow angry. "Hercules, you take grave risks! Remember you are mortal. There are gods who would crush you like an insect if you spoke to them with such insolence."

"I see," I said again, and briefly bowed my head. "Very well, Lord Messenger, I dispute with you no more. I have sworn I will do this service for my father, and I will. Where is Olympus? Tell me that much at least, and I'll be on my way."

This time I really did expect a simple answer. But instead of giving me one, Hermes only seemed to grow even more uncomfortable. He hurled the fruit core from him, only a casual motion of his arm, but the soft missile went ripping like a slung stone through the leaves of another tree.

Turning back to me at last, he said, "That is another thing I cannot tell you."

"The location of Mount Olympus?" I was incredulous. "Cannot or will not?"

The Messenger now looked more ill at ease than I had ever seen him, though it seemed he had reasoned himself out of his anger, or got rid of it some other way. He said: "I can give you a rough idea of where it is, and Prometheus, too. But I cannot reveal to you his precise location, or that of Mount Olympus, either, because I no longer know. The truth is, I have forgotten both. I had forgotten the very existence of Prometheus until Zeus reminded me."

There was silence for a little while, and I could feel a cold chill creeping down my spine. Eventually I nerved myself to ask: "Lord Hermes, is one of us mad?"

"*You* are not mad, Hercules. As for myself, the question is not so simply answered—but yes, I *am* partially deranged, at least when it comes to memory. And so is every god I know."

I sat there for what seemed a long time, not knowing what to say. For the first time I began to realize how grim was our situation regarding the Giants.

Eventually Hermes began to speak again. It came out that all the gods, or all of them with whom he had had any recent contact, had fought skirmishes with Giants who used their secret weapon, or had been attacked by their great enemies from ambush, and all the gods, or almost all, had forgotten pretty much the same things.

I was under more than ordinary strain, and my temper got the best of me. Also I was very young and had not yet been much pounded by my world. I said: "So, your brains have all more or less gone rotten."

That got me glared at again, and for a moment I was afraid that I had indeed gone too far. In a voice that made me wince and recoil, despite myself, he barked out: "Hear me, mortal! We who appeal for your help are the wounded veterans of a great war!"

I apologized for my rudeness. But presently I had taken up the argument again, though on a considerably lower key. "You, a god, expect me, a mortal, to find Olympus for you, as well as this fellow who is somehow bound to a rock?"

Hermes tried to be reassuring. "The search may occupy you for some time, Hercules. But there is every reason to believe you will succeed."

Most of the citizens of Cadmia were really pleased to see me looking for my club and making other preparations to leave home again, though of course they expressed their regrets when I told them I was going. Young king Eurystheus was especially two-faced. As he peered out from under his bronze lid during my farewell audience, I could see in his eye a glint of self-satisfaction at how cleverly he was blocking my plans to seize his throne. Meanwhile he halfheartedly offered me an escort of warriors on the expedition I was about to undertake. I courteously declined, not wanting to be burdened with a squadron of mouths to somehow feed, of minds to argue with, and of bodies to keep out of trouble.

Before leaving, I made sure that Megan and little Hyllus were established comfortably in our new house.

After telling Megan that I was ready to push on, I informed Enkidu before telling anyone else, more or less assuming that he would choose to accompany me again.

But when my nephew heard the news, his eyes did not light up as I had expected. He briefly hesitated, and then told me: "I'm not going with you this time, Herc."

"Ah." For a moment I was astonished, but as soon as I took thought on the matter, surprise vanished. My nephew was now almost fourteen years old, and he told me he wanted to stay home and marry the girl who had grown to be attractive in his eyes. Once my mother and Amphitryon had intended that I should marry her, but there was no longer any hope of that. Also the wealth that would come with the wedding was beginning to loom up real and solid in Enkidu's eyes.

I reminded my old comrade that if he settled down and stayed home, the army, and the chronic war, were waiting for him in a year or two, as soon as his father thought him old enough to fight.

But Enkidu had already taken these matters into consideration. "I know, but it sounds like the war's about over. At last. And by the Underworld, Unc, you don't need me. You can get anyone you want to come with you now. You're really getting to be famous."

When it came time for me to depart from the happy cottage where Megan and I had enjoyed a sort of honeymoon, I took my leave with some regret, made sharper by the tears of my young wife. But in my heart I had never abandoned my quest to learn all I could about my father and finally to confront him face-to-face. And however attractive home and hearth might be, particularly after a long wandering, it was a man's business to be out and active in the world.

Getting back to the place where we had left the *Skyboat,* and where I hoped to find it waiting for me, would entail a long overland journey. But this time I was riding a good cameloid from the start. On the eve of my departure, a number of people offered various gifts, all calculated, as I thought, to speed me on my way. A few others, would-be adventurers, had volunteered to accompany me, though I had told no one where I was going or on what mission. None seemed desirable as companions, and firmly I told them that I preferred to go alone.

Up to that point my solo journey was uneventful. I was just about to step aboard the *Skyboat* when some inward sense told me that a god was near. Ready for another argument with Hermes, I turned around to confront a tall male figure. But the face I saw was not the one I had expected.

This time, in the appearance of the image before me, there was an undercurrent of something infinitely more terrible than any Messenger. This time I confronted Apollo himself.

I had never laid eyes on the Far-Worker before, but somehow I knew him instantly and unmistakably. The movements of my body seemed automatic. Letting my club slide from my shoulder, I went down on one knee before him, something I had never thought of doing before Hermes. My mouth had gone dry, and I began to know, perhaps truly for the first time, what it is to be afraid.

Not that there was anything intrinsically awe-inspiring in his shape, though he was certainly impressive. Apollo stood before me in the form of a beautiful, beardless youth, a little taller than I, his lean, muscular body draped in white tunic and cape, with Bow and Arrows slung on his back and a small lyre fastened to his belt. His face and arms would have been naturally pale, but they were tanned, and his curly hair grew strangely, in an entangled mixture of red and black.

When the great god spoke to me his look was grim at first, and his greeting came with the sound of a harsh accusation.

"You are Hercules," he growled.

"I am, lord."

He made an impatient gesture. "All right, Hercules. Who are they? Tell me their names, the gods and humans who plot against me."

I was too bewildered to attempt any reply.

My situation must have shown in my face. Apollo shook his head, and some of the stiffness went out of his pose.

His voice became lower and less threatening. "But no, there are too many logical reasons against that, and deep in my heart I feel it cannot be so. And Daedalus and the prince Asterion speak well of you, Hercules. Hermes does, too, but he . . ." He left the phrase unfinished and stood staring at me uncertainly.

At last it was up to me to break the silence. "Lord Apollo, Hermes has explained to me that his memory is damaged. Is it possible that you have suffered in a similar way?"

"He said that, did he?" The Far-Worker glared at me again for a moment, then relaxed a little further. "It is only too possible, I fear. Only too possible."

"I am sorry to hear that."

Suspicion was rapidly being replaced by uncertainty. "I must admit, Hercules," said Apollo a moment later, "that my own memory of Olympus, its nature and whereabouts, is regrettably inadequate. In fact, the more I contemplate the situation, try to estimate the number of things I must have forgotten, the more it alarms me."

"Then you, too, have fought the Giants, lord."

"Yes, fought them indeed. When I was in an earlier avatar." His right hand rose for a moment to touch his slung Bow, then fell back to his side. "Destroyed a few, but at a cost. And part of the price I paid was that for a long time, many months, the mere existence of the Giants seems to have been blotted from my memory."

Now Apollo asked me more questions, fortunately free of accusations. In response, I told him about my repeated meetings with Hermes, and what Daedalus and Prince Asterion had told me.

The Far-Worker had had his own meetings with those men, some of them comparatively recent. But he had partially forgotten them, and he found my point of view on the subject very interesting.

"And where is Hermes now?" he wanted to know.

I had no idea.

"Lord Apollo, if you have come to ask me, or command me, to do what my father has ordered, you should know that I need no special urging. Hermes has convinced me of the need. It was only that I needed another day here at home, to set my affairs in order."

"It isn't that," Apollo said. Now his manner was much milder than it had been on his arrival. "I had forgotten so much, certain things began to seem so inexplicable, that I began to think there was a conspiracy against me . . . but now memories are beginning to come back.

"Fortunately, the damage that the Giants do to gods is not always permanent." He ran distracted fingers through his hair, an action that drew my attention again to the strange mixture of red and black. But I was not going to offer any comments.

Suddenly the Far-Worker's suspicion flared again. "You," Apollo challenged me, "seem to know more about Zeus than I do. Can you explain that?"

When confronting the Messenger, I had been able to summon up a brash defiance. But in Apollo's presence that attitude had utterly evaporated, and I felt like a small boy called by some powerful authority to account for his misdeeds.

"Sorry, my lord Apollo, but I can explain very little. I know that great Zeus is my father, but nothing of any conspiracy."

For the first time he favored me with something like a smile. Gradually the Far-Worker seemed to be completely conquering his suspicions.

At last he relaxed somewhat. "Call me Jeremy, if you will. My mortal name was—is—Jeremy Redthorn. Actually I'm still rather new at this god business. I was younger than you are now when I put on Apollo's Face, and I seem to remember that my hair was all red . . . that must have been about two years ago, though keeping track of the past has become a matter of uncertainty. Maybe in another year or so it will be all black."

"Oh. Yes, your hair, of course." While Apollo had been speaking, my perception of the figure before me shifted. Before me I saw an unsettling combination of youth and majesty, uncertainty and imperial power.

In the midst of our discussion Apollo paused, as if suddenly struck by a new idea. "Have you ever been to Vulcan's workshop and laboratory?" he demanded.

"Never."

"It would be a good thing," he announced, "for you to pay that place a visit. Daedalus is working there, too, you know, and he and the Smith will want to hear everything you can tell them about this Antaeus. I saw those jars of muck you sent, and they made me wonder."

"I agree," I said. I had for a long time been curious as to what the gods were doing with the material I had provided them. "I would be delighted and honored to see the workshop where Hephaestus works his wonders. But how am I to get there?"

"How are you to get there? I can take you, easily enough. But Zeus says that learning all we can from Atlas must come first."

EIGHTEEN

The Man on the Rock

*B*eginning to feel a little more at ease with my divine companion, I tentatively suggested to him that we could both ride in
the *Skyboat.* But great Apollo brushed this idea aside. He raised a
hand and made a slight gesture. From out of somewhere, I could not
tell where unless it was the empty air, there came a magnificent chariot, empty of passengers, that looked much like the one I had seen on
the island of Corycus, belonging to Dionysus. But as it rolled to a
stop beside us I could see that this one was pulled by horses instead
of leopards. They were a pair of huge, white, fiery animals, obviously
as much creatures of the supernatural as was Apollo himself.

The Sun God leaped in and seized the reins. "Come, Hercules,"
he said. "I have some vague idea of where this Prometheus may be."

"Near Olympus."

"Yes, and I also have a vague idea about that. Between the two of
us, we ought to have a good chance of finding him."

I was not eager to board the chariot, but it seemed I had little
choice. Taking my club in hand, I boldly climbed in, and a moment
later we were airborne. Flight of any kind was a new experience for
me, and moments later my eyes were closed, and my two-handed grip
on the rail before me was crushing wood and metal.

Apollo urged me to relax. "Don't look down, if it bothers you. I'll
try to make the ride as smooth as possible."

Making an effort of will, I succeeded in opening my eyes. Trying to
take my mind off the fact that I was now hurtling through the air, several hundred feet above the ground, I asked the Far-Worker how we
were going to find Prometheus, and Mount Olympus, if neither of us
knew exactly where they were.

"I have a vague idea," Apollo repeated. "Say, within a couple of
hundred square miles. But no clear memory of the exact spot." He
rubbed a hand over his handsome face, the gesture of a man brushing
away cobwebs. "I do seem to remember that there are Giants in the

vicinity. If they allow us to complete this little trip, I'll take you on to Vulcan's laboratory."

"Hermes warned me about Giants, too." I discovered that it helped to keep my eyes raised, watching the clouds instead of the earth.

"He did, did he? I suppose the Messenger has also skirmished with them. . . . I tell you, Hercules, if I could even recall much about the enemy who has robbed me of so many memories, I might fear to face that power again. But as it is . . . in ignorance is courage." Apollo shook himself and straightened his shoulders. "Enough of that. Why exactly are we looking for Prometheus?"

I explained to my new companion that Zeus now wanted his former enemy rescued from his endless punishment.

"Because it seems," I went on, "that only this Prometheus can tell us where the Giant named Atlas is to be found—can you remember anything of Atlas?"

"Afraid not. Almost nothing."

"Oh. Well, Atlas, in turn, is important because he knows something, or can do something, that Daedalus and Hephaestus dearly want to find out, or accomplish." I was having to shout above the rush of wind. "I don't understand the details. Maybe when I meet Zeus he'll fill in some of them for me."

"Ah." Apollo shrugged his powerful shoulders. "Well, if Hermes says Atlas must be located, then that's what we'd better do. The Messenger may have retained more of his wits than I have of mine."

That was not the most reassuring thing he could have said. The chariot flew on in silence, except for the continual rush of wind. Now and then Apollo mentioned certain landmarks, towns and mountains, streams and lakes, as they passed below, while I for the most part kept my eyes fixed firmly on the horizon. To judge by the rapidity with which the earthly features hurtled by, our passage through the air was amazingly swift, much faster even than *Skyboat.* Fortunately our conveyance was also much steadier than the *Argo,* whose motion had once made me seasick.

No more than an hour had passed before our flight path began tending downward. We descended to lower and lower altitudes, until we were only skimming over a remote and rocky wasteland. There was no body of water in sight, not even a small stream. I had to agree that *Skyboat* would not have been of much help in reaching this land-locked region.

Now that we were at little more than rooftop height, I found I was able to watch the ground without being overcome by terror or illness. Apollo guided our team of unnatural beasts to and fro in a methodical search pattern. We spent a long time flying back and forth before we located the rock we wanted.

"There he is," my companion suddenly announced. Apollo's eyes were, unsurprisingly, much keener than mine, and it was he who made the discovery. "That looks like a man, lying on a rock." And with a touch on the reins he sent the chariot into a sharp bank.

Soon we were directly over the forlorn-looking individual on his slab of stone, and I looked down and nodded. "That must be the fellow we want. Few would choose this place for sunbathing."

There was no sign of any human settlement, not even a hunters' or herders' track, anywhere nearby. Prometheus had been chained down atop a small, rocky hill between two slightly larger heights. Occasionally, during the minute or two while we were making our close approach, he moved his head or limbs, and once or twice let out a hoarse cry of pain.

His situation was amazing, and horrifying. I had never seen anything remotely like it.

As we approached more closely, we saw a naked man, of muscular build and indeterminate age, chained flat on his back on a stone bed. As far as I could see, he was totally exposed to day and night, heat and cold, sun and rain. Obviously something out of the ordinary kept him from dying, in this situation where ordinarily a man might have expected to live and suffer for only a matter of hours, or a few days at the very most. What kind of nourishment was keeping him alive was more than I could guess.

His beard was not gray, but it had grown so long that it wound almost entirely around the rock.

But mere exposure was not the worst that Prometheus had to endure. A kind of hunchbacked vulture, parts of its body naked of all feathers, flapped into view even as we drew near. The great bird landed on the rock, as if on some familiar perch, and immediately began tormenting the victim, the sharp beak opening a bloody wound in the man's side.

As we approached, the creature looked up, spreading its wings to their full ten-foot span, a drop of blood falling from the tip of its beak. Apollo touched his Bow, and the bird sprang into the air and flapped away, screaming.

Moments later we were on the ground. Leaping out of the chariot even before its wheels ceased to roll, I rejoiced in the reassuring feel of solid earth beneath my feet.

At once I hurried to the side of the onetime enemy of Zeus, whose chains yielded promptly to my strength.

Prudently I remembered my father's command, passed on to me by Mercury, to leave some fragment of the chain still fastened to Prometheus so that the oath of an earlier avatar of Zeus need not be broken. I left a circlet, with a single link attached, on his left wrist.

The man on the rock had not reacted to our approach and hardly stirred even when I broke him free. Though his eyes were open, I quickly decided that he could not be fully conscious, but rather in a kind of suspended animation.

Now Apollo came and took him by the hand, and now Prometheus sat up and frowned at his rescuers in puzzlement. A touch from the hand of the God of Healing, and the ugly wound in the victim's side closed over and ceased to bleed.

But now, even as Prometheus seemed on the verge of recovery from his ancient ordeal, the predatory bird reappeared, looking ready to deal him a setback.

A moment later an Arrow from Apollo's Bow produced a sharp midair explosion, after which only a feather or two survived to come drifting to the ground.

After disposing of the ugly bird, Apollo stood watch, brooding with his Bow in hand and a second Arrow ready, while I pulled from the rock the anchor bolts with broken chains attached, so that no one else might ever be held captive in the same place.

Prometheus was now standing on his feet and beginning to look about him. He took no notice of Apollo, who was a step or two behind him, and he paid little attention to me, though I stood right at his side. Obviously his mind was far from clear as yet.

But at last the man did speak, gasping out: "But is this real? I am now truly free?" I could barely comprehend him, his accent had such a strange and antique sound.

"Truly free," I assured him. "By order of Zeus himself."

"Ahh!" It was a kind of groaning noise that might have expressed either pain or triumph.

"What can you tell me about Atlas?" I demanded, seeing no reason to waste any time.

Seeming to come more fully wake, Prometheus frowned at me. His voice when he finally spoke was scratchy, as if it had not been used in a long time. "Why do you want to approach Atlas? Do you know what you are asking for?"

I exchanged glances with Apollo. "Probably I don't know everything I should," I admitted. "But I am here in the service of Zeus himself, trying to locate Atlas the Giant."

Prometheus seemed surprised by my last words. He knotted his hands in his long beard and tugged at it nervously.

"A Giant?" His hoarse voice almost broke. "No. Not Atlas. Well, maybe he once was. I expect there may be Giants about. But the one you are looking for is nothing as simple and uncomplicated as a mere Giant." And from the corner of my eye I saw Apollo turn his face to us, concentrating on this remarkable response.

Meanwhile the man we had rescued was turning back and forth, studying his surroundings in every direction, as if he needed to orient himself after his long, tormented sleep. When he at last took notice of Apollo, he merely acknowledged the Olympian's presence with a slight bow, as if gods in general were truly familiar sights to him. An arrogant attitude, I thought, that might well have got him into trouble in the past.

Then Prometheus raised an arm, from which a single link of chain still dangled, and pointed off to the northeast.

"You will find the one you say you are looking for in that direction," he said. "No more than a few hours' walk. See, there, that peak on what looks like the very edge of the world?"

I stood behind our informant and peered along the length of his extended arm. He seemed to be indicating the top of a rugged, truncated cone, blue with distance, that fitted into a notch in the rocky horizon. I doubted that it was really the edge of the world, though at the time I could not feel absolutely sure.

"You will find Olympus there," Prometheus was telling us, "in the middle of a flat space ringed by hills. Seek Atlas on the top of the central cone. He'll be there still . . . though I haven't seen him for centuries."

Apollo was standing close beside us now and gazing into the distance. He seemed to have no need to shade his eyes from the lowering sun.

"Olympus? Yes, that may be it," he murmured, in the tone of a man who is talking chiefly to himself. "That may well be the place." Then he rounded on Prometheus. "If you haven't seen him for centuries, what makes you so sure that he will still be there?"

Now it was the former captive's turn to appear puzzled. "He's not going anywhere—how can he, when he supports the heavens?"

Apollo and I looked at each other. "We thank you for your information," he told Prometheus.

Then the god made a sign to me with his head, a slight but commanding nod, and I followed him as he began to walk in the direction indicated, leaving Prometheus behind. The chariot followed us, just keeping pace, the rims of its wheels turning slowly a foot or so above the uneven ground.

"If there are truly Giants about," Apollo observed, when we had trudged along for a hundred yards or so, "it might be a good idea for us to walk the rest of the way. A man-sized shape on the ground is a much less conspicuous target than a flying chariot."

In the past, folk who have heard my description of that day's events have asked what happened to Prometheus after he was freed. I can only tell my present readers what I told them, that I do not know. The Far-Worker and I had many other things to think about. My last glance at the man we had rescued showed him standing with one hand on the rock that had been his place of torture, gazing out over the land in the opposite direction. His back was straight, his wound was no longer bleeding, and the tormenting bird was dead.

* * *

It crossed my mind as we walked that perhaps I ought to persuade Apollo that my duty was to report to Zeus before doing anything else. But how could I be sure that Atlas had now been located unless I saw him for myself?

My companion set a brisk walking pace, but not one that I found impossible to keep. As we moved along, with the chariot keeping pace behind us, Apollo described his own mind as like a painting on a canvas, one that had been torn full of holes, so that the scene depicted was now barely recognizable.

He added: "I ought to remember something about Atlas, and almost I do. But 'almost' is no help to us."

"What I can't understand, Lord Apollo—Jeremy—is how can any being, however great, support the sky?"

"I suppose that's one of the things we may find out, if we keep going."

I walked on, trying to picture what Atlas could be like, trying to picture what might happen if he simply got tired and let go. And again I thought to myself: *The edge of the world?* But no, one of my early tutors had taught me that wise folk had demonstrated in several ways that the world was round.

As we hiked along, Apollo told me the little he could currently remember about Atlas. As time passed since his last brush with the Giants and their exotic weapon, some details about the case were starting to come back to him.

"I am now beginning to recall a certain legend," he added. "One that says Atlas represents another case of fearful punishment inflicted by one of your father's predecessors in the endless chain of avatars of Zeus. That earlier Zeus sentenced a certain particularly rebellious Giant to bear the weight of the firmament, for all time to come."

"The firmament. I suppose that means the sky?"

"That is correct."

"Is this some poetic figure of speech?" Somehow I could not imagine that even I myself would be strong enough for that.

"My thought is that it must be." And Apollo turned and looked at me, as if the fact that I might think about poetry had surprised him.

As we trudged on, the chariot still following us at a little distance, my companion added suddenly: "If we happen to meet a Giant, and if I should fall in combat with him—"

"Zeus forbid it!"

"I doubt your father has the power to forbid such things. So, listen to me, Hercules. If I do fall, you must press on, to do the next thing that Zeus asks of you."

"If we meet a Giant," I said, "other than this Atlas, who of course must be questioned, to find out what he knows—the first thing I'll do with any other Giant is beat his brains out with my club." And I made it sing through the air.

"I wish you success in the endeavor."

"I've fought one of them already," I assured my companion. "Antaeus tried to use his memory-destroying magic on me, but it had no effect, as far as I could tell. So, it might be wise if I went first. It might save you from losing another chunk of memory."

Apollo seemed to give the matter serious thought, then came to a prompt decision and nodded his agreement. With divine assurance, he judged himself too valuable to our cause to risk his life unnecessarily; and the risk to me in fighting another Giant would probably be minimal.

We held a brief conversation, after which Apollo waited for his chariot to catch up with him and then climbed into it. He promised to keep an eye on my progress from a distance and to come to my aid at once if I appeared to be in trouble.

When I turned again to look around, neither god nor chariot were anywhere to be seen.

Pushing on alone at a steady pace, I came in two or three hours to the cone-shaped hill and began to climb. The slope looked much longer now than it had from a distance.

The day was far advanced by that time, and presently I sought a place to rest for the night. I am a creature of daylight, basically, and I also thought my ally Apollo would be at his strongest when the sun was bright.

The stars were over me when I drifted off to sleep, and my last clear thought was something to the effect of how ridiculous it was that any creature of the earth could hold them up.

I slept soundly, and in the morning resumed my climb. On top, I found a spring where I could slake my thirst. Looking about me, I gradually convinced myself that I had found what seemed to be the place that Prometheus had described.

The big hill I had just climbed had on its top a cup-shaped indentation perhaps two hundred yards across. In the middle of this, in turn, stood a small hill. And it struck me that from a vantage point atop this small interior elevation the whole sky would seem to be spread out for comfortable inspection. So I went there as soon as I had caught my breath.

After my encounter with Antaeus, I thought I had a pretty good idea of what Atlas would be like, but it soon turned out that I was wrong.

The small hill had, again, a small depression at its summit. This concavity was no more than ten yards wide, and it seemed to have been paved at some time in the remote past, for remnants of a regular layer of stones or tiles showed through the clumps of grass and deposits of dry earth that overlay it now. And at the middle of the small depression stood an object that inevitably drew my attention, first because of its position, and second because it looked something like a tree stump, at the very center of this concentric series of otherwise completely treeless hills and hollows.

With a faint chill I realized that its rounded upper surface had some vague similarity to what I imagined the grainy head of a bald Giant must be like. But the resemblance was still greater, I thought, to a tree stump.

Something like a tree stump, about four feet high, and half that in diameter. But the substance of it did not look like wood, but rather like a pillar of rock, or of compacted earth. In fact the color of it and the grainy surface made me think of Giants' skin. Around the base of this pillar, or stump, the earth was muddy, and I supposed that any hard rain must cause quite a puddle there at the bottom of the once-paved bowl.

I went to stand beside the peculiar stump, rested an arm on it familiarly, and looked around. For all I could tell, I was indeed now positioned at the very center of the earth and sky, my line of sight clear to the remote blue horizon, which seemed equally distant in all directions.

Then it occurred to me to wonder if Atlas, for all his strength and possible bulk, might be invisible, like a sprite; and that possibly the giant pillars that held the sky, if any, were invisible as well. But I could walk in every direction around the central stump without bumping into anything of the kind.

When at last I grew impatient, and called out for Atlas, no one and nothing answered, leaving me feeling a curious mixture of disappointment and relief.

On becoming even more impatient, I took hold of the strange tree stump and began to exert the force that would soon have wrenched it from the ground.

Then at last a great voice, that seemed to come from everywhere around me, boomed out, commanding me to stop.

You may believe that I stopped at once.

"I am Hercules of Cadmia," I informed the world, and the invisible owner of the voice. "I have come here in search of one called Atlas."

The top of what had looked like a dead stump clicked open suddenly, an abrupt flowerlike blooming that revealed not petals but what I took to be a huge eye, glassy and translucent, staring back at me with an intensity I took to signify intelligence.

"I am Atlas," said the same voice, at last, now diminished to a more reasonable volume.

Had I been even ordinarily susceptible to fear, I would probably have taken to my heels at that moment. As it was, I recoiled a couple of steps, then demanded of the thing bluntly, "Are you a Giant?"

The voice regained its former volume. "A CASTLE CALLED DOUBTING CASTLE," it boomed out. "THE OWNER WHEREOF WAS GIANT DESPAIR."

"I do not understand you."

"THE PEACE OF GOD, WHICH PASSETH ALL UNDERSTANDING."

It certainly passed mine. I stood silent for a while, trying to think. If this—this *thing* confronting me was all there was to see of Atlas, he certainly bore no resemblance to Antaeus.

At last I said: "You are no Giant, then. And you are certainly not a man. Nor like any god that I have ever seen or heard described."

"YE SHALL BE AS GODS, KNOWING GOOD AND EVIL."

"I do not understand you. I am trying to determine if the legends about you are true or false. They say that you hold up the pillars on which the stars are supported."

"AND WHEN THE STARS THREW DOWN THEIR SPEARS, AND WATERED HEAVEN WITH THEIR TEARS, DID HE SMILE HIS WORK TO SEE?"

"I assume that question is somehow rhetorical. Yes, yes, very well. What can you show me, or tell me, about whatever it is that holds stars in their places?"

Finally I had managed to ask a question of my own that evoked something like a real answer.

And then there occurred something so far beyond my understanding that even now I have difficultly trying to describe it. Somehow Atlas conjured into existence, atop his stump-head, a much larger visionary space, spread before me like a kind of stage.

The apparitions on this stage were clear and brilliant, and moved in a way that seemed perfectly lifelike. Yet it seemed to me that none of them had ever truly been alive.

I regretted that Apollo was missing this show, and even more that Daedalus could not see it.

A voice spoke to me, in my own language, and the marvelous pictures came and went. I have neither the space here nor the inclination to set down all that Atlas told me on that day. But among other things, it was revealed to me that every star I saw in the night sky was really another sun—and that many of those stars were actually bigger and brighter than the sun that gave us all life, and that our poets called the Eye of Apollo.

The voice from the pillar spoke to me also of inconceivable times and distances.

And gradually I came to realize that, in a symbolic sense, what the legends said about Atlas was quite true. When later I had a chance to talk to Daedalus again, I had this thought confirmed: Atlas indeed supported the celestial sphere, sustained the structure of the Universe, in the sense that he retained and preserved many basic truths about the world that would otherwise have been utterly forgotten.

When I asked Atlas where the Giants came from, he told me that they had issued from the earth.

The beginnings of new understanding grew in me. My imagination relaxed, glad to be relieved of the effort of picturing huge pillars, by which the weight of the whole sky might be transferred to one unimaginable set of shoulders, part of some Giant body sitting or standing in this spot.

As I continued to question Atlas about the world, another thing he showed me was a parade of human shapes, or images. And he told me also about something he called the machinery of Olympus, which still diligently made such records of certain folk, records in the form of images, which were then caused to appear in the Underworld.

But I was no longer listening carefully, because my imagination had been truly caught by that one phrase. *The machinery of Olympus.* Those words, if they meant anything, must mean that Olympus still existed somewhere.

Meanwhile, the strange being who dealt in the tree stump, or issued from it, spoke on, telling me about the spritelike creatures who had made the shadow images that I watched, in pursuit of some vast project that all human and Olympian minds had long since forgotten about.

There was more, more than I will attempt to set down now, more than I can even remember. When at last the demonstration ceased, I fell into a kind of reverie of contemplation.

Apollo had to call me twice to rouse me. I looked around to see him standing in his chariot, behind his pair of magnificent white horses. All the marvelous display that Atlas had stunned and enlightened me with was gone, and the day was far advanced.

I thought the Far-Worker was looking at me strangely. He said: "My curiosity got the best of me, Hercules. What's going on?"

I pointed at the peculiar central column. "Atlas, here, can probably explain things better than I can."

"This—is Atlas?" But the god did not stay for an answer to that question. Instead he immediately faced the tall stump and demanded: "Tell me, oracle—where is lost Olympus?"

The reply this time must have come in a form perceptible only to divine senses, for I saw and heard it not. But Apollo understood something, because he grabbed me by the arm and pulled me back into the chariot. A moment later, the horses went bounding away at top speed.

I thought at the time that our hasty departure was probably a mistake, and now, looking back, I am sure of it. The god and I might both have learned much more from Atlas, had it not been for Apollo's eagerness to find his way back to Olympus, and my eagerness to be at his side when he made that discovery.

How far we traveled, or even in exactly what direction, I could not have said, for our flight was extremely rapid, and the sky around us was full of clouds much of the time. When Apollo and I finally came to the place that he said had once been Olympus, we discovered it deserted now, another almost barren mountaintop.

We landed a short distance below the summit, dismounted from the chariot, and began to climb. The danger of being seen by Giants had apparently been forgotten. I felt my ears pop on the ascent.

The air was so thin and cold, and there were moments in my short stay there when I had trouble breathing.

"Was this it? Yes, I think . . . but I can't be sure." Coming to a temporary halt, Apollo pressed his fists against his temples.

Old memories, long forgotten, began to come back to him. He tried to convey them to me, sometimes stammering in a most ungod-like way, and I could tell he felt a grievous sense of loss. Once this place must have had the appearance of an earthly paradise, but now it was only dust and blowing tumbleweed.

As we advanced, the Far-Worker began to tell me, in a dreamy, abstracted voice, about another mountaintop he had visited, only a few years ago, and in his current avatar. There, for a brief time, he had thought he had rediscovered Olympus.

"It was the similarity between that place and this that half awoke old memories, made me almost think that I had really returned here."

I murmured something.

He went on: "Somehow, when I found myself facing a sudden howling wind that stirred piles of old bones—it reminded me of this.

Of the last time I, Apollo, saw Olympus—that was many years before Jeremy Redthorn was born. Oh, many years indeed."

But I paid little attention to what sounded like an old man's reminiscences, coming from the lips of a beardless youth. Instead I was caught up in trying to discover more marvels somewhere on the dusty, barren, flattened hilltop where we were now. Alas, that effort was doomed to disappointment.

Evidence of one kind and another, visible to us on every hand— broken glass and tile, shreds of what might once have been fine cloth—suggested that the site once known as Olympus had been raided, perhaps occupied for a long time, one way or another ruthlessly despoiled by Giants. Apollo told me that for years all the gods and goddesses had been afraid to show their faces there. And then, what was worse, almost all of them had totally forgotten.

I shuddered faintly, inwardly. For the moment, Jeremy Redthorn seemed to have disappeared, and it was the Sun God, the Far-Worker, who walked with me around the blasted mountaintop. But he was still a mentally crippled deity. As we progressed, he sometimes thought he saw the remnants of familiar landmarks, but in no case could he be really sure.

For a time, Apollo sat on a rock with his face buried in his hands. When he looked up, it was to tell me that before the Giants' first onslaught, this had been a place of surpassing beauty.

"I gathered that much, Lord Apollo, from what you have already said."

He sighed. "Memories are coming back, a little at a time. Do you know anything of that war, Hercules?"

"Nothing, my lord—nothing, Jeremy."

My companion did not seem to be listening, or to care which name I addressed him by. He said softly: "It must be a thousand years. But if I stop now, and close my eyes, I can almost hear the music again . . ."

And to my amazement—though I really should not have been amazed—I saw tears on his young face.

Downed

$\mathcal{My}$ recent adventures had wearied me, in mind more than in body, and left me profoundly confused. In the course of the last few days I had confronted the awesome deity Apollo, had almost incurred his enmity, and then had finally joined forces with him. Together Apollo and I had rescued Prometheus, and then had managed, or at least survived, an encounter with the entity called Atlas. *That* meeting in itself would have been enough to befuddle me. But when it was over I had been privileged to walk beside the Far-Worker as his comrade while he rediscovered and explored the ruins of Olympus.

The two of us left Olympus together, once more riding the chariot, cruising at low altitude behind slow-pacing horses. At first it seemed to me that we had no definite destination.

I could only hope that my experiences since leaving home had begun to teach me something about the world. Certainly they had begun to reveal to me the depth and breadth of my own ignorance. Physical strength could give a great advantage, and sometimes it could be vitally important. But I had begun to realize that it did not guarantee success in any but the crudest trials.

Very little of the knowledge I had gained so recently and with such difficulty was reassuring. In fact, the more I learned about the world, the more I felt that it was on the verge of collapsing around me, and I was not sure what to do next.

Looking back over my shoulder, I cast a last look at the rugged slopes of what had once been high Olympus.

Apollo's mood seemed to mirror my own, a readiness for rest and reflection.

As we were crossing a small stream, he turned the chariot and brought it down for a soft landing on the grassy bank. Getting out, I promptly sat down in the grass, feeling tired in body and mind.

Apollo said he would be back very soon, clucked to his magnificent white horses, and drove away.

The appearance of the surrounding land struck me as restfully neutral. It was less barren than the hills we had just left, but there were no rich crops or lush forests to be seen. The scenery was soothing rather than dramatic, with gentle hills of grazing land and a few trees here and there. Such surroundings were peaceful after the wonders I had just experienced. It seemed an undemanding spot, and I welcomed the opportunity to relax.

I dozed off, but could not have been sleeping for very long when I heard the soft rushing sound of the chariot moving through the air, and opened my eyes to discover that my companion had returned. He brought welcome food and drink, both of a quality worthy of the gods. Then we rested for a time, well out of sight of the place that had been Olympus, and well away from the immediate effects, which had been greater on my companion than they were on me, of our encounter with Atlas.

While resting, Apollo and I compared notes on what we had seen and experienced there.

We came to the conclusion that nothing Atlas had told us had any direct bearing on the outcome of the gods' struggle against the Giants—except possibly we now had evidence confirming our enemies' earthly origins.

When we had reached that point in our discussion, the Far-Worker repeated his advice that I should pay a visit to the laboratory where Daedalus and Hephaestus were working with the materials that I had gathered for them.

"I am ready to do so, Lord Apollo—Jeremy. Where is it?"

He gestured with the piece of fruit that he was eating. "On a secret island, far to the north of here. Let us rest a little, and we'll go. They will certainly want to hear everything we can tell them about Prometheus and the strange encounter we had with Atlas. I don't doubt they'll have many questions to ask. Anyway, I have an urge to see the very latest achievements of the wizards on their island."

When we had finished our repast, the Far-Worker leaped into his car and grabbed the reins. He gestured to me, and I climbed aboard.

*   *   *

Once more the earth swiftly fell away beneath us. As we flew, my escort told me that the two wizards of technology, one divine and one human, were anxious to talk to me as soon as possible.

"Daedalus will want to know whether you managed to gather any new samples while you were having your encounter with Atlas."

"I would as soon have tried to take a sample of some god's hide as to dig into that little pillar. I consider myself lucky to have come away from that meeting with my life. All I gained was—the experience."

"That can be the most valuable prize of all."

My companion told me that my mentors yearned more than ever to fathom the mysteries of the enemy's weapon that robbed gods of their memories.

"I would not be surprised if Atlas was equipped with even more marvelous weapons than that," I told him. "But I saw nothing of any of them."

The god and I continued our discussion as the chariot carried us along.

We were flying over land, just above a patchy layer of thin clouds, and the god who was transporting me was talking to me about something when he was cut off abruptly in midsentence.

The chariot swerved suddenly, and I had the impression that some gigantic, invisible hand had swiped at us, almost knocking us out of the sky—for a moment I did not understand that the only real impact we had suffered came from some Giant's magic weapon, which was felt in Apollo's mind, and from there transmitted through his hands and the reins to his great white horses.

I thought that Apollo was able to recognize our attacker, for he cried out a name: "Alkyoneus!"

Even as we lurched about in midair, my eye fell on a towering figure that stood on a hilltop hundreds of feet below us. It was a Giant, both arms raised, fingers extended and pointing straight at us. This was Antaeus writ large, the tufted hair, blank eyes, and grainy skin, equal to the worst my imagination might have done. I stared at a figure of the same almost-human shape as the Giant I had killed, standing among trees as if they were small bushes, kilted in what seemed a patchwork sail of animal skins, but enlarged, engorged, to what appeared in my shocked eyes as a height of perhaps a hundred feet.

In a moment the weapon struck again, an invisible club whose impact seemed to be felt only in my companion's brain. Nothing happened to affect the chariot directly, nor the wondrous animals who bore it after them, nor even me, the helpless passenger. But this time the blow to the god's memory was severe enough to make him lose all control. His hands jerked awkwardly at the reins, as if he had no idea of what he ought to do with them.

My escort was now clinging to the rail as desperately as I was. Apollo turned a strangely distorted countenance in my direction and was looking at me wildly, as if he had never seen me before. As if he did not know who I was, what we might be doing together, or where we were going.

I grabbed him by the arm and tried to shake him, but it was like gripping a marble statue.

In the next few moments it became plain that he had utterly lost control over his chariot. It seemed that he could only stare stupidly as the ground came rushing up at us.

As in my battle with Antaeus, I was not directly affected by the weapon, or curse, or whatever the right name was for the thing that struck at us. But now it seemed quite possible that I was going to die anyway.

As we spiraled lower, I was able to get one last clear look at the man-mountain who had shot us down. His great, slab-sided, rock-grained face was as blank in triumph as I supposed it would have been in defeat.

Now we were so close above the treetops that from time to time the chariot's wheels tore at a branch. My last glimpse of the Giant showed him walking, his huge body moving with surprising quickness, as he attempted to get in one more invisible shot. I had the impression that he was uncertain of his aim, and I could only hope that this time he would miss.

Looking at the form beside me, I saw to my horror that my god-pilot had temporarily lost consciousness. I again tried to rouse him, but failed.

The magic team that pulled the chariot still retained their full strength. But the injury to their great master had upset them, thrown them into a panic. We were flying low now, barely skimming the tree-tops, and still performing wild gyrations.

I grasped the reins and tried to exert control. I shouted commands at the backs of the great plunging beasts that pulled us through the air, but the animals ignored me. I might have pulled harder, but feared that if I did so, I was going to break their necks.

In seizing the reins, I had released my two-handed grip upon the railing. As the chariot swayed back and forth, scraping tall branches in a wild ride, a sharp turn suddenly hurled me out over the side. At the last moment I grabbed desperately for something solid, but the whole equipage was already far out of my reach.

My body was as helpless as a falling doll, but fortunately some-what tougher. Shielding my face with my hands, I crashed violently through a screen of branches, then bounced off a trunk to hit the ground. Any normal human would almost certainly have been killed by the successive impacts, but I suffered no serious damage and a moment later was getting to my feet, feeling only a few sore spots.

Trees stood close to me on every side, the branches of the nearest showing new white wood, splintered by the shock of my fall. The forest had swallowed me up. Flocks of disturbed birds were racketing around over the treetops; but attacking Giant, wounded god, and speeding chariot were all out of sight and sound. As far as I could tell from where I lay, they might never have existed.

And on top of all my other problems, my club was gone. Either it had remained in the chariot, and so was possibly many miles away by now, or it had been thrown out and there was no telling where it had come down—in either case, there was little hope of finding one small log in a dense forest, and I was going to have to do without it. Partly to settle my nerves, and partly because I did not know what else to do, I began to make myself a new one.

Finding a sturdy trunk of suitable wood took some time, and so did shaping it to the right size, using only my bare hands; but when it was done I had regained a measure of control over my destiny.

Now I thought it was time to reconnoiter. On a slight rise in the forest I found a promising-looking tree and climbed it to scan the sky and the horizon for signs of Apollo and his chariot—or for the Giant, who I swore would suffer grievously for his ambush if I could catch up with him. But nothing was visible but trees and more trees. After the high-speed flight and its sudden unplanned ending, I really had no idea where in the world I was.

My first act, on finding myself in this situation, was an amateur's attempt at magic, trying to summon *Skyboat* to me. I closed my eyes and concentrated fervently on the vessel as I had seen it last, in a place that must now be many miles away.

I had no reason to believe that I was anywhere near a river, or the sea. Even if *Skyboat* responded to my call, there was no reason to believe that I would see the vessel again for many days. I was going to have to find my way on foot out of this trackless forest.

I also tried to imagine the humming presence of the invisible sprite, and call it to me that I might employ it as a messenger; but I was unpracticed in all matters of magic and could not be sure I had succeeded.

The only map of the world that I could visualize was, I feared, too woefully inaccurate to be of any use. My travels, since that distant day when I was sent out to herd cattle, had already convinced me that my early tutors had taught me practically nothing about real geography, especially with regard to those parts of the world that lay at any substantial distance from Cadmia.

It would obviously be hopeless for me to press on and try to reach Vulcan's secret laboratory, as I had not the least idea where it was. Even in my confusion, it was obvious that regaining my homeland, or even Corycus, would entail another long journey, and something of a weary one, as it seemed likely I would be compelled to do it all on foot.

After several days of almost aimless wandering, during which I saw few people, had little to eat, and gained no clear idea of where I was, I found myself crossing a small stream, which as it turned out represented a border between kingdoms. As I waded out of the stream and on the eastern side, I found myself confronted by a warning sign. The message, in several languages, was carved into a broad wooden panel, which in turn had been nailed conspicuously to a tree.

KNOW BY THESE PRESENTS
THAT ALL MEN ARE FORBIDDEN ENTRY HERE
by order of
HER ROYAL MAJESTY MOCTOD
QUEEN OF THE AMAZONS

This suggested rather forcefully that I ought to consider turning back. But over the last few days I had come to believe, though my grounds for doing so were not very strong, that the Great Sea lay in the direction I had been walking, and that my *Skyboat* might very well be cruising through it even now, drawing closer to me at every moment. If that was indeed the case, swift transportation might be awaiting me only a few miles deep in Amazon territory, along the coast, or up a river.

The sign confirmed what legend had long held, that the Amazons did not much care especially for men, except as occasional partners in sex or commerce. But still I dared to hope that a lone traveler, unarmed and hungry, might be charitably received.

Of course I could hardly be considered unarmed as long as I was carrying my huge new club. But I had invested some time and effort in its making, and I decided to wait at least until I was challenged before throwing it away.

So I boldly crossed the river, and shortly after met a lone woman, rather elderly, gathering firewood. When I asked directions, she told me I had now entered a land called Themiscyra, on the river Thermodon, and if I followed the river downstream I would come in a few days to a good-sized city. While telling me these things my informant stared at me as if she had never seen a man before. Perhaps she was intimidated by the sight of my huge weapon; in any case, she made no objection to my presence.

Taking the downstream path, on the theory that it must lead me eventually to sea, I soon encountered a shrine to Diana, standing at the next river ford. This gave me strong confirmation that I was really in the land of the Amazons.

I had long known, in a vague way, as everyone did, that the Amazons were worshipers of Artemis. (That goddess, as everyone knew, was generally identified with Diana, traditionally thought to be the twin sister of Apollo. Legend called her a virgin huntress who carried Arrows and a Spear, was of a vindictive nature, and enjoyed a close association with the Moon.) If I could get the backing of Artemis/Diana, in some convincing way, then the warrior ladies ought to be cooperative.

It was true that most humans lived their entire lives without ever encountering a god. But since beginning my wanderings, I had personally met several, and so far had had good results. So perhaps it was not strange that I began to nurse hopes of somehow confronting the goddess Diana, in this the land of her worshipers, and then making her my friend by claiming acquaintance with her twin brother.

Somehow, in this later time when I am writing, certain legends have twisted the facts around to say that my trip to the country of the Amazons was a deliberate foray, undertaken to capture the girdle of their queen.

I find it hard to understand how my obtaining this garment would have inconvenienced the Giants, mighty enemies of the gods, in any way. And now, as long as the subject has come up, it strikes me that this might be the time to review the whole business of my supposed Twelve labors. These are tasks which are often said to have been imposed on me—the gods alone know why—by King Eurystheus. The list is given differently in different sources, but the following sequence is widely accepted.

1. Slaying the Nemean lion, whose skin I was supposed to have worn ever afterward. I feel I have already discussed this at sufficient length.
2. Slaying the nine-headed Hydra of Lerna. I have said how this came about, and how, because there were credible witnesses, my fame began to grow.

3. Capturing of the Hind (in some accounts the Stag) of Arcadia. Purely fictional. In this case, legend, unadulterated by any facts at all, provided this stag with antlers of gold and hooves of brass, and sent me chasing it for a full year in a determined effort to bring it back alive.

4. The wild Boar of Mount Erymanthus. In this tale, as in the next item on the list, there was a good deal of truth.

5. Cleansing the Augean stables.

6. Shooting the monstrous man-eating birds of the Stymphalian marshes. The second purely imaginary adventure in the list. The story may have been based on a dream I once endured, though how the stuff of private dreams could be transmitted into legend is more than I can fathom, unless someone with the talents of Prince Asterion might have been responsible.

7. Capturing of a mad bull that had terrorized Corycus. A very twisted transformation of my activities in cooperation with the prince.

8. Ditto the man-eating mares of King Diomedes of the Bistones. Some authorities on my career omit this tale altogether, as well they might. I believe Enkidu in his own memoirs classifies it, correctly, as mere legend. Certainly unnaturally carnivorous horses (possibly something to do with centaurs) were supposed to be the property of the Thracian king, Diomedes. And I, in an effort to inflict condign punishment, fed the mares Diomedes himself.

9. Seizing the girdle of Hyppolyte, queen of the Amazons. Most sources even name the wrong queen here. I am shortly going to introduce Her Majesty Moctod into my narrative; let me only add here, parenthetically, that the gods never really favored the idea of my marrying and settling down—I was too useful to them as a footloose adventurer. On the other hand, the Titans would probably have supported my adopting a sedentary lifestyle, had they been consulted.

10. Seizing the cattle of the three-bodied (alternately, three-headed) Giant named Geryon, supposed to live in the island of Erythia, somewhere in the remote west. On my way to pillage Geryon of his cows, I supposedly strangled one Cacus, a three-headed shepherd who puffed flames and lived in a cave decorated with the bones of his victims. A number of factual events seem to be confabulated in this adventure, along with some creditably artistic lies; disentangling them would take more time than I am willing to devote to the subject.

11. Bringing back (I think to King Eurytheus) the Golden Apples kept at the world's end by the three sisters called Hesperides. We have already seen something of the real Apples, and will see more. I think this needs no further comment from me, except that the king in his bronze box would not have had the faintest idea what to do with them.

12. Fetching up Cerberus from the Underworld. We will soon come to the basis of this tale.

It was said of Queen Moctod and her followers that they kept a few men around as servants; that at designated times they sought out strangers and lay with them to accomplish the reproduction of their race. Boy babies resulting from these unions would be sacrificed, or given for adoption to neighboring tribes. Each young girl suffered the amputation of one breast—generally the left, presumably in early childhood—to facilitate the use of the bow.

An alternate version was that every girl was required to kill a man before she was allowed to take a husband. My own thought was that women meeting this qualification might soon face a real shortage of prospective bridegrooms.

Early on in my visit to the Amazons' country, I observed some evidence that other male adventurers had recently intruded in this space presumably reserved for women only, and even that some of my own sex were still on the scene.

One distant figure, dark-bearded and almost breastless, labored in a field, guiding a plow pulled by a cameloid. Almost certainly a man, I thought, but very possibly a slave.

The only children to be seen were girls. If there were any pregnant warriors about, they seemed to be making an effort not to appear in public.

Evidence of a more recent intrusion could be seen in the occasional glimpses I had of wounded women warriors, limping, or nursing the stumps of missing arms or legs; and once I saw in the distance what appeared to be a funeral, but whether the death might have been a result of recent combat I had no way to tell.

Again, I once glimpsed on a stout limb of a distant tree three dead bodies, hanging by their necks. Whether men or women I could not distinguish at the distance, but they might have been three pirates when they walked and breathed.

It seemed to me distinctly possible that the rule against men, like many other rules in many other lands, was not strictly enforced, and as I have mentioned, some adult males, probably slaves, were in fact to be seen. Also I could imagine exceptions being made for merchants or skilled workers.

There were also the charred remnants of some ship to be seen, along a muddy riverbank, and the painted symbol still visible on certain planks suggested it had been a pirate vessel. This was of course encouraging in that it suggested I was somewhat closer to the sea than I had thought.

The weather was mild, and sleeping out of doors posed no problem to an experienced traveler. Water was plentifully available, but food was another matter, and before long I was ravenously hungry.

Almost the only people I saw anywhere, at least for the first several days, were women, who did (or at least officially claimed to do) all the heavy work of farming and hunting. Of course it was hardly unknown in my own land, or any other, that females should perform these tasks, but it was strange to see no men at all. An ignorant stranger, coming on the scene, might have supposed that the entire male population had been wiped out in some war. Which, when I thought about it, seemed possibly the truth.

*   *   *

Not until I had been several days in the territory of the Amazons was I challenged by an armed patrol—and I was lacking any *Skyboat* in which to flee from them.

I was facing in the other direction when I heard a shrill voice call: "Over here, girls. Looks like another of that damned gang of pirates."

Other voices responded, and there was a general trampling and crashing in the underbrush. Presently nine sturdy figures came into view to stand with weapons ready, gazing at my solitary figure.

"You're right. I thought we'd seen the last of 'em, but here's another."

All of the women confronting me were young, vigorous, and well armed. They wore a kind of uniform consisting of short skirts and sandals, and each was bound across her upper body with a kind of sash that covered the right breast, passing also across a flattened area that showed the left had been removed.

Unhappily I considered the one-breasted warriors and their spears and arrows. They all looked lithe and agile, and I doubted very much that I would be able to outrun the slowest of them. Most carried bows, and each had a short shield, shaped like a half-moon and dabbed with gilt paint, as well as a sword. The fact that I had dropped my club voluntarily kept them from trying to cut me down at once. Meanwhile I thought I might be able to retrieve the weapon later, and that the lack would mean no more than an inconvenience.

The patrol commander barked again: "One more damned pirate. We know how to deal with your kind!"

"I hope so, ma'am," I assured her. "But I have my doubts."

When I thought about it, I could hardly blame them for their mistake. If I was not a pirate, where was the ship that had brought me across the sea? Anyway, I looked more like a pirate than a merchant. I did not attempt to disabuse them of this notion, calculating that there was no chance they might believe the truth.

As you might expect, I prepared to strongly resist any attempt to take my life. It was my evident readiness to face their several blades that gave them pause, I think.

Raising both hands in what I hoped would be interpreted as a peaceful gesture, I said: "I consent to be your prisoner."

"You do? How noble of you!"

"If I am your prisoner, then it would seem that you ought to feed me."

"We should hang him right away!" The second in command decided briskly. I gathered that was what had happened to the last straggling pirate to be discovered.

They bound my hands at first, of course, and I allowed this on the theory that it might be easier to talk to them if they believed me to be quite helpless—alas, they paid no more attention to my peaceful protestations after my hands were trussed up than before.

Then they hoisted me up to sit on the back of a phlegmatic cameloid they were using as a pack animal, tossed a rope over an overhanging limb, and soon had a noose around my neck.

But of course, when they drove the cameloid out from under me they were disappointed with the result. There I was, hanging in midair as they intended, but a slight tensing of my neck muscles enabled me to keep on breathing easily enough and even to carry on my argument as to why they should let me pass freely through their territory. Not that the women were listening. But presently they cut me down, and were recoiling the rope in preparation for starting over when a superior officer arrived on the scene.

While this officer was receiving the report of the patrol leader, I renewed my worries about what might have happened to Apollo. But I could not be sure that the flying chariot had crashed, or where it might have come down. Possibly a hundred miles away.

Actually my hopes of being able to summon the *Skyboat* had grown somewhat brighter. It was encouraging news that some pirate ship had evidently been able to make it within a few miles of this spot, and gave me reason to hope that my little craft could approach even closer. Once *Skyboat* was positioned as near me as the sprite could bring it, it could lie there in its mode of concealment until the sprite found me again and guided me to my means of escape. But how much time must pass before the magic vessel might be able to accomplish this approach I could not guess.

*   *   *

And only now, for the first time, did they search me thoroughly, without finding additional weapons, or anything that might qualify as stolen treasure.

The officer now in charge made a sound of disgust at the failure to discover anything incriminating. "I'd say you threw away the tools of your trade as soon as you saw you were about to be caught. But it won't do you any good."

After a short discussion among the leaders, they agreed to keep me alive until their queen had had a chance to question me.

There was some discussion of binding and dragging me, but I saw no reason to put up with that, and laid hold of a stout tree trunk, this one rooted firmly in the soil, and would not be persuaded to let it go. Blows with fists and blunt instruments failed to make me change my mind.

One had her sword poised above my wrists when the officer ordered: "Don't hack him! It'll be easier to deliver him to the queen if he's all in one piece."

The fact that my would-be captors were all women was not what kept me from more violent resistance, but rather it was my reluctance to be drawn into a full-scale battle with any nation. Surely that would have to be a losing proposition for me in the end.

After several minutes of fruitless effort, their complete inability to pry me loose began to convince some of my captors—if that was indeed their status—that I was a god.

I got the impression that male gods would not be welcome in this land, any more than mortal men.

One stood back panting. "If he is a god, why doesn't he say so?" she demanded of her comrades.

"Just bring me to your queen," I kept on patiently repeating.

"Shut up! I'll cut off your head first, and bring her that!"

"You won't cut my head off. You can't. And if you could, I'd insult your queen by refusing to answer any of her questions."

Some took me for a madman, and some for a god, and others were quite ready to make an all-out effort to kill me first and then decide into which category I might fit best.

Again the possibility of real fighting loomed. One or two women I might have overpowered harmlessly, just as I had Hector the Trojan. But someone would be sure to get hurt in a general onslaught, with weapons waving and thrusting in every direction.

Eventually their contemptuous abuse began to make me angry. I said: "I have not killed women before, but I imagine you will die as easily as men." And I loudly regretted the fact that I had thrown away my club.

When they gave up trying to tear me loose from the tree, I let go of it and stood there flexing my arms and fingers, which were somewhat cramped, waiting to see what approach their commanding officer decided to try next. Fortunately she proved willing to be reasonable.

TWENTY

Amazons

soon reached the conclusion that the lands ruled by Queen Moctod could not be very large. When we reached the capital city of the women, I thought it surprisingly small, and the royal palace little more than a middle-sized fort. Fortunately word of my capture had already reached the queen, and she was curious to see me. When at last I stood before her, several days after being taken into custody, she looked me up and down, her expression a mixture of contempt and puzzlement. My hands were still unbound, and no doubt she found this odd. Meanwhile, the women who had brought me in were telling her that I was more impressive than I looked, but still the queen, naturally enough, failed to understand.

Having evidently just come from the practice field—or, I thought, perhaps from punishing some other band of pirates—she who faced me now was fully armed with a steel sword, a shield of bronze and wood and leather, and a helmet of fine workmanship. Not as hard, I was sure, as some of the fine helms I had seen, first on Amphitryon and on a number of others since, forged of black iron; but so beautiful of workmanship that I could see how it might be the superior choice to carry into combat, for the impressive effect that it would have on one's opponent.

The queen's size, her evident strength, and above all her attitude convinced me that she would be more than a match for most of the male warriors I had ever seen.

Moctod wore no binding on her upper body, and where her left breast ought to have been there was only an old, pale scar, so faint and puckered that I could well believe it resulted from a wound made in infancy. Her right breast was full and firm.

"Why did you not tie his hands?" she at last demanded sharply. The queen's voice was strong, in keeping with her appearance.

The patrol leader cleared her throat. "He made a lot of fuss when we tried that, Majesty. Whereas if we left him unbound, he was willing to walk along with us. . . ."

"Your prisoner 'made a fuss,' you say? So you asked him politely to walk along?"

My old antagonist seemed to wilt. Almost I was able to feel sorry for her. She said: "Actually we had to fight a sort of skirmish with him, ma'am."

"Almost a dozen of you, and he made it a fight? I don't think it could have been much of a skirmish, as none of you seems to have been wounded in the process."

The junior officer raised her hands and let them fall, a helpless gesture. "Ma'am, he is . . . very strong."

The queen raised her eyebrows and let them fall, as if to say that she was accustomed to having a lot of strange problems brought before her—that was all part of the job—and she felt quite capable of dealing with this situation, as she had with all the others.

"'Very strong,'" she repeated the words under her breath, as if trying them as an incantation. Then Moctod looked at me and made an imperious gesture with one finger. "Come stand before me, outlander," she ordered. "What is your name?"

I did as I was bidden. "I am Hercules, Your Majesty. Hercules of Cadmia."

And I saw at once that my name meant nothing to the queen; celebrity was not going to be my problem in this country.

Moctod, now focusing an intense, blue-eyed gaze on me from under her steel helm, was an inch or two taller than I. People usually view extra height as conferring some kind of an advantage. I often do not take that viewpoint seriously.

The queen said: "You seem to have impressed my soldiers as a mighty fighter. They say you were carrying a club. Did you knock their swords out of their hands with it, or what?"

One of the fighting women was now carrying my improvised bludgeon over her strong right shoulder.

I shook my head. "Majesty, I voluntarily threw my club away when I encountered your patrol. At first I was even willing for my hands to be bound. I claim no skill at all in combat. I have never practiced with the sword, or even clubbed another human being."

"But you *are* very strong."

"Oh yes, ma'am, that is true enough."

The queen nodded slowly. "One of you loan him a sword and shield. I want to see a demonstration of this strength that so impressed my fighting women." And she drew her sword. "Do you think you are strong enough, Hercules, to keep me from killing you?"

"I am not afraid of being killed, Your Majesty."

And the queen, her voice sharpening, said: "Then perhaps you should learn a little fear. Just because it has not happened to you yet, you seem to think that it cannot. Let me tell you, men as a rule die very easily. I have proved that to my own satisfaction often enough."

There was a murmuring among the elder women who served as the queen's counselors; evidently my seeming bravery had already made something of an impression upon them.

Experience had convinced me that usually the fastest way to get past the difficulty of an unwelcome fight, or proposed test, was to appear ready, and even eager, to go through with it. Leaving the offered shield where it lay on the ground, I bent and picked up the sword, running my gaze over it as I did so, just as if I knew what I ought to be looking for. The blade looked keen and true, and I suppose it might have been as well made as the queen's own weapon. Then I stepped back and nodded to the queen, signifying that I was ready.

My opponent was angry now, of course; insulted that I had scorned to take the shield. But she was too experienced a warrior to take even the most unlikely-looking opponent for granted. She approached cautiously, circling first right, then left. The sword in her hand made feinting movements that I suppose were meant to provoke certain reactions in a trained fighter, but of course they were entirely wasted on my ignorance.

I was not minded to prolong the farce. Let her defend herself, I thought. Doing my best to convince without killing (which certainly would not have made my situation any easier), I struck with an overhand swing, applying what I hoped was a nicely calculated amount of force.

The queen had no need to move her half-moon shield, and caught the stroke on it quite neatly. But the impact, of course, was far beyond anything she had been expecting, or could possibly have been ready to withstand. Her shield, of tough leather bound with bronze, was cut nearly in half, the arm that held it dislocated at the shoulder, and any counterblow was rendered totally impossible. Her balance broken in an instant, the Amazon went staggering back to hit the ground in an ignominious fall. My borrowed sword had broken, the blade staying pinched in the ruined shield, while most of the handle remained in my hand.

A cry of shock and outrage went up from the watching circle. The ring of watching warriors first drew back, then raised their weapons and would have assaulted me en masse—but the queen, still on the ground, raised her voice and stopped them.

When the Amazon elders saw the strength of my sword arm, even those who had earlier favored killing me now entirely abandoned the idea—not, I think, out of fear, or serious doubt that they would be able to accomplish the job, but because I had suddenly become greatly desirable as the father of some of the next generation of female warriors. Now I understood what all the talk of testing had been about.

A babble of discussion rose up, then quieted almost at once. They were now universally agreed that I should be invited, or if necessary compelled, to stay on as an honored guest until I had impregnated at least several dozen women—what might be done with me after that still seemed an open question.

The queen, like any other serious warrior, was angry at having been bested. A physician had to be called to pop her dislocated joint back into place. But she bore the pain stoically, suppressed her personal feelings, and went along with what her people wanted.

It was up to Moctod to put the matter to me officially: "We invite you, Hercules of Cadmia, to live with us for a year, and in that time to get as many of us as possible with child."

I muttered some kind of a response, which was probably not as gracious as it could have been. Many young men would have wholeheartedly accepted such an offer on the spot, and indeed I felt tempted; but as matters stood, I had to be about my father's business. Still, an outright refusal would only have made my task more difficult. First of all, I wanted sleep and food.

But what response I made did not much matter, for no one was really listening. It was taken for granted that I was going to consent, whether I agreed or not. My new hosts pointed out a kind of villa, a large house with stuccoed walls and a peaked roof, built against a hillside, which they said would house me for the duration of my stay. Wearily I made my way in that direction. I was vaguely surprised, and amused, to see that now I was apparently going to be left unguarded. Either they could not imagine a man wanting to escape from confinement on such terms, or they could not imagine one succeeding.

As I approached the villa set against the hill, I heard, somewhere inside the house, a deep voice singing. I could only hope that its owner was not one of the women I was expected to impregnate.

A short, sturdy, rather ugly servant girl came to meet me at the door, then stood back, gaping in surprise at the sight of an unfettered man. A shrine to Diana, only a little smaller than the one beside the border road, occupied most of the entryway of the house.

Investigating a little further, I discovered the singer and was relieved of my latest worry. He was wrapped in a silken robe and relaxing on a pile of pillows, and courteously enough he stood up to say hello. He was a handsome man, too youthful for any gray to have come into his fair hair and beard, though sun and wind had started to carve lines in his face. He was tall enough to tower over the servant girl and me. Had he introduced himself as a god, many would have taken him at his word without an argument; but in fact he said that he was Theseus, and acknowledged that he had come to the land of the Amazons as leader of a pirate expedition that had proved a trifle too ambitious.

"I've heard your name," I offered. I did not doubt this introduction for a moment; this, indeed, was how the famous Theseus ought to look.

"Most people have." He smiled faintly. "I trust you heard nothing too good associated with it."

"You can feel at ease about that. Nothing in your record as it was told to me would make me envious. Mainly tales of piracy."

Theseus laughed at that and seemed well satisfied that it should be so. He, too, as it turned out, had been invited to stay among the Amazons, for the same reason as myself. He said he had been on the job a month and thought he was already well along in his task of siring a new generation of warriors. When I asked what had happened to his men, his face darkened, and he did not reply at once. It seemed to me that it would be unwise to pursue the subject, and I let it drop.

Theseus was obviously wondering why *I* had been recruited for the stud farm. Nor did it take him long to put the question plainly. He squinted at me thoughtfully, looked me up and down, and scratched his bearded chin. "I wonder why they gave you such a special invitation, sprout?"

I smiled faintly and stuck out my hand. "Try a turn of arm wrestling?"

He looked at me in some surprise, then shrugged. "Don't mind if I do."

Several turns were necessary, the result of the first being put down to some kind of unmanly magic or trickery. It was even necessary to squeeze his hand a little to finally make my point. But once it had been made, Theseus accepted it philosophically.

Ten minutes later, the two of us were sitting side by side on a comfortable couch in the main room of the guest house, sipping cool drinks brought by the servant girl (yes, said my new colleague, she was one of those selected for breeding purposes; he supposed one of us would get around to her, in time) and having a peaceable discussion.

"Understand, Hercules, that in the first place, these women are not, on the average, anywhere near my ideal of feminine beauty. I've seen one or two, here and there . . . and one in particular . . . but the ones they keep sending to my bed to be plowed and planted aren't. In the second place, whatever other merits some of these girls might have, it grows monotonous when a man finds only half the usual number of breasts available for his enjoyment." Unconsciously he had begun massaging his own right hand, the one that I had squeezed.

"I understand," I said. To me also it had seemed likely that the largest and strongest Amazons, rather than the most attractive, would be selected for our attentions. Vaguely I wondered whether there would be many eager volunteers. And of course politics would play some part, as it always seemed to do.

I went on: "I, too, find the prospect of a long stay in these parts not all that alluring."

It turned out that Theseus, too, had fought a duel with the queen. He complained that it was never in actual combat that he lost out, but in the complications that arose when people were trying to make peace.

"I'll admit it to you, Hercules—I had a long struggle, trying to put her down without doing her any serious harm. Of course I managed it in the end, but I have no doubt that in a fair fight, one on one, she'd kill nine out of ten of my men; and my men are—were—hardly milksops. Maybe even nineteen out of twenty."

From the moment that Theseus had spoken his name to me, I had been ready to dislike him, knowing his ill repute for vile deeds as a pirate—there was no doubt that in his case it was justly earned. Another reason to feel aversion for him, if any were needed, was that in appearance, Theseus was everything I would have liked to be, tall and handsome with bulging muscles and graceful movements—sort of a blond, sun-bleached Jason. I could well imagine that the new warriors he sired for the queen would match the very Amazon ideal.

But at the same time, he gained my respect by refusing to either be afraid of me or fawn on me, even after he felt my strength. In this he was unlike those so-called heroes of the Argosy, or at least that faction among them who had resorted to base trickery to get me off the ship.

Another matter that Theseus and I discussed was to what extent we were really prisoners. As far as he could see, he told me, the house was completely unguarded, and no one followed him when he walked out of it and strolled about. No specific rules had been spelled out to either of us, but we were both certain that any attempt on our part to leave would have been strongly discouraged.

Our peaceable conversation was soon interrupted by another young woman, whose name, as I soon learned, was Antiope—she was the "one in particular" he had mentioned earlier. Antiope had originally been one of the pirate's assigned bed partners (and, according to my taste, much better-looking than the average of them) who, while playing her assigned role, had fallen desperately in love with the handsome intruder. She was obviously quite willing to be abducted by him.

When he caught sight of her looking in at us, he called: "Come in, sweet one. This is Hercules, he's just arrived."

My name meant no more to Antiope than it had to Moctod. She

looked from one of us to the other, and appeared pleased. "I see that you are friends," she commented.

"We're working at it, honey," said Theseus, and kissed her.

Antiope adopted a friendly attitude toward me as soon as it became apparent that I posed no threat to her beloved. And when Theseus strongly hinted that I was not to consider her as one of my own clients in our joint fertility program, I assured him that I would take no girl or woman to my bed who was unwilling to be there.

With these points settled, the three of us conversed as friends. I found myself rather liking Antiope and silently hoping that the man she now adored would not desert her, if the pair of them did succeed in getting away to the great world.

Theseus talked for a while about what might happen to any of his crew who still survived, if he escaped on his own. But it seemed practically certain they were all dead.

I am not sure how many warriors I actually fathered for Moctod, but quite possibly there were several. However, the number cannot be vast.

Not many days after my arrival, the sprite whose arrival I had been hoping for came in secret to me at night, making its presence known when I was alone in bed. The creature seemed as incapable of speech as ever, but I took its cheerful buzzing to mean that the *Skyboat* was conveniently nearby—or at least as near as it was going to get by water—and that the sprite would somehow guide me to it when I was ready.

I told Theseus nothing of this visitor but, when the two of us were alone, let him understand that I had some magical reason to believe the time had come.

No doubt it was my strength that made him consider me trustworthy. He and I made our getaway from the Amazons in a cooperative effort.

He began to outline a plan that would have involved killing to get our hands on a boat, but I strongly urged that we do no harm, if we could avoid it, to any of the women—I reminded my colleague that there was no point in offending Diana unnecessarily by injuring her worshipers. I also let my companion know I had reason to believe that we would find a boat available.

With these facts in mind, my nonviolent method was adopted. Rising from our respective beds in the middle of the night, we joined Antiope, who had made her own way to the rendezvous and was waiting for us with provisions. The three of us then headed into the hills, in the direction of the nearest stream that was big enough to carry a small boat. If anyone had seen us, Antiope would have played the role of slave master, conducting two docile males to some new farmland where there were plows for them to pull.

To my great relief, my sprite had materialized again on cue and kept buzzing invisibly in my ear, so softly that no one else was aware of the inhuman presence. Naturally Theseus was curious as to how I could know that a boat would be waiting in a certain place. But he was ever ready to take a chance.

As we trod our way as silently as possible through the moonlit woods, I thought Antiope was quietly but almost hysterically happy at the thought of having her lover to herself, away from all those other women, for as many days and nights as the two of them might choose. I thought her a lovely creature, even if she had only one breast. And she had fallen desperately in love with Theseus and was eager to get away. Again, I hoped that he would treat her kindly.

I have no doubt that had Theseus still possessed even a remnant of a crew, he would have considered it essential to his honor, and to his reputation as a commander, to recapture his ship somehow. He would also have made a valiant effort, at least, to get his crew out of captivity and take them along. But as matters stood, he had only himself to look out for.

Gray dawn was lightening the sky when we reached the bank of a small river. "There she is," I said, and pointed.

When Theseus got his first look at the *Skyboat,* I let him think that it was the means by which I had come traveling to Amazon country. Not that the question of my mode of travel, of no immediate practical value, concerned him much.

At the first sight of the little craft, he had no high opinion of it—but when we three climbed aboard and it began to move, even before we had so much as touched a sail or oar, that was a different matter.

The way we went skipping and darting down small streams, even harmlessly through rapids, to plunge triumphantly into the sea at last, soon convinced the master pirate that there was more to this mode of transportation than at first met the eye.

For once Theseus was almost at a loss for speech. But finally he said: "I swear, Hercules. Ordinarily, I'd be sorely tempted to take a boat like this one away from its owner, whoever that might be. But I'll make an exception in your case." He showed white teeth in a smile. "Of course one reason, though not the only one, is that you'd break most of my bones if I tried anything like that." And he threw back his head and laughed with an infectious joy.

"I can show you another reason, too," I said. "Take the helm for a moment; give it a try."

Impressive as was the outward appearance of our compass-pyx, the experienced captain soon discovered that our vessel was no better than a small and barely seaworthy rowboat when it came under his command. The box of ivory and ebony lay inert against his forehead. Only Enkidu besides myself had been entrusted with the power of control, and my nephew, I supposed, was still peacefully at home. Where now I, in truth, fervently wished to be. I had had enough, and more than enough, of adventuring for the time being.

Soon after leaving the land of the Amazons, the pirate king and I separated, still under conditions of mutual respect. I put my pair of passengers ashore on an island of his choosing, on the margin of the Great Sea, from which he seemed supremely confident of being able to make his way to anywhere he wished. And we parted wishing each other success in our respective endeavors.

Antiope gave me a brief wave and then fixed her gaze once more on the man beside her, the one she so adored.

I set my course for home, as well as I was able.

Thanatos

*I*t has been my fate, in common with the great majority of humankind, to meet Death on the surface of the earth. What made my case out of the ordinary was the fact that my first encounter with Thanatos was not my last. As I write these words, I believe that the final confrontation between the two of us is yet to be. I have heard some say that I am now truly immortal, but in human minds and mouths that word has as many meanings as does human life itself.

But let me tell things in their proper order. The first occasion on which I stood face-to-face with Death (I am here using no mere figure of speech) took place some time before I ever managed to force an entry to the Underworld.

When, in the course of my laborious return alone from the realm of the Amazons, I sailed my *Skyboat* along the coast of the land called Pherae, I found that my reputation had somehow preceded me. It was a fair land, displaying many signs of prosperity, and none at all of recent war.

On most of the islands where I stopped, and in the coastal villages, many people recognized my name and stood back from me in awe. But here and there a few were ready to challenge me to a fight, just for the sake of challenge; and some of these, seeing my youth and unimpressive size, and the fact that my body bore no scars, refused to believe I could be the hero who had slain the Hydra, crushed the ribs of mighty Antaeus, and clubbed to death the sea monster that would otherwise have devoured a Trojan princess. Such would-be rivals I usually managed to put off with soft words and a steady gaze, though one or two required a firmer hand. With a sigh I acknowledged the fact that the days when I could wander the earth in carefree anonymity were gone, and would never return, unless I began to travel in disguise.

*   *   *

When the people I spoke to along the way told me that I had reached the realm of King Admetus, my spirits rose. Here I ought to find at least a friendly welcome. Many days ago I had learned, indirectly, by word of mouth from various folk, that I was formally invited to visit King Admetus and his queen, at their court, in a town described as being "below the peak called Chalcodon."

The invitation reached me first when I was in Cadmia, dallying with my new bride, and it had been carried there in a somewhat garbled form. I pondered at the time whether the invitation might be some result of my having saved Hesione from the sea monster, or whether there existed some alliance between these people and the grateful folk at Troy, who might still be trying to find some way to reward me.

The truth, as I discovered later, was somewhat simpler and had little to do with any personal reputation I might have gained: Every member of the original crew of *Argo,* along with their immediate families, was included in the invitation. At least one of Jason's heroes was a native of Pherae.

While I am again on the subject of the Argosy, I should mention that there have been for some years several lists of those names, all differing in detail. Each nation, sometimes it seems each city, puts forward a compilation in which its own representative is prominent. There is inevitably dispute about who joined Jason's crew and when, and who dropped out or died along the way. In some of these rosters, you will find the name of King Admetus himself, which is a mistake.

Imagine, then, my dismay at arriving at the court of Admetus only to find that the whole capital city, if not the entire nation, was in mourning and disarray. The grief the people showed was obviously genuine, and disfigured almost every face. The palace, like many other buildings in the city, was draped in swaths of black, and I entered its precincts to the sound of harsh gongs beaten intermittently. Meanwhile the air, indoors and out, was thick with bitter smoke and a fine drift of ashes from the sacrificial fires.

However, the prospect was not one of unrelieved gloom on my part. I had scarcely arrived when I saw a vision which lifted my thoughts momentarily out of the realm of death and sorrow—Deianeira, the sister of Meleager.

Several other guests happened to be present when I arrived in the torchlit courtyard, and my eyes studying the small group immediately picked out green eyes, straight brown hair, and a slender female body, clad in the finest of translucent linen.

I approached Danni at once, and we exchanged friendly greetings—like all other conversation in the palace, less cheerful than they might have been, because of the funereal atmosphere.

"Is it Fate that brings us together, or only chance?" I asked, when we had gone through the customary forms of speech and handclasps.

But Danni had little interest in such questions. Hardly had she greeted me before she was asking if I could tell her any news of Meleager—naturally she had not seen him since the day I pitched him into the harbor at Iolcus, and she had thought that Mel was still with me and the others on the Argosy.

I expressed my regret that I could not give her any news about her brother. In turn she told me that she had come here to the court of King Admetus in response to the general invitation. She was the only representative of Meleager's family who could make the trip.

"My uncle Augeus was unable to leave home, or so he claimed, and we agreed it would be rude for no one of our family to appear. So, here I am."

"And I am glad you came, and that your uncle stayed home."

I learned that the ship that had brought her to Pherae was in the harbor beside my boat. And I was attracted to her at once, though instead of declaring the fact I told her about my marriage.

When Danni heard that, she mentioned, almost casually, that since our last meeting she had been betrothed, to one of her uncle's neighbors, an arrangement for which her uncle had been responsible. But the elderly neighbor had died before the marriage could be solemnized.

"My condolences," I offered.

There was a flash of something bitter in the green eyes. "You may save them for another time. It was a fortunate escape for me."

"In that case, my congratulations."

Our talk turned to the Argosy again, about which many rumors swirled. I now told Danni the story of how I had become separated from her brother and the rest, and she hoped that Meleager had not been involved in what had amounted to my nephew's kidnapping.

"How unfair of them!" she declared. "Are you much saddened, Hercules, to have been left behind, to have missed all their glorious adventures?"

"I have had little time to think about what adventures they might be having. My own life has not been exactly dull."

After some polite conversation with the other guests, I took Danni aside for a more private talk. At the moment I was less interested in telling her my history than in hearing more of hers.

When we were quite alone, she said to me: "My uncle Augeus is insisting that I move in permanently with him. Everyone says it is unseemly for a young unmarried woman to be maintaining her own household."

"I wouldn't want to live with your uncle," I observed.

"Nor do I, and so far I've managed to put him off. My worst fear is that he will get tired of waiting for Mel to come back, and decide to arrange yet another betrothal for me."

That would be tragic, I thought. But the funereal gloom of the real tragedy with which we were surrounded cut short our discussion of other matters. "What has happened here?" I demanded in a lowered voice, waving my hand to include the courtyard and the palace.

Danni was not yet certain, either. But the question was answered by one of the minor court officials when he realized we did not know. "Woe to us all! Our lovely queen is dead!"

Any coherent information on the cause of death was hard to come by, and details were impossible. Contradictory reports were circulating. Yet the main point was inescapable: The beloved young queen was dead. Tragedy had struck the royal family less than a full day ago, and the news was only now being carried by the outlying portions of the realm. Yet tradition, as inflexible here as in many other places, decreed that an appointment made with foreign visitors must be kept.

When the king at last made his appearance, the look on the face of our royal host was so lost, so doomed, that I could not keep from bursting out: "My lord king—my greatest sympathy!"

Admetus turned his gaze in my direction, but he seemed to be looking through me—not out of rudeness, but in pain. He was young. I suppose no older than his wife had been, and seldom have I seen anyone so nearly bereft of his wits by grief. Now I could see that tears were glistening on his bearded cheeks. It was hard for him to choke out even a few words.

"My wife, my queen—is dead."

We all hastened to offer such condolences as we were able. I said to him again: "Majesty, my heartfelt sympathy! Is there anything I can do to ease your pain?"

But the king could say no more at the moment, and abandoned himself once more to quiet weeping.

The traditional feast of welcome, a form required by rigid local custom, was of course no feast at all. Indeed it was a meal in name only, as a succession of elaborate dishes came to the table and were taken away again untouched by any who sat there. Dancers and musicians there were none, but only the harsh sound of the distant gongs at random intervals.

As soon as custom and courtesy allowed, the king arose, murmured a few indistinguishable words, and retreated to his quarters.

At that the gathering broke up. Moments later, I, too, had risen from my chair. We were told that the king would see us again, later in the evening; meanwhile, we were free to move about the palace.

Having located the room where I was to spend the night, I joined the other guests in wandering, and fell in with Danni and a young girl serving as her attendant.

At any other time, the royal art collection would have made a considerable impression, but now our minds were too absorbed in tragedy. As we traversed a hallway, I was able to see, from two or three rooms away, where the dead body of the beloved queen lay in state, gowned in black on a bier of carven ebony. Around her a circle of armed attendants was standing motionless to form a guard of honor. Her comely face looked marvelously pale against the darkness of cloth and wood. Yet her body did not seem shrunken or wasted, or otherwise damaged in any way that I could see.

The official to whom I had spoken earlier, and a court physician to whom I was also introduced, told me in response to my questions that a strange illness had come upon her very suddenly.

Danni was moved again to tears.

I tried to imagine what it would be like to hear that my own beloved Megan had been seized by death; but I soon shuddered inwardly and gave the effort up.

"What was the nature of Her Majesty's illness?" I inquired when next I saw the court physician, no more than an hour later.

"Nothing contagious," he answered shortly. Somewhere in the background, voices quavered in shrill mourning.

"That was not my concern."

He looked at me again and seemed to relax a little. "It was no disease, good Hercules. Nor was it violence, in the ordinary sense."

The physician paused a moment and looked behind him over his shoulder before continuing in a lower voice. "The truth is that she fell victim to a visit from the God of Death himself."

Still I did not quite understand. "I suppose we all do that, Doctor, sooner or later. But—?"

He was shaking his head. "I am not speaking figuratively. I mean that an avatar of Thanatos was here, within these walls—may still be nearby, for all I know—as an active enemy of our king."

"Ah. The king and the god had some dispute?"

"It is a long story, and a tragic one. Suffice it to say that our good king has made an enemy against whom no mere mortal can have any defense." He shuddered slightly. "I don't know if you can understand. Few people have ever actually confronted any god, face-to-face."

"I have," I said. And from the corner of my eye saw Danni turn her face toward me.

"I see." It seemed that my informant believed my claim, and that had made me rise somewhat in his estimation. "Then perhaps you can understand. But *this* god . . ."

Other people were approaching, and our conversation died away.

* * *

I might have retired early to my room, except for the king's promise that he would see his guests again, later in the evening. As matters fell out, I never learned precisely what was planned, perhaps some ritual of mourning that would have required the presence of us all at midnight. I was standing in a courtyard of the palace, in the presence of the king himself and several others, guests and members of the household, waiting to be told more, when to the surprise of us all, Thanatos actually appeared.

The God of Death manifested himself, bearing in his arms the queen's dead body. He had emerged from one of the dark doorways leading into the far wing of the palace, looking as if he had every right to be where he was—and I am sure it is the same with any home he enters.

I saw before me a human figure, that of a strong man somewhat taller than myself, draped in a long cloak of black and red. An unkempt dark beard rimmed the lower half of a fierce countenance. And there was just a hint, gone again before I could focus my mortal vision on them, of red and ghostly wings sprouting from broad shoulders. And I understood that once more I was looking at a god. At the same time, the figure before me was thoroughly human. In some way, that made it more frightening, but it was not nearly as overwhelming in its presence as Apollo, or even Hermes.

Danni was outraged, and she clenched her small fists. "Ah, gods, this is unbearable!" Her voice was not loud, but in the silence clearly audible. Death seemed to pay it no attention.

In the next moment she had fastened an appealing gaze on me. "Oh, if only we could do something! Ah, if my brother was only here! But no, Mel is only human, as mortal as you and I."

I tried to find some words of comfort, but there were none. Meanwhile, Death was carrying the dead queen easily in his arms. So, it is said, Death conveys all whom he harvests to the Underworld; but we all stared, for none of us had ever seen the like before, and I hope I never see it again.

We all, as I say, were standing as if paralyzed, and Thanatos would almost certainly have borne away his prey unchallenged, had he not chosen to delay. But as he walked across the terrace toward the open garden, his eye fell upon me. It was obvious that he recognized me and was not going to let the occasion pass unmarked.

When I saw the way he looked at me, I wondered why such enmity. Was this avatar of Death perhaps a friend of Hera? A question crossed my mind as to whether the God of Death might have defected to the Giants' side, in hopes of being placed in some position of authority when they had finally broken the power of the Olympians on earth. Or was he simply, cravenly, hoping that the Giants would allow him to survive, when all the other Olympians had been wiped out? I had known for some time that Zeus had enemies among the gods, though I doubted that any of them were going to try to strike at him directly.

On the other hand, I supposed it might be possible that Thanatos really cared little, one way or the other, about what Zeus might think. And that this was simply some feud of his with the local king and had nothing to do directly with the great war on which all of my attention had been focused.

He let the black-draped body of the queen slide casually from his grip, as if it had been no more than a slaughtered sheep or deer. Then the God of Death, keeping his smiling gaze fixed on me, assumed a negligent pose with folded arms and empty hands, leaning against one of the columns supporting the roof of a cloister. It was a gesture of leisurely arrogance that seemed to say he wanted to establish himself in a position from which he could give me his full attention.

A tomblike hush had fallen over the entire courtyard; all was so quiet that I could hear the very faint crackling noise of one of the torches in its wall sconce. But more and more people were gathering, and it seemed that with every heartbeat a new face appeared in one of the windows on the upper level, or on the open side of the courtyard, where terrace sloped and blended gradually into a formal garden.

The god allowed the pause to build dramatically before he finally spoke, in a cracked and grating voice.

"You are Hercules." He seemed to make the mere statement of my name a kind of accusation. Somewhere in the distance, one of the gongs of mourning made its random, crashing sound.

"I am," I replied. About then it crossed my mind to wonder

whether the Death God was perhaps upset that I had slain Antaeus, with whom Thanatos might have formed some kind of alliance.

Thanatos nodded with the air of a judge confirming a verdict; it was as if I had pleaded guilty, and he now prepared to pronounce the appropriate sentence.

"You are a mortal who has grand ideas about himself," the god went on. "I understand that you are trying to find your way to the Underworld?"

Nothing had ever been further from my thoughts. But I had no intention of meekly submitting for Death's approval any itinerary I might decide on. "And if I am?"

"I can arrange swift passage there for you." And Thanatos smiled an evil smile.

My anger was growing rapidly, driving my own fear before it, and I said: "Before I decide whether to accept your invitation, God of Death, there is a question that I wish you would answer for me."

The dark head bowed. An emanation of cold seemed to proceed from the powerful, twisted figure. "Out of courtesy to your father, I allow you to ask it."

"It is this. What kind of human would deliberately put on that Face that you are wearing? What sort of man are you, who wanted to become Death? What kind of—of creature—would pick up that ghastly *thing,* the Face of Death, and press it against his own eyes and nose and mouth, eager to have *that* sink into his brain?"

Even before I had finished speaking, a very faint hushed gasp went up from the still-growing crowd.

My contempt and defiance were harsh and plain in my voice, and Death was almost gaping at me, as if he could hardly believe either his eyes or ears.

I had one more good look at Danni, and even from the corner of my eye I could see that her eyes were wide, whether in fright or exhilaration I could not tell.

Presently my antagonist recovered himself sufficiently to speak. "You do indeed have grand ideas. You think that you are strong, young mortal Hercules. It is time you learned something about real strength." Having got over his moment of shock at my defiance, he was as smug, self-satisfied, and certain as any Linus or any lion had ever been.

After a pause he added: "One touch of my hand and you will die."

"I do not think so," my anger answered him.

"I am a god," the slayer said.

"And I, the son of a far greater god than you."

Death's eyes glittered, and I saw the fingers of his right hand working, as if they hungered to grasp and smother. "That may be so, but your father is not here now to save you. I have seen a thousand sons and daughters of Zeus, and gathered them all in. Whether or not he will think you worth trying to ransom, we will discover. Now come along." And he reached out his hand toward me, the gesture of a parent commanding a reluctant child.

A Brawl with Death

I stepped forward and walked toward Thanatos, not in obedience but with a purpose of my own.

Death abandoned his lounging pose, stood up straight, and fastened his grip upon my left arm. Cold fear struck through me, but I was determined not to yield.

At the moment when Thanatos touched me, I felt a great drain of power and strength, of the very force of life itself. Yet so deep was the reservoir with which Zeus had endowed me that my life stayed in my body, and my body retained its strength. Instead of standing meekly in the grip of Death, I raised my right fist high and struck at him. It was no skilled boxer's blow, but still a solid punch, one that would have killed a mortal man. It grazed his bearded chin and hit him in the chest, and his grip on my arm was broken and he fell back awkwardly, his cloak of red and black swirling about him.

Briefly I had the feeling that I was once more grappling with the Giant Antaeus, but that image did not last. The force arrayed against me now was far greater, though of course Thanatos was not nearly so large as the Giant had been. He was tougher than the Hydra, and I was handicapped by not having my club immediately available.

I had to pummel my opponent with my fists for some time to do him any damage. Meanwhile he struck no real blows, nor did he even attempt any common wrestling holds. Instead he continued to paw and grapple, in the way that only Death can do, trying to draw my life out of my body; but the power of life in me was too great.

Without taking my gaze from my opponent for a moment, I could see from the rim of my vision that the courtyard had become a kind of informal boxing or wrestling ring, surrounded by what must have been half the population of the palace, the other half having precipitately fled.

I bombarded pawing Death with another flurry of punches, and again he went stumbling backward, circling slowly in retreat. From his mouth there came a keening wail of astonishment and rage, along with a trickle of blood, and now I heard the first, soft, unbelieving murmur from the watching crowd, who earlier must have been too shocked to breathe.

Death stepped back, and I advanced.

I was awkward and unskilled in fighting, but so, as I soon realized, was my opponent. Again and again I landed awkward, untaught, swinging blows, any one of which would have pulped the skull or crushed the ribs of any mere human, mangled any natural beast that walked the earth. They did not kill the God of Death, or even break his bones, but again and again they staggered him and knocked him down. Now I saw in his eyes the beginning of understanding that it was truly my father's power that lived in my blood and muscles.

Yet so strong were pride and hatred in my enemy that again and again he leaped to his feet, his cloak flying and the shadowy images of his wings, and hurled himself at me once more.

My own pride, and my anger, were now at full tide. I sent my right fist deep into my charging enemy's midsection, as hard as I could throw it, so that the god gasped and stood for a moment paralyzed, bent almost double. In that moment I drove my left fist down against his head, directly overhand, as if I were pounding a spike through iron. The stone of the patio cracked beneath my victim's feet.

Thus the Death God fell, for the fourth or fifth time. Even under such an impact, Thanatos still did not lose consciousness. But he, and I, and everyone who watched us, knew that he was hopelessly beaten.

I stepped back, like a sportsmanlike boxer, waiting for my opponent to try to rise again.

He raised his face, forehead all smeared with divine blood, and gave me a strange and desperate look, in which terror and disbelief were mingled. Then he began to crawl away. After crawling a few yards Thanatos regained his feet, but kept his back to me and did not pause in his limping, staggering retreat. The circle of watchers, silent again in awe, parted rapidly at his approach. This avatar of Death was not yet dead, but it seemed that his vitality was dangerously low.

At first he hobbled toward the spot where he had set down the pale queen, as if still determined to take her; but I moved quickly to stand in his way, and the God of Death shuddered and reversed himself again.

Thanatos abandoned to me not only the field, but his victim as well, and it seemed he had all that he could do to drag himself away. Before his creeping progress had brought him to the edge of the terrace beside the garden, where anxious onlookers went scurrying ever farther at his approach, his body briefly became transparent and then disappeared. The last I saw of him was the malignant look he turned at me, over his shoulder, just before he vanished.

I turned to look for Danni, but could not immediately locate her in the suddenly milling crowd.

Alcestis the queen, her face as pale as the fate that she had just escaped, still lay where Death had set her down. Her eyes were closed, but we all saw with a shock of joy that she was breathing now. Thanatos had drained her life force away almost to the dregs, but when he was punished, his own existence threatened, what he had drained flowed back to her. Her loving family and her attendants flocked around her with cries of rapture. Soon, in the arms of her rejoicing husband, she had recovered fully from her seeming death.

All the crowd who had watched the fight were awestricken by the power I had demonstrated. Some were already prostrating themselves before me, as if in worship of a god; but I made known my displeasure, and they quickly got to their feet again.

When King Admetus could finally tear himself away from his young wife, he came to me and swore his eternal gratitude, and made extravagant promises of the rewards he was going to give me; and I was very young, and I admit that I believed him for a time.

His cheeks still streamed, but now his tears expressed his joy.

"Half my kingdom, Hercules! I swear by Zeus and by Apollo, that half of everything I own is yours!"

Perhaps I am unjust, and he would really have honored his promise, had I not declined the offer.

"I have no need of kingdoms, Majesty. To give me charge of such immense and complicated matters would only inflict on me an enormous burden."

Then Admetus changed his offer, to endless amounts of jewels and gold and slaves, and swore that he would hear no refusal on my part. But when the promises later turned out to be empty, I was not much upset. The truth was that there was really nothing I needed that was in his power to give.

On that night a certain servant, attendant in the palace, asked so winningly for the honor of sleeping with me that I agreed, and the question never arose as to what otherwise might have happened between me and Meleager's sister.

When full sleep finally claimed me, I was granted only a few hours of peace before Prince Asterion showed his horned head before me in a dream. Even before he spoke, I understood that he had come to give me warning. It seemed to me that the prince and I were standing in a vast, dark room, or hall, swept by a cold wind that blew through open doors and windows. I had the feeling, the inward knowledge, that what he was about to say was so terrible that I awoke, sweating and gasping, before I heard even the first words of what he said. The young attendant who shared my bed was frightened and hurriedly left the room, never to return.

On the next morning I left the king and queen behind, amid a clamor of rejoicing bells. I waved farewell to Danni's haunting green eyes and slender form, and climbed into my little boat and sailed away, my ears almost deafened by a renewed chorus of prayers and good wishes, eager to get home and see my wife and son again.

Now I must pause here in my writing to gather strength to deal with what must next be told.

I have known for some time that for some tasks, even the strength of Hercules may not be enough.

The next leg of my great journey was uneventful. Not many days after departing the kingdom of Admetus, I arrived again in my homeland. Having the speed of the *Skyboat* at my disposal meant that much of the known world was only hours or days away, instead of weeks or months.

On drawing near my homeland, I left the boat at the same place I had moored it on my previous visit, and took to my feet with a light step.

When I was almost within sight of the walls of Cadmia, trudging eagerly up a narrow road, I caught sight of a lone figure standing ahead of me, straight and unmoving in the very middle of the road. It was an ebony figure of shadow, outlined against the mottled clouds of a red sunset. At a distance I could recognize the hair of curly black and the protruding ears. Enkidu had come to welcome me, but he did not advance to meet me, so whatever news he had could not be good. My heart turned over in my breast when I drew near enough to see the look upon my nephew's face, and that he wore the ragged clothes pre-scribed by tradition for one in mourning.

"Enkidu, you are alone," I said as I approached.

"Everyone else was too much frightened to come with me," he answered softly. His arms hung loose at his sides, and he tried to avoid meeting my eyes.

"Frightened of what?" I asked. Although as I now look back, it seems to me that I already knew.

My nephew had put on weight since I had seen him last, and also gained a little height, but the rags of ritual mourning hung on him loosely. And now his face was so pale that he only looked ill, and not like a young man prosperously married.

His voice, too, seemed unnatural. "Hercules, the prince Asterion appeared to me in a dream and said that you were coming home. He said also that I must be the one to go to meet you."

There followed a long and terrible silence. Then somehow Enkidu managed to speak the necessary words, so that at last I heard the blunt facts, the terrible news of how my wife and child had been horribly murdered. The hands that had done the deed were more than human.

It was as if my spirit had been forced partly out of my body by the shock. The next thing I remember is as if I were observing the scene from outside. I have a kind of vision of myself, sitting helpless in the dust of the road, while Enkidu bent over me, avoiding giving any real answers to the horrible questions that thronged up in my mind. In a kind of madness I kept demanding more details.

What he did tell me was that the bodies of my wife and child had been buried, with honors that made the ceremony almost worthy of a royal funeral. The king had seen to that. Eurystheus had been much saddened by the tragedy, and he sent word that he hoped soon to be able to express his condolences in person.

Enkidu had to help me to my feet. Then he and his young wife took me into their large house, where first servants, and then physicians, were brought to attend me.

There followed a period of time, lasting for days, when fits of senseless violence came over me, and things were broken; fortunately none were human bodies. But eventually such seizures passed, and a time came when others felt safe in approaching me.

From what people told me of the horror of the days just preceding my return home, I realized that Thanatos must have come to wreak destruction on my family as a means of revenge for his humiliating beating.

No other Cadmians had been struck down. None had tried to defend Megan—how could they? I felt no special anger at any of them, from King Eurystheus on down, for their failure. My time for real anger had not come as yet. Never did I see the king, and indeed I had almost forgotten him and his bronze box.

Instead, I was struck by the supreme irony that I had been concerned for what my son would be when he grew up. For that was never going to happen.

Weeks passed. Day after day I sat alone in a room in my nephew's house, or sometimes on a terrace, while all, or almost all, feared to come near me. Once Amphitryon came, and from a little distance murmured his condolences.

It seemed that even before my own arrival, the news had already reached Cadmia of what feat I had achieved at the court of King Admetus. People avoided me and spoke of me in hushed whispers, as they might of any blasphemer who had made an enemy of a powerful deity.

Once—but I am almost sure that this visitation was only in a dream—Apollo himself came to speak to me in soothing words. When I dared to threaten him with my fist, he withdrew himself again—but I was almost sure that it was only in a dream.

And again—and that *this* was a dream I had no doubt—Prince Asterion came to me. He confronted me calmly, even though in the dream I raised my fist against him, as I had in waking life against my other friends. This time he had no words to say in his strange voice, but blessedly he turned aside a nightmare that had begun to ride me, so that I could sink into a kind of rest, oblivion.

And so in time the full madness of grief passed from me, as all things must pass. A day came when I was again aware, however dully, of the songs of birds outside my guest room's window. And somewhere in Enkidu's household a servant's child was crying, and I could find some reassurance in the fact that there were still children in the world.

Pulling myself together, I stood up and tore off the torn and wretched garments of my mourning. I put on a clean tunic and went out of the house in which I had been hiding, to breathe again the outdoor air of the living world.

It seemed that I was doomed to live on for a time, and now I could begin to face the prospect without shrinking. Quietly and reasonably I called for servants to bring me water for a bath, and oil with which to anoint my hair and my youthful beginnings of a beard.

People approached me, cautiously, and now I could speak to them rationally enough. Presently I requested that simple preparations should be made, for I would soon be departing on a journey.

And I called at last for food, for though I had only the beginnings of an appetite, I knew that I would soon need my strength.

For the first time in weeks, I took notice of what I ate, and thought the taste of it was pleasant. I was drinking a bowl of soup when Enkidu came to see me.

"What will you do now, Hercules?" my nephew asked, when he had assured himself that I was largely recovered from my madness, but saw that I was determined to leave. His young wife and her attendants stood looking over his shoulders.

"I am going to look for Death," I answered, carefully setting down the bowl.

It took my hearers a moment or two to be sure that I was not talking about suicide.

I was sure now, had finally accepted the fact, that my wife and son were beyond rescue. He who was Death would have made very certain, in this case. I had not seen their bodies buried, but I went to look one final time upon their graves, and this time the sight brought almost the same feeling of finality.

"I will come with you, then," Enkidu said. I think the words cost him a considerable effort, but they were firmly spoken. His body was heavier than it had been, but his cheeks were still quite beardless.

"No, my friend, my comrade," I told him immediately. "I thank you for the offer, but where I am going this time you may not go." And I saw his young wife, still standing behind him, suddenly relax.

Some prominent citizens of Cadmia came to see me. They were worried that Death would return to harry their land again, now that I was gone.

"And so he will," I told them. "Death comes everywhere. But sooner or later he will again find himself in the same place with me."

Now I was determined, as never before, to enter the realm of Death himself and make him pay. Selecting a log of seasoned wild-olive wood, I fashioned myself a new club.

"How and where I do not know," I said, "but somehow I will find his world. He cannot hide from me forever." And I picked up from the dirt of a flower bed a small stone that felt as hard as granite, and between my thumb and fingers absently crushed it into powder.

It seemed to me that no other purpose remained to me in life, except to find my way to the Underworld, and there to have my revenge upon Thanatos.

But when it was actually time to depart, I had to overcome an urge to hesitate. I would take the road back to where the *Skyboat* waited—but then in which direction was I to seek?

Kneeling in the bottom of the boat, I rested my forehead against the ivory box of the compass-pyx that had once—it seemed so long ago!—been given me by the gods. Then I let my thoughts flow as a dark stream. I would leave it to *Skyboat* to find the way to Hell.

Tartarus

$\mathcal{T}$he *Skyboat's* compass-pyx reflected only shadowy images
into my mind as I fed it with my hatred—what better fuel for
a voyage to Hell?—and the urgency of my need for revenge.
Presently my craft jerked into motion, and we were under way. The
effort took me a long time—weeks passed, perhaps a month, and
whenever I truly relaxed we drifted aimlessly—but in the end I was
successful.

The powers of the *Skyboat* were even greater than I had imagined
them—or perhaps I give them too much credit. It may be that success
was due to my own human, mortal will, stronger than either my
friends or enemies had calculated, and to the fuel of hate.

My entrance to the Underworld lay in a strange and unfamiliar land,
and I reached it near sunset, following a day of oppressive weather,
when storms threatened, but no lightning had yet struck to purge
the air.

The magic *Skyboat* brought me as far as it could, down one stream
and through the Great Sea, then up another watercourse through several branchings, until the stream at last became too shallow, and I was
forced to abandon my vessel.

I had left home with a substantial supply of food and still had
enough left to maintain my strength for perhaps another week. I carried also a waterskin, which I refilled when I could. These modest
supplies, and my club, made up the whole of my equipment. Now I
began to climb on foot beside the rivulet, and the sprite, buzzing invisibly as usual, came with me.

Climbing the rough hillside for a hundred yards or so, I came to a
growth of cypress and a thicket of cedar on a small shelf of land. In
this hidden place the stream I had been following was born, in a pool
fed by deep springs. Another and lesser trickle of water fell incon-
spicuously from the same pond, pouring away out of sight over a nar-

row lip of stone, vanishing through a hole that opened into a lower darkness between two tilted slabs of granite.

When I put my head into this dark hole, I could hear, rising from far underground, the muted thunder of a small waterfall. Also my nose was attacked by a foul, sulphurous smell, which I took as a hopeful sign. Surely this was the path for the Underworld, to which my boat had done its best to carry me.

I took it as another favorable sign that now the sprite who had come with me on my last climb deserted me abruptly.

I silently waved good-bye to the invisible creature, and to my abandoned *Skyboat,* now also out of sight behind rocks and trees. Shouldering the most recent version of my club, I tried to wedge my body into the dark hole, following the subterranean waterfall.

At the last moment the start of my descent was delayed. The hole in the rock was not quite large enough for me to work my entire body into it; briefly I laid my new club aside, and a moment's work with my two arms wrought a minor dislocation in one of the small bones of the mountain, affording my body now room enough to pass.

Whatever drama might have been inherent in my thus beginning a journey underground was somewhat spoiled by an anticlimax. The way beyond the entrance opening was dark, but never quite too dark for me to find my footing, though I could not determine any source for the faint light.

Minute after minute, and then hour after hour, while the last traces of daylight faded and vanished far behind me, I trod a path that seemed to have been worn into the earth and rock by the passage of innumerable feet. Yet paradoxically I encountered no other travelers. Certainly, I thought, no such army as the silent majority could ever have passed between those granite slabs without leaving many traces. If all the dead of all the world were somehow required to traverse that narrow opening, I'd have encountered such a crush and press aboveground that I'd still be trying to get through.

No, I thought. The Underworld must receive its recruits, or the great preponderance of them, through some system more complex than that.

When at last I grew weary from my long trek underground, I

paused to rest, in a place where dry dust made a pillow softer than plain rock, and fell into a slumber.

As I slept, Apollo appeared to me in a dream, to offer his sympathy on my tragic loss. He also told me he was pleased that I seemed to be recovering from the shock; and he reassured me that his memory, damaged in the Giant's assault that had aborted our journey to Vulcan's workshop, was now largely restored again.

Vaguely I was aware that the prince Asterion was arranging this communication, and from time to time I could see his horned head in the background.

It seemed to me that in my dream I asked, or tried to ask, Apollo whether he could, or would, try to join me in the realm of Hades. And I thought that the Sun God concluded by telling me: "I am not welcome down there, and my appearance would only provoke another terrible fight with Hades, one that our cause can ill afford just now. But I will see you again, Hercules, in waking life, soon after you emerge from the Underworld—provided you are able to do that."

Groaning and sneezing with the dryness of the dust that made my pillow, I awoke from sleep, not knowing for a moment who I was, or where, or why—but then I remembered where I was, and why.

While still only half awake, it seemed to me that I heard a great dog barking in the distance. This made me wonder whether the entrance to the Underworld that I had found might be the one where Cerberus kept watch—or perhaps, I thought, that story was nothing but legend.

When I was fully awake, I heard no barking. Groping around me in the dimness until I found my club, I set it on my shoulder and moved on.

That next portion of my descent lasted for what seemed many hours. Where the shadows were thickest I went probing the way ahead with the length of my club, sometimes on a declivity so steep that I had to use it as a staff and grip rock with one hand to keep my balance. Though the darkness was unending, still it never became quite absolute. The tortuous path beside the gurgling rivulet of water at last flattened out into a level space, and the close rocky walls fell back. As

I went lower the air grew warmer, but at the same time became thick and foul.

On the way I had had plenty of time to ponder where I was going, and what I was about. I remembered an ancient story that one of my early tutors had required me to memorize: It told of a cave of immeasurable depth, its mouth hidden by the darkness of a forest on the shore of a black lake. No birds flew over those waters or in those woods because of the foul air rising from the lake, whose name, Avernus, meant that it was birdless.

Presently, as I went farther and farther along the level way, the stench that had assailed my nostrils as I reached the depths began to fade—or at least, as is the way with most foul smells, I ceased to notice it.

And then, to my considerable astonishment, I came upon a deserted village—scattered houses, built much in the style of peasants' homes I was familiar with above. It was hard to imagine what fields the villagers might farm, what crops they grew; yet I was unable to shake a feeling that these dwellings ought to be occupied, that very likely there had recently been people in them, and they would be inhabited again as soon as I looked away.

But I knew I must not expect to find things here as they were in the world above. Now I felt that I was truly in the realm of Hades. I had gone beyond worrying over what might happen to me. But it did strike me as odd that so far I had encountered not another soul, neither human, god, nor demon.

Whether there was any longer a solid roof above my head or not, I could not have said. But for a long time now, the stars had ceased to be visible.

The whole place was unrelievedly dim and shadowy, with, as far as I could tell, not so much as a mushroom growing anywhere. Still, enough light to let me see where I was going came from somewhere, but I could not identify the source. Such was the effect of those surroundings on my mind and soul that I never doubted that these conditions were doomed to persist eternally. I would have taken an oath that Apollo's blessed sunlight had never touched that gray and lifeless scene, and I could find no reason to believe that it ever would. It seemed I could feel as much as see the clouds that weighed above me, and patches of fog seemed to spring up out of the barren ground.

On I pressed through the forbidding landscape. Looking back now, I suppose that I must still have nursed a faint hope of being able to save my wife and child, a hope so faint and distant that I dared not acknowledge it to myself—otherwise I might well have been over-come with terror to find myself in such surroundings. No mere curiosity, no thought of material treasure, not even the bitter anger that still held me in its thrall, could have driven me further on.

Somewhere, far behind me now, the stream I had followed from the Upper World had trickled away into the rocks and disappeared. But now again there was water somewhere ahead. I could smell it. It impressed me as the same odor that arises from some deep, natural wells, not quite foul and yet not invitingly clear. One would have to be thirsty indeed to drink willingly from that fount.

And now, with every step that I advanced, I felt more certain that my feet were on the true descending path. Here I noted that a groove per-haps a foot wide had been deeply worn into the solid rock, as if by the feet of innumerable numbers of the dead, who had come this way be-fore me. Still, no one beside myself was using the passage now.

There was a murmur of speech from somewhere ahead, voices rising louder now and then, as of two or three people in grim argu-ment. Advancing a little farther, I emerged from the narrow passage into a vast, dim cavern. At a distance of a hundred yards or so, I could perceive dim shapes, as of several people standing on a shore, near a long boat bobbing in the dark and shallow water, almost at their feet.

It seemed to me that everyone in the world must remember, from sto-ries heard in childhood, that Charon was the boatman who ferried the newly dead across the river Styx; and I had no doubt of who this boat-man was, from the moment I first saw him. My adventures since meet-ing the Hydra had considerably strengthened my faith in legends.

Pacing steadily closer, I could see the boatman and his clients all more clearly. Charon was a wizened figure, wrapped in dark rags. What little I could see of his face and hands suggested that he was incredibly ancient, yet the way he waved his arms about proved him still briskly active. His boat was as dark as the water it floated on, and some thirty feet long when first I looked at it, though later it seemed shorter. He was alone in the boat now, standing in the rear, from which position he seemed to control his vessel easily with his single pole.

I suppose I might have waded or swum the river, taking my chances with whatever dangers might lie concealed in the dark water. But I preferred to bend Charon to my will, rather than seem to be avoiding him. It was as if I sought out obstacles for the sheer raging joy of forcing my way through them.

By now, I thought, my eyes were as well accustomed to the eternal darkness as they were ever going to be. The Styx was broad and gloomy and slow-moving, with the opposite shore visible only as a suggestion of disturbing shadows. Now and then a few bubbles from some unknown source came rising out of the depths.

Those who stood onshore disputing with the boatman were dim, dark figures, hard to see in any detail, even when I came near them. I took them to be the shades of five or six folk who were new arrivals, like myself. Without thinking about it I at first assumed that, unlike me, they were dead and engaged in the traditional ritual of passage.

But when I came right in among them, I could perceive these others clearly enough to see that two or three were steadily, audibly breathing, and one even seemed to be gasping in terror and exhaustion. Then they were no more dead than I was, at least not finally. I was reminded of the strange condition of Queen Alcestis when Thanatos had her in his grasp.

Most of the legendary tales agreed that at the point where I had now arrived, it was necessary for the newly arrived soul to bargain for its passage. In fact, at the moment of my arrival, one of the men in the group was shrilly demanding to be taken across even though he could not pay.

One of his fellows was nervously trying to calm him, calling him Menippus. I elbowed my way in among the others, stood by the arguer, and would have taken his part in the debate with Charon, except that Menippus glared at me with resentment the first time I opened my mouth on his behalf.

Charon resented my intrusion, too.

"I am Hercules, of Cadmia," I told the boatman when he rounded on me with hand outstretched for payment. And in the next breath I demanded: "I have come to this wretched place looking for Thanatos. Where is he?"

Now Charon looked at me closely for the first time, and his ancient, rheumy eyes went wide. It was doubtless the first time in his miserable life that he had ever heard that question asked; and I saw by his terrified reaction to my name and question that my reputation had preceded me even into Hell. There was no room in his image of the world for any intruder like me. So I waved my club and terrified the boatman into cooperating.

His voice was quavering, though he tried to make it brave. "Lord Hercules, there is the matter of payment—"

I had no patience, either, with one who would ask me to pay for this kind of ride. "Payment? Payment! How do you dare to ask me such a question, you damned unhuman monster? How dare you ask such a thing of anyone?"

"It is . . . it is the custom, sir . . ."

"To the Underworld with your custom!" I roared out, then paused, thinking that the way I had phrased my defiance somehow did not make sense.

Next he protested that his boat was too fragile to take the weight of living flesh and bone, but I disallowed that argument, having already seen that some of the other passengers were breathing. With the exception of Menippus, they all seemed willing to be herded along like sheep.

At last we were off, and I had to put up with no more nonsense from our boatman about being charged for the ride. Charon drove his vessel energetically across the broad, dark river, displaying a vigor that the appearance of his crinkled form suggested was quite impossible.

The moment the prow ran ashore on the Hellward bank, I stepped out onto land. As I turned my back on them all, I could hear Menippus resuming his own dispute with the boatman, even after having been ferried across. Now the unhappy passenger was demanding to be returned to the other side, and Charon was responding with abusive threats.

Later, the legends would tell how Charon was punished with a beating by some lieutenant of Hades for allowing me, a live and breathing man, to pass unhindered. It may be so. Still, I suppose it was not the beating he would have absorbed had he tried to stop me.

But the fate of the feckless boatman has little to do with the story I have set out to tell. From the shoreline the land sloped up gradually, inland, for thirty or forty paces, and beyond that inclined down again. As I groped and stumbled my way deeper into the Underworld I began to encounter frightening shapes, which I took to be the shades of those who were truly dead.

Here and there across the dark landscape I became aware of slowly moving groups of faintly glowing, marching images, as well as an occasional individual in isolation. Now, in this much later epoch when I write, I realize more clearly that only a few of all the world's dead could have been represented in that place, even by such tenuous forms and shadows. And when I was there I could distinguish, at first glance, between those who moved in solid form, and the others who were only images.

Sometimes both types of figure responded when spoken to, and sometimes the words they spoke seemed to make sense; but no real thought or feeling was behind them. They were images that moved and walked and sometimes uttered words; but when I steeled my nerves to touch one, my hand passed right through, so that my palm and fingers for a moment were brightly lighted.

At first I was truly frightened, for the first time since I began my lonely journey. But when I looked more closely at those that were mere apparitions, I was strongly reminded of the images Atlas had shown me—sometimes these, too, were clear and brilliant, and moved in a way that was almost lifelike. Yet it seemed to me that they were much more like reflections in a fine mirror than they were like spirits who had truly been alive.

Some of these people were trapped here—or at least their images seemed to be—in the same way Prometheus had been trapped, held by the same kind of fetters as those I had once broken. It occurred to me now that his punishment had been a form of Hell on the surface of the earth.

*   *   *

Gradually but steadily the impression kept growing on me that who-ever or whatever had created Olympus seemed to have manufactured Tartarus as well. There were certain similarities, giving the impres-sion, when I thought about it, of common construction units of some kind. Here again I saw stubby projections from the ground, with a re-semblance to tree stumps, but that had an artificial look about them.

Certain others among the frightful shapes only looked at me, and fled in terror when I tried to question them.

Every time I thought some individual among them took notice of me, I demanded of her, or him: "I am Hercules, of Cadmia. Where is my wife, Megan? And where is our child?"

And, when those questions failed, as they did each time, I fol-lowed with: "Where is the God of Death?"

But never did I get a useful answer. None of those I sought were anywhere to be found.

It was with mixed feelings of joy and fear that I encountered the shade of my own mother, dressed as I had often seen her in sunlight and in life. Almost I expected to see her sewing basket in her hand. But though the figure had come walking toward me, as if drawn by some mysterious affinity, it was only an image and, when it came within arm's length, ignored me.

I staggered, and then for a moment I could not move at all. "Mother!" I cried out.

But the eyes of Alcmene's shade were terribly clear and empty, and they looked through me, and then looked on, as if I had not been there at all. There was no awareness in them.

And what wrung my heart almost beyond endurance was that I was granted one last look at the shade of Megan, and that of our babe held in her arms. I believe the only thing that saved my sanity was what I had learned from Atlas, regarding how the machinery of Olympus still made such counterfeit likenesses of many people at the point of death. How such bright shadows were created and preserved, in pursuit of some vast project whose purpose all living minds had long since forgotten. So I knew, even as I saw her, that it was not truly

Megan who walked before me, but only an image, like a reflection in a pond.

I realize that this explanation leaves uncertain the fate, the nature, of other individuals I encountered in Tartarus, those who still retained their bodies as solid and breathing as my own. But it seems to me that people in that situation have merely been drained of life force, like Alcestis. As we will see, sufficient life remained to certain dwellers in the Underworld to allow them to move and speak, behaving almost normally. I later had good evidence of the fact that when some of these were able to regain the surface of the earth, they were not much the worse for their dread experience.

Since my visit to the Underworld, I have spoken with wise counselors and have come to understand that human bodies, when imprisoned long enough in that dark realm, change fundamentally, acquire a different nature than the one they were born with. With ordinary mortals, the transformation need not take long—but of course I was protected by my father's power, inherent in each atom of my body.

For one thing, they became immortal, or so long-lived that they are sometimes assumed to be immune to death. Charon was an example.

But it is possible for humans in such a situation to be restored to their original natures, if they return to the more mundane world above, where they were born, and where they naturally die.

Later, when I had more time to ponder these events at leisure, it occurred to me to wonder whether Charon himself might be one of these, no longer truly human. Yet what was he, if not human?

But at the time when I was buried in the Underworld, as when I had confronted Atlas under the great bowl of the sky, my mind simply reeled under these complexities and I made no progress in unraveling them.

The general movement of all the shades and breathing folk around me tended in a certain direction, and I took that heading, too, after pausing to eat the last remaining portion of the food I had brought with me.

I drank from a small cold stream, right at the point where it came trickling from the rock, and hoped that it was not the beginning of Lethe, the source of all forgetfulness.

The scattered population whose movement I had been following gradually thinned out in numbers; where the individual shapes were going, I could not say, but there were ever fewer and fewer of them, and in time I was alone.

After descending a great distance, I was led by a burgeoning red glow to come upon an impressive archway, higher than the walls of Cadmia. This opened into what had to be the throne room of the King of Hell.

Once I had entered this vast chamber I paused, involuntarily, to gape about me. The height of the ceiling seemed impossible, made more so by the clouds of reddish mist that concealed its true distance.

At the far end of the great room, the length of a sports stadium from where I stood, there towered high a great black throne, which seemed of a size to seat a Giant comfortably—but the figure occupying it now was no bigger than a man.

At this depth, the air around me was beginning to turn hot again, and the floor of rock was growing warm beneath my sandaled feet. Drawing a deep breath of the tainted atmosphere, I started the long walk to the throne.

My hopes rose as I advanced and could see that the black throne was indeed occupied. But he who sat on it was not, to my great disappointment, my enemy Thanatos. Instead, the enthroned figure was one I would have no hope of pummeling in the way I had served Death. After all, Hades, called by some Pluto or Dis Pater, was, with Zeus and Poseidon, one of the three who ruled the universe—or so I had been taught.

He slouched on the throne, legs crossed, watching my approach with not enough interest to cause him to sit up straight. A crown of some dull metal, formed into a jagged shape, sat crooked on his great, bearded head, and he was twirling some small object in one hand. I was within a few strides of the foot of the throne before I could feel sure of what it was. And then I knew a shock of disappointment: if the Face of Death was here in the hands of Hades, then the last avatar to wear it was surely dead, and all my hope of revenge was in vain.

This was another god whom I had never seen before, but he knew me, for he nodded and smiled at my approach. I had no doubt that it was Hades himself who sat twirling the Face of Death, which looked like a clear, glassy mask, around his finger, stuck through one of the mask's eyeholes. The thought crossed my mind that he might be pondering which mortal ought to be invested with the powers of Thanatos next. I had no doubt there would be willing applicants.

Hades had a booming, bellowing laugh, which sounded when I drew very near. I had heard such laughter before, on the bright surface of the earth, but only from the hopelessly insane.

"Hail, Hercules," the voice of the Lord of the Underworld boomed out when I stood close before him. "I have been more or less expecting you for some time. But I thought you might come riding on some centaur's back. Have you run out of labors to perform in the world of the living?"

Again it seemed my fame had run ahead of me. "Greetings to you, Lord Hades. I am looking for Thanatos."

"Is that the real reason? Well, this is not the place to find him." In rambling and disjointed words, and with many repetitions, the Lord of the Underworld explained to me that Tartarus was actually a very poor place to look for Thanatos—the Death God spent almost all his time in the world above.

This was not how I would have expected Hades to act. The behavior of the god before me strongly reinforced my suspicions of true madness; I wondered whether being struck by a Giant's weapon might produce that effect. I also wondered whether I should raise the question, but soon decided there was nothing to be gained by doing so.

"Plenty of work up there to keep him busy." He gestured with a great thumb toward the rocky ceiling, and once more he laughed. "Up on the surface is where Thanatos does his work—if you can dignify what he does by that name."

Meanwhile, another handful of ghostly, semitransparent figures trooped by, paying no attention to me, nor even to the ruler of this fantastic domain. As far as I could tell, none of these wraiths had any purpose in their movement, but wandered aimlessly.

"Why do you stare at them, Hercules?" the Lord of the Underworld demanded. "What did you expect to find here, festivals of sunshine?"

"I stare because I still wonder if Thanatos is among them."

"And if he were?" Hades went on in his rambling, disjointed speech. "These are mere witless, lifeless shades, no more than shadows on a wall. What point is there in punishing a shadow?"

I replied to that question with one of my own. "If these are only shadows, tell me this: What is it that casts the shadow? What of their true souls?"

The mad god squinted at me horribly and pointed one great arm in my direction as he nodded for emphasis. "Now *there* is a question. There is a *pro*found mystery. I myself have often wondered about that. But if such things still exist anywhere in the Universe, it is certainly not here."

He paused, then added with a chilling laugh: "If you see *my* true soul anywhere, will you let me know? I fear that someone's stolen it away."

He made a sudden motion with his great right arm, as of scooping up an object I could not see clearly, and putting it on his head. For just an instant, I thought he might be grabbing his true soul. And a moment later I was startled when the figure of Hades abruptly vanished from my sight. Another moment and he was back, still occupying his throne, and laughing his hideous laugh.

It came to me that he must be putting on and taking off his famed Helmet of Invisibility, which had been resting—itself invisible, until he picked it up—beside him, on one broad arm of his throne chair.

Great Hades shifted his weight on his royal seat and looked around, as if seeking someone who ought to be present but was not. Then, in a brief return of mental clarity, he seemed to recall his situation.

"Where is that damned zombie who—? But no, I forget, they've all gone. I am unattended." Leaning a little forward, he fixed me with a terrible gaze. "Would you believe it? *They say I have gone mad.*" The last words came out in a ghastly whisper.

"I suppose I might believe that if I tried."

That, at least, seemed to be logical. If Hades had indeed gone mad, then his consort Persephone and all his usual attendants might well have fled his presence in terror, not knowing what atrocity he might commit on them at any moment. So he sat on the black throne, all alone in the vast throne room, and seemed to pay no attention at all to the ceaseless passage of time.

He did ask me some questions, though. Some of them I do not remember, but some I do.

"Hercules, tell me, have the sun and moon yet fallen from their places? Is the end of the Universe at hand?"

"Not according to Atlas."

"Have you seen *the stars, at bloody wars, in the wounded welkin weeping?*" Again the terrifying whisper.

"I do not understand you," I protested.

"You are no poet, then."

"I never claimed to be."

And then the Lord of the Underworld wondered aloud if I was the first intruder of many who were going to seek shelter in his domain, when that of sun and stars and sea was falling and burning up around them.

Rather than stand tongue-tied, I continued to do my best to answer Hades. I gave him what reassurances I could about the stability of the world above. Also I reminded him about the war.

"Zeus fights the Giants, does he? Well, I could tell him a thing or two about that. I myself went out fighting Giants once . . . yes, I was a true god once, though you might not believe it to look at me."

"Oh, I believe it, Dark One. You are not the only deity who is sometimes called insane."

Hades thought no more of receiving the insult than I, in my current state, of giving it. Perhaps he did not even hear it. He went on rambling, and playing with the god-Face in his hands, while I looked around me for any evidence that Thanatos might be going to appear. Alas, I found none.

When the Lord of the Underworld had babbled on a little longer, I suddenly pricked up my ears. He seemed to be claiming that he was now allied with Zeus, Apollo, and other gods of the Upper World. And in later days I was able to verify the fact: he had signed with them a pact of mutual toleration and nonviolence, until their common enemies, the Giants, should be disposed of.

But there was still no sign of the one I had come here seeking. I supposed it might be possible that when Hades learned that I was coming into his domain, he had warned Thanatos, either the old avatar or the new, and sent him to hide somewhere else. But that would require some other explanation of the Face my host was twirling.

At last I said: "I have no quarrel with you just now, Master of the Underworld." Raising an arm, I pointed off to my right. In that direction a different quality in the light, or in the dimness rather, strongly suggested some kind of a broad doorway, at only a moderate distance. "What is there?" I demanded.

"What is anywhere, bold mortal? And why should you care? For a dead man, Hercules, you display an inordinate amount of energy."

"If you think that I am dead, Lord of Hell, watch closely and learn better. Now tell me, is Death hiding in that room?" Once again I jabbed the air with my finger. "Do you fear to give me a plain answer?"

"I fear nothing, dead man!" And he hammered the right arm of his great chair with his clenched fist, so hard that the floor of Hell quivered beneath my feet. "The Thrones of Lethe are in that room. Go see for yourself. Now go away, bother me no longer, I have work to do. Can't you see? A tremendous amount of important work!" And he sank back on this throne and closed his eyes and resumed his twiddling, twirling of the Face of Death.

I turned my back on His Dark Majesty and moved away. But when I had gone only a few paces, he called after me: "What else you find in there may surprise you, Hercules!" And suddenly the laughter of Hades boomed forth again.

Turning my back again on the mad god, I walked steadily away. Ahead of me the outline of a large doorway loomed more clearly through the dimness with every step. And in the same direction I thought I could now hear the sound of men's voices, raised as if in drunken song.

TWENTY-FOUR

The Harrowing

*N*ow I heard the drunken singing, in two voices, from close
ahead. The louder and clearer voice was rather deep, and it
seemed to me strangely familiar.

On passing through the arched doorway I found myself in another chamber of the Underworld, this one fully as long and wide as
the throne room, though not as high. Frozen drops of rock, looking as
if they had once been molten, hung from a ceiling that was in places
low enough for a tall man to bang his head. I was not tall enough to
need to worry. The vast space, mostly empty, was strangely lighted by
wall-mounted torches that burned with flames of evil red, flames that
shot up to play against the lowering overhead rock without doing very
much to relieve the surrounding blackness—and here, as Hades had
predicted, I came upon a sight which brought me to a halt in sheer
surprise.

Clouds of shadow or dank fog—I suppose there were some of
each—filled much of the huge chamber. But when I had walked half
its length, I could observe a pair of men occupying two of a long row
of low chairs, or perches; knee-high, stumplike projections rising
from the ebony floor. It seemed to me at first glance that all the other
chairs were empty.

Hades had said something about this room containing the Thrones
of Lethe, which sounded to me like seats named for the legendary
River of Forgetfulness.

For some reason the two men were arrayed in festive garments,
creating a totally incongruous effect in this buried dungeon. They
were sitting in slumped positions, the one on the more distant chair
looking almost comatose, his bearded jaw moving intermittently as
he tried to sing. The other was turning his head from side to side as I
approached, but at first he paid me no attention. Their faces remained
almost entirely in shadow.

In the gloom, it took me a few moments to determine that the
pair were bound in place on their stumps, with shackles around their

waists and ankles. They also wore strange-looking caps or helmets, each headpiece connected by a thin cable to the Throne below.

The relatively active man, he who was sitting nearest to the door where I had entered, had somehow managed to get his head almost free of this restraint, so his metal cap had slid far down over his left ear. But his limbs were still firmly bound by chains, much like those Prometheus had endured, and there seemed no possibility that he could ever free himself entirely.

As I drew near, this one stopped turning his head from side to side and focused his gaze on me. "Are you real?" the familiar voice inquired of me as I approached.

"Of course I am," I said.

A well-remembered figure put out a human hand, large and muscular yet trembling, to try to touch my arm. A shaky whisper asked me: "Have you solid human flesh and bone?"

"I have, and I intend to keep them."

After a shocked pause, there came a one-word question: "Hercules?"

My amazement at this encounter was at least as great as his. I had last seen Theseus well aboveground and apparently in good health, in the company of the lovely Antiope, when we parted following our escape from the land of the Amazons. His companion in this grotesque dungeon I could not recognize, but even semiconscious he, too, had a piratic look about him.

Seeing my evident uncertainty, Theseus introduced me to his comrade, naming him Pirithous. It was hard to estimate sizes when both men were sitting down, but I thought Pirithous was nearly as big as Theseus, and more thickly built.

Theseus seemed to think it important to tell me more about his companion. "He was a Lapith chieftain—Hercules, this damned fool once tried to steal some sheep from me, did you know that?"

"No," I said.

When Pirithous would not respond to verbal urgings, Theseus kicked him and swore at him and finally managed to rouse him a little from his stupor.

Meanwhile I was asking: "So how in hell did the two of you ever find your way down into the Underworld? And how long have you been here?"

Theseus frowned and shook his head. His lips moved as if he were making an effort to count something.

"Just got here," said Pirithous, his bass voice full of misplaced confidence, as he added a string of blasphemies against a formidable array of gods. Though he now gave the impression of being more or less aware of his surroundings, it was obvious that neither he nor Theseus had any real idea of how much time had passed.

As I have already mentioned, the row of stumps, or Thrones of Lethe, extended into the distance. A hint of shadowed movement, yards away, suggested that not all the Thrones were empty in that direction.

I was more perturbed, and fascinated, by the prisoners' unique surroundings than they themselves seemed to be.

"Is there no decent *light* down here?" I demanded. "No torches, candles, a simple oil lamp even?" I still could not identify the source of the faint illumination that suggested more than it revealed, and rendered hideous the few details that it did make clear.

Theseus strained against his bonds as if he had suddenly just noticed them, his mighty muscles quivering for a long moment before he slumped back. In an ordinary man, his posture would have suggested something like despair.

"Hercules, can you get us out?"

His voice now sounded muted, and that was the least arrogant thing I had ever heard him say.

"It's possible," I told him. "I have yet to see the bond I couldn't break."

I bent to make a closer examination of the links and clamps that held the pirates to their stumps. The material of the Thrones strongly resembled that of other ancient odylic devices I had encountered recently. Each consisted of a flat seat attached to the top of a short pillar of white stone, smooth as marble, with odd devices connected to it, things that I supposed must have some magical import. The confining chains, like those that had bound Prometheus, were of brass or bronze or iron (it was hard to be sure in the dimness), fastened with clasps of what looked like ebony and ivory to hold the captive's wrists and ankles.

I took some links between my fingers.

"Slain in some sea fight at last, were you?" I demanded of the master pirate. Not that I really thought him or his companion dead—there was too much breath and sweat and profanity about them. At the same time, the shackle holding the right arm of Theseus let go with a ringing snap. Seconds later I heard a metal fragment land on hard rock in the distance.

"No. No, nothing like that." His handsome eyes were clearing now, with activity and the prospect of freedom. "Hercules, it is really you? Damnation, but I think it is. Who else could break these things? So, Thanatos has collected you after all."

"Like hell he has! I'll collect *him* if he comes within my grasp. I'm very much alive."

But there was no use trying to explain my situation to Theseus now, or obtain any useful information from him. Suddenly he was almost comatose again. I pulled his tilted helmet entirely off his head, but that seemed to make little difference. As long as he remained sitting on a Throne of Lethe, it seemed impossible to rouse the Prince of Pirates from his trancelike state for more than a few moments at a stretch. He could only respond feebly when I shook him and called his name.

Exerting my strength against one after another of the material bonds that held him—the chains were tougher than I had expected, but in the end I had my way—I managed to free Theseus entirely, and pulled him to is feet.

He staggered but did not fall. As soon as he had broken contact with the Throne of Lethe, the master pirate gazed at me like a man freshly awakened from some hideous dream, and I saw the sweat break out on his living, breathing face. In the next moment he tore off the festive garments in which he had been dressed, and stood in the noxious darkness naked, his whole body trembling.

Casting another glance down the row of chairs, noting again that there was a third one, in the distance, that also seemed to be occupied, I asked what had happened to the Amazon princess, Antiope, who had been with him when we last met.

Theseus answered shortly that she was not here.

Meanwhile I was methodically working to free Pirithous, who let his festive garments stay on when he got up. He, like his captain, gave every indication of being still actively alive.

I remarked on this, and they emphatically agreed.

"We're no more dead than you are, by the balls of Zeus!" growled Theseus.

"I'd say a lot closer to it, though. Well, if the pair of you were not killed in some sea fight, how *did* you get into this situation?"

"We were hunting Persephone," Pirithous admitted in a mumble.

For a moment I was sure that my ears had betrayed me. "You were hunting *who?*"

"You know, Hades's queen."

"I know who Persephone is; the queen of this place, consort of Hades, or call him Dis or Pluto if you like." Planting my fists on my hips, I shook my head. "What I find hard to believe is that anyone could be stupid enough to try a trick like that."

Theseus shrugged and seemed to revel in the freedom of movement he had now regained. Somehow he was not angered by my harsh words; looking back, I think he was actually pleased to find himself in the company of someone strong enough to assume a kind of authority, for this allowed him to play his favorite role of carefree rebel.

He went on: "My friend Pirithous here had taken a fancy to her. And, well, when that happens, what can a man do? We were going to carry her away. I thought that once we got back to our ship . . ." He shrugged again and let the idea die away.

"You *thought?* That you would simply carry away a goddess? I wouldn't call that thinking. And how did you manage to get in here, anyway? And where's your ship?"

"There's a river, called Acheron, that has it source in the Upper World but drains into a cave. We took that route. But I'm afraid the ship is gone."

I nodded. "It did seem to me that there had to be more than one entrance," I remarked. "Maybe there are many."

Slowly Theseus shook his head. "Not such a good idea, was it?" he admitted. "Well, we were both a little drunk at the time."

"I wouldn't call that an idea at all, kidnapping the consort of Hades! Even a pair of stupid pirates should have known better."

Pirithous groaned something inarticulate. I supposed that Hades, even in his craziness, must have been impressed by their audacity, but certainly not amused by it. When he caught these intruders, the mad Lord of the Underworld had told them they were invited to a banquet, and had dressed them in festive garments. But then Hades had placed them on the Thrones of Lethe, and they were fortunate indeed that he had not yet got around to doing worse.

Theseus had now recovered enough of his wits to feel deeply shaken by the experience. "Were you ever caught up in the hands of a god, Hercules? You may be strong, but . . . just grabbed up, like a child, and then tied down like a laced shoe? There's not much a man can do when that happens to him. Not even a man as powerful as you are."

"No, not much. Let me ask you again, now that you're fully awake: I don't suppose you've seen Thanatos anywhere around here?" Hades had shown me what looked to me like the Face of Death, and told me a story to go with it; but the urge for revenge would not let go of me that easily.

Pirithous shook his head. Theseus said: "No, we've seen no one like that." And now his tone, for once, became suddenly plaintive. "Hercules? Get us out of here?" And Pirithous, with a kind of inarticulate groan, seconded the plea.

"I'll try. But first, I think there's someone else, down that way. Let me see who it is." And I turned away and began to walk along the line of Thrones.

Before I had taken many steps, I heard another strained and strangely familiar voice call my name from that direction.

In another moment I was close enough to get a clear look at the face of Meleager, Danni's brother, who sat chained to another stone tree stump.

I had no surprise left in me.

This third prisoner, dressed in an ordinary tunic that he might have worn while on his Argosy adventure, was more fully conscious than either of the buccaneers had been when on their Thrones.

"Hercules?" he croaked.

"It's me. Hold still, and I'll have you loose in a moment." And I set down my club again.

"I died foolishly, Hercules!" Meleager was plainly in a mood for agonized repentance. "Wickedly abandoning my responsibilities to my family in the Upper World."

"You haven't died at all, not yet," I counseled him. "Not entirely."

Spang went a chain. Again the spray of fragments, making a fine pattern on distant stone.

"I am dead." Mel contradicted me flatly, speaking in the solemn tone of one who wanted to be finished with all mortal life. "I couldn't be here otherwise. I'm dead and undergoing a just punishment for the evil I have done. For all the good I have failed to do." He paused, wrinkling his brow. "Whereas you're really still alive, aren't you?"

"My body is as solid and hale as ever," I assured him. *Spang.*

Now he was trying to wrench the helmet off his head, but not having any success. "Hercules, if you ever do manage to return to the Upper World alive—"

"I suppose that might happen." I really believe that until that moment I had not thought about it, one way or the other.

"—I entreat you to marry my sister, Deianeira."

His words struck me speechless, and my hands ceased their work for a long moment.

"Hercules, she is an innocent young girl. As yet she knows nothing of the ways of Aphrodite, charmer of men."

Remembering our meeting at the court of King Admetus, I was not totally sure about that, but in any case it seemed irrelevant.

"How do you know that you were killed?" I demanded of Meleager, changing the subject. Meanwhile, every time I looked at him or touched him my conviction was reaffirmed that this was indeed a living man. I could watch him breathe, and feel the solidity of his limbs as I peeled away their bonds.

In another moment he was completely free, but seemed unable to give my question a clear answer. "Something hit me in the head. Then there was another fight, and it seemed to me I drowned . . ."

*　　*　　*

As far as I could tell, there were no other captives in the great prison room; hasty introductions were performed, and the four of us began to look for some way out. I felt reluctant to go back through Hades's throne room; and I got the impression, trying to see through fog and shadow, that the door in that direction was now closed.

Meanwhile, Meleager was not yet fully satisfied that he still breathed. "How could I be here if I wasn't dead?" he insisted, after a few moments of thick-witted attempt at thought.

I shook my head at this. "You're no deader than the rest of us."

Meleager now resumed his attempts to arrange a marriage. Before his plunge into the Underworld, he had been the surviving male head of the family, and as an honorable man had considered his sister his responsibility.

"Hercules, I should never have gone off with Jason on that mad expedition. Not when it meant abandoning my family responsibilities. I have failed in my duty to my sister, because it was entirely up to me to see to it that she makes a good marriage. Now more than ever she needs a decent husband. I'm serious, I entreat you to take her for your wife."

"Why 'more than ever'?"

"Because—I'm dead."

"Oh yes, I had forgotten. Well, finding an acceptable husband for Danni should not be difficult at all—she is a lovely woman."

"That she is." Meleager paused, looked at me closely. Then in a loud, firm voice, he said: "As for 'acceptable,' my standards are quite high. Hercules, if you are able to return to the world above, I charge you with the duty of marrying my sister."

I stared at him, realizing that he was not just dazed, and wondering if he had gone as mad as Hades. But then I remembered that Meleager had not seen me since the day, long months ago, when the Argonauts had left me and my nephew stranded on the shores of Mysia. How long ago that seemed! So it was highly unlikely that Mel could have heard the news of my marriage to Megan, or her recent death.

I find it hard to reconstruct, or understand, my own mental state at this time. Possibly my grief for my lost loved ones had burned so fiercely that already there were only ashes left. Still, it would seem

that no thought could be farther from my mind than that of contract-
ing another marriage. But I can only report what truly happened, and
the fact is that I heard myself agreeing to Mel's entreaties—perhaps
in those circumstances I would have said anything to stop his raving.

Besides, I had to confront the fact that my search for Thanatos in
Hell had failed. Before I went elsewhere seeking Death, I might as
well take the opportunity to cheat him out of three more victims.

"Stay close behind me, men," I told the trio who now—yes, even
Theseus—were looking to me for leadership. "I'm getting out of
here, and I don't think anyone will try to stop me as I leave." Privately
I told myself that I would welcome any such attempt.

I chose the direction in which the ground beneath our feet
seemed to rise a little as we moved, and set out.

Meleager, as we progressed, tearfully confessed that he felt a
great responsibility for the kidnapping of Enkidu, which had resulted
in the lad's being thrown into the Pool of Pegae, all because most of
the Argonauts wanted to delay and get rid of his powerful uncle. Mel
said he had not been directly responsible, but he had failed to properly discourage the attempt.

"I am sorry now that I didn't try to stop them, Hercules." His
honest face was woebegone.

"It's over now, and no harm done," I told him shortly. "Let it be
forgotten."

I gave serious thought to the possibility of summoning my *Skyboat* to come cruising right along the Styx, or the Acheron, and enjoyed a moment of sardonic amusement at the thought of Charon's
reaction to such competition. But then I thought of the long, long detour the boat might have to travel to get from the nameless stream
where I had left it waiting, and decided it had best stay there.

The fact was that I had virtually given up trying to find Thanatos in
the Underworld. Since entering Hell, I had repeatedly encountered
folk whom I could recognize, a state of affairs which seemed unlikely, considering the vast number of people who must have died
since the beginning of the world, and of all those who must be dying
now, hour by hour and minute by minute, in every nation and in many
of the ships at sea, with or without the personal help of Thanatos or

any other god. In an Underworld so heavily populated, why, out of all those thousands, nay millions, should I keep encountering so many people I had known?

Surely something more than mere chance must be involved. So, were the Death God here, I thought, I would have found him by now. Since he was not, I would have to seek him elsewhere.

Besides, there had been something convincing in the way that Hades, whether he was insane or not, had twirled what appeared to be the Face of Death around his finger.

As the four of us moved on from room to room, an obstacle to our departure soon presented itself. There came a huge whining and shuffling in the darkness, and then we saw it: what I can only describe as a three-headed dog, shaggy and elephant-sized, though built closer to the ground than any elephant.

When I was on Corycus, several people had told me that at least two versions of Cerberus had been destroyed in recent years—but here was yet another duplication, or perhaps it was a new edition, of the great dog.

Cerberus was stranger than any beast I had encountered on the surface of the earth, perhaps even more bizarre than Antaeus. He, or it, was neither beast, god, nor human, but rather an artifact of the mysterious odylic process.

Each head was equipped with a pair of wide-set yellow eyes and supported by its own set of forelegs, so that the creature walked and ran upon eight legs in all. Each set of jaws was filled with long, sharp teeth.

Pirithous and Meleager retreated hastily, for which I could not blame them. Theseus danced about alertly, keeping out of reach of those six big jaws.

"I think I can grab one leg and hold it, Hercules," he calmly proposed. "Or would you rather I took the tail?"

I thanked him politely but suggested that his best move would be to stay clear. Then I stepped in close to Cerberus, catching all three of its slow brains by surprise, and stunned the one in the middle with a punch. The two remaining heads howled and snarled and snapped. Both tried to get at me at once, with the effect of paralyzing their shared body with contradictory commands.

A bit of scrambling about was necessary before all three heads could be rendered unconscious, and while that was in progress I considered the idea of bringing back to Hephaestus and Daedalus some sample fragment of the great dog's flesh and bone.

Or, for that matter, the whole thing, as I had once brought the Boar. I could picture myself throwing Cerberus down at the feet of Hermes, or of Zeus himself. "Here, you are so obsessed with monsters, take this one!"

But I soon gave up on that plan. Getting the whole beast out alive, with the three heads probably regaining consciousness at random intervals, would certainly have required a terrific struggle.

Pirithous and Meleager soon returned, and the four of us walked on, leaving the monster dog where it had fallen. We had not gone far when it began to whine and whimper in the gloom behind us. But those sounds faded gradually as we moved away.

Finding my way down into Hell had been comparatively easy. But once the decision had been made to get out again, I realized that I faced something of a problem. Simply retracing my steps seemed out of the question; I had the feeling that the scenery here was slowly and continually shifting, so that finding the right way would be hopeless. Theseus and Pirithous had no more idea than I did of which way we ought to go; and Meleager could not even remember how he had been brought into the Underworld.

Doing the best we could, we groped our way through one room and passage after another, praying for providential guidance and trying to climb when we came to anything like a stair or ramp.

Now the stench of sulphur mounted in my nostrils. We had reached the hinterland of Hell, a dark and smoky place enough in its own right, bathed in some kind of volcanic fumes, and frightening in the way that all deeply unsettled things can be.

How long we kept at it I cannot say, but eventually determination was rewarded. What had looked like only more hellish space, only mere fogbank dimness, turned out when I bumped into it to be a solid wall, painted or naturally colored gray, in shadings that gave it the look of fog when seen from only a few feet away.

As soon as I felt it was solid wall, and had made sure there was no door, I hit the blank surface with my fist, putting some energy behind the blow. Something cracked, in the circumstances an encouraging sound. I hit it again, still harder, and then again. Pieces began to fall away, and presently I succeeded in breaking my way through.

Emerging on the other side of the wall, we immediately felt a movement of what smelled and tasted like fresh air. The other aspects of the world were not much changed, but the refreshing draft gave us hope. Finding an ascending slope, we pushed on with fresh energy, drawing in deep breaths.

After a long climb, during which the world around us underwent a gradual alteration, we came to a place where we were undoubtedly aboveground, and the blessed light of Apollo's sun, or Diana's moon, was visible at least dimly, and there were living, growing things about.

I had found my way down into Hell, then fought my way up and out of it again.

But as soon as all immediate challenges had been disposed of, the pointlessness of it all struck me with overwhelming force. The fact that I had survived another adventure was ultimately meaningless. I had really won nothing at all.

Megan was still dead, and so was small Hyllus, whose life I had, without fully realizing it, begun to consider in some ways more important than my own. I saw the world before me as a dark, blank space, devoid of significance.

And when that thought came I collapsed again, sitting on the ground, not knowing what to do or what was to become of me. I felt like most of my self had been consumed in the fires of my own rage and hate.

On my emergence from the Underworld I more than half expected to find Hermes waiting for me, ready to congratulate me on my accomplishments and to tell me that my divine sponsors had a new job for me to undertake. Oh, the Messenger would probably be very glad to see me, having a good reason to fear that a valuable worker had gone to Hell and would not be coming back. And of course he would have good reasons why neither he nor Zeus had gone to Tartarus to look for me.

Not that Zeus was ever going to speak to me directly. But I knew exactly what I was going to tell the Messenger when next I saw him: "If any of you gods have seen my father, I would like to see him, too. No matter if he is not in fact all-powerful. No matter even if there are a hundred Giants stronger than he is, or if he has now gone as mad as Hades. I won't hold any of those things against him. But I have done all that I swore to do, and more; and I intend to hold him to his promise to meet with me. There are some words I want to say to him."

As soon as we could be sure that we were out, my three companions wept tears of joy and hastened to offer prayers and promise sacrifices of thanksgiving. Meleager, finally convinced that he was still alive, was in ecstasy. Their demonstrations of delight evoked in me nothing but the dregs of my rage at Thanatos, and loathing for the world.

The sky in the east turned light, and presently I could see the sun again, but at first the sight meant nothing to me. The light of sun and moon and stars was only mockery.

When my three companions in escape offered me words of comfort and tried to inspire me to new hope, I raised my fist and roared at them. Two of them prudently retreated. Only one remained, who was still standing near me when I once more raised my head. Again I raised my fist menacingly, but the figure before me did not move.

Theseus, the scoundrel and pirate, was the only one who defied my stupid threats and remained with me. Pirithous had taken to his heels—and so, I observed, had Meleager, who an hour or so ago had pledged himself to me in eternal gratitude and friendship. I groaned out curses at the remaining pirate and warned him to be on his way, too.

But when I looked up again, some minutes later, Theseus was still standing there, exactly where he had been.

He said in a firm voice: "Pull yourself together, shipmate."

I gave him a look that would have driven ten ordinary men away. But Theseus stared right back at me.

He said: "Hell of a thing, what Death did to you. Robbed you all at once of everything you had. I don't know if I could take a punch like that—hell, I know I couldn't. I've never had the guts to live that kind of life. Love people and have them love me, knowing it could all be lost. Which is doubtless why I could never pick one woman and . . ."

An interval of silence passed, while my companion looked away from me, as if he pondered the evils of the world, or perhaps had been surprised by something in himself. Then he came a little closer and squatted down at my side. Presently he sighed, and went on:

"I'm older than you, Hercules, and there's some things I do know. When the whole damned world has fallen on a man's head, he's got to suck in his gut and keep going. Do that, and you can still win. Law of nature. Win, even if the bastards kill you. But if you don't do that, then you've let them win."

"I . . ." It was excruciatingly hard to get out any words at all. "I wanted to find Death. Whether I could beat the hell out of him again, or whether he got me this time . . . but instead there sat Hades, gone completely mad. He had the Face of Death in his hands, and he sat there, twirling it around his finger."

My faithful companion nodded, as if he understood. At least he sympathized, and at the moment that was more important. Later I realized that the pirate's understanding went in some ways deeper than my own.

After a while he reassured me: "You'll catch up with him. Sooner or later."

Theseus stayed with me yet for a while longer. Until, I suppose, he saw in me some sign that in my mind I had turned some kind of corner and was going to heed his advice.

"You'll be all right now, Hercules. Yeah, I think you will. Let your friends help you."

And at last he quietly moved on.

TWENTY-FIVE

Wrestling

kyboat had not yet rejoined me, and I began to travel on my own two legs, looking for a sizable stream where I might hope that it would soon be able to meet me.

After my descent into the Underworld, and after Theseus had given me his necessary pep talk, and I had made my way through the rest of the limbo of the borderlands, I craved a face-to-face meeting with my father even more desperately than before.

Now I was traveling alone again, even though more than ever I needed to talk to someone who could make sense out of what had happened in my own life, and was still happening in the world. I would have given much to have even an hour with Daedalus, but that was not to be.

Danni's green eyes and slender body kept intruding upon my thoughts, and I yearned toward her as if I might find in her a place of refuge from grief and fear and turmoil. Again in memory I saw the face of her brother, deep in Tartarus, and heard him urging me to marry her. The words took on the character of some mystic revelation.

The first time I feel asleep after returning to the world of the living, I had a dream in which I found myself dueling somehow with my father. I thought in my vision that Zeus, huge, gray-bearded, the image of a quintessential patriarch, came at me armed with the sword and shield of the Amazon queen, and my club was awkward, and suddenly it became too heavy for me to lift at all.

It was all unclear in my mind as to whether the duel had anything to do with my promise to marry Danni.

I crossed a small stream or two, but still had not regained the *Skyboat*. I was wandering in an unknown country, far from home, vaguely hoping somehow to regain contact with Apollo.

In my alienated state of mind I kept wondering if all the gods that

I had ever met had been deranged or even killed by some effort of our terrible enemies. The dream in which Apollo appeared to me was reassuring, but he might of course have fallen in battle after that.

In the course of my waking wanderings, I came to a town of modest size whose name I did not know; nor was I at all certain what border I had last crossed. But I could understand the speech of those I met, or enough of it to meet my needs, and this satisfied me for the time being.

The townsfolk greeted me with a simple, courteous welcome. It seemed that I now found myself in a land set apart from most of the world's wars and upheavals, where the people seemed simple and for the most part honest. Here and there were simple shrines to the usual gods, the figures considered most likely to be helpful and dependable.

The town's mayor, a gray-bearded elder with massive eyebrows and a pleasant face, came out to offer me official welcome, and did so without indicating that he knew he had a celebrity on his hands. I got the impression that any well-behaved traveler might have been given the same reception.

There was a small speech that I had given often since the beginning of my wanderings, and now I used it yet again.

"My name is Hercules, and I am an honest man. I am also a stranger among you, far from my own home, and I ask for what you can spare me in the way of food and clothing."

"That seems a most reasonable request, and it is granted." The old man, who had shown no reaction when he heard my name, briefly paused to study me before he added: "But will you do us one reasonable favor in return?"

"Very likely. What is it?"

Leaning a little forward, he pronounced the one word carefully: "Wrestle."

"Wrestle?" For a moment I wondered whether I had heard him correctly. "Wrestle who? And where, and why, and when?"

The man looked a little pained, as if the speech he gave me had been enforced upon him. He said: "There is a certain competition pending, in which it is crucial to us that our town should not be utterly disgraced. Understand, stranger, that whether you actually win a single match or not is of small importance. All that really matters is that you make a creditable effort."

"All right." I could feel myself relaxing inwardly. "I can manage that, and it doesn't seem a lot to ask. Far be it from me to bring disgrace upon my hosts."

The mayor smiled. "Good. We will feed you first, of course. We want you to be strong." And he looked at my unimpressive frame with optimistic eyes.

While I attacked the substantial meal that was soon set before me, washing it down with a flagon of good local beer, I heard the explanations of the townsfolk as to why they were in need of another wrestler.

The whole business seemed a little odd, but reasonably straightforward. The wrestling matches were part of a local tradition of competition with a neighboring town. Each town's chosen competitors formed a single line, the two lines approaching each other head-on, from opposite sides of the wrestling ring. The losing contestant in each match, two falls out of three, was eliminated, and the next man in line stood up in his place. When all the members of either one line or the other had been thrown, the opposite team was acclaimed the winner.

Meanwhile, the general populations of the two towns mingled freely; scores of women, children, and elders all gathered outside the ring to watch and to cheer on their respective local heroes in a festive, almost carnival, atmosphere. Similar contests between towns existed in Cadmia, and in my wanderings I had encountered others. As such affairs went, this one seemed notably unbloody. For that reason, I thought, if for no other, it deserved to be encouraged.

I was not surprised to see that most of the other contestants, on both sides, were bigger than me, bulkier with bone and muscle. When we had stripped, put on the traditional loincloths worn in wrestling, and had taken our places for the event, my hosts' line was notably shorter than that of their opponents. As a relatively small man of unproven skill, I was placed at the tail of it, with the stoutest champion at the head.

After a few speeches, mercifully short, the match got under way. Women and children cheered on the sidelines, and the elder men looked on with varying expressions.

My hosts were somewhat downcast, though not especially surprised, when the opposition proved more powerful and our line was soon depleted. When I stepped forward, the opposing line was only a little shorter than it had been at the start, with almost a dozen men remaining. In contrast, I was the last hope for our side.

Still, I would have been willing to lay a small wager that we were not going to lose.

Methodically, I began to work my way through the opposing wrestlers, who, as I had expected, presented no particular problem. For a time I amused myself by throwing them in alternate directions, one this way and the next one that. I allowed each one to struggle and strain for a short time before disposing of him. Of course I grimaced and grunted at appropriate moments, trying to cloak my series of victories in an air of difficulty.

I had gone through six or seven opponents in this fashion, creating something of a sensation in the audience. And now here came the next man in line. His body was muscular but not spectacular, his size was no greater than ordinary, and there was nothing in his face to capture my attention. Some gray was sprinkled in his dark beard, making him seem a little older than his teammates, though still far from ancient.

Reaching out, I seized the rolled cloth belt of his loincloth with one hand, and one of his arms with the other, taking care not to crush the bones and flesh. With gentle force I pulled and pushed—

—and found myself swept helplessly right off my feet, spinning in midair, the world's whirl ending only when my flight ended, with a great thump that left me flat on my back and staring in stupefaction at the sky.

My head was still spinning as I scrambled quickly to all fours, then up into a kind of wrestler's crouch. My opponent was in roughly the same position, looking at me keenly, his expression indicating wariness rather than the triumph or surprise I had expected.

The crowd around us, instead of closing in, had drawn back in apprehension. For a moment there had been shocked silence, and now there was a steady murmuring.

Now at last I took a good look at the man who had actually over-powered me and thrown me to the ground. If he was indeed a god, and I had to assume he was, his appearance still gave no clue to his exact identity.

There was a louder murmuring from the crowd as word spread of the remarkable thing that had just happened. From what I could over-hear, I gathered that the onlookers were as amazed as I was, and no one seemed to have any idea of the stranger's identity.

We closed and grappled with each other once again. This time it seemed to me that though my opponent's strength was absolutely fan-tastic, every bit the equal of my own, he was not as skilled as other men I had encountered, whose skills had of course availed them nothing.

Here and there during my wanderings, including my earlier matches of the day, I had without even trying picked up a trick or two, simply by observing what one wrestler after another tried to do to me.

Attempting one of these tricks now, I put something like my full strength into the effort, and was rewarded by seeing the mystery man swept off his feet, to land awkwardly and with a heavy thud.

To judge by his expression, he was every bit as surprised as I had been—and a moment later, every bit as determined to have revenge.

We grunted a few terse comments at each other.

The noise of the crowd drowned out all else, as we closed and grappled for the third time.

As sometimes happens, more often when neither contestant has much skill, the fall was inconclusive. We staggered and came down together. Before we could regain our feet and try again, eager voices were being raised on all sides. I heard that the mayors of the two towns seemed to be declaring a truce, both of them eager to conclude that the contest had ended in a draw.

By mutual consent my opponent and I let ourselves sink back to the ground. We sat there in the worn dirt, staring at each other, while the sound of my own racing pulse in my ears gradually died away, and the heaving of my chest for air subsided. The man who had managed to throw me to the earth was wearing a little smile now, as if he was quite pleased with the result of our tussle. His face, everything about him looked staggeringly ordinary. And obviously he was waiting for me to speak first.

I tried to speak, failed, and tried again. A third attempt was necessary before I could get out the words, "You are my father."

The smile that great Zeus was wearing broadened, making pleasant creases in his face. I noted that somehow my father's skin was more weathered and lined than mine was, or would ever be.

He said, in a voice that just missed being ordinary: "And you are Hercules. Every bit as strong as I had hoped you would be. Come, we must have a talk."

Jumping to his feet, as if to make a point of the fact that he was fully recovered from our gasping struggle, he offered me a hand and pulled me up. Then he linked his arm with mine and led me away to a place where, for some reason, none of the curious onlookers followed. I could hear them somewhere in the middle distance, marveling loudly over how the pair of champions had suddenly disappeared.

After all my efforts to bring this moment about, I came perilously close to not knowing what to say.

"You are—" But somehow I could not get out the words.

"I am your father. Yes, you were quite right the first time." The Thunderer wiped sweat from his face and chuckled in a very human way.

Despite his show of jumping quickly to his feet, we were both still breathing heavily. At last I managed to find some words: "So, I have outwrestled Zeus himself."

"Only in one fall out of three! I would not brag, upstart, if I were you." Though the words were harsh, the tone in which they were spoken told of pride and even a kind of love.

Then the most powerful god in the Universe cast back over his left shoulder a look that was almost furtive.

"Besides," my father said, "the less closely the world can keep track of my whereabouts, the better. In particular, the Giants are not to know anything at all of where I am, or what I'm doing."

I made an awkward, sweeping gesture. "This whole wrestling contest—"

He nodded. "All designed just so you and I could have this meeting. I have taken considerable pains to arrange it. I wanted to keep it as secret as possible from our enemies, and to make sure that you would be unlikely to refuse to take part."

"I am honored."

"You deserve to be honored. You have done well."

"Thank you," I said. And then: "I have prayed for this meeting."

"That was well done." It seemed a perfectly sincere comment.

"Do gods really hear all their worshipers' prayers?" I asked my father. "There must be thousands and thousands every day."

"More like millions and millions, Hercules. But there is no need for the gods to hear every single one of them, because we know what they are. What they always are, have always been."

I thought that over for a little while. "And do you, great Zeus, know the details of the lives of all your thousands of children?"

"Zeus has thousands of offspring, true. But without his Face in here"—and my father raised a hand to touch his forehead—"I would still be a man; and the man who now wears the Face of Zeus"—he thumped himself on the chest—"has only a very few children whom he calls his own."

"And I—"

"And you, Hercules, I am proud to say, are one of them."

We talked for a time of other matters, but inevitably came to the matter of the Giants.

We talked for what seemed a long time, and I do not remember all of what we said. But at one point, I know Zeus told me: "Mortals are always wondering why we have so often withdrawn ourselves from human affairs for extended periods. But few if any have guessed the correct answer."

"Which is simply fear."

"Fear indeed. A god, or goddess, appearing openly among humans will inevitably soon draw a crowd. And crowds are conspicuous and make it easy for our enemies to keep track of where we are."

And I said to him: "Apollo told me that his true name—his first, human name—is Jeremy Redthorn."

"I'm well aware of what the young man told you. But don't expect to hear any similar revelations from me. There are good reasons."

"I don't doubt it, sir."

And then my father began to talk about me. I will not set down here everything that he said, but it turned out that he knew many details of my childhood that I had imagined no one but myself would ever know.

As soon as I had the chance, I began to question him about Hera, the goddess proclaimed by tradition to be his consort, and who, I had some reason to believe, had once sent snakes to kill me in my cradle.

My father frowned. "Sadly, there is some truth in the story. I regret I was not alert enough to prevent it—more proof, if any were needed, of my own distinct lack of omnipotence. But that's all over and done with."

He heaved a sigh, and his face regained cheerfulness. "Hera exists now in a new avatar—have you met her yet?—never mind, you will. No reason to think of her current version as my wife, but she and I are on good terms. No, Hercules, as far as I know, you have nothing to fear from any god or goddess."

"That's good to know, sir." I paused, then added: "But there is one god who has much to fear from me, if I ever get my hands on him again."

"That avatar of Death is himself dead," said Zeus. Then he added: "Of course I would have stopped the horror he committed against your family, had I known in time what he intended. But you must understand that I have my limits, too, especially since I began to encounter Giants. And you must be careful what you do to gods, even the most minor ones. Almost all of them are jealous of our power and status and want no humiliation at the hands of mortals."

"I understand that, sir."

"I remember the day Amphitryon flogged you with a belt," Zeus went on, smiling faintly. "That was one time when there was obviously no need for me to intervene on your behalf."

"I should not have broken his fine dagger."

"No, that was wrong of you. But you were very young; and I, too, have broken many things that I should not, while lacking your excuse."

I wondered, silently, if my father had also been watching on the day when I first made love to Megan. Some part of me wanted to ask him that, but a greater part would not.

And then there was the sad hour in which I had killed Linus. But we did not speak of that time, either.

Now Zeus was looking at me in a way that made me wonder if he could indeed see everything that was in my heart. He said: "Today is a good day, as far as my wits are concerned. I seem to be recovering as rapidly as can be expected from my last duel with a Giant. That is why—that is one reason—I have chosen it for our talk."

We talked, at last, about the final fate of Megan and little Hyllus. "I hope and pray," I said, "their true souls are not wandering lost, somewhere in the Underworld."

"That much I can promise you," my father said.

"Indeed," I said, "I was pretty well convinced that there are no true souls there. I saw strange empty images, and a few bodies that lived and breathed, as lively as my own."

"'We each of us owe God a death . . . ,'" said the man who was supposed to be the greatest god himself, and I had the impression that he was quoting something. "Someday, Hercules, you and I must have a talk on the subject of life and death."

"In a way, sir," I said impulsively, "you remind me of Daedalus."

"Do I, indeed? I take that as a compliment. I hope the Artisan would feel the same way."

At last, so Zeus told me, he had available the results of the analysis, performed by Vulcan and Daedalus, of the Boar I had brought in alive, and of the other samples of flesh and bone from an assortment of monsters, including Antaeus.

And he got to his feet, with the air of a king about to take his leave.

But before departing, he said to me: "You are my son, and I am proud of you."

"Father!" The word still sounded strange in my own ears. When he paused, I demanded: "When will I see you again? Tell me, what am I to do next?"

Zeus shook his head. "If only I were really as all-powerful as the legends have me! All I can tell you with certainty is that I must go now, and I will see you again when the proper time has come. Meanwhile, here is another you have met, and you must go with him."

My visit with Atlas, and my sojourn underground, had revealed to me too much of the Universe for me to any longer imagine that Zeus or any other individual might be its ruler.

And when my father had said good-bye, I was not much surprised to see Apollo waiting for me in his chariot, ready to convey me to the secret laboratory.

The Far-Worker and I greeted each other joyfully, and I learned with great relief that he had once again regained his mental faculties, and practically all his memory.

He said to me: "We gods are resilient. But how many more times our minds may be so damaged, and still recover . . ." The god shook his head pessimistically.

And yet once more, taking my courage in both hands, I boarded my friend's chariot, not knowing if we could reach our destination before some Giant's weapon, like an invisible arrow, shot us out of the sky.

This time we flew far, and higher than before, so high indeed that my lungs worked hard for breath. My imagination peopled the earth below us thickly with Giants, towering forms who scanned the skies for targets—like hunters with bows and slings, who look for ducks. But if in fact there were any such enemies around, they could not see us, and we were not attacked.

Vulcan's Workshop

*L*ike everyone else I knew, I had been hearing stories about Vulcan's workshop all my life. It was one of the great establishments of legend, in which, from time immemorial, all manner of marvels had been and were still being produced. And at the end of my second ride in a flying chariot, which concluded much more successfully than my first, I was able to confirm with my own eyes the truth of some of the strangest tales.

By the time we began our second hour of flight, I knew that we were farther north than I had ever been before. As we approached our destination from the air, there appeared before us a rocky island, bound by glaciers, a mile out from the ragged, fog-bound shoreline of a northern ocean, under the slanted light of a western sun. Gray, sullen seas beat on the sharp rocks of the little island, far less than a square mile in area. I would not have wanted to attempt to reach that goal by sea, not even in the *Skyboat*. Even the name of this ocean was unknown to me, and I realized that its waters were connected to those of the Great Sea only by a long, circuitous route.

But thoughts of geography and navigation were secondary at the moment. I scarcely felt the icy wind that tugged at my hair and beard, or the warmth of the low sun in the bright sky. I was no stranger to earthly palaces, but never had I seen, and scarcely had I imagined, anything like this. Looking at the island, and the structure occupying most of its surface, I would never have guessed that it had ever been inhabited by either gods or humans.

The location seemed to have been chosen with the idea of making the fortress on it not only unassailable, but approachable only by gods, or by other beings with a comparable talent for flight.

The whole building—for such my escort assured me it was— seemed little more than a huge slab of dark, slippery rock, perhaps a hundred feet high, tilted only a few degrees out of the vertical, and emerging from a rocky platform only a few feet above the level of the sea. The only sign of artifice was a few reinforcing bands of strong metal, inlaid into the otherwise almost featureless rock.

As the chariot bore us down toward a landing on the platform base, I was puzzled at still being able to see no doors or windows in all the flat expanse of walls. There were indeed huge panels, almost flat and smooth, whose appearance from a quarter of a mile away had suggested that they might be enormous doors. But as we drew nearer still, our flight slowing almost to a stop as it neared its end, I saw that their surfaces were devoid of any lock or hinge or joining, and there appeared to be no way to get a grip to try to open them.

Either Apollo was reading my mind or his powers of observation allowed him to determine just what I was looking at.

"Once I tried my full strength against those portals," he informed me. "And as you see, they are still standing."

I looked at him, and at the rock, and back to him again. "The lord Vulcan must build well, and deserves his reputation," I said.

"Indeed he does. But this time we come with a key and know the secret of the lock."

Apollo's pacing horses seemed to know just where to bring us down, without specific orders from their master. We landed on a small, flat space just in front of the largest flat panel that might have been a door. I believe my escort was just about to put a key into a lock (thought I could not discern the keyhole) when the door was opened for us by the life-sized figure of a slender maiden, completely nude and seeming to be made entirely of shining gold.

As long as we were still airborne, the chariot had glowed with a kind of inner warmth, which had sufficed to keep my mortal flesh from freezing. But when we came to a halt and I jumped out, the full arctic blast of Hyperborean wind struck at me, and I was very glad to follow the gesture of the golden maid, who beckoned me to her through the doorway, into a place of comfortable warmth and cheerful light.

I started to speak to the maid as I hurried past her, but before I had finished a sentence I was completely sure that the figure before me was neither human nor god, but only a device of metal and magic, cunningly formed into the shape of a young girl. Apollo, entering the fortress right behind me, ignored the golden marvel and strode on down a long hallway, halloing ahead in the manner of a man entering a familiar house. The maiden promptly closed the outer door behind us.

Moments later my divine companion and I were standing in a vast room, almost as big as the hall of Hades in the Underworld, furnished with chairs and tables of heroic size, and lit by the orange glow of a distant forge. Another moment after that, and we were being welcomed by a marvelous company, in which Daedalus, the only mortal present besides myself, made the least impressive figure.

Half a dozen tall, formidable figures were gathered in the hall, and most of them turned their heads to look at me as I entered. Their faces wore a variety of expressions, and presently I was being introduced to Hephaestus, also known as Vulcan, or the Smith.

The Smith's hands were big, with gnarled fingers, and he limped on a right leg that was slightly twisted and deformed. His muscular torso was bare and sweating, and he was gripping some tool I did not recognize.

Before I could start to worry about any possible awkwardness in my being introduced to Hera, the thing had been accomplished. I bowed low before a majestic woman in formal robes, who responded with a gracious nod. A golden circlet crowned her head, and a peacock was strutting at her feet.

Close beside her was standing Mars, also called Ares, unmistakable with his armor and his spear. I knew a strange sensation down the back of my neck when the God of War nodded to me with respect.

I was sure that my first glance on entering had shown me several other deities in the group, but whoever they might have been, all were gone now, vanished like a rainbow when the sun is suddenly engulfed in clouds.

Daedalus said he had important business to transact with me, now that I was available, and he called me away from the gathering of gods and goddesses as soon as he could without offending any of that company. With one of the golden maidens to assist him, he was prepared to show me the important work that he and Hephaestus were engaged in. Meanwhile I started to tell him about my experience with Atlas.

Gladly I followed the Artisan into another room. I had pictured the inside of this establishment, when I tried to picture it at all, as a gigantic forge or foundry, filled with flame and smoke and the clang of metal, and all of these were present in the central hall; but the first workroom I actually entered was equipped and furnished very differently. Most of the laborers, it seemed to me, were as invisible as so many Dionysian sprites.

Now Daedalus showed me an ongoing laboratory experiment, in which he and the Smith were hand-forging helmets out of a special alloy of bronze, containing a slight mixture of the residue of a fallen Giant's body. Daedalus had hopes that this alloy would effectively shield the wearer's brain from the Giants' destructive rays.

Naturally I rejoiced to hear this news. It was obvious from past experience that the assembled divinities would need some kind of protective devices if they were going to have any chance of making a successful fight of it in the open.

At the time of my arrival, Hephaestus had only one helmet ready. Conferring with Daedalus and his magic helpers, he tried to get a production line going.

Ordinarily, Zeus and his colleagues wore gold or silver, when they encumbered their comely bodies with any metal at all. I got the impression that they all considered helmets, like their other accoutrements, as purely decorative. In the ordinary course of events deities needed no protection, from either violence or weather.

Vulcan put his experimental helmet on his own head. He wanted to demonstrate his own handiwork by getting someone to accompany him in an airborne chariot while he hunted for a Giant and attempted to attack him.

When the Smith's devine peers heard of this planned demonstration, they were upset, and all agreed that he was too important to the cause to risk himself in such a fashion. Naturally no mortal human would be of any use as a subject in this case, and so it was decided to call for volunteers among the lesser deities.

But as soon as word went out from Hephaestus and Daedalus that they were seeking some minor god willing to be experimentally befuddled, Dionysus volunteered at once, saying that such a mental state was nothing out of the ordinary for him.

"I fear my esteemed colleagues do not understand," proclaimed the Twice-Born. "I am no hero. It's just that I expect to experience little difference between the mental state brought on by this experiment and the ecstasy I commonly share with my worshipers."

The Smith shook his head doubtfully. "Then it seems we ought to find some other volunteer for our test. Who else is available?" And this discussion, too, seemed likely to dissolve in hopeless wrangling. I feared there was no way that the important test could be accomplished anytime soon.

After I had been given a preliminary tour of the secret workshop, Hephaestus called me aside, saying he had prepared for me special gifts. "Hercules, I have heard much of you, and I like what I hear."

This came as a complete surprise to me, but you may believe I followed with alacrity. In another room, where the fire of a smaller forge was burning, he showed me that he had ready a suit of chain mail, forged from a different metal alloy than the gods' helmets, and padded with fine wool. This, he promised me, would be just what I needed. The garment had been forged and trimmed with divine skill into a shape that fit me excellently well.

I put it on at once, found that it allowed me perfect freedom of movement, and once more thanked its creator. It would offer considerable protection from any weapon the Giants might strike at me with, and from the arctic blasts of freezing air as well.

I thanked the Smith as politely as I could, while keeping to myself my serious doubts that I would ever need armor of any kind to shield me in a fight—on the other hand, if we were going to fight in a cold climate I would certainly be grateful for something to keep me warm.

Daedalus, who had come to observe the fitting, cautioned me that the suit's materials had not been tested against burns or poisons.

And Hephaestus said: "Since I have been told something of your strength, I have not stinted on the armor's strength by trying to reduce its weight. Few mortal men who wore this would be able to lift their arms, or even move their feet. But you should have no difficulty."

He also told me that his mortal name was Andy Ferrante. "You might as well call me Andy, Hercules. I'm even newer at this game than Apollo is." And he put out his hand for me to shake.

And in the course of our talk, Hephaestus mentioned his dream of someday, somehow, gaining the power of manufacturing Faces. But any such effort would have to wait until the war was over.

When I was dressed in my new suit, and after I had allowed myself a few hours' sleep and had eaten, I resumed my study of the research projects that were currently under way.

There was another golden maiden here, and other inhuman helpers who were less spectacular, if only because they were invisible.

By studying the materials and processes that the Giants had used to create the monsters, the Smith and the Artisan between them thought they had gained some important insight as to the nature of the Giants, and some clues to their special weapon as well. Though the Boar and Hydra, and the sea monster that had almost eaten the Trojan princess, were of course of different species than the Giants, they, too, were designed creatures, incorporating odylic magic.

Part of the work recently accomplished by the Smith and the Artisan had been the building of a kind of greenhouse on a remote high ledge of Vulcan's fortress, and the planting of Apple seeds therein. So far there had not been enough of a crop to allow much in the way of experimentation.

Daedalus told me as he suspected that the Giants, whether moved by some intellectual curiosity or only acting on instinct, had also been experimenting. Not with helmets, unfortunately, but with means of turning all native earthly life into monstrous variations that would cease to reproduce. So far they had had only occasional success.

"And we still don't know with any certainty where the Giants themselves came from—I find it fascinating that Atlas told you they issued from the earth. I wonder if he meant that the first ones grew like plants? Oh, how I wish I had been there when you were talking to him!"

"I wish so, too," I told the Artisan. "Maybe when this war is over we can go back and talk to him again."

Almost all the Giants with whom people had reported having encountered were male. But my tutors assured me again that female examples, Giants who seemed to have been modeled in more or less crude imitation of human women, were not unknown.

Though Giants rarely spoke to gods or humans, there had been a few dialogues between the two species over the centuries. Generally these communications consisted of little more than shouted threats, challenges, or warnings. Presumably the Titans communicated more frequently among themselves.

The life span of each Giant seemed to be enormous, though probably not comparable to that of a god.

Neither Daedalus nor Hephaestus had yet been able to learn exactly where on earth the Giants had first sprung to life, or when—except that it must have been in the remote past.

Or whether, somewhere in the dim past, they had actually been human—to me that was the most chilling possibility of all.

The more I thought about our race of enemies, the more I realized that I knew almost nothing about them. I spoke my thoughts aloud to Daedalus. "I wonder, are there Giant infants somewhere?"

"I suppose everything that lives must pass through some stage of immaturity. Antaeus, as you describe him, Hercules, must have been quite young, as Giants go."

"That had never occurred to me," I remarked, trying to cast back my thoughts. "True, he had no beard, and I think no hair on chest or belly. It may be he was but half grown." I tried to compare his remembered image with that of the Giant who had shot Apollo's chariot out of the air with me aboard.

As later research demonstrated, those Apples of Hesperides were essential to the Giants' reproduction and important in their nourishment, if not essential to their absolute survival.

"If we can eliminate the Apples entirely from the earth, that ought to make the survival of our enemies much more difficult. It might even finish them off entirely."

It was perfectly true, several deities assured me, that the Giants sometimes sexually assaulted women, and even goddesses. A number of cases had been recorded down through the years. But Daedalus now contended that their assaults on females were only being misinterpreted as sexual.

Hera, who had quietly approached and was listening to the lecture, was not pleased with that point of view and issued a stern decree that the rights of women should be everywhere defended.

The next point to be argued, by some of the other gods, was just what those rights should be. Our discussion was going nowhere when Zeus suddenly joined us, materializing apparently from out of nothing, surprising everyone already inside the laboratory. My father was dressed simply, though much more regally than when I had seen him in the wrestling ring. Especially astonished were those gods, chiefly Vulcan, who thought that all intruders had been effectively excluded. But when they saw who this intruder was, they only shrugged their shoulders.

Diplomatically Zeus sidestepped the debate on women's rights. It seemed that a council of war was about to get under way, and as I was so important to the Olympian cause, I was invited to attend. Zeus now publicly acknowledged me as his son in front of his assembled colleagues, none of whom seemed in the least surprised.

Hephaestus, pleased that I had taken to his customized armor with such enthusiasm, was ready now to show me my new club, which he said he had made from a particular oak tree.

This weapon was no larger than other clubs of similar shape that I had used in the past, but it was certainly heavier, and stronger. This one had been loaded by Vulcan with metal weights, and strengthened with steel bands and rods. I understood that the Artisan had been instrumental in its design.

It was so heavy that Daedalus, after one abortive effort to lift it cleanly, did not try to carry it to me himself, but employed one of the golden maidens for the job. The slender metal figure bore the weapon with an ease that not even an Amazon could have matched.

Daedalus said to me: "An ordinary man would be considered very powerful if he could even lift this weapon, let alone use it. It is designed especially for one of your size and strength."

I swung it a few times in the air, reveling in what seemed perfect balance, and looked about for something to hit.

*   *   *

The inconclusive wrangling of the gods was cut off in midsentence by a Titanic blast, which shook the floor of rock beneath our feet.

My divine allies and I were startled, and some of us were staggered, when rock over our heads shuddered, as if Thor's hammer had struck home, and a fine sprinkling of dust came sifting down.

A moment later, the speeding figure of the Messenger came darting into the vast room from somewhere to warn us all in a stentorian voice that the Giants had taken the offensive and were now bombarding Vulcan's island laboratory with huge rocks, while an actual invasion was about to get under way.

The walls and roof of Vulcan's laboratory, as I have said, looked almost unimaginably strong. But still I had a feeling in my bones that they would give way if that bombardment were continued. Each direct hit sent tremors through the solid rock beneath our feet, shook down a shower of fine debris, and produced an almost deafening gonglike reverberation in the ears of all who occupied the fortress.

The Olympians' immediate response to the attack was to plunge into an argument as to whether the rock and metal walls of the fortress could be depended on to shield their vulnerable brains from memory depletion, as long as they remained inside.

"To the Underworld with memory depletion!" shouted a deity I could not recognize. "We'd better get ourselves out of the way of flying rocks!"

Mars pounded the butt of his spear on the stone floor and roared out his contempt of such a cowardly attitude. Shrinking out of sight of the enemy was no way to win a war.

Meanwhile, I was more than ready to enter combat. Gripping my new club in both hands, I almost cried aloud for joy as I ran toward the place where, as I remembered, a door led to the outside.

Zeus now echoed the War God in a ringing call to arms. And now indeed the numbers in our company were growing. I could not recognize most of the new arrivals, nor tell where they were coming from—perhaps from some other chamber in the fort.

I learned a little later that before the fighting started, Zeus had been sending out messengers, summoning every god and goddess whose support he had any hope of getting, to take part in a climactic battle. He had meant to convene a conference of deities, where he could present to his colleagues a reasoned case for all-out warfare against the Giants; but that argument had now been made for him, and forcefully.

Sprites had done most of the messenger work, maintaining a fairly effective communications network on our side, leaving only a few of the most vitally important missions for Mercury to handle personally.

The invitations, or urgent summonses from Zeus to join the fight, had gone only to his fellow deities—this was not a matter in which mere mortal humans could be expected to be of any help. All the kings and high priests of earthly power would have to remain standing on the sidelines, beside the humbler members of the human race.

Meanwhile, in the main room of the workshop, the molten, carefully blended bronze alloy was being poured into ingots, which were then in turn hammered and welded into the shape of the desired helmets. Something like a production line had been established, operated chiefly by the Smith's two golden metal aides, with help from some Dionysian satyrs, and other creatures I could not immediately identify.

The great building shook under the impact of another enormous boulder as the bombardment continued.

Still, some of the Smith's clients were unhappy with the helmet design. Rarely have I known any group of mortals as prone to argument as were the gods. Some of their number insisted on debating the question of whether Vulcan had got his proportions right in that alloy, and even the relative efficacy of bronze, as compared to iron, or cloth, or simple unalloyed tin or copper.

As I listened to them, there dawned on me suddenly something I ought to have realized before: that deities were no braver than anyone else, when facing what they thought might be a real danger. Some eagerly embraced even the weakest excuses to put off the moment of real testing.

Certain other deities, of course, were at the opposite extreme of readiness. Blustering Ares now demanded that he be given the first helmet. Hephaestus complied, and as soon as Mars had the bronze casque on his head he lived up to his reputation by actually leading the way into combat. The metal was still so hot from the forge that it was almost glowing, but Mars did not appear to notice the heat as he gripped it in both hands.

"If you are looking for some guarantee of perfect safety," he barked at his timorous colleagues, "we will not find it here inside this fort, or anywhere!"

Some of the gods railed at Ares for his bragging, but others shouted their readiness to follow him into battle.

Mars pointed at me and sought to shame them by my example. "Will you stand back and allow a mere mortal to lead the way?"

I was hardly leading the way at the moment, but the War God's point was made. Some responded angrily to this challenge, and others ignored it. It seemed to me that a sizable majority of divinities took to their heels, fleeing through the air invisibly (as they hoped), or tried to hide in an effort to avoid the weapon they could not withstand. At the present rate of production, it seemed that hours or even days must pass before Vulcan's helmets would be available to all the gods who wanted them.

The fact that a great many gods were ready to delegate their fighting to a mere mortal like myself did not disturb me. I understood their necessity for doing what was necessary to protect themselves, at least until the enemy's most effective weapons could be somehow countered. If all my powerful allies should be wiped out, my own chances of success would vanish utterly.

And I thought I had yet to meet the Giant who could do me any deadly harm—I suppose my state of mind at the time could be generously described as the overconfidence of youth.

Battle

$\mathcal{S}$eeing that I was trying to get out-of-doors and into the fight as quickly as possible, some goddess equipped with flying Sandals—to my embarrassment I could not recognize her—effortlessly picked me up and carried me high into the upper reaches of the laboratory's vast interior.

I had entered Vulcan's laboratory through a door at ground level, but now came out through an opening high in the peaked roof. There my benefactor silently put me down and flew away. On emerging into the open air, I was much comforted to find that my new armor protected me effectively from the arctic blasts of cold wind; I had dreaded being frozen more than I feared anything a Giant was likely to do to me.

As when I entered the fortress, the sun was low in the sky; but now its light fell from a different direction, and I realized that a night had passed while I was inside.

As soon as I got outside I could see that not only was a bombardment in progress, but a strong force of Giants was approaching the island, advancing in a rough semicircle along the fog-shrouded shore a mile away, and out across the water.

Looking down from my high vantage point, it seemed to me that the tallest of the attackers might be closer to fifty feet in height than to a hundred. Even at a distance of half a mile, Alkyoneus was already recognizable, conspicuous among his fellows by his size and bulk. His appearance was also odd, this time, because his body gleamed, as if with metal, from head to foot.

To my further amazement I saw that some of the attackers were actually afloat in the choppy sea, in several kinds of ships and rafts. Even more astonishing, some, supported by enormous balloons, were airborne over the water.

"Don't tell me they can swim!" barked some minor godlet, hovering just over the sharply peaked roof where I was balancing. "I'd expect them to melt to mud with a good soaking."

I would have expected much the same thing, but that was not the case. Actually the attackers were approaching across and through the water, their weight partially supported by enormous balloons, their stony feet only dragging a little in the waves.

I brandished my new club and announced my readiness to fight.

As soon as I had my feet solidly planted on the peak of the roof, I could see how the outer walls of the fortress had already been damaged, great irregular peelings of stone spalled away by the bombardment, like bark splintered from a tree. Huge rocks were still flying toward us on curved paths out of the gray sky, some of them from clear over the horizon, one arriving at or near the laboratory every few seconds. While still at a distance some of these boulders seemed to float like giant snowflakes, or tufts of thistledown, but as they drew near I could see that they were actually hurtling faster than arrows. Some were so small and approached so swiftly that it taxed my mortal vision to catch sight of them at all.

"So, they are using trebuchets? Or catapults?" I demanded.

The head of the goddess turned in my direction. "I believe they are simply picking up rocks in their hands and throwing them, my lad. Giants can do that."

I was impressed.

Meanwhile, the actual invasion was steadily progressing. Those Giants supported by balloons came floating toward us almost entirely above the water, only dipping in their feet from time to time, taking advantage of an offshore breeze to stay on course to the island. Their massive feet were encased in bundles of hollow reeds that must have given them some buoyancy. It struck me at the time that our monstrous enemies must be very brave to risk the depths of the ocean thus; it seemed to me hardly possible that any of that earthy race could swim, but that rather they must sink like the stones they almost were, once plunged in without support.

Something, it might have been the day's first Arrow from Apollo's Bow, or a slung stone from Mars, punctured the supporting balloons of one advancing figure, and with a great bellowing cry the Giant fell into the ocean. He disappeared completely in a titanic splash, but moments later his head and shoulders surfaced. Plainly he found the water only chest-deep at his point of entry, and he managed to survive, his earthy body more resistant to melting than I had expected.

*   *   *

His fellow Titans were not discouraged by his fate. Anyway, comparatively few were depending on balloons. A majority were paddling enormous boats, approaching our fortress island from several sides at once. The nearest of this latter group were almost ashore now and had abandoned their boats to go wading in the sea, as if indifferent to its icy cold and to the pounding of the surf.

Meanwhile, other attackers continued hurling huge rocks at our fortress island, some from very far away. I was glad to see that the enemy effort was not well coordinated, so that the members of the landing party stood in some danger of being brained by their own side's long-range bombardment. At the same time I wondered how those distant throwers could ever know whether they had the proper range or not.

Even as I watched, the first of the invading Giants actually set his huge feet on the island. And now about a dozen more were just about to follow him. Their seamed and craggy faces loomed not far below me, some bearded and some smooth, all of them hard, all loathsome in my sight.

Now Ares, reining in his black horses so that his chariot hovered in midair, was shouting at his colleagues, trying to convince them that the numbers made this a serious attempt to take the fort, and not just a harassing raid.

Zeus raised his voice and said: "Whatever their intentions may be, here they are, and we'd better start to fight them."

Mars began to roar out orders, but Apollo at the same time seemed to be commanding yet another course of action.

Impatient of watching and waiting, I decided to take the initiative. The way our leaders were contradicting one another, I could hardly fail to find myself acting in obedience to one chief at least, no matter what I did.

Wary about putting myself directly in the path of one of the huge incoming missiles, I impulsively tried catching a small splinter from one of the near misses. A head-sized fragment was arcing toward me slowly enough that I could get my hands in its way. Catching the heavy object spun me around with its velocity, but I was able to keep my grip on it while still retaining my balance on the peaked roof.

In another moment, I had hurled the fragment back, aiming for the spot on the horizon whence most of the big rocks were coming, and putting what I then considered to be nearly all my strength into the throw. Two or three such attempts were necessary for me to get the distance approximately right, as nearly as I could judge from the distant splashes of ice and snow; but it seemed unlikely that I would hit any of my targets, which were invisible to me with distance. I thought I had better direct my energies to matters close at hand.

By now, four or five of the Giants' invasion force were already ashore, looking about for enemies to smite, while an equal number of the enormous figures, with more following in the distance, were now wading knee-deep, or thigh-deep, in through the breaking surf.

And now the long-range bombardment ceased abruptly, as if some signal had been given. I wondered if the throwers' sight was keen enough to see the situation from miles away.

Our enemies' willingness to immerse themselves yards deep in water proved to be a mistake when Poseidon, Lord of the Oceans, and some of his lesser associates entered the battle on our side.

I saw Neptune's bearded head above the waves, but only briefly. This first thrust of Poseidon and his forces into combat scored some success for our side. The waves erupted around the ships that were still carrying Giants, capsizing the oversize passengers into the almost frozen sea. Salt water seemed to boil around those wading ashore, and mammoth breakers pounded them against the rocks, bruising and tearing their hard bodies, spilling thick Giant blood into the sea.

Again I saw Neptune riding in his golden chariot, pulled by white horses, with his trident raised high, leading his forces into battle.

Unhappily the Sea God's head was still unprotected, and a Giant mind weapon soon disrupted his attack. He and his escort of lesser gods were driven off with failing memories.

With startling suddenness the huge waves died away, leaving the sea around our island almost calm. The natural sea creatures, killer whales and others who had been following Neptune's orders were left leaderless. Some who persisted in their assaults were scooped out of the sea in Giant hands and hurled against dry rocks.

Finding the surf a perilous place to be themselves, Giants hastened to scramble up onto the shore.

Now a few more of the gods, their noble heads newly ensconced in bronze helmets, came flying out of the fortress, some in chariots and some running like deer with flying Sandals, in a wild sortie.

Immediately several Giants' arms were lifted and pointed at them, blasting the deities with their special weapon. But this time our foes were confounded when the devices for the first time failed to work, or had only marginal effect, even at close range.

Roaring in triumph, our gods, using their own characteristic weapons, struck down a number of Giants, and the rest fell back in a disorderly retreat. The lightning of Zeus struck left and right, the Arrows of Apollo flew, the spear of Mars thrust again and again, with effective violence.

I saw more than one of the Giants' balloons explode into flames, flaring spectacularly when lightning struck, and dropping their weighty burdens on rock or into the sea.

One came down very close to where I stood. The gasbags that gave the huge body buoyancy were pierced by missiles. The Giant's huge frame tottered, and he stumbled on his massive, slow-moving feet. Missiles of his own, that he had not had time to throw, cascaded from his hands to crash hard on the distant ground, and his vast arms, with fingers spread, went groping blindly. More lightning bolts seared down, to right and left, each momentarily painting one side of his body a pure electric white.

His body hit the earth with a crushing impact. The frame of any Giant who fell for any considerable distance broke to pieces on contact with the ground.

The losses were not all on one side. I saw some lesser god, whom I could not recognize at that distance, struck down, mashed flat by a huge rock. The victim's god-Face came bursting from his head and went spinning away to fall into the sea. I believe the only human to witness that loss was myself, and I neither needed nor wanted whatever extra powers that Face might have conveyed. If the tales of magic that we all believed were true, then sometime, somewhere, it would be washed ashore where human hands could pick it up.

Meanwhile I still had taken no part in the fight myself and was frantically casting about for some way of actually getting into action. So far, none of our adversaries had come within my reach. (I knew that with a little exertion, I could jump for a great distance; but occasional practice sessions, early in life, had convinced me that I could never be exactly sure just where I was going to come down.)

Months ago, on entering my combat with Antaeus, I had expected a struggle not intrinsically different from an ordinary wrestling match. But now, having survived and profited from that experience, I had some idea of what I was up against. I could only suppose that the truly huge Giants would be vastly stronger even than Antaeus, their bodies tougher and harder to wound or break. I wanted to take full advantage of my new, bigger, heavier club, but I also vowed to tear my opponent apart with my bare hands, if that proved necessary.

I contemplated jumping, or falling, to the ground and attacking one of the advancing Giants at foot level. But Fate provided a more promising opportunity. From the high roof of Vulcan's enormous dwelling I could look right down on the shaggy head of one of the taller Giants as the huge intruder tried to break his way in through what looked like the laboratory's front door.

The business was slightly complicated by the fact that he was actually wearing a kind of helmet, which appeared to be made of several thicknesses of tough leather. But I thought that ought to make little difference to my club.

Boldly I leaped onto my adversary's head, and with my free hand I clutched a handful of his coarse, shaggy hair to keep myself in position. Then with my club I belabored his padded skull.

In such a position I could strike only awkwardly, so it seemed to me that I was only tapping. Still my victim screamed and fell to his knees; his skull was thick, but it was not hard and thick enough.

I had been expecting my gargantuan opponent to collapse as soon as his head was severely damaged, but the collapse was not as quick or as complete as I had hoped.

I pounded him some more, and then leaped free when his body crashed face-first along the stony shore.

*   *   *

Several Titans, having identified me as the mortal who was causing them huge problems, surrounded me with the obvious goal of trying to finish me off. They pounded at me with giant clubs, actual tree trunks stripped of branches, whose impact on the island rock I narrowly avoided.

Others came balloon-skipping across the half-frozen sea, carrying oil-soaked tree trunks as great burning brands. Quite a sight in the gray, near arctic twilight, but a poor choice of weapon with which to assault Vulcan's stony stronghold.

But these special weapons were not meant to breach the walls. They were intended to kill me.

Almost the only real pain I had ever felt in my life had come from internal causes—the common bellyaches and toothaches of childhood. The peculiar blister raised on my hand during my fight with the centaurs was a notable exception. I did have good reason to believe that my skin was much more heat-resistant than that of any ordinary human, but whether it could withstand prolonged exposure to fire I did not know, and being reluctant to put it to the ultimate test, I did all I could to avoid the burning tree trunks.

Now the voices of several gods were raised in excited cries, sounding a familiar name. I turned to see that the enemy champion was at hand, and I recognized him as the Giant who had shot down Apollo's chariot with me aboard. Alkyoneus had come ashore and was standing on one rocky tip of the laboratory island. The archenemy of the gods was leading the other invaders.

This was my first really good look at Alkyoneus, and I stood stunned, for he was even more impressive when seen at close range. He was clad from head to toe in some kind of metal armor, or at least in a net of chains, the lower links dragging on the earth.

Apollo brought his chariot to a sudden stop beside me, and in a few terse words proposed that we attack this Giant together.

Gripping my club, I stared at the enemy champion. He differed from the others in being not only larger, but more powerfully built. Just as a wrestler is easily distinguished from other men at first glance, so Alkyoneus stood out from his fellow Giants.

"Anytime you're ready, Jeremy Redthorn," I said, over my shoulder.

But before Apollo and I could agree on a plan for our attack, the chariot of Mars came hurtling past us at full speed. The War God was charging directly at our common enemy, howling a challenge and raising his mighty spear.

Alkyoneus struck out with one mighty arm, and I gasped in surprise as the rushing chariot of Mars was knocked aside before the god could thrust with his spear.

And in the next moment, the Giant moved in our direction with amazing speed. Before I realized what had happened, Apollo, too, had been somehow beaten to the ground, where his horses lay tangled in their harness; his chariot spun its wheels in the air.

In the next instant my Titanic opponent had somehow spotted my tiny figure and had turned on me with arms outstretched. Perhaps my fame had spread even among Giants, and he knew me by the club I carried. All of his enormous fingers were pointing at me, and he was obviously using the exotic weapon that his kind used against the gods—whether or not the word of my invulnerability had spread among our enemies, he wanted to try for himself whether the special weapon had no effect.

Mighty Alkyoneus was not stupid enough to persist with his useless magic after he saw that it was ineffective.

I ran toward him, but he moved away—not out of fear, I was sure. Rather he was intent on rallying, in a voice of thunder, some of his fellow Giants who were obviously contemplating a retreat.

Another, lesser Giant came at me and repeated another of my earlier opponent's mistakes by trying to step on me, like a man killing a beetle or a mouse. But I was a different sort of mouse than this creature had ever seen before. Bracing the butt end of my club on the ground, like a soldier's pike, I gave him a punctured foot.

The enormous body of my most recent opponent took a long time falling, like a tall tree. The arms were extremely powerful, and by no means clumsy, but still ineffective in breaking the fall. The heavy impact on rock took a lot out of him, and I suspect it cost him a few broken ribs, with likely internal injuries. But he was a fighter, and his fingers kept spasmodically attempting to grab me up. I had to disable most of the fingers before I could get inside the reach of his arms, close to his body, and finish him off.

Just as I did so, gods brought down another Giant only a short distance away. One outflung arm splashed into the ocean. The vast head split open like a melon when it came down hard on a sharp outcropping of rock, and blood and brains spilled out.

Unable to drop upon my opponent's head this time, I started the process of destruction with the big toe. My experience so far indicated that the process of killing a Giant could never be accomplished with a single blow, no matter how powerful.

The first blow of my metal-loaded club shattered the hard skin and splintered the even harder bones of what, even seen at close range, looked superficially like a giant human foot, down to the toenails and the small tufts of hair that grew upon the toes.

It seemed that the bigger the Giant, the tougher his flesh and the stronger his bones. All of these Giants were vastly more powerful than Antaeus had been.

My latest foe hopped and bellowed, as a man might if stung on the big toe by a large wasp.

Another wallop, and a crack appeared in the skin of his feet, running up the ankle, then the calf. Another hard blow on the ankle completed the disabling of the left leg.

One more blow, and he was down on one knee. When the Giant put one hand to the ground for support, I began to destroy that hand even as I had destroyed his foot.

In a way the Giants' size put them at a disadvantage. Daedalus and others have explained to me that it is simply a fact of nature that huge bodies are more vulnerable than small ones to certain common mishaps—such as tripping and falling down.

When I had finished destroying my second or third victim in this manner, I leaned on my club, gasping, and looked around. Our surviving foes were now in general retreat. The enemy attack on Vulcan's laboratory had been beaten off, at least for the moment. Apollo was on his feet again, shaking his head to clear it, calming his magic horses and trying to restore his chariot.

A distracted Giant was unaware of the radiant presence of Apollo, at a range of only about a mile, until an Arrow smote home like an explosive bullet, blasting and scattering pieces of tough, claylike Giant flesh in all directions, along with shattered fragments of bone.

And with that the fight was on again.

The battle that was eventually to decide all of our fates had started almost accidentally. Certainly our side had not chosen that day outside of Vulcan's laboratory as the time and place for a decisive confrontation, and maybe the Giants had not planned it that way, either. But as the fighting went on, both sides kept pouring in reinforcements.

The majority of participants on our side arrived on the scene by air, while most Giants came by water. A few of our enemies seemed to have made a long march overland, then had to find a way to cross approximately a mile of open, relatively shallow water between them and the island.

Daedalus and I were the only mortal humans to witness the entire battle, though the fate of our whole race hung in the balance.

Many more gods, perhaps a majority of all those in the world, chose not to take part, or were simply off on the other side of the world somewhere—I thought that many gods, despite all the educational opportunities that they enjoyed, had probably never realized how truly big the world was. And now it was sadly true that many others were no longer able to remember the size of the earth. And of course most mortals had never suspected the truths of geography, or even thought much on the subject.

The bodies of the Titans, when they employed their huge balloons to assist them in rapid movement, went drifting over sea and land like a flotilla of flying gods . . . still, only one or two, most notably Alkyoneus, could move as fast as most of the gods.

In actual combat, with their huge feet planted firmly on the ground that nourished them, Giants turned and bent and straightened almost gracefully and with amazing speed, their huge arms flailing. Few of our enemies bore weapons, though some had fashioned shields, and some brandished clubs. Most depended on their boulder-sized fists, and the strength and accuracy (which was considerable) of their throwing arms, and with them poured out a hail of devastation, which at one time or another must have knocked to earth a score of gods. On that terrible day, more than one god-Face was forcibly separated from its late wearer's human head. Any human who came within their reach, whether enjoying the powers of a god-Face or not, stood in some danger.

More than once I was hit by a stone or by some Giant's fist or club—my body was sent flying for a considerable distance, or it smashed into a rock wall. Under one such impact the rock cracked, but I still survived without disabling injury. My real test came when the experience was repeated, and I began to realize that there were limits to even my toughness.

Some gods appeared only briefly on the battlefield and then withdrew again. I have already named some who were present, and some I will name, and tell what they did. I will pass over the behavior of certain others in tactful silence.

And there were still other deities who never put in an appearance at all, a few of them for the simple reason that they did not learn of the battle until it was over. A few more were more deliberately circumspect. As far as I knew, Hades himself was still ranting in his madness, while remaining safely and snugly underground. And I thought that perhaps there was some method in his madness after all.

When we had beaten off the Giants' renewed attack, Mars and Zeus assigned a garrison of some less combative deities to hold the laboratory against any possibly renewed assault. Meanwhile it seemed that we ought to take the offensive with the bulk of our forces—but of course in that company no decision so momentous could be made without a lengthy conference and argument.

While we were resting from our exertions, and while several gods were polishing their arguments, back inside the laboratory, Zeus told

me more of my own history. Some years ago, the then-current avatar
of Zeus had figured out a way to invest a human, or mortal, with divine power, without burdening him with the new vulnerability of a Face.

The idea was that the presumably enormous capabilities of this
"designed" human would be immune to the Giants' most effective
weapon. But exactly what those capabilities were going to be was
very difficult to predict.

Everyone was well aware that such a weapon would take years to
develop.

"Perhaps twenty years must pass before it is fully ready," Zeus
had argued at the time. "But neither we nor the Giants are going anywhere. And they are not, thank all the Fates, in any hurry about arranging our annihilation. Therefore certainty is more important than
speed when we plan our move against them."

Early on, several of those who advised Zeus in his planning de-
voutly expressed their hopes that this new man, or woman, should not
be physically deformed, like Prince Asterion. It could be catastrophic
to the plans of Zeus if this planned savior were to find life a burden
and be angry at those who had brought him into the world. And what
if this human being should be corrupted, to turn against the gods who
had created him?

"But it is rarely the obviously deformed who find life an unbearable burden," Vulcan reminded his leader now.

"That is true, I had forgotten. It is so very long since I was merely
human."

I never learned what process of selection had been employed. Whatever it was, it indicated that Alcmene, wife of the Cadmian general
Amphitryon, would be the ideal candidate for this breeding. One consideration must have been that the blood of divinity ran in her veins.

"That could be said of a great many people," I observed.

"Not nearly as great a number as would like to claim it for themselves. But Alcmene was indeed a special case." Daedalus, who had
evidently been making a study of the matter, went on to explain that
Zeus was my mother's great-grandfather on her father's side—and had
also been, probably in another avatar, a remote ancestor of her husband.

"An incestuous business," I commented, bleakly considering my own origins. "Or would be, if the same rules applied to gods as to humankind."

"There's no use speaking of gods and rules in the same breath," said Daedalus, and looked around to see who might be listening. "I suppose we will come one day to the point where every human being on earth is descended in some way from Zeus."

My father, as I eventually discovered, had planned to wait until I was somewhat older before throwing me into the front line in the struggle against the Giants. But through the years of my childhood, the Giants kept posing a greater and ever greater threat. When my father learned that I had already slain a monstrous lion, and shortly after that the Hydra, he decided I was already old enough, and pushed on with his plan.

(I had the feeling that my father was on the point of telling me something more while we were resting between battles—but that, for good or ill, he could not quite bring himself to do so.)

Some hours passed thus in the laboratory, while we talked and rested (it seemed to me that gods wanted rest, whether they actually needed it or not), and some of us rearmed ourselves before going on with the next phase of the battle. There were some gods ready to fight who still lacked helmets.

Mars ranted and raved, urging us to lose no time in rushing after the fleeing foe. We should strike while the momentum was with us, and before the enemy could find some way of counteracting the protective helmets that had so suddenly provided our side with an advantage. Several times I reminded various deities that whenever we launched our attack, I would need a ride in someone's chariot if I was going to keep up. Zeus assured me that there were fighting gods who lacked the power of flight, so Daedalus and I would not be the only wingless passengers; but there were chariots enough for all to ride.

While some counseled a quick pursuit, other gods were already convinced that the Giants no longer presented an immediate threat to the Olympians' dominance of the world, and that it was time to declare the war won and go home.

Here Zeus did his best to assert his authority, proclaiming that the war was only getting started. In future either gods or Giants would rule the earth, and there could be no compromise.

TWENTY-EIGHT

We Go A-Hunting

*W*hen we had rested for a few hours after beating off the enemy attack, Zeus, Hephaestus, and Apollo convened a council of war inside Vulcan's fortress. Daedalus and I, the only mortal humans for many miles around, reentered the vast building and stood by listening, though for some time no one acknowledged our presence.

All the gods recognized the need to follow some unified plan in following up our victory, but there was wide disagreement as to what that plan should be.

Gods and goddesses began to scribble maps on the flat, blank surface of one of Vulcan's interior walls. Someone knew, or claimed to know, where most of the Giants dwelt. Another informed us that Alkyoneus had been seen fleeing in that direction.

Zeus had the place of honor in all ceremonies among the gods, or at least in all of them I ever saw. Hades and Poseidon were next in rank, but even when Hades was not at war with Zeus, or suffering through a bout of madness, he kept almost entirely apart from the others. Poseidon was no enemy of Zeus, but until today he had not been much concerned about the problem posed by Giants.

"Speaking of Poseidon," asked some goddess I did not recognize, "does anyone know if he survived that little skirmish?"

No one could be sure. In any case, Neptune exercised an independent command over his own marine forces. Several witnesses reported seeing him caught without a bronze helmet, and I spoke up to confirm that observation. It was then assumed that he had not joined the council of war because he could not longer remember who he was or what he was supposed to be doing.

Mars, for all his hard fighting and dynamic speeches, failed as an effective leader because he paid too little attention to what his comrades in arms were doing and saying, what they feared and wanted. Though he claimed to be the war chief on land and in the air, a number of his fellow deities were disinclined to listen to him when he began shouting orders.

I was, and still am, no expert on military affairs, but it needed no experience to see that we were not going to present any kind of disciplined, highly organized opposition to the enemy.

Daedalus proclaimed in a firm voice that when at last we set out to carry the fight to the Giants in their own territory, he was coming with us.

Hephaestus announced that he wanted to come, too; and that if we waited a few more hours, his workers would have produced enough bronze helmets to protect everyone. Unfortunately, neither Vulcan nor Daedalus had been able to come up with any weapon that would be especially effective against Giants.

The first phase of the battle had demonstrated that the Smith's defensive helmets were not a total success. Deities fighting with their heads encased in bronze still suffered some loss of memory when the Giants' strange weapon struck at them heavily and repeatedly. However, the helmets did help enormously, and almost every god and goddess who meant to fight was now demanding one. It was still uncertain what would be the long-term fate of those who relied on bronze for protection in battle.

I knew that I could still play an important role in the fighting, but it was now possible to imagine that the gods might win even without my help.

There came a time when the bickering in the great hall died down, and I realized that most of the assembled company were looking at me, and that I was the subject of discussion.

In the background I could hear someone muttering about a prophecy supposedly once made by Hera: that the gods would be victorious in the war only if some mortal human clad in a lion's skin should fight beside them. And there was an old tradition, or superstition, regarding Giants, that their mother, the earth, had made them proof against all weapons of the gods—not, however, against weapons of mortals; and knowing this, Athena was to arrange the birth of a great mortal hero.

*   *   *

Dionysus was saying: "It took the enterprise and the strength of Hercules to make some of the gods realize that the Giants were neither invulnerable nor omnipotent. Humanity invested with the power of gods, but without the need for Faces, could fight and win against them."

Someone else impulsively put forth the proposal that, as soon as an appropriate Face became available, I be granted divine status, as a reward for my success in battle.

I heard this offer with mixed feelings. Of course it was an honor to be so admired, but I was immediately disinclined to accept. There was no Face of Hercules, and I was not at all sure that I wanted to become someone other than who I was.

But already the council had moved on to a discussion of our enemies. The Giants had shared the earth with us for a long time. Ancient descriptions spoke of them as towering, terrible creatures, who for the most part sported long beards, and in some cases wore snakes' tails instead of legs.

Humans called some Giants by their own Titanic names, while for others we knew only the names we had devised for them ourselves. Here and there was one who had at some time introduced himself to humanity, on one of those rare occasions when a meeting was peaceful enough to allow for such civility.

Daedalus (who kept reminding everyone that he wanted to accompany our attacking forces) told me he was convinced that the powers giving the special weapon its effectiveness were related to the magic-tech by means of which the race of Giants themselves had somehow been born.

Slowly, over centuries, there had come to be more and more Giants on the earth. I suppose we humans, including the earthly gods, could only thank whatever power truly ruled the Universe that our enemies' rate of reproduction was so low—else we would have been overrun, wiped out, many human generations in the past.

Someone said of the Giants: "The damned creatures are just very hard to kill. Sheer physical force still seems like the best bet, but it will have to be applied on a scale that will strain our resources."

And Mercury reported: "They do sometimes have spasms of lust, in which they yearn to force their will upon goddesses. And of course it takes a lot of food to fill their enormous bellies. Hercules and others have seen them eating cattle, chewing up entire bovine bodies like so many little sausages."

After all, I had watched the first Giant I ever saw as he roasted and ate a sheep. I imagined that they might like to eat people even more than sheep or other animals, but like everyone else were forced to take what they could get.

For a time, certain deities who made a practice of studying their opponents thought that Giants might be mutated humans. That idea struck me as extremely strange when I first encountered it, and nothing I learned later made it sound any more reasonable.

What these awkward imitations of ourselves might eventually want to do with the uncountable kinds of other life that grew on earth, once they had established their dominion, was more than any god or mortal in our ranks could say. The Titans were here, and they were hostile to humanity, and that was about all we could be certain of regarding their purposes.

The Smith and the Artisan, basing their arguments largely on evidence I had gathered, tried to convince the assembled Olympians that the Giants were not alien to the earth. They had not come from somewhere out among the stars but were only a part of the earth's own life—a part that in ancient times had been twisted into a strange shape by magic, what some called odylic science.

This suggestion of worlds other than our own sharply called to memory other mysteries that I had recently encountered.

"Atlas was beginning to show me something of the kind," I said, and saw many gods' faces turn toward me in surprise. "But only beginning. We didn't have a chance to get very far with any revelations."

The great contest between Giants and Olympians had gone on for many years. I understood now that it went a long way toward explaining why the gods have been for long periods absent from world affairs.

"But leaving Giants alone does not get rid of them," Zeus reminded his colleagues. "They do not spontaneously disappear. Rather they continue, in their patient, methodical way, to spend their time and energy becoming more and more troublesome to humanity. By means of the strange monsters they create, if for no other reason."

For many years the gods had been trying to keep their problem of vulnerability a secret from the bulk of humanity, fearing that if men and women knew their relative weakness, they would take the Titans' side against their own relations.

At one point Zeus said: "I can see now that trying to preserve secrecy was a mistake, and we should have put more trust in our fellow humans." Looking at the only two mortal humans present, he added: "It would be natural for you to side with us rather than the dirt-faces."

Daedalus agreed. "And siding with the Giants would have been a great mistake on our part. In a world ruled by Giants, ordinary people would be reduced to the status of cattle. The centaurs have chosen poorly."

I was sure that some of them, including Pholus, would not be on the Giants' side.

One of the gods philosophized: "After all, we *are* humans, however much we like to call ourselves immortal. Our Faces that we boast about, that other people worship, are only masks that we put on."

Eventually our expeditionary force got under way.

When the time actually came to move out, Apollo reached out an arm and scooped me aboard his chariot. Beside us drove Mars, behind a pair of magnificent black horses, their hoofbeats thundering on air.

Thanks to the speed of movement afforded us by the divine Sandals and chariots, we were able to travel more than a thousand miles to the south in only a few hours. Most of the flight was at high altitude, but the chariot of Apollo provided warmth and somehow even air to keep the Far-Worker's passengers, Daedalus and myself, almost comfortable.

The sprites had provided our leaders with accurate intelligence, and at the expected time we came in sight of a village, built on a gigantic scale, in the midst of a green and sunlit land. Looking over the rail of my host's chariot, I could catch a glimpse in the distance of a broad blue arm of the Great Sea; but it was too far away to let us obtain any help from Neptune and his legions.

A score or more of flying chariots came sweeping in rapidly on a cluster of huge buildings, each tall enough for its builders and owners to stand upright inside. The construction materials used were the trunks of many large trees and huge stone blocks. Roofs had been thatched with giant plants.

The air was much warmer here than it had been around the laboratory's desolate island, and things were green and growing. We had seen only a few humans on our final approach to our objective, but in this climate it seemed likely that Apples could be grown easily and plentifully. As we were on the point of landing, I looked out over long rows of budding trees that would be huge when they had got their growth; another orchard nearby held a smaller number that were already grown and producing fruit.

The inhabitants must have been warned somehow of our approach, for we found not a single Giant in any of the buildings or nearby fields.

Here and there as we came sweeping in, movement swarmed on pairs of tiny legs, no bigger and much weaker than my own—ordinary mortal humans who had been dwelling here with the Giants, or by their sufferance.

"Do they not know that we come to save them from the Giants?" I demanded of the world.

Daedalus shook his head. "They probably realize that we bring war. And a war between gods and Giants is not something that most humans will want to watch at close range."

There were also penned and pastured animals, doubtless being bred for food, that we dispersed by breaking down the fences. I also caught a glimpse of a few centaurs galloping away, but all my thoughts were on other matters at the time.

"I don't suppose this place is the Giants' headquarters," the Artisan observed to me. "But it must be the nearest thing to one that our scouts could find."

"I suppose they must have other orchards elsewhere," I agreed. "There certainly can't be many Giants in the world, if this is their biggest town."

He nodded. "It seems a fair assumption that somewhere they have other settlements and orchards, ten times the size of these."

And then we were on the ground, the silence shattered by a loud rumbling of wheels while our vehicle jolted to a stop. Daedalus prudently stayed with Apollo's chariot, while I jumped out and joined some of the bolder gods in prowling through the buildings, seeking for our foes. They were not to be discovered in that place, but their property was everywhere, in the form of gigantic tools and furnishings.

One of our more bellicose gods was shouting: "Come out, Alkyoneus, come out and play! Where are you hiding?"

But no one, it seemed, was ready just then to join us in another game.

"These are the Apples of the Hesperides," cried Zeus, pulling open a huge bin of fruit, calling everyone's attention to the fact. Everyone could recognize them, from the sample I had earlier obtained. It was impossible to mistake them for any other kind of fruit or vegetable. The yellow, melon-sized fruit were in all the buildings, arrayed on racks or snuggled one or two in a nest, like the eggs of barnyard fowl.

As we broke into the place and battered our way through it, my companions and I stumbled upon an indoor nursery for seedlings, roofed with a kind of oiled paper that let in much sunlight. I pounded the trees and their containers into splinters with my club, and the gods to the right and left of me wrought similar destruction.

"If Hades were here," some minor god suggested, "he might generate a nice earthquake and tumble these walls down."

"It seems we'll have to do as best we can without him," cautioned Zeus.

We also found another huge building, in which the balloons used in the attack on the island had evidently been manufactured.

But we were not going to be allowed to pillage and ruin the enemy stronghold unopposed: In a nearby grove of towering trees forces had been gathering to oppose our invasion, and now they were ready to strike at us. The counterattack was signaled by a new barrage of flying rocks.

The counterattack did not really take us by surprise, but we were too near that situation to feel comfortable about it. Yet another Giant now advanced on me with murderous intent.

Apparently some of our enemies were still ignorant about me. Certainly this advancing Titan, like the others I had faced, must have believed I was a god—or he would not have wasted his special weapon trying to disable me.

Like the others I had so far confronted, this one misplaced his confidence in the magical beams he could project from his fingertips.

As the long day of fighting wore on, I saw some minor goddess struck down, whose name I did not know. Her head was shattered, a sickening display of colors punctuated with pieces of white bone, making a portrait of beauty and power brought low by overwhelming brutal force. If she had been wearing a bronze helmet, it had offered no protection against such a ferocious blow.

I looked at her feet for flying Sandals, thinking that I might gain speed enough to let me catch up with my opponents.

But either she had not been wearing Sandals, or someone else had taken them ahead of me.

Moments later, I saw something I truly had never expected to behold: a momentarily victorious Giant, still feeling desperate enough, or perhaps simply adventurous enough, to try on a Face. He picked it up from the body of his comparatively diminutive slain opponent.

In the hand that raised it, the Face was a tiny, insignificant thing. At a little distance it looked like nothing more or less than a translucent mask designed to fit a mortal human head. It was no match at all for the Giant's great, pale, rocklike sketch of a countenance. And it remained stubbornly unabsorbed when he tried to press it between his eyes with one huge finger.

The Face was still stuck on the end of his fingertip when I got his attention by beginning to cut him down.

Again Alkyoneus, the archenemy of the gods, appeared, clad in rattling strips and chains of metal armor, inspiring the Giant forces to renewed efforts.

Many of the gods recoiled as the Giants' champion strode forward. But again Mars chose to meet him head-on, howling a challenge. Alas, Ares had no more success in this joust than in the previous one.

But our forces rallied, the thunderbolts of Zeus flew thick and fast, the Arrows of Apollo killed and wounded. I could see that Alkyoneus was hurt, but he kept to his feet.

Mars was slower to climb back into his chariot this time, slower to plead with his fellow Olympians that we must pursue the enemy as quickly as we could. Zeus added his own urgings, but it did not matter. Most of the surviving gods insisted on having time to rest.

Not that any who had come this far were ready to quit. We were determined to hunt down and exterminate the fleeing enemy, or at least get rid of Alkyoneus.

Even at the much later date on which I write, the ideal of complete extermination has so far proven impossible to achieve. Some minimize the continued threat. And Poseidon and some of the other gods, who had been deranged and driven early from the field, in later days rejoined divine society having forgotten that there ever was a battle at all. To this day some of them do not remember it; and a few even believe, or pretend to believe, that the whole story is an utter fabrication. My own memory of these events is probably better than that of any god, simply because I never fell victim to the Giants' magic force—and that indeed is one reason why I am writing these memoirs.

I was surprised to see how, despite their heavy bodies, the Giants could move quite rapidly over long distances, outpacing racing cameloids when they were forced to make the effort. And I was surprised also at their numbers in their counterattack around their village. Obviously their survivors from the earlier fighting had been reinforced.

In the fierce battles of that day there were perhaps a hundred gods in all, arrayed on one side, and perhaps as many as two hundred Giants on the other—along with certain centaurs and whatever other creatures might have been induced to join them.

At the beginning, and again later, whenever events allowed us a breathing space, the strategic questions were fiercely debated—such as, whether it was possible, or even desirable, to concentrate our forces in one place. But, as I suspect happens in most battles, once the fighting started, fine plans and strategy were all but forgotten by both sides as we concentrated on the mechanics of destruction, and on keeping ourselves alive. On every side the fighting was spreading like wildfire, and the commanders could no more manage it than they could have regulated a conflagration.

Many of the gods who did join in the fighting were comparatively minor figures, and some achieved more than their more famous colleagues. I hesitate to name names.

Even Mars was accused of cowardice by some. He could not be everywhere, and others who fought missed seeing him at all.

His appearance whenever he did show up inspired terror in many, including some of our opponents, if one could judge by the speed with which they fled from him.

At one point I saw with horror that the God of War had lost his helmet.

Shortly after that, the Giants scored on him with their special weapon; but in the case of Ares the effect was not what his enemies had hoped. Even when he had almost entirely lost his memory, he charged ahead, caring for nothing but killing.

I saw him send home a spear-thrust that felled a Giant, then whip his chariot horses on in pursuit of his next target.

Running up to one of my huge opponents at the level of his ankles, I prepared to swing my club with force enough to annihilate one of his leg bones, bulging beneath the skin. But the stepping motion of his leg changed at the last moment, and again I lost respect for our enemies' intelligence. This Giant, like several of my earlier opponents, was prepared to stomp on me with a gigantic foot—a moment later he reacted as if he'd stepped on a sharp stone. Partly the result of the fine steel armor with which Hephaestus had provided me—and partly because I held up my club on end to prick his foot.

*   *   *

Some have assured me that Giants have always had a special fear of lightning. But what mortal creature does not fear the thunderbolt? Whether the enemy particularly dreaded them or not, the fulminations of Zeus had a powerful effect. Even when the Thunderer failed to score a direct hit, his blasts still did considerable damage. Daedalus later discovered that the iron component of my club had been magnetized strongly enough to pick up nails.

The Thunderer also gathered thunderbolts into loose magnetic spheres and rolled them at his enemies like bowling balls. On contact they tended to produce truly satisfying explosions.

But Alkyoneus was obviously possessed of some form of immunity. It was as if his whole body served as a kind of lightning rod, conducting the power harmlessly down into the earth.

Later we discovered that his armor, which he had had designed specially for a duel with Zeus, offered an all-metal pathway that kept his body inside it safe.

Neither was I to be outdone when it came to throwing things, small though I was. Zeus and all other gods were able to magically extend the reach of their hands and arms, enabling them to uproot and move whole mountains, or at least small hills, and hurl them as projectiles.

"What's *that?*" I called out in amazement. Around us the whole earth seemed to be shuddering.

"One of them," said Zeus, "is throwing mountains at us."

I choked out something stupid, I am sure, for I could not believe the fact. Later I saw convincing evidence.

"It's true enough," my father told me. "Well, I will show them that I can do the same."

When a god or Giant literally uprooted a mountain, the whole earth quivered for many miles around, and clouds of dust billowed up, darkening the sky. When the Giant or god hurled such a missile, the huge mass cast a cloud-sized shadow in its passage. If it was thrown hard enough, the shock wave in itself was enough to knock down trees and lesser vegetation.

I on the other hand remained limited in my reach, even if my strength was equal to the Thunderer's. I had not my father's power to exert force outside my body, and could never get my arms around such a huge object. But once I had boulders in my grasp, I could propel them with the velocity of pellets shot from a crossbow—or even faster, faster than the eye could follow, if I put all my strength and will into the throw.

Never before in my life, not even, as it seemed to me then, not even in my wrestling match with Zeus, had I ever exerted my full strength.

My aim was not too good at first, and I missed my target by a quarter of a mile—a visible splash, startling white against the wine-dark sea, or a fountain of dust on land, showed where the missile struck—but my skills rapidly improved with practice.

Whenever one of my missiles struck home, it cracked a Giant's skull or ribs. I think I saw one lesser Giant's head carried entirely away, but at that distance it was hard to be sure.

Any lesser being I hit, such as a centaur, was of course obliterated by the impact.

And when a mass of earth or rock, hurled by some Giant, came toward me far too fast for me to dodge, I could only brace myself and try to withstand the impact. A deafening roar was followed by smothering darkness—and then, gasping and choking, I had to dig myself out from under several yards of soil and broken rock.

Some have said that when our battle for the Apple orchard had run its course, certain Giants who had been captured alive were locked away in Tartarus by Zeus; that the Thunderer for some reason wanted to spare their lives but doom them to eternal exile. I think this is extremely doubtful. Another legend has it that a remnant of our foes retreated to some portion of the Underworld as to a last defensive redoubt; and the gods decided that the difficulties of digging them out of any fastness so well fortified would have been so great that even Hades had doubts of being able to accomplish it.

Later legends have stated that the gods could do no more than stun the Giants, and depended in every case on the arms of Hercules to provide a finishing blow. In fact, Giants were wounded and killed, often without any help from me, in a number of ways, some particularly gruesome.

Some of our opponents on that day were no bigger than Antaeus had been. But none, I think, were any smaller.

Of course legend has played its role in history, as usual. One hears, for example, that the superhuman giant Tityus, when his body was stretched out at full length, covered nine acres. And Enkelados was so energetic that the whole weight of Mount Aetna was barely enough to keep him from bursting free. These were definitely exaggerations.

To my astonishment, some have lately questioned whether the Giants ever existed, and put forth the foolish argument that if they had, surely some of their bones would still remain as evidence. But the truth, as I have been trying to explain convincingly in these pages, is that when they died, their bones, along with the rest of their vast bodies, soon decayed into a substance indistinguishable from ordinary dirt and gravel.

Diana, traditionally called the twin sister of Apollo, appeared from somewhere to take part in the fighting. She was said to be a virgin huntress, who carried arrows and a spear and was of a vindictive nature.

I saw her kill the Giant called Gration, riddling him with pointed shafts, and I was mightily impressed.

Several of our enemies were especially impressive, too, each in his own way. Briareus in his furious efforts almost proved true the legend that credited him with a hundred arms, while Typhon practically played the part of a volcano, breathing out fire. At various times most of the gods showed some fear of these beings, though not to the degree ascribed by legend, in which the Olympians all fled to Egypt and hid themselves under various forms.

The renewed fighting around the devastated Giant village turned fierce indeed.

Porphyrion, while trying to seize Hera, perhaps as a hostage, was overpowered by a team of gods, and Enkelados was slain by Athena. Ephialtes died when one of Apollo's Arrows struck him in the eye.

Apollo in general played a major role in the fighting, his Arrows doing almost as much damage as Zeus accomplished with his mighty bolts of lightning.

Hephaestus also battled fiercely, angered I suppose by the attack upon his laboratory. I saw his figure, looking larger than life-sized, carrying in each hand an enormous gobbet of what must have been molten iron, which he hurled at any of our enemies who came in range.

Alkyoneus was not to be defeated, but soon the landscape was littered with the bodies of dead Giants, and he gave his surviving colleagues the signal to withdraw.

○ *TWENTY-NINE* ○

The Last Word

Our pursuit of the fleeing Alkyoneus and his band of surviving Giants carried us closer and ever closer to the part of the world that I associated in my mind with Danni.

The Giants had been airborne when they embarked on this latest leg of their retreat, and yet here we were, following their footprints in the earth. There should be a better word to describe the marks made by their tremendous feet—they were not mere prints, but great crushed craters. Bushes, small trees, and fences were smashed down when in the way. I remember the trail's crossing an abandoned farmyard, where a couple of outbuildings had been flattened, too.

Each segment of visible trail extended for no more than about a hundred yards. Then it would cease abruptly, showing exactly where the massive bodies of our enemies had once more gone airborne. But then after a short flight, usually no more than half a mile, at least one or two Giants returned to earth once more and ran for a short distance on their great legs. Remembering how quickly I had seen them step in battle, I could well believe that their steady running pace would be impressive.

"It's almost as if they wanted to make sure we don't lose their trail," shouted someone flying near me.

I had what I thought was a better idea: that our enemies, depending on the earth for sustenance far more than humans did, could not or dared not remain out of contact with soil and rock for more than a few minutes.

As the miles flew by and the day advanced, and the direction taken by our quarry did not change, I began to feel some immediate concern for Danni, and I promised myself that before I left the area of the estate, I would see to it that she was safe. Several times I told myself that there was no reason to think she stood in any special danger. But my uneasiness persisted.

I had known for some time the approximate location of her home and Meleager's, near the port city of Iolcus—Mel had told me as much, during the brief time when we were Argonauts together. And now I remembered that he had mentioned it again when we were climbing together out of Tartarus. He had been trying to make some preliminary arrangement for my formal betrothal to his sister, while I in my black mood had been paying little attention.

And certainly I remembered where the estate of Augeus was located, whose stables I had once so thoroughly cleansed. And it bothered me that the trail left by the fleeing Giants was now tending in that direction. I thought it was quite possible that Danni happened to be visiting her uncle there again, or that she had been forced by family pressures to relocate in her uncle's house.

As the suspicion grew in me that the Giants were deliberately planning to use her, I wondered: Had word somehow already reached my enemies that Danni and I were now formally engaged, or about to be? Some being had overheard me talking to her brother, down in Tartarus? Plenty of time for the word to spread, while I was wandering around the Upper World again and wrestling with my father.

At nightfall we broke off our pursuit and stopped to rest and eat and make plans for the next day. Whether gods absolutely required physical nourishment or not, a number of them were not going to forgo it for themselves or for their horses, just because we happened to be at war.

By the time we stopped, Daedalus and I were both in serious need of rest. My last sleep, just before that last battle, was a troubled one.

I dreamt that Hades had sent the Face of Death to me by a special messenger, and that I was free to make what disposition of it I wished.

I tried to tear the clear, glassy stuff in two, but the fabric was strong enough to resist even me—which I found a strange sensation indeed, even in a dream. At last I threw the damn thing from me, into a small stream, knowing that it would be washed into a larger river, and then yet a larger one, eventually finding its way to the ocean—let find it who would.

I dreamt that battle was raging again, and that Zeus had been struck down by two mountains hurled at him at once by two Giants, catching him between.

Where my father had been standing, there was now only a huge hole in the earth. I borrowed a chariot and flew desperately toward the center of the crater, which was almost a mile in diameter.

Desperately distressed, I dug frantically into the rubble, sending huge rocks flying this way and that.

At the bottom lay one small human body, somehow still almost intact—or at least recognizable.

I dreamt then that as my father lay dying in my arms, the Face of Zeus came working its way up out of his eyes and forehead, like some long-sunken vessel rising from the deep; and with great reluctance, but a sense of inevitability, I picked it up and put it on.

And then for a time, still dreaming, I reveled in the powers of Zeus. My perception widened, in a way that not even Atlas had been able to accomplish, so that I was granted some idea, some feel, for how great and magnificent the earth was—the deep sky had suddenly become too frightening for me to contemplate.

Great, grumbling, black-bellied cloud masses churned their way across the sky, in obedience to my will. Grand crooked forks of lightning fell from them to devastate my chosen targets. I could see Giants, now shrunken to the scale of small and frightened humans, running for their lives.

Eventually Prince Asterion appeared in my dream and told me he had come to help me out of it and to wish me well in the coming fight.

I woke from my troubled sleep to find my living father standing looking at me. Zeus, as God of the Sky, had the governance of lightning, as well as wind and storm in general. And his powers extended beyond the earth, somewhat above the thick blanket of air that Atlas had once shown me. By the commanding power of his will alone, the Thunderer could deflect the rocks that flew unendingly in airless space, when natural causes brought them near Earth, and then guided them like slung missiles against his monstrous enemies.

And the Giants on their side were far from weak and helpless. As whole new hosts and legions of their enormous bodies came tramping or drifting toward us over land and sea, I realized that there were more of them in the world than I had ever imagined. From the talk I heard around me, I understood that at least some of the gods were similarly astonished.

When the fighting resumed, the Arrows of Diana struck home in concert with those of Apollo, and no Giant could stand against that double impact.

When a strong god and I attacked as a team, no Giant whom we challenged could stand for very long before us. Mighty Arrows flew from Apollo's Bow, faster than any human could have aimed and shot them. As the bewildered target tried to fend them off, I moved in close for the attack.

When I had a chance, I looked around for Alkyoneus; but always some other opponent intervened.

In that climactic battle, Athena once more played a considerable role. She fought wearing a helmet, wielding a spear, and guarding herself with the shield called Aegis, which at that time was not yet as famous as it has since become.

As I have already said, there were many other gods engaged on that field of combat, and there are too many stories for me to attempt to tell them all.

It was with a sense of some inevitable fate come due that I saw the Giants' trial lead at last directly to the estate of Danni's uncle Augeus, the same man who had once claimed to offer a great reward for the slaying of the Hydra and had so urgently craved the cleansing of the stables.

The trail led straight to that place, and through it, apparently without pause, as if our enemies' flight had followed this path only by the sheerest accident. Later, of course, I learned that that was not the case. There had been a plan to take Danni hostage and use her somehow against me. But our enemies' plans, like our own, were subject to confusion in the fog of war, and she was never captured.

But I of course demanded that we land, and soon Apollo's chariot came down on the front lawn of Uncle Augeus, and moments later I entered the house, with such an escort as only young men in legends ever have. And Danni was there, of course, free and unharmed, and I will never forget the look in her green eyes when I strode in, with the Lord Apollo half a stride behind me, an Arrow nocked to his Bow.

I think it unlikely that Augeus, in his shocked state, immediately recognized in me a young troublemaker who had once cleaned his stables. But even if he did, he was not about to refuse me permission to marry his young niece—especially not when he had every reason to believe that an army of Giants was about to descend on his estate and trample his accumulated prosperity into dust.

As soon as Danni saw me, she came to me and took both my hands in hers. I could see she was afraid, but I thought that most of her fear was for me, not for herself.

She said: "Mel has told me of the loss you suffered. It is so terrible, I wonder how you endure it."

"I couldn't endure it. But other things have happened to bring me past it."

"Other things—having to do with me, Hercules?"

"One of them does. Very much so." I suppose my manner indicated that I would be more specific when the right time came, and sensibly she did not press me at the moment.

We talked of Mel, who had set out to be a hero, and of our current situation regarding the Giants.

"You've cut your hair," I said. It was still straight and brown, but it only just hung past her ears.

"Do you like it?" She shook her head to make her tresses dance.

"I do, whether it is long or short. But then I like everything about you, and it has been that way since the moment we first met." Without pausing, I rushed on:

"I have sworn a solemn oath to marry you."

Danni's face showed no great surprise, and I realized that Mel must have told her of the conversation he and I had shared in Hell.

Suddenly there was a daring glint of humor in her green eyes, and she asked: "Sworn it under what compulsion?" Now I thought that she was testing me, ready either to laugh or to flare in anger.

"Don't you know me better than that? It is impossible to compel Hercules, son of Zeus, to do anything he does not want to do."

"Oh, has that been proven? But I have not tried my hand at such a feat." And I rejoiced to see a spirit of mischief dancing in the green eyes, ready to do battle with anything, especially with fear and sadness. "It would be an interesting challenge."

Now it was my turn to reach out with both hands to her. "Danni, will you be my wife?"

"Hercules, you must know I will. I have been aching to marry you since the day you threw my brother off the dock."

And Zeus himself found time to preside at a brief and simple ceremony, where several other gods and goddesses honored Danni and me by their presence—the business took only a few minutes.

But the wedding feast was going to have to wait, and so was the wedding night. Some people on our side were surprised at that, believing the battle was basically over and that it only remained for us to hunt down Alkyoneus and the other Giants who had fled.

"The battle may well be over," the Thunderer assured them, "but the war certainly is not."

And even those who thought the battle over were seriously mistaken. Now Alkyoneus was in the process of hunting me down, and came raging after me.

For some time now, when traveling long distances, he had been using a pair of flying Sandals, stolen or captured from some unhappy god, which worked as well on his enormous bulk as on a body of merely human size. But when it came time to fight again, he put the Sandals off, so he could better plant his feet and swing his club. He was running at us now, in solid contact with the earth, and it was plain he meant to fight.

And yet again Apollo, bronze helmet and all, had been knocked out of the air by a club in the hands of Alkyoneus, and the Sun God had to take a moment or two to regain his senses.

My case was similar. I never saw the blow that hit me when I came running near, doing my best to get within reach of the Giant's feet. I suppose it was his long club that he swung to swat me off the ground and send me flying—as I had once, long ago, propelled a lion through the air.

It must have been only moments later that a pair of centaurs found me lying stunned, after that terrific blow had bounced me off a rock or two.

Meanwhile the final, desperate battle still raged all around us, but I was only dimly aware of it. At first the centaurs' voices seemed to reach me from a great distance and to be partially muffled. They were debating between themselves as to what to do with me. By now I was beginning to regain my senses.

Kneeling beside me, the two six-limbed beings first tried to pry my club out of my immobile fingers, but I maintained my grip on that glorious weapon even while I continued to feign unconsciousness.

Now I could more clearly hear the centaurs, and recognized one voice as that of Nessus. The words of their debate began to make more sense in my shocked brain.

"Should we kill him immediately?" one asked.

"There's only one way we can do that." The voice of Nessus carried the calm of great insanity. "Are you ready for the sacrifice?"

The nameless centaur sounded considerably more normal than my old enemy. "We have talked that over again and again. No need for any of us to die, if the loss, the donation, is shared among us."

At the time, this made no sense to me. And then, just as I was about to leap up and smite them, Nessus said: "Anyway, we must first take him to Alkyoneus, who wants to see what he is made of."

Struck by a sudden inspiration, I lay still, restricting my impending movement to a few twitches.

"Shall we tie his wrists?" the nameless centaur asked.

"Tie the arms of Hercules?" Nessus was contemptuous. "That would be a useless exercise, wouldn't you say?"

Presently I was lifted and slung over a horselike back. Still I gripped my club, so one end of it went dragging on the ground as I was carried, and I thought surely that would make my would-be captors suspicious. But no, they were certain they had captured me, and I went along with the game as the only means of catching up with Alkyoneus. By now I was convinced that he was too fast on his feet for me to have any chance of overtaking him. Meanwhile, a temporary lull had fallen over the battlefield.

"Put him here," boomed out an enormous voice, and I was

dumped from a centaur's back onto a surface as broad and flat and leathery as the floor of an expensive tent. And now the tent floor was moving up, bearing me and the two centaurs with it.

Cracking an eyelid open, I made sure that I had been set down on the palm of a Giant's hand, and that currently I was being held at the level of his chest while he inspected me. The palm of his hand was easily ten feet wide. Taking an iron grip upon my patience, I ordered myself to wait until I could be sure of landing on the great Giant's shoulder if I jumped, and to wait until I had my feet planted on his shoulder before I swung my club.

Presently I heard the Giant's enormous, booming voice again, this time from deafeningly near at hand, conversing with the centaurs in some language I did not understand.

By this time I suppose Alkyoneus was about half convinced that I was finally dead. Now at last he was incautiously holding me close to his head so he could examine me closely. Maybe he was near-sighted. I was prodded, gently, with the tip of a finger that felt like the end of a big log.

Getting my feet under me in a sudden scramble, I suddenly realized there was no need to jump from his hand to his shoulder before I swung—his staring right eye was only a few feet from my face.

But Nessus and his comrade reacted quickly when I moved. Their natural unconsidered instinct was to seize me, and they were quick enough to get some parts of their bodies in the way of my swing when it was launched into the Giant's face.

Thus it was that my club, propelled with all the strength that I could summon up, hit centaur flesh and bone by accident, hit and passed through on its way to its intended target.

What the effect of my unaided swing would have on Alkyoneus I do not know, for just at that moment a timely contribution came from Apollo—one of his Arrows entered the Giant's left eye, detonating a powerful explosion inside his head, even as I knocked the staring right eye of Alkyoneus clear out of his enormous face.

Two slain centaurs and I fell with the great Giant's hand, and fortunately the corpse of Alkyoneus, almost beheaded by the double impact, did not land on top of me; but still a moment later I was writhing and screaming on the ground, in agony from a poisoning by the centaurs' blood. Some of it had splashed me, soaking through the wool with which my suit of Vulcan's chain mail was lined; and I tore desperately at the garment to get it off.

Even in my frenzy, I realized that Danni was there, trying to help me.

Moments later, I fell into a swoon from which I only recovered when the battle was practically over.

The armor made for me by Vulcan, and the quick action of my bride-to-be, had saved me from a worse fate, but I had still been severely burned, as if by acid.

Zeus had failed to warn me, fearful that I would at last turn against him if I knew the secret vulnerability he had designed into my nature.

In planning my existence, Zeus had been as crafty and suspicious as a god could be with the experience of ages to draw upon (at least in those portions of his memory that were not riddled with lacunae). He had feared to create a rival who might someday pose a threat to his own rule. Therefore he had provided his hopeful new monster with a secret weakness, by means of which he would be able to arrange my destruction, if that ever became necessary. The answer, what he thought was an acceptable answer, was found in the chemistry of centaurs' blood.

Apollo had survived the fight without any additional damage, and presently he came to do what he could to ease my suffering; and what he could do was quite a lot. Pain subsided to bearable levels, and some of my strength returned.

A small crowd of victorious gods was gathered around the fallen bulk of Alkyoneus; and now it was possible to study the design of his armor, which conducted thunderbolts harmlessly to the ground.

The surviving centaurs had all fled the field; and to this day I have never learned why certain of their race so hated me that they tried to arrange with their Giant allies an elaborate plan for my destruction.

*　　*　　*

My friend Hephaestus still had not abandoned hope of someday discovering the secret of creating Faces. He has told me that he will someday be able in his laboratory to forge the Face of Hercules, who must henceforward be a god. Oh, not great enough to challenge my father, as Vulcan hastens to make clear, or to cause Zeus any uneasy moments. The god Hercules would lack some of the Thunderer's key attributes, while still matching him in general strength and durability.

But if the day ever comes when Vulcan succeeds, I do not think I will accept the gift. Not unless Danni receives her own immortality at the same time.

Certain gods remind me, from time to time, that I am still only mortal—as if the fact gave them cause for worry. It does not much concern me. I have already faced Thanatos once, and in my heart I still believe what I suppose I have always believed, that some inner essence of humanity is naturally immune to death. So, I am no more and no less immortal than Danni at my side, or any of those who envy me my strength—or than any of you who read my words.

Besides, even gods must die, as was thoroughly demonstrated in our war with the Giants. And if Vulcan is ever able to grant me such a gift, and I accept it, then when I die the Face of Hercules must pass to someone else.

Here I conclude this story of my life. But my life is not yet over. Danni will bear me sons and daughters, and I do not think any god will be so foolish as to try to serve me as Zeus once served Amphitryon.

Free Public Library
Township of Hamilton
1 Municipal Drive
Hamilton, NJ 08619